DeeJay
&
Betty

DeeJay
&
Betty

A Novel by

ANNE CAMERON

HARBOUR PUBLISHING

HARBOUR PUBLISHING
P.O. Box 219
Madeira Park, BC Canada V0N 2H0

Published with the assistance of the Canada Council and the Government of British Columbia, Tourism and Ministry Responsible for Culture, Cultural Services Branch.

Cover painting by June Huber
Cover design by Mary White
Page design and composition by Vancouver Desktop Publishing Centre
Printed and bound in Canada

Canadian Cataloguing in Publication Data

Cameron, Anne, 1938-
  DeeJay and Betty

  ISBN 1-55017-112-7
  I. Title.
PS8555.A53D4 1994   C813'.54   C94-910736-0
PR9199.3.C35D4 1994

For my children
Alex
Erin
Pierre
Marianne
Tara

for my grandchildren
Daniel
Sarah
David
Terry
Sheldon
Jen
Andy

ACKNOWLEDGEMENTS

Nobody makes their way through life alone, and I have been blessed with siblings and cousins who took into a second generation the love and support I received from my mother, my aunts and my uncles. I know they have often been puzzled, hurt, even angry with some of my life choices and have often felt they might never "understand" what it is I think I am doing with my time on earth, but they have never made me feel that I—me—this flawed person—have been "wrong." For this I thank them. I feel very lucky and am even learning to be comfortable with Baboo.

My friends have hung in with me and for me for many years; they may be few in number but they know who they are and I love them.

Stanley and Nancy Colbert were there for me back when I had yet to enjoy major publication, and have been true, honest and loyal friends in all the time since. I think their personal support of writers has been a boon to many of us; a few more like them and this might not be such a lonely kind of life.

Mary and Howie have made pleasant that which all too often is a right total pain in the face.

Jim and Rod are true friends, and who would believe it's been that many years?! Tempus sure does fugit!!

And to Eleanor, who has been a stalwart in my life for so many years, my thanks, my appreciation, and my love. Whatever your little heart desires, kiddo! Couldn't have done 'er without you.

"A friend is someone who stands beside you, even when you're beside yourself."

Book I

1

DONNA JEAN BANWIN'S MOTHER PATSY WAS, to put none too fine a point upon it, a hype. Had Patsy's arm not ruled the rest of her body and mind, Donna Jean probably would never have been conceived, but a hype can only feed her veins by peddling her ass and some two a.m. trick hit the bull's eye. Patsy found herself up a stump, and life could have started out a lot worse for Donna Jean than it did, but Patsy got herself busted for laying bad paper and wound up doing six months in the provincial jail. There was no tapering off, no weaning, they let her do it cold turkey, and God in her mercy alone knows what that did to Donna Jean, who at the time wasn't Donna Jean at all, but just a glob of multiplying cells. But whatever the cold turkey did do, it was better than what would have been done if Patsy had been out on the street stuffing her arm, shoving strange substances up her nose and drinking anything she could get hold of that had alcohol in it, up to and including vanilla extract and Mennen Aftershave. .

Patsy got out in time to go to the welfare, get an intent-to-rent form and find herself a place to call home for the time being. She moved in and put groceries on the shelves, went to the Goodwill and told them the sad story of her life, filled out a form and got some donated furniture, diapers and baby clothes.

Patsy had no intention of handing her kid over for adoption. It wasn't any overdeveloped maternal instinct, just the cold realization she'd get one helluva lot more on welfare with a kid than she'd get on her own.

She wasn't even chipping when she went into labour. She wasn't taking any chances that the baby would go into withdrawal, the nurses tell the doctor, the doctor report it as child abuse and the welfare scoop the kid who was going to be the means whereby Patsy had some sort of income. So Donna Jean came out seeming as healthy and ordinary as any other kid.

Patsy stayed three days in hospital, learning how to put on and take off diapers, how to mix and store formula, how to feed and burp her daughter. Then Patsy got into a cab and took the kid back to the motel unit on the side of the highway, the place she called home.

There were lots of babysitters in the motel. There were lots of other kids whose mothers were no more together than Patsy, many of them for the same reasons or lack of reason. Any of those kids was so glad of a chance to get the hell away from the old lady for a while they would fight to be the one who sat on the sagging sofa watching the flickering TV and playing with Donna Jean, who was quickly renamed DeeJay.

Some nights Patsy came home and some nights she didn't. Once in a blue moon she came home alone. On those nights when she came home and wasn't alone DeeJay got the chance to sleep in a basket within sight and sound of almost any damn thing the human mind could invent.

Then Ricky started hanging around on a more or less full-time basis. Ricky was referred to by the local cops as a scuzzbag. For once they were bang on, he was as big a scuzzbag as anyone would care to encounter. One of his economic endeavours was to get drugs as cheap as he could and sell them for as much as he could. Had he restricted himself to things legal, he might have been an entrepreneur, most certainly had he gone into real estate he'd have been considered a sterling example of the capitalist persuasion, might even have been elected to government and graduated to a Senate seat. But Ricky had other aspirations and became, instead, a recognized creep.

With Patsy's welfare ensuring the rent, and her streetwalking taking care of the kid's food, Ricky's ventures provided them with whatever else they needed, including a constant supply of shit. Patsy was well and truly wired before very long, which meant she was pathetically eager to do just about anything Ricky decided he wanted done. DeeJay got to witness much of that, too.

Then Ricky and three or four others became ambitious and decided there was no need to go through life as a bunch of ankle-biters when they could just as easily go for the throat. But when you're a scuzzbag you hang out with other scuzzbags and if heaven has ordained you an ankle-biter the throat is well beyond your grasp.

All they had to do was stay cool. They knew the office manager of the feed store took the day's take to the night depository at the same time every evening. The feed store stayed open until half past six so the farmers with day jobs had time after their shift ended to drop by and pick up ten sacks of pig feed or a dozen bales of hay. Sometime between six-thirty closing and seven p.m., the manager took the black vinyl zippered-shut bag to the big metal depository on the south wall of the bank and dropped it through the slot. It was easy. Foolproof.

The proof of what fools they were was in the slapdash higgledy-piggledy way they tried to pull it off. They stole a car and waited, engine idling quietly, until the woman came in sight. Then Ricky pulled a stocking mask over his face and moved from the car to the alley. As the manager reached out to drop the bag in the slot, Ricky grabbed the bag. "Don't get brave, lady," he warned. She very wisely didn't get the least bit brave. She gasped, but didn't even try to turn her head to see who was taking the bag. She just opened her fingers and released her grip.

Ricky laughed and started back toward the car. That's when the manager pulled the spray can of oven cleaner from her purse and let him have it, just like using Raid on shit flies. Then, while Ricky was gagging and choking, pawing at his streaming eyes and trying to stagger away, the woman reached for the little red painted metal hammer and obeyed the instructions "in case of fire break glass."

Ricky made it to the car, he made it through the open door, and flopped on the back seat, gasping and cursing. The car took off, pedal to the metal, mere minutes ahead of every emergency vehicle in town. The first vehicle to arrive ran over the black vinyl bag Ricky had dropped. The woman pointed and yelled a description of the car, the driver of the vehicle grabbed the walky-talky and every cop in town knew where to head and what to look for.

Ricky was still coughing and rubbing his eyes when they tried to run the roadblock and instead ran right into it. The stolen car rammed the cop car broadside, pushed it three or four feet. The driver slammed the stolen car into reverse for another try and wound up with a slug in the mess where his face used to be. Everyone else just raised their hands and gave up, then and there.

The lot of them were arrested, fingerprinted and sent off to the big prison to wait for the various lawyers to prepare their cases. Only then, more than twenty-four hours after the manager of the feed store let him have it, did anyone look at Ricky's eyes. He'd been weeping, wailing, crying, bitching and whining the whole time that his eyes were burnin' out of his fuggin' head but nobody did anything about it. They believed him, they just didn't do anything except say to each other they hoped to Christ the little horror wound up blind. He didn't. Close, but no cookie. No white cane, either. Just very thick glasses with cheap plastic frames. Nothing that would keep him out of General Population. For once, Ricky found out some of what is required to go from ankle-biter to throat-snapper. The small-town mutt was exposed for several months to some big city ones, and it was an education.

He got sent back to town for the trial, which dragged on for all of two and a half days before they were found guilty and sentenced to ten years. But while in the local pokey, Ricky's lawyer had got him permission to see Patsy. They hugged and smooched and called each other honey, and whispered sweet nothings to each other, then Patsy left, wiping her eyes and sniffling.

The day they were shipping them all off in the armoured van Patsy came down to wave bye-bye and sob bitterly. She had DeeJay with her and just as they were about to shove Ricky into the van and slam the door shut, Patsy wailed, gave DeeJay a shove and the kid, rehearsed for hours, raced forward yelling "Daddy, Daddy!"

"Oh God, my *kid*!" Ricky wailed and whirled, scooping up the two and a half-year-old charmer, hugging her, kissing her face and begging the cops to give him a half a second here, Jesus man, it's my kid, how would you feel if you weren't going to see *your* kid for the next ten years?

But rules are rules and DeeJay, who had started wailing and

howling, was pried from Ricky's loving arms and sent back to her mommy. Ricky got in the van, wiping at his eyes. The van drove off with the convicted securely locked in the back.

Patsy took DeeJay home and used alcohol to get the grey sticky goo off the almost raw skin on the kid's back. The grey sticky goo was what was left of the adhesive tape Ricky had ripped loose. That's what had made DeeJay start wailing and howling.

In the back of the van the flat-sided straight razor nestled up the sleeve of Ricky's jail coveralls. The van drove ten miles to the airport where the small plane was waiting to take the convicted off to prison. They drove the van right out on the tarmac so the paying customers in the airport waiting room wouldn't have to put up with the stream of filth coming from the rejects.

Ricky was the last one out of the van. The other two were almost to the little steps leading up to the small plane when Ricky came out and slashed open the face of the deputy.

The deputy let out with a high-pitched wail like a rabbit who has just caught a foot in a trap. Ricky slashed again, and then it was like all the stories about the whirling dervish, with blood spurting and flesh gaping.

They didn't have a hope in hell, not any of them. There had never been the slightest chance three ankle-biters with a straight razor could organize things well enough to get the keys, undo the handcuffs, steal a car, then make a getaway. And the deputies had no hope in hell, either, of avoiding that straight razor.

Ricky was laughing. That's what the horrified paying customers in the airport lounge saw through the plate glass window. A total lunatic laughing like hell, causing blood to spurt, deliberately grossing them all out by rubbing the blood on his face and cavorting madly.

The sheriff raised himself from the pool of his own blood on the tarmac, pulled his gun and fired twice. The first shot nailed one of the accomplices and that was that for him. The second shot got Ricky in just about the last place Ricky had ever wanted to be got. The customers in the airport lounge heard his scream even through the sound-insulated wall. Some of them became very ill.

Eventually, when the fuss had calmed down a bit, they put two and two together and came up with something somewhere between three and a half and five and two-thirds. By then there was no proof Patsy or DeeJay had done anything other than go down to wave bye-bye to Daddy and howl a bit. But it sure put Patsy in the bad books in town. Especially those bad books as were kept by the constabulary. "And for what?" she mourned dramatically. "Even if they let him out tomorrow, he'll never be able to fuck again."

The cops took some kind of grim satisfaction in that, and even more and grimmer satisfaction in the thought of what the old-time long-term cons were going to find for Ricky to do now that he couldn't actively fuck. "I hope the son of a bitch is raw end receiver for a long long time," the sheriff said more than once. You could hardly blame him for feeling a tad bitter, he'd spent weeks in hospital trying hard not to die, then had to undergo plastic surgery on his face and restorative surgery on his hand, wrist and arm. They got that all sewn together again and did the best they could, but he never regained the use of his middle, ring or baby finger, which left him nothing but his thumb and his pointer. "Enough to pull the trigger and send that bastard low-life to hell if he comes near me again for as long as either or both of us live, though," he promised. "I'll kill the fucker, with or without a goddamn excuse."

Ricky was put to work in the kitchen of the prison. Everything the cops had hoped the hardliners would do to him got done to him. This made him bitter and sent him even deeper into his own particular brand of craziness, and to get revenge on them all, he began fucking the meat he was supposed to be cooking for supper. He couldn't do much with anything warm and alive, but he could go through the motions with the food. Limp and flaccid or not it was all the same to the fryers in the waxed cartons. "Eat it you fuckers," he'd yell as he served chicken stew. "Munch it down you corn-holing queers," he'd yell, flipping overcooked hamburger patties onto their plates. "Munch 'er up, gearbox," he invited, spooning stew on mashed potatoes. "Num num num, grubbytime!" They all thought he was as crazy as a tier rat until someone saw what it was he was doing by way of tenderizing and let them know what it was they'd been eating for all those months.

Someone stole a spoon, broke off the bowl, rubbed the handle on the concrete floor until it was sharp enough to slam like a nail into a piece of wood. Then that same someone held the shiv by the wooden handle and sharpened the rest of the spoon handle into a vicious little stiletto and planted it like a concord grape whip between the fourth and fifth ribs. Ricky's fourth and fifth ribs. "Nummy nummy your own damn self," was the last thing Ricky heard.

Patsy was doing the streets and DeeJay was learning all about survival. She was hungry so much of the time that there was never any need to tell her "eat your supper or you won't get dessert." DeeJay didn't know what dessert was and any time there was food she just sat down and packed it away until there either wasn't any more food or she couldn't ram another bite into her belly. She got left alone so much she invented new ways of feeding herself and even scoffed away uncooked oatmeal by the handful. Wieners and beans were DeeJay's equivalent of steak dinners, and Krap dinner figured big in her mind, too.

When she was four Patsy got busted and the welfare came to the motel. DeeJay went to a foster home, and if she'd known about heaven she'd have thought that was where they sent her. Three meals a day with snacks in between, a swingset in the back yard and a sandbox. The cat used it as a crap box but that's probably what the little shovel and sifter was for, to get the mess out before you started to play.

Patsy did four and a half months and was let back out on the street again. She had to "prove herself fit" before they'd let her have DeeJay back, but by the time DeeJay was five and a half she had been banished from heaven and was back in the motel with her ever-lovin' mommy. "You're an awful kid," Patsy told her. "I never knew no kid before who *asked* to be sent back to the whoofare!"

Patsy was pregnant again, and for a while DeeJay thought she might even get a baby sister or baby brother. The welfare gives just about twice as much money to a woman with a kid as they give to a woman on her own, but after the big raise for the first kid, they only add fifty dollars per month for every other kid. "Can't do much on fifty bucks," Patsy groused. "Hardly even buy potatoes for it."

She went to the hospital, had the baby, and came home without it. When DeeJay asked where the baby was Patsy told her to shut up and stay shut up. "I signed it for adoption," she said flatly. "It's gonna have a real family, with a dad and everything. Prob'ly wind up with a pony and a big Irish setter dog!" DeeJay thought that was great for the baby. She wondered why she'd been disqualified from any of that good stuff and put in a motel unit on the side of the highway. Didn't seem fair, somehow.

Patsy was sort of hanging out with Jack by then. Jack was known as an asshole in more than one town on the coast. He was even known as an asshole in a couple of cities. While Patsy was peddling her low-rent wares, Jack was busy whapping senior citizens on the head and stealing their old age pension, or hot-wiring cars and stripping them for parts easily sold to various greasy garages, where the only questions asked were "can you get more?" and "know anywhere I can get some good grass?" Jack's answers to both questions were in the affirmative.

Then Jack, bright as a nit, decided to become a back alley entrepreneur. He stole some money to buy some dope and sold it for enough profit to buy more dope and sell it at a bigger profit. He managed to stay ahead of the law for all of two weeks and so impressed the drug dealers they fronted him for a fairly sizable load. The responsibility was too much for dipshit Jack, he started feeding his arm and Patsy's arm and while ripped got the bright idea he could burn the dealers.

The first thing DeeJay knew about anything, four men were in the motel unit calling themselves "uncle" and asking where Mommy and Daddy were. "Out," she said. The uncles told the babysitter she could go home now, they'd look after the kid, and they even paid her for babysitting. That was such a novel happening the babysitter, who was at least eleven or twelve, memorized their faces.

DeeJay sat on the stinking plaid sofa watching the television and the uncles sat around smoking cigarettes and cleaning their nails with the sharp shiny blades of their knives. When she got hungry, DeeJay went over to the cupboards and started looking for something to eat. Even the nail cleaners were disgusted when she hauled out a little packet of instant noodles, ripped it open and started to gnaw on dry noodles.

"Fuckin' Christ," one of them growled. "Go get her some food for Chrissakes." The youngest, a mere apprentice, nodded and left the motel. Less than ten minutes later he was back with half a dozen Big Macs, some fries and several milk shakes. None of the nail cleaners had any appetite so DeeJay ate as much as she could and stashed the rest for later.

All that food on a stomach which had been empty for far too long sent her blood sugar plummeting and she got very sleepy, so she pulled the dust-impregnated crocheted afghan from the Goodwill up over her and went to sleep.

She woke up quickly though when Patsy and Jack came home and the ruckus broke loose. Patsy screamed and screamed and screamed and screamed but DeeJay couldn't scream, she just cowered on the couch, her eyes bugging out so far you could have whapped them out of her face with a stick.

They didn't use the knives, they smashed a chair and used the splintered legs of it. They beat Jack into nearly two hundred pounds of raw meat and then, in coarse and graphic detail, told Patsy what they were going to do with the splintered chair legs if she didn't get her ass out on the street and start making money to pay off Jack's debts.

Patsy didn't have a hope in hell of making that kind of money and they all knew it but she nodded, and wept, and nodded and sobbed and nodded until they yelled at her to put a sock in it goddamn it, wash her fuckin' face and get her fuckin' ass out on the street.

"Can I call him an ambulance?" she asked.

"Call him any fuckin' thing you want, just get busy makin' money."

Jack lay on the floor for hours. Eventually they got sick and tired of looking at him. They picked him up, threw him on the bed and left him there. They left the motel and headed off to collect money from Patsy. She was working for them now.

"Hey, kid," Jack managed. "Get me a drink of water, will you?"

DeeJay got him a drink of water. Then she went back to sleep. When she woke up, she ate one of the cold Big Macs and went outside to try to find something to do.

"Can you find me something to eat?" Jack groaned.

"There isn't nothin' to eat," she lied. Damned if she was sharing her Big Mac with *him*!

He had to pull himself together and save his own ass until Patsy came in and could be browbeaten into looking after him. She cried while she did it and cursed him out thoroughly. "Some protection you are," she whined, "look at you! And look what I have to do! Because of you!"

"Shut up or I'll fix you good," he vowed.

"You touch me and they'll rip off your stinkin' head! I work for them now!"

And she did. Full time. They gave her just enough for her arm to keep her from coming apart. It might have worked out halfways okay, they might have managed to keep her just high enough and wired enough to do what she was told but not so much she forgot how to do what she was supposed to be doing. Every now and again someone delivered Big Macs or Chinese food or something to DeeJay. Jack tried to take it but he couldn't move around very fast and after a while he gave up and wobbled off to find his own.

He didn't come back for a week or so, and when he did he was still a mess but some of his spunk had come back. He told DeeJay to make him a sandwich and when she said no he backhanded her and knocked her across the room, so she got up and ran out of the motel.

Turned out he'd done her a favour. She was over by the motel office stroking the motel cat when three of the four guys came back, with golf clubs. The motel manager said later she hadn't thought they looked much like golfers but you never know about things like that. When they left they took the clubs with them. But something about the way they left, running, jumping into the car and taking off, tires squealing, tipped the motel manager. She went to the unit, looked through the open front door, screeched, and ran for the phone. The kid who had been the babysitter the first time the guys showed up remembered enough of what they looked like to give the police a solid description but nothing much came of it. Maybe they didn't look very hard.

DeeJay, throughout the whole furor, stayed with the cat so she never had to see what they had done to Jack with the golf clubs and the guys did her a favour because she never again had to put up with Jack. The cops came, and then the whoofare came and just like that, DeeJay was in a foster home. Not the same one, but it too had food, and a clean bed, and toys and a TV that didn't flicker all the time.

She was there from before the start of grade one to the end of grade two, and then all the good stuff was gone and she was back with Patsy. By this time she didn't know Patsy very well and didn't have any memories that inclined her to think kindly of dear old Mom.

"Fine thank you I get," Patsy maundered. "Look what I done for you, and what thanks do I get? Any? No, by damn, not a bit. My own flesh and blood and it looks at me like it never seen me before. That's some thank you."

School was the escape. School was where there were crayons and water paints, where there were pencils and plenty of paper, where all you had to do was get the work done, and done right, and then you could do just about anything you wanted to do. It seemed fair to DeeJay. If they wanted her to add up some numbers, fine, she'd add them up, and be as neat as a pin about it, too. Once that was done she could hand her work over to the teacher and then go play in the reward corner until it was time for the next lesson and the next piece of work. She could take coloured plasticene and use it to make little animals, or little toys like the ones she saw on TV. She could make panda bears or she could make space aliens, the teacher didn't care, as long as when you were through you took it all apart and put the proper colour in the proper bottle, with the top on so it wouldn't all dry out and be useless.

The more words you got right on your spelling tests, the more time you got with the fingerpaints. It was easy. It was fair. And fair meant a lot to DeeJay because it was such a rarity in her life.

Grades three, four, and the first part of grade five she was with her mother. Somehow that didn't seem fair, but nobody had asked her about her own wishes. She knew by now that most of the kids in school were under strict orders from their parents not to play with her, not to go to her place to watch TV and not to invite her to their places. She knew why. She almost understood. But she didn't think that was very fair. She wasn't the one who was drunk a lot of the time, and high a lot of the time, and rowdy nearly all of the time. She knew there was one way to talk at home and another way when you were at school, or around nice people. You might tell Patsy to fuck off and leave you alone but you didn't say it to a teacher, or a nice kid, or the parents of a nice kid.

The time with Patsy ended after the first part of grade five. Patsy came home one night with three or four men and a couple of other barfly women and they smoked up some weed and then started drinking the wine they had brought home, the kind that comes in the big cardboard imitation kegs with a plastic spigot and the wine in a plastic bag inside. One of the men brought out something he had in his pocket and they got out the spoon and candle. Patsy got her fit from where she hid it in the box of sanitary pads in the little cupboard-thing under the bathroom sink, and they said things like aaaaall right and way to go. There wasn't enough for any of them to get very high, but it was enough to give them a fast buzz until the weed and the plonk started to work.

DeeJay thought she'd been crafty enough to feel safe even with a bunch of rounders in the house, she'd taken her pillow and the quilt under the bed and made her nest there. Usually not even Patsy thought to look for her under the bed. She went to sleep and that was probably mistake number two. One of the men reached under the bed, grabbed the quilt, dragged it and DeeJay out from what she had thought was safety. She wakened then, but she was, after all, not quite ten years old, and skinny from never quite getting enough to eat. What he did to her hurt. It hurt real bad. It hurt so bad she couldn't screech, or yell, or even cry. And what good would it have done, anyway?

She couldn't get back to sleep after that, not just because she was afraid but because she hurt so bad it made her feel sick to her stomach. So when it was time she got dressed and went to school.

The grade five teacher was used to having DeeJay fall asleep at her desk. Usually she just ignored it, and let the kid sleep. But there was something about how pale DeeJay was, something about the dark half moons under her eyes, something about her pinched mouth that made the teacher move to the desk and that's when she saw that DeeJay was sitting in a little pool of blood.

The teacher didn't yell or gasp or do anything to draw attention to what she had found. She just stood by DeeJay's desk and said very very quietly, "You know, I think you've all worked so well this morning that you should have a little reward. Why don't you very very quietly go and get your jackets and very very quietly go out to the playground and have some extra recess time. Quietly, now, or the other classes will hear and then you might not have the swings and slides all to yourself."

The kids grinned and got up quietly. "Jocelyn, would you stop by the office and ask the secretary to tell Mr. Franson that I need to see him right away, please?"

When Mr. Franson got to the room the teacher already had DeeJay bundled up and ready to go. The principal didn't even ask any questions, he just lifted DeeJay and almost ran for his car.

When DeeJay woke up it was the middle of the night and she was lying in a bed with sides on it, like a crib, only shiny. There was a needle in her arm, and a tube from it to a plastic bag hanging from a stand. A nurse was bending over the railing, smiling. "Hello, there," she said in a very soft voice. "So you've decided to wake up, have you?"

"Not really," DeeJay whispered.

"If you want to go back to sleep, you can."

"Okay," and she tried, but she couldn't get back to sleep.

"Do you hurt anywhere?" the nurse asked.

"Yes," and she pointed where. The nurse nodded and the next thing DeeJay knew she was being given a shot in the upper leg. That took away the hurting but she couldn't get back to sleep and finally realized it was because she was so hungry her stomach was cramping.

"Well, and we can fix that, too," the nurse told her.

DeeJay ate a bowl of chicken noodle soup and three crackers, drank a glass of milk, then lay down and slept until breakfast time. After breakfast the social worker came to ask her some questions. Then she left and the next time she came she had a policewoman with her. They had some more questions. Then they left and Dee-Jay had lunch. It was a really good one, too. Two big pieces of meat loaf with gravy, two scoops of mashed potatoes and some nice bright green peas. And something sweet with a sauce over it, for dessert.

She slept a bit and when she wakened the social worker was back, and so was the policewoman, and they had a sort of a camera thing. While the camera thing whirred, they asked questions and DeeJay did her best to answer everything as well as she could. They asked a lot of questions, and sometimes they seemed to be very upset, but nobody yelled at her and then they left and took their camera with them.

She didn't have to go to court or anything. She never saw the policewoman again, just the social worker, and then, when she was out of the hospital and in the foster home, she didn't see the social worker much, either. She did not see her mother for a long long time, and lost no sleep about it.

DeeJay thought the first foster home she got put into when she got out of hospital was really great. Other kids to play and fight with, a room in the basement for a bedroom, which she shared with two other kids, both fosters, and another room down there where all the toys and games were and all the kids played in after supper or on rainy days. Later, when she had something to compare it with, she realized it wasn't great at all, it was just okay, but for the time she was there she thought she'd been sent to the outskirts of paradise. The next place wasn't very nice at all, even at the time she knew it. Pray, pray, pray, and DeeJay had no experience with that at all. The prayers themselves were easy enough, you just memorized them, and DeeJay was good at memorizing. It was what happened after the prayers, where they'd ask questions of the "what if" kind.

What if you found ten dollars on the sidewalk, what would you do with it?

"Spend it," DeeJay said promptly. "I'd go to a cafe and buy a real nice meal. Maybe a steak dinner or something like that."

"No," the woman shook her head. "No, Jesus wouldn't like that."

Jesus wanted DeeJay to try to find out *whose* money it was and give it back, like a good Christian little girl.

"First person you asked would say it was his, whether it was or not, and he'd take it."

"Then he'd be a sinner."

"Yeah? Then *he'd* get the steak dinner!"

But they still wanted DeeJay to try to find the owner and then, if she couldn't (fat chance!), give the money to Jesus.

DeeJay was starting to feel as if that steak dinner actually existed and these people were trying to deprive her of it. "Jesus don't need no money," she mumbled, stubborn.

"But those who labour in his fields do. They would use the money for good works."

DeeJay said nothing.

"Now, what would you do if you found ten dollars on the sidewalk, dear?"

"I'd keep it," DeeJay insisted. After all, didn't Jesus want her to tell the truth? And wouldn't it be a lie if she said she'd give it to Jesus? He'd just have to find some other way to pay the labourers in the fields. If DeeJay ever got any money, it was going for steak dinner.

"Go to your room," she was told. So she did. Seemed Jesus wanted her to sit on the edge of her bed and contemplate her sins. Seemed Jesus wanted her to pray that he unharden her heart. DeeJay didn't know her heart was hard. She thought everybody had the same kind of heart, big and red like a Valentine, only probably made of meat, like the rest of your body.

She wasn't there long and the worker came and talked to her, but most of what got asked was as big a puzzle as Jesus and the damn money. The worker realized there were too many concepts which either went over DeeJay's head or flew right past her ears on their way to somewhere else. She tried to explain to the foster parents what DeeJay's background was, tried to explain that the child was as ignorant as any foreign heathen of the concepts of Christianity, but it's easy to deal with the foreign heathen, you just drop two dollars in the collection plate. The heathen at the hearth are there all the time, wanting steak dinners and not welcoming any chance to be hugged to the bosom of Christ.

So she went to the next place, and that was fine. There were lots of kids there, three of them full-timers, two of them long-termers and several others like herself, part-timers or short-termers. During the day when all the kids except for her youngest were at school, the lady ran a sort of daycare service, and sometimes the little pre-schoolers were still there when DeeJay came rushing in to change from her school stuff into play stuff. Then, if she wanted to, she could maybe take a small one out on the swings for a while or, if it was raining, sit and play with the crayons or playdough or something, amusing the small ones while the mom got ready to make the supper.

She finished grade six at that place and had part of her summer holiday there, then she must have rolled sevens or something because the worker told her to pack up her stuff because next Tuesday she was going to go to what they hoped would be her long-term placement.

DeeJay felt anxious about long-term placement. What if it was a bunch of oh-holy-ole's again, with Jesus figuring in every conversation? One of the other short-termers had been in one place where they gave you a string of some kind of love beads or something and you had to kneel and say a prayer for every bead. Every night before bed. Christ almighty, eh!

If you have to go live on a farm, get your first sight of it at the beginning of August, when the first plums are just starting to fill out and ripen. DeeJay fell in love. But her blast of glee was followed almost immediately by the chilling realization it wouldn't last. Nothing ever did.

She had a little bedroom all to herself, with a bunk bed and a four-drawer dresser and a closet big enough to park a bike in if you had a bike. And before long, DeeJay had a bike. It wasn't new, but who gave a toot about new, it worked, and it worked really well. On it, she could go to the lake for a swim, or go to the creek to watch the frogs, or pedal with a packed lunch down the highway to the skidder trail that led down to the beach where the waves moved toward the shore, away from the shore, toward the shore, away again, cycle after cycle, day after day, forever and beyond, turning driftwood logs to slivers and rocks to sand.

There was work to do but everyone did it, and DeeJay was never asked to do more than her share. At first it was just ordinary stuff, like dishes and dusting, but then she got to stand on the little running board thing and watch Bud on the tractor. Sure was a lot of stuff to remember about driving a tractor. Worse than a car, looked like.

And then haying, and she couldn't do much about lifting the bales onto the conveyor thing that took them from the wagon up to the loft of the barn, but she could at least take cold drinks out to them, and sit on the steps peeling spuds and watching the tractor go back and forth across the field. Then, when everyone came in all sunburned and aching, she could make sure there were towels for everyone and the table was set. They'd smile tired smiles at her and nod and say "Thanks, kid," then sit at the table and pack away food until you couldn't believe anyone could eat so much.

When the hay was done they had a great big party. DeeJay had never been at anything like it. There was this old hot water tank behind the woodshed, at least six and a half feet long. Someone had taken a welder or something and cut it in half, not around the middle like a belt, but the long way, so what you had was like a great big long shallow tub. They stood it up on some bricks and filled it with two sacks of charcoal briquets, then got them burning and when all the charcoal had turned white hot they put a big rack of some kind over top and brought out the steaks they'd made from the half-grown steer.

Everyone showed up with different kinds of salads and someone brought a great big thing full of scalloped spuds with grated cheese melted on top and turned crispy in the oven. Cakes and pies and God you couldn't begin to imagine what all was brought, and everyone was laughing and teasing each other. A guy who was just about twice as big as the strong man in the circus showed up with six salmon and put them on the barbecue, someone brought chops from a pig they kept calling Tubbers and someone else brought a big blue canner half full of chicken legs soaking in what they called a marry-nad.

DeeJay sort of hung back because everybody obviously knew everybody else and had done for a long time. You can't just bust in on something like that, you have to bide your time, people might get proddy, you just don't know. But then Jeannie hollered, "Hey, DeeJay, what's the matter, the cat got your tongue? Or are you just shy by nature?" and before DeeJay had time to even think about what she was going to say, she said it. "I'm not shy, I just don't want to butt in is all."

There was a little bit of a silence and then the big guy who brought the fish stood up and made his face grin. "Hey, gimme a break here, kid," he said softly. "You got *invited*, you're not butting in." He gave her a little shove on the shoulder, then followed that with a quick short squeeze that wasn't quite a hug. It was better than a hug, really, because it didn't last long and didn't make her feel squirmy.

That party went on until DeeJay was too tired to eat or boogie any more. When she went off to bed some people were still sitting on big pieces of wood around the bonfire they'd built, and other people were up dancing on the hard packed place where usually they parked the car and the pickup truck. DeeJay kept on all her clothes because you don't easily forget getting hauled out from under your own bed like had happened that time, but nobody came within a hundred feet of her.

She was up before anyone else in the morning and went outside so's not to disturb the ones still sleeping. She picked up some paper plates that had been overlooked in the cleanup, found some styrofoam cups, tossed them on what had been the bonfire and then generally tidied up, even taking the big bucket of scraps and leftovers out to the pigs. She almost felt as if it had been her party.

Food figured big in DeeJay's life, probably because there had been so little of it for so long, and not much of it was good. When you think two-day old cold Big Macs are good food, something is very much awry. Jeannie thought food was important, too. "I hardly ever peel spuds," she said, scrubbing the skins with a special brush. "The vitamins are just underneath the peel, and if you pare that away you wind up giving the best part of it all to the chickens. They don't need the vitamins as much as we do, they've got balanced feed plus they free-range and fill up on bugs'n'stuff."

"Food is just like we are," she grinned. "You rush it, it gets tough. Eggs, especially. Cook an egg when you're in a hurry and you've got white leather. At the same time, you can't just let it putz away for a long long time with nothing much happening, that'll make it tough, too. Just give it some respect, is all. After all, it's what keeps you perking."

"Beans. I like pinto beans best, but I couldn't tell you why.

What you do is rinse them, because there's apt to be gravel and grit in with the beans themselves. Then put them in cold water, put it on the stove, bring it to a boil and let 'er rip for a few minutes. Then turn off the heat and let 'em soak in that hot water for oh, maybe a half hour, an hour. While that's happening you brown your onion. Whenever you're using onion, you brown it first. That's what starts the taste, so get it started right at the beginning. Then your tomato sauce, your spices, then your pinto beans and then a handful of macaroni. It'll cook down to nothing much at all but it's good thickener and it does something else, too, to balance the vitamins and such. And rice, always put rice in with your beans. No matter how you're cooking beans, put in rice, too. For one thing," she grinned again, "you don't fart as much."

"When do you put in the salt?"

"I don't, myself. There's more than enough salt in the tomato paste. And if you salt the first water the beans don't seem to ever get soft. I don't mind a bit of a bone in carrots, or even in green beans, but I can't stand baked beans with bones in them. It's like gnawing away on buckshot or something. And I will *not* eat broccoli with a bone in it. Some of the others say they like theirs crunchy. Well, I'll cook them the way they like them and if they want crunch broccoli, fine, but you might have noticed I serve theirs first and leave mine in another three or four minutes. I am not eating bony broccoli, and that's that."

"I'll eat it that way," DeeJay admitted, "but I like it better if it's cooked all the way through. Seems as if there's more taste." She tried to copy Jeannie's easy grin. "Mind you, with or without taste, there's not much in the way of food manages to sneak past me."

"I noticed. We figured the budget deficit was from trying to feed you; the whole damn province is gonna wind up on the skids just from picking up the tab for your grocery bill."

"Ah, g'wan with you, I'm worth it!" She was starting to learn a little bit about humour, too, and if she was still clumsy with it nobody seemed to mind. "I'm a lot better-lookin' than those politicians and if the money wasn't going for my food it'd be going in their pockets."

"That may be the God's own truth, kiddo. Whoops! Don't cut lettuce, rip it. If you cut it you get a bowl of wilted green stuff rapidly turning brown."

Sometimes at night DeeJay would wake up in her own bed in her own room and she'd feel as if what she really wanted most to do was pull the pillow over her head and just cry, and cry, and cry, because it was all just too good to be true, and whatever was good didn't last. She didn't know what it was she'd done, but she must have been real little when she did it. She must have been so little she couldn't remember doing whatever the bad thing was she did that made God mad at her. So mad God just kept punishing her over and over and over again for that thing she couldn't remember doing. It didn't seem fair, somehow, to be punished for something you'd done before you were old enough to know what you were doing was punishable, or even to know you'd done it. It wouldn't change anything, probably, but she sure would like to know why God was mad at her.

2

DEEJAY WAS ON A LADDER, up a tree, in the orchard, picking fruit when the social worker's car turned off the paved road and started down the driveway, kicking up a little streak of dust. DeeJay looked at Jeannie who looked back at DeeJay.

"Shit," said Jeannie.

"I don't wanna," DeeJay blurted.

"Me neither, kid."

She came down the ladder fighting tears. They had just about picked all the golden plums and should have started on the transparent apples next, but DeeJay knew she wasn't going to be in on that part of the harvest. She knew. She wanted to be strong, she wanted to be tough, she wanted to keep it inside herself, and she couldn't. She couldn't even do what Jeannie had been trying to teach her to do, which was not worry about a thing until it happened.

"My God, you're like the White Queen in Alice in Wonderland," Jeannie had said, over and over again, "you worry yourself sick about things before they even start to happen. Give it up. Remember that old thing about sufficient unto each day is the evil thereof."

"What's that mean?"

"Means don't worry about the sky falling until it hits you on the head."

"And then you'd never have time to duck."

"Duck schmuck, you'll give yourself ulcers."

She was sobbing so bad she got the hiccups, and they weren't even out of the orchard. The social worker got out of her car, but DeeJay couldn't see her for the flood of tears. She just kept putting one foot in front of the other, feeling Jeannie's arm around her shoulders, feeling Jeannie's warm body pressing against her side. Then, all too soon, damn it, she could see the social worker in her nice clothes and shoes with just a film of driveway dust on the shiny leather tops.

They went into the house and sat at the table. Jeannie made a pot of tea and put some cookies on a plate in the middle of the table. The social worker put her leather briefcase on the table, opened it, brought out some papers and checked something, then nodded. "Well, Donna," she said brightly, "I have some very good news for you."

"No you don't," DeeJay said coldly. "You've got shit news for me. You're moving me, aren't you?"

"Your mother has finished her substance treatment and has made application to have you returned to her care."

"Oh, goody goody," DeeJay shouted. "Now I get to go sit in the fuckin' motel on the side of the highway again! How could I be so lucky. I am fuckin' overwhelmed."

The social worker told DeeJay she wasn't making a very good impression.

"I'll make a fuckin' impression, bitch. I'll put the impression of my knuckles right on the end of your pig-Irish nose! You want an impression? How about the impression of my goddamn shoe right up your arse?"

The social worker looked at Jeannie as if she expected her to put DeeJay across her knee and spank, but Jeannie was busy examining the cookies she'd baked that morning and didn't seem to notice anything was amiss. So the social worker forced a smile. "You'll be all settled in and reacquainted before school goes in."

"Yeah? And what am I supposed to do? Jump in the air and sing four verses of the national anthem? I don't want to go. If you can't hear that I can shout louder. Better yet, maybe we can all chip in some money and buy you a hearing aid. I do not want to go!"

"Your mother is prepared to apply to the courts for custody."

Powerless in the face of an authority which paid attention only to itself, denied any chance of choice, DeeJay put aside everything Jeannie had taught her and called, instead, on what she had learned in the place to which the whoofare biddy was determined to return her. She resurrected her garbage mouth and let loose.

"My fuckin' mother is prepared to get an increase in her welfare cheque is what she's prepared to do. So that she can prepare herself to go back to more of the same goddamn thing she's been doing since as long as I can remember. When do I get *my* chance to apply to the fuckin' courts? How come you can divorce a husband or a wife but you can't divorce your fuckin' parents? No. No. No no no no no no *no!* Is that clear? NO! Write that on your form. Come on, I want to see you write it on that fuckin' form. Find a line and if you can't find a line write in the margin. Try 'subject child voiced strong opposition to the idea'. Try 'DeeJay protests', try 'no no *no!*' I like it here. I've been here a long time. I'd like to be here a couple of years more. I'd like to finish school, okay, and finish it right here. That woman is nuts. *Nuts!*"

She knew it wasn't going to do any good but she did it anyway. She yelled, she shouted, she thumped her fist on the table and she even promised that one day she'd kick the fuckin' shit right out of the social worker.

And a week later she was in the back seat of the car, being driven away from Jeannie and the farm, back to live with Patsy. "Now, DeeJay, if you just give it a chance I'm sure it will all work out fine," the social worker said. "Try to approach things positively, dear."

"I'm positive this is bullshit, okay? I'm positive you're being paid good money to do a bad job. I'm positive this is going to be just awful. And I'm positive that if it's awful for me it's going to be ten times as awful for everyone else!"

"If you go through life with that attitude you won't go far," the social worker warned.

"Oh, fuck you and the people you work for!"

DeeJay refused to help take her stuff out of the car. She refused to put it away. She just sat on the bed in what Patsy said was her bedroom and glared, arms across her chest, hugging herself, so angry she could taste something in her mouth that made her think of being little and putting a penny under her tongue. The social worker left hurriedly. Patsy came into the bedroom and stood at the door smiling as if everything was just hunky dory.

"It's nice to have you back," she said.

"Go get fucked," DeeJay answered.

"Watch your tongue, little girl," Patsy warned, the colour draining from her face.

"Sure," DeeJay smiled. "And it'll be easier to watch if it isn't hidden behind my teeth." She stuck her tongue out at Patsy.

"I can see we aren't going to get along any better this time than we ever did." Patsy tried to sound like a school teacher, all haughty and dignified. "I never did understand how it was I got such an unnatural kid. Well, you can leave your tongue hanging in the air until it dries out, it's no skin off my nose."

"Eat it. Leave me alone. This is all your idea, not mine. If it'd been up to me I'd'a never set eyes on you again."

"*Why* are you like that?" Patsy screamed. "*Why?*"

"Maybe because I got stuck with a stinkin' junkie for a mother. Maybe I got stuck livin' like a ditch rat because you spent grocery money on some kind of shit for your arm, or some kind of shit to push up your nose or some kind of shit to drink or some kind of shit you put where the sun don't shine. Maybe you snorted my supper one or two times too many, Pat-see. All you ever did for me was fuck up my life, okay? I was doing just fine without you. And one day I'll off-load you and do just fine again! Now get outta my sight before I whap you a good one."

Patsy left. After all, DeeJay was two inches taller and probably fifteen pounds heavier and had been lifting hay bales, and it showed. DeeJay sat in her room, determined not to have Patsy see or hear her crying. Anyway, she'd done nothing much else for over a week and what good had crying done, other than give her such a stinking headache she had to take Tylenol.

Her grade eleven teacher thought there had been some kind of mix-up in the school records. The transfer files showed DeeJay was a good student with a cheerful attitude and excellent work habits. The DeeJay she had to deal with slouched in her seat, refused to answer, stared at the wall and broke her pencils into little pieces. The transfer papers said DeeJay took responsibility but what this snarly little madam took was a hike any time she felt like it. She might be there at the beginning of English and five minutes into it she'd get up and just walk away, leaving her books on the desk.

The principal tried to talk to her but DeeJay wouldn't even sit down, she just leaned against the wall and yawned in his face. Three weeks after school let in, DeeJay didn't show up at all. After two days they phoned to see if she was sick, but there was no answer at the other end.

Patsy didn't hear the phone because she had got her cheque on Welfare Wednesday and was in never-never land by nightfall. When the phone rang Friday afternoon, she was passed out on the couch with the TV flickering and the drapes drawn. DeeJay wasn't even in the apartment.

DeeJay was in town, just hangin' out near the arcade. She had about twelve dollars in her pocket, money she'd lifted from Patsy's purse, and she had no intention of going back home ever again. Fight, fight, fight, even when they weren't yelling at each other they were fighting in silence. And Patsy with her smarmy goddamn smile, saying "You'll be all right here on your own, won't you?" as if DeeJay was five again. For that matter, even when DeeJay *was* five, Patsy hadn't worried if she'd be okay on her own or not, she'd just put on her sleazy hooer clothes and pitty-patty in her spike heels off she'd go, across the apartment and out the front door, then tipper-tapper down the steps to the outer door. Click click click along the front walk and tippy-tappy down the sidewalk to the bus stop. DeeJay would kill time until anywhere between two and four in the morning when Patsy would come back, carrying her shoes most likely, usually with some two-on-a-scale-of-one-to-ten coming along behind her.

"Ssshhh," Patsy would hiss. "Sssshhhh, m'kid's sleepin'." "Yeah? Lemme see what your kid looks like." They always wanted to take a peek at the kid.

So DeeJay got a big can of water ready and as soon as her door opened she fired the can at the opening and yelled "Get the fuck outta here, y'asshole!" She only had to do it a time or two. Patsy caught on and after that she didn't even mention the kid. "Ssshhh," she'd hiss, "the downstairs neighbours are cranky."

But then there was morning, and waking up. Provided, of course, you'd been able to get to sleep. Clothes scattered around, empty beer bottles all over the top of the table where you were supposed to eat your crunchy-munchies yum-yum-yum. Stinking shoes or socks littered around the place. Maybe a sweaty tee shirt over the back of a chair. "For crying out *loud!*" she yelled, "Don't you know these guys only come here because they got no place of their own to go to? They wait in the bar hopin' some fool like you will bring 'em in outta the rain so's they don't have to flop in the park."

"Shut up. What do you know about anything?"

"Jesus, sound asleep I'm smarter'n you are when you're wide awake."

And no use going back to the farm. That's the first place they'd look for her. Jeannie didn't need whoofare workers and cops and who knows what all coming down on her like flies onto cow patties.

Besides, you could actually have some fun here. Not all the guys hanging around here were skipping school.

"So what d'ya say, Dolly? You wanna come dancin'?"

"They won't let me in. I don't have ID."

"So we'll go where they don't ask for ID. No prob-lehm. C'mon, we'll get us into a cab and get the nice man to take us to where I know there's a party goin' on. We can boogie all we want."

"I don't even know your name, mister."

"I'm no mister, dolly. I'm Sid."

"I'm not Dolly, Sid. I'm DeeJay."

"Hi, DeeJay."

"Hi, Sid."

"So why aren't you in school?"

"Because I'm here. Why aren't you at work?"

"Because we're on two-week shutdown is why. They'll fly us back into camp a week from the day after tomorrow. You be sure to remind me, okay? I'd hate to miss the plane."

"Why not?" she laughed. "After all, we both missed the boat."

"I never missed no boat." He waved at a taxi. "Come on, DeeJay, let's go find the party."

The party was all over a little shingled house set three-quarters of the way back on a long thin lot at the far end of town. The faded paint had peeled off the shingles, the front steps sort of leaned to one side and wobbled when they walked up them, and the two-bedroom-living room-kitchen-and-bathroom place was full of people, most of them with long-necked bottles clutched in their fists.

The stereo was going, but not loudly, and what was coming out of it was sixties mouldy oldies. Everyone seemed to know all the words to all the songs, and some of the drinkers were pretending to be singers, but nobody was convinced, not even themselves.

She knew she'd be the youngest there. She thought everyone would tease her but the most that got said was a comment directed at Sid. "You figure it's worth a stint in the crowbar hotel?" "Eat your heart out, mung mouth," Sid laughed. "Eat your fuckin' heart out."

DeeJay didn't really like the taste of beer but that's about all there was, except for some stuff that was worse. She figured if she just kind of held onto it she'd look as if she was drinking without having to drink.

Sid noticed even before he went to the fridge to get another for himself. "You don't like beer?"

"Not much."

"What do you like?"

"I don't know." She decided to lay it on the line and let him decide for himself if she was just too dumb to be bothered with. "I never drank anything before."

He grinned. "What else haven't you done before?" and she felt her face going brick red. He laughed softly and moved to plug in an electric kettle. DeeJay drank tea for a while, then someone yelled he was heading off on a beer run and Sid went over to talk to him. When the guy came back Sid took a couple of bottles from him and mixed a drink for DeeJay. "Try this," he said, "see how you like it."

She tasted it tentatively. "It's okay," she dared, "it's a bit like lemonade."

"Lemon gin," he told her. "There's nothing better for a starter."

It was okay, but it wasn't really good. She just sipped at it, but Sid didn't seem to think he'd wasted his money. And at least she could get it down, which was more than could be said for the beer.

They danced, then danced some more. People came and people

left. There were some more beer runs and two guys got into some kind of fight but the others pushed them out into the back yard and ignored the stupidity.

Someone turned on the lights and DeeJay realized it was getting dark outside. Talk about time flying. Didn't seem like they'd been there any length of time at all and the entire afternoon had just vanished.

"You getting hungry?" Sid asked. "I'm about ready to eat a horse and chase down the rider."

"I guess so." She didn't quite know what was expected of her. Well, it was okay, she had hamburger money in her jeans pocket.

Someone was heading off in a car and Sid yelled at him to wait up, they'd catch a ride with him. DeeJay found her jacket, and Sid's, and then they were in the back seat of the car but she couldn't remember going out of the house or down the steps. Sid was sitting with his arm around her shoulders, singing with the country and western coming from the static-y car radio. DeeJay kind of moved closer to him and dared to rest her head against his upper arm. He grinned and winked.

They went to the Golden Dragon and had the Number Three Special for Two, and then, because Sid was still hungry, they shared a plate of deep-fried prawns in golden plum sauce. Sid put away a couple of beer but DeeJay had Chinese tea because she knew the waiter wouldn't believe she was old enough for a drink and she didn't want to be confronted.

She wasn't quite as bleary when they left the restaurant as she had been when they went in, and yet she felt almost giddy.

"So, what's next?" Sid asked, sliding his arm around her waist. "Where would you like to go and what would you like to do?"

"I'd like to go to Paris," she told him, "and stand on a bridge over the River Seine."

"Me too. And see pyramids and the Great Wall of China and maybe those pagodas in Thailand, too. Think we got time before I have to head back next week?"

"Probably not," she agreed. "Anyway, I don't think these jeans are exactly what they've got in mind as travel wardrobe."

"Oh, I don't know. Looks good to me. We can go back to the party we were at or we can find us another one."

They went back to the party but the house was so jammed there wasn't room to dance. Someone was passing around some home-grown and DeeJay took a puff, but it didn't do anything for her. She didn't think she felt any different after the second puff, either, or the third for that matter. Here she was drinking and toking and still no hint as to what it was about all this that was so tempting Patsy had dedicated her entire goddamn life to it. Oh well, takes all kinds.

They went to another party and if she'd been asked she'd have sworn on a stack of bibles they were only there a half hour or so, but it must have been longer than that because when they walked into Sid's hotel room the electric clock said half past three and then some.

Sid did something with the TV and then phoned the desk clerk, and the screen bounced a bit before settling down to show a movie. There was a little fridge kind of thing against one wall and he put the lemon gin in it with a two-four of beer, then went out of the room and down the hall. When he came back he had a couple of cans of Sprite and a cardboard tub of ice cubes.

"So any time you want to go home you just say so," he told her, pouring lemon gin over three or four ice cubes and adding about two tablespoons of Sprite.

"Not much to go home for," she laughed. "By now my mother will either be passed out over the table, puking in the john, or entertaining some friggin' loser."

"Easy," he laughed, "that friggin' loser might be my old man!" And they both laughed.

"Oh well," she shrugged, "everybody's got a sad song to sing, they just can't find an audience, eh."

"Yeah." He ripped open a bag of Cheezies and dropped it in her lap, then sat beside her. "So if I start kissing you, are you going to scream for help?"

"Not very loudly."

"Yeah? That's nice to know. When do you start to scream loudly?"

"I don't know," she gulped at her drink, then coughed and felt stupid. "I never was in a hotel room before in my life. And I don't have any idea what it is you expect."

"Really?" He looked as if he didn't believe her. DeeJay couldn't think of anything to say that he would believe so she said nothing, just looked down at the floor and turned her glass around and around, making the ice cubes clink against the sides. "Well, maybe I'll go visit the ice machines again," he said and he was gone, leaving her to watch the grotty movie on the television. It was pretty rank, and pretty stupid, too. You wondered how anybody got the money together for a piece of garbage like that and once they got the money why didn't they hire some good actors instead of those people who looked as if they ought to be sweeping streets instead.

He came back and sat next to her, then kissed her. She didn't know what to do with her glass, or with her hands, or anything. After a while she got a crick in her neck sitting with her head turned sideways. She kind of squirmed and he took the glass from her and put it over on the table next to the TV. "What a piece of shit," he said, and switched off the grot.

A while later he took off his jeans and jockey shorts and sat on the sofa digging in his jeans pocket. He brought out a little square cardboard box and from it took a foil-wrapped wafer. "Dispenser down by the ice cube machine," he grinned. She didn't understand until he opened the foil and she saw what it was he was putting on his thing, then she felt suddenly shy and at the same time less scared.

It wasn't too comfortable on the sofa, but then afterward they had a shower and went to the bed and that time it wasn't too uncomfortable at all. When he was finished he grinned at her and licked her belly, then went to the fridge for beer. She would have rather had a Sprite but she drank the beer, and they smoked a joint he pulled from his shirt pocket.

She napped, but only briefly because Sid woke her up again and when she kind of cringed away he looked puzzled. "Kind of sore," she admitted. He beamed as if she'd just finished singing happy birthday or something. He spit on his fingers and rubbed her, and that stung too, but she didn't say anything because he thought he was making it easier for her. Well, it wasn't, and it lasted a long long time, she was starting to get really uncomfortable when suddenly he was making a lot of noise, gasping and grunting and saying Jesus Jesus and thank God it was finished with and they could move a bit and she could get the cramp out of her back.

She would have loved the chance to go to sleep but by then the sun was coming through the window and the traffic was hooting and tooting up and down the street and Sid was making noises about eating horses and chasing down the riders again.

They got dressed and went to Smitty's for breakfast, and DeeJay didn't know she was hungry until the food came. In the women's room she got a pad from the dispenser to catch the dribbles. She supposed she'd have to go home for some clean clothes, and she wasn't looking forward to that, Patsy would probably scream and yell and make a real good impression on the visiting company.

"I guess I have to go get some clothes," she told Sid. "That ought to be fun."

"Yeah, your old lady will probably shit bricks. Why not pass on the idea? There's stores in town and I got three months' wages burnin' a hole in my pocket. Time enough for strife when you can't find a way to avoid it," and he winked at her. "Besides, I don't really want to meet your mother."

"Neither would any other sane person."

She would have just picked up some underwear and maybe a toothbrush, but once started Sid was a fool for sales tags. Then they had lunch and went back to the hotel room for the fashion show. Nothing fancy, jeans and tee shirts, some socks and a bright blue satin jacket with a big #1 on the left sleeve.

"How about number four?" Sid lay on the bed, his arms under his head, and grinned at her. "And five and six and so it goes."

And so it went, right up until the following Sunday when he got into the float plane. She stood on the dock and waved until the plane took off, then she trudged back to the apartment with her shopping bags and her new stuff.

"My daughter the slut!" Patsy screamed.

"Put a sock in it, will you?"

"Where have you *been?*"

"Not here!" DeeJay snapped. "And not with an old fart like you!" Patsy hauled back to give her a slap in the face and DeeJay dropped her shopping bags, clenched her fist and held it out where Patsy could see every knuckle. "You just fuckin' dare," she gritted.

"I'll give it right back to you!" Patsy dropped her hand. DeeJay lowered her fist. And that was that for family discussions.

Sid had given her some money before he left "so's you can buy stamps and stuff and write me letters." She bought writing paper and envelopes and stamps, but she bought some groceries, too.

"I didn't know you knew how to cook," said Patsy, packing away hamburger patties with gravy, mashed spuds and salad.

"I can cook."

"I never learned."

"Oh you don't have to tell *me* you never learned to cook," Dee-Jay sniped. "I'm the one had to gnaw her way through burnt offering, remember?"

"Yeah, well, this is good."

Somehow they got into a routine. The whoofare cheque would come in the door, Patsy would sign it, DeeJay would take it to the supermarket and get a shitload of groceries, then hand over the change.

"Know what they do? All the prices in this end of town are higher than they are over in the other end where people have got cars and stuff and can drive right past a place if they don't like it. Funny, huh, the ones with enough money to be able to afford goddamn near anything at all wind up with the best bargains because the stores want to keep their business, and those of us without cars who have to bring our bags home on the bus, we wind up paying way lots more because we can't troop all over the place lookin' for cheap stuff. Got ya comin' and goin', don't they."

The MiniMart was only two blocks from the roach palace they called their apartment. DeeJay was on her way for groceries just as the manager was taping a hand-lettered sign to the glass door. Help Wanted, it said.

"So," she grinned widely, "you gonna give *me* that job?"

The manager knew her slightly. "What qualifications do you have?"

"Well, for one thing I do my shopping here. And for another I only live down the street so I'll hardly be late for work. Besides," and she grinned again, "you can probably get me for cheaper than you'd get a human being."

Human beings got about twice as much as she got, but what

she got was one helluva lot more than she'd been getting. She worked from two in the afternoon until closing time at ten at night and her mealtime was any time she could grab a bite without leaving customers unattended.

"The whoofare finds out you're working and it's going to bugger up my money," Patsy warned.

"That is your lookout, lady, not mine. I got better things to do with *my* life than sit on my ass waiting for you to take the whoofare cheque to the bar."

"Jesus Christ, how did I get stuck with a bitch of a kid like you?"

"You fuckin' *made* me live with you, remember? I was doin' fine where I was."

"Why *they* wanted you I'm damned if I know!"

"Yeah, and I love you too. I think not."

"The least you could do is chip in on the rent."

"I do. I buy groceries. You don't. You wouldn't eat nothing but shit if I wasn't bringing home groceries."

"Just my luck. I prob'ly gave away the *nice* one!"

"More likely the lucky one! Lucky enough she never had to see your ugly face or hear your whine, whine, whine."

It was true. Patsy whined. Even when she had a smile on her face there was an ingratiating fawning undertone to her voice that was guaranteed to set a person's teeth on edge. The day DeeJay figured out Patsy's age was a day that, even at the time, she knew she wasn't going to forget. She looked at her mother, the realizations started to strike, and DeeJay just stared. Patsy was thin, not very tall, and from behind, if she would just straighten her shoulders, she might look like a teen-ager. There was something half-formed or tentative about her hips and waist. The slumped shoulders told the cold truth, though, and made you wonder if Patsy had ever really been a kid, maybe she'd been born weary. Her face wasn't so much lined as permanently sagged; you could have turned loose the makeup artists of Hollywood and no matter what they did, Patsy would have looked the way she looked with no warpaint on her at all. Almost exhausted. Her eyes were like scorch marks and when she got up the energy to smile it was enough to make a body wish she hadn't bothered trying. And Dee-

Jay went cold when she realized she had been born at a time when her mother was no older than she was now.

"Do I have any grandparents or anything?" she dared.

"Why d'you want to know a thing like that?"

"Well, don't I have a right to know? How come there's never been a grandma on the scene? You an orphan or something?"

"I'd'a been better off if I had been. We'd'a both been better off if I'd'a been an orphan." Then she laughed. "Next best thing to it, I guess. "

"Well?" DeeJay persisted.

"Leave me alone about it, okay?"

"No."

"They kicked me out, all right? You happy now? I got the boot. The old one-two-three-heave-*ho!*" and she waved her arms as if emptying water from a rusty pail.

"Why?"

"It's none'a your beeswax. Drop it."

"Why?"

"I am not going to rehash all that old shit. They kicked me out. Period. And I stayed kicked out. Period two. And then I was up the stump with you and that ripped 'er for all time. Period three. And nothing's got any better since then, either! So put a cap on it."

"Where do they live?"

"Why do you want to know? You think you're going to put on your Sunday-go-to-meetin' jeans and tee shirt and show up on their front door ringin' the old bell, so that when they open 'er up you can give 'em a big dental display and say Hi, I'm your granddaughter Donna Jean and you're just gonna fall in love with me?"

It was so close to what DeeJay had started imagining that she almost choked.

"Well, forget it, kiddo. Far as they're concerned apples don't fall far from the tree. If you're my kid you're the spawn of sin and the sins of the mothers shall be visited upon their children, and all that good Christian forgiving crap and corruption. They'd gladly pay ten bucks for the chance to throw horse puckies at both'a us. Besides, I haven't seen 'em in nearly seventeen years. How'n hell am I supposed to know where they live?"

42

"So where *did* they live at the time?"

Patsy stared at DeeJay for a long time then went to the fridge and got out a bottle of cheap wine. She unscrewed the cap and threw it in the garbage, then got a jam jar and went back to the sofa and sat on it, glaring as she poured wine. Finally she nodded. "Okay," she said tiredly, "okay, you got your rights, I guess. You wanna go and see 'em, you take yourself to Vancouver. And in Vancouver you go to the bus depot. . ." Step by step by step she outlined the directions, her voice flat and expressionless, so flat and so expressionless DeeJay knew Patsy had been making this trip in her mind so often it had become a boring commute. "And right about then," she said, looking up and glaring bitterly, "is when they'll empty the thundermug on your head."

"Nice bunch," was all DeeJay could think to say.

"And just think, after the last trumpet sounds heaven will be *full* of 'em! The thought of spendin' eternity with that bunch might well be what spurred me along the road to hell. So now you know and don't you even so much as *ask* ever again or you'll get the old heave-ho, just like I did!"

"No," DeeJay snarled. "I couldn't be that lucky. If I'd'a had any luck at all I'd'a been born in a ditch."

"For all you know you were."

They bickered bitterly all the time except when they were screaming and practically coming to blows, each holding the other responsible for all the errors and omissions of life itself.

Sid came out of camp again and instead of a hotel room for the duration, he got himself a tourist cabin on the bank of a small river five minutes' walk from the bus line. He already knew from letters that DeeJay was working, and where, so he didn't waste any time checking with Patsy or going around to the apartment, he went to the MiniMart. DeeJay grinned from ear to ear when she saw him, but there were customers in the store so all they did was touch hands briefly, and laugh softly.

"Hey, you," she said. "About time you showed up, I was starting to think you'd flushed yourself down the john."

"Yeah," he agreed. "Been too long. So how you been?"

He went across the street and down a block to wait in the beer parlour until her shift was over. She worried he'd forget the time and she'd wind up standing on the sidewalk asking people who were going in to tell him she was waiting, but he was as keen to see her as she was to see him and when she left the store Sid was strolling back from the pub.

"Hey, there." He put his arm around her and gave her a tight hug. "Sure is good to see you. You wanna go party hearty?"

"You know it," she agreed. She'd have gone to the river to watch spawned fish die if that was what he had in mind.

They joined up with some friends of his at a motel and for a few hours they danced, told jokes or listened to others tell them, but finally they quit pretending there wasn't something else they would rather do, and they called a cab and went to Sid's tourist cabin.

"Oh, it's not that bad," he yawned, lighting cigarettes for them both and lying back against his pillow. "I mean the average guy he works five days and gets two off, right, and what does that give you time to do? You can't even work up a good drunk in that time, not when you have to be back at work and wide awake come Monday ay-em. So I get the same days off, I just get 'em all in a swell foop, and I like it that way. We work from as soon as you can see until just before you can't see any more, then ride the crummy back down the access road to camp. Time for a hot shower and some clean clothes, then over to the cookshack to fill up on what Cookie's been slavin' over all day while we been cuttin' sticks. So by the time you've fueled up and packed away some groceries, hey, it's just about time to go get your teddy bear and bunny-foot jammies."

She laughed at the image of Sid in Dr. Dentons, padding down the hallway with a Pooh bear tucked under his arm. "What's funny?" he asked, and she told him. He chuckled with her, then stubbed out his cigarette and yawned. She passed hers to him to stub out and they snuggled down together comfortably, bare skin touching.

"Listen, you, I'll turn you both over if this doesn't stop!" Patsy yelled, her face flushed with anger. "She'll wind up with the whoofare and you, mister smart-ass big-time Charlie, you can cool your pecker off in the crowbar hotel!"

"Ah, go find something to jab into your arm! I only came for some clean clothes is all."

"Clean clothes is all, huh? What about your damn job?"

"Don't you worry about *my* job!" DeeJay yelled. "You don't know job from snot so don't give me any lip about it. My job is fine, just fine. More than can be said for any goddamn job *you* ever had!"

"T'hell with her," Sid raged. "Grab a whole buncha stuff while you're at it. Who needs this crap? Do I need this crap? I don't need this crap!"

They left Patsy flipping out in the apartment and stormed off, Sid carrying the plastic garbage bag stuffed with clothes. DeeJay went to work, still angry, and Sid took the bag of clothes back to his tourist cabin. When DeeJay's shift was done, Sid was waiting, leaning against the plate glass of the big front window.

"Hey, sweetheart," he laughed softly. "What do you say to a nice steak supper?"

"I had the idea first." She held out the brown paper-wrapped package. "The best in the store and an employee discount, too."

She took her time and she fussed over the late supper, remembering everything Jeannie had told her. She even ripped the lettuce instead of cutting it with a knife.

"And to top it off," Sid laughed, "she can cook!"

The day before Sid went back into camp, DeeJay took her garbage bag of clothes and another of kitchen stuff they had left over, like fancy lemon-spice-and pepper mixes for seafood and five-spice for Chinese food and Greek seasoning for salads and lamb, back to the apartment. Patsy glared at them bitterly, her face bruised, her lip swollen, one eye half-shut and darkened.

DeeJay shook her head. "What happened to you? Talking when you should have been listening?"

"Go ahead, gloat," Patsy answered. Then, surprisingly, she grinned. "Just another case of the innocent bystander catchin' the flak is all; and for the first time in my life the cops were on my side. That just about finished me. The old heart near stopped when the cuntstable said I should press charges and sue." She shrugged. "So you gonna spend the night here?"

"No, but I'll see you tomorrow after the plane takes off," DeeJay said. Patsy just nodded, as if she'd known as much but had to ask anyway, for the sake of politeness, or something.

Sid came out of camp early, because of snow in the bush. There was next to no warning at all, in fact the first DeeJay knew about it he was standing in the lineup at the cash, grinning from ear to ear with a pushcart of groceries.

"I didn't even see you come in!" she gasped.

"Fooled ya, huh?" He would have kissed her if it hadn't been for the people in line behind him. "Well, here I are, as they say. And don't make any plans for supper because that's all taken care of, okay?"

They went to the Golden Dragon and pigged out, smiling at each other often and reaching across the table to touch hands.

"Gonna be out for a while," he told her. "Probably won't go back until oh, April, maybe. Think you can put up with me for that long?"

"I think so."

"Good. Maybe we ought to look for something a bit more perma-hoozie than a tourist court, what do you think? We might find us someplace with the old white picket fence or something."

"Jesus," she breathed. "That's kind of heavy."

"Yeah, well, you got a strong back."

"But I could still keep workin', huh?"

"Fuckin' right you're gonna work!" he laughed heartily. "You think I'm gonna spend time with a lady of leisure? You can work and I can find out what it's like to take advantage of the good things in life."

They didn't get a place with a picket fence, they didn't get a place with any fence at all. They got an apartment, with no yard, just a parking lot and a little brick thingamy with some dirt in it which they made jokes about each time they passed. "Damn nice of them to build a box for the neighbourhood cats to crap in," Sid said. "Maybe we should grow us some em-jay in there and I could put up a stand and sell it to the passers-by."

DeeJay had to leave the apartment at one-fifteen to catch the bus to the MiniMart stop. That meant she got to work early but if she waited until the next bus she would have been late and the boss was crusty at the best of times. It made for a long day but it also meant if anyone on the earlier shift wanted to leave early, DeeJay could cover for them so that if something came up, they would cover for her and she wouldn't have to worry about losing her job. Theoretically it was a good deal all the way around, but she figured the first time she needed a favour someone's grandmother would be sick or there would be an appointment couldn't be broken. Still, you never know until you try.

For her seventeenth birthday Sid got her a pretty little watch with a gold expansion bracelet and roman numerals on the dial. "My sister had one like it," he explained, "so I thought ... I like 'em better than those other ones with the blinking lights and flip-flopping numbers."

"It's gorgeous," she blinked back tears. "I never had anything this nice before in my life."

"You're gonna have *lots* of nice stuff," he promised.

Their apartment came furnished and the stuff had the look of the sale catalogue but it was better than anything DeeJay had known except for the foster home stuff, and that had never been hers or anything close to hers, even at the time. She got some tablets to drop one at a time into the toilet tank to keep things clean and stop any smells, she got spray stuff that would clean the bathtub without scratching the porcelain, she got stuff to put down her drains to keep them from belching back gases, and she tried half a dozen different spray cans of furniture polish before she found the one she liked best. She got room deodorizers for each room, evergreen and spice in the bathroom, floral for the bedroom, cinnamon for the living room because Sid smoked almost nonstop and she didn't want the place to smell like an old ashtray, the way Patsy's place sometimes did. There was blue stuff in a spray bottle to do the windows and mirrors, there was stuff to sprinkle on the rugs and carpets before you vacuumed, and other stuff to hang in the closets so the moths wouldn't eat your clothes. There was even stuff you could put in your fridge to keep it from smelling like old coffee cream, green onions and ripe cheese.

But it seemed as if nothing she bought and nothing she did with what she bought could make the place inviting enough or comfortable enough for Sid. "I just got to get used to being settled, is all," he said. "I'm just not used to it, DeeJay. I mean usually I come out and buy new jeans and the party starts, right? And we haven't been partying, we're as stuck in a rut as if we'd been married for ten years or something."

So they partied, but it wasn't the same. DeeJay could hack it for a day or two but she started to feel as if she was short of sleep, and if the party decided to hop into cars and head off to Victoria for breakfast she had to say no, because you could guarantee they'd never be back in time for her to go to work.

"Well quit the goddamn job why don't you!" Sid yelled. "It hardly pays worth the shoe leather to walk to the goddamn bus stop anyway!"

"Don't *you* tell me what to do!" she answered. "The day I gotta take orders from a shortass like you is the day I turn in my belly button and resign from the human fuckin' race!"

"Kiss my ass, bitch," he laughed. "You don't have me so pussywhipped you can run the whole show your own way."

They made it up, of course. Nobody even slammed out of the apartment. Nobody went off in a huff, nobody even went off in a cab. They just snapped and snarled at each other for a while then both of them said "I'm sorry," and they agreed to put it behind them.

Sometimes DeeJay would come home from work and Sid would be sitting watching TV and sucking on a beer. Other times she'd come home from work and the place would be empty, the lights out, the TV off, and the scent of room deodorant winning, for a change, against the smell of his cigarettes. DeeJay didn't mind. She'd grill a cheese sandwich, have a little tub of yogurt, soak in a nice scented bath and crawl into bed hoping she could sleep without dreaming about the cash register and the groceries coming toward her on the little lazy susan. Sometimes Sid came in around three or four, sometimes he showed up for breakfast, a couple of times he phoned her around nine in the morning to say he was in Ladysmith, or Parksville, and would see her when she got home from work.

"Listen, kid, I got some not-so-hot news for you," Patsy told her.

"If it's not so hot keep it to yourself," DeeJay answered, putting hot croissants on the table between the teapot and the jar of strawberry jam.

"Well, no, I don't think so." Patsy smeared jam on a roll, and tasted it tentatively. "Bugger's hot," she remarked, but she bit into it eagerly all the same.

"Well, at least let me get my bum on the chair before you pull the sky down around my ears. What is it? You get arrested again?"

"Your old man was in the bar last night."

"I know he was, what do you think, he sneaks out the window or something? I know he was in the goddamn bar. And then he went to a party. And then the party went to Duncan."

"Yeah? Well the party mighta gone to Duncan but he didn't. He's fuckin' around on you."

"Bullshit he is."

"He is, too. And I can tell you who with."

"You'd like the chance, wouldn't you? You'd love the chance to just ruin it all and then sit back and say I told ya so, and laugh up your fuckin' sleeve!" and she slammed her hand on the table, but the tears were already pouring. "Why don't you tell someone who *cares*, Patsy?"

"Yeah, you fuckin' big-mouth bitch!" Sid sighed from the doorway to the bedroom.

"You gonna deny it?" Patsy dared, finishing her croissant and reaching for another. "You gonna stand there in your underwear with your hairy chest shoved in the world's face and try to convince my daughter you weren't in up to your pubes with Caroline Macy? Who happens," she sent the arrow in as deep as she could, "to be the kid sister of the guy I had breakfast with today! Who happens to have shown up in the coffee shop with no-sleep-for-me bags under her eyes and a grin like a cheshy cat because she'd'a paid ten bucks for the chance to tell me she was cuttin' hay in my daughter's pasture! You stinkin' pussy-bandit bastard!" Patsy smiled pleasantly. "You ain't from this town, eh? You don't *know* people, see? So you don't got enough sense to know who you can bugger around with and not get caught and who's gonna blow it for you just as fast as possible. I live here, eh. I got friends here, eh."

"You got no friends, you cheap hunk of shit," Sid answered.

"All's you got is a bunch of bloody barflies gathered around the same shit heap as yourself."

"Ah, g'wan back to bed and try to think up some excuses she'll believe after I've gone and you start tryin' to cover your ass."

"I never did," he said, after Patsy left. "I don't care who told what to who or where they were when they did it, and if you want, you can phone anyone who was at the party and they'll tell you."

"Oh, sure, I'm going to phone around checking up on you the same as if I was your mother and you were six years old or something. Sure, I am. And have 'em all laughin' like hell, too!"

"Well, I never did!" he yelled. "You heard what she said! The damn lyin' bitch woulda paid ten bucks for the chance to make trouble. But she didn't have to, your old lady was ready to jump for no money at all! Jesus H. Christ what a fuckin' hole of a town, I can hardly wait to get back to camp where the only thing you got to worry about is a fuckin' tree comin' down on your head or a snapped cable bustin' your back or somethin'!"

"Just tell her she's full of shit," DeeJay said to Patsy. "Tell her on her best day she ain't woman enough to get anythin' but leftovers."

"If that's how you want it, honey," Patsy agreed. "I wouldn't give up without a fight myself, can't expect you to, I guess."

They hung in until Sid went back into camp but by the time he climbed into the float plane they both knew they'd had the best of it and it would never be anything but warmed-up leftovers from now on. DeeJay almost cried, but she was damned if she'd give the watching world the satisfaction.

"You be careful," she warned. "You watch out for those busted cables and all."

"You, too, darlin'," he smiled, but it wasn't the ear-to-ear smile, it was the one that looked as if there was a whole bunch of stuff he wanted to say and didn't quite know how to put into words.

So she moved back in with Patsy and they both acted as if nothing of any consequence had happened.

"Well, Jesus," Patsy sighed, "the son of a bitch done 'er on purpose."

"He did no such thing!" DeeJay yelled. "People don't *do* things like that on purpose!"

"You'd be surprised what people do," Patsy answered, glowering darkly. "On purpose. People do the damnedest stuff and do it on purpose just to flush other people's toilets. Stuff that makes no sense at all gets done just to drive home a point."

"God, the people you hang out with must sure be the world's prize examples of something-or-other."

"Hey, darlin', the people I hang out with are the people *you* hang out with, too, you know!"

DeeJay had been stepping out with Patsy for the past three weeks or so. It seemed as if she just couldn't quite manage to unwind after work, no sense going back to Patsy's stinking apartment and sitting staring at a TV that had seen its better days when Sgt. Bilko was still a hit. She knew others no older than herself who could pass in the pub, and anyway, Patsy knew where to get some ID that said DeeJay was two years older than her actual age. As long as she kept a low profile she'd be okay. After an hour or two of listening to jokes and watching people lurch sideways into the jukebox, even the apartment and her fold-out couch seemed like a great place to be, and she could sleep until it was time to wake up and start coming to life for work.

So that much of what Patsy said might have been maybe half true. But the other part was just stupid. DeeJay knew what it was. It was those last two or three nights where both of them were trying hard to convince themselves and each other that something hadn't gone flat and stale between them. And no sense blaming Sid. If there was to be any goddamn blame, hang it around her own neck, she should have gone to the doctor lots earlier, everyone knows rubbers are only about ninety percent effective at the best of times.

"It's not too late," Patsy said hopefully. "We could go to the doctor and get it flushed. I'd hold your hand."

"You'd likely spit in it," DeeJay snapped. "Anyway, I'm not flushin' it."

"You ain't *keepin'* it!"

"There's always the good old family tradition of giving it away."

"Shoulda give *you* away and that's no lie."

"You don't know how friggin' true that is. I mighta been lucky and been adopted by a serial murderer and his next chosen victim. Been better'n what's come down so far, believe you me, lady."

"So you say," Patsy laughed. "But you'd'a still been so stupid as to believe he was just reading the National Geographic with Susie Cream Cheese there, and you'd'a still been stupid to think them damn sausage-skin gumboots don't leak, and you'd'a still been stupid enough to wind up the butt of the oldest joke in the history of mankind."

"He did not," DeeJay countered. "He's not that kind of person. Maybe the people *you* know are that kind of person, but don't send other people to hell for your own wrongdoings."

"Christ, and now it's turned into a preacher. Don't that top the cake."

She was about four months along and just starting to show when out of nowhere at all, surprises never cease, there was Jeannie in the store lineup with a little kid DeeJay had never seen before and a collection of popsicles and Joo-sees.

"For crying out loud!" Jeannie said happily. "Who you don't see when you don't got a net, eh!"

DeeJay grinned until she thought her face would split. "What are you doing in the low-rent end of town? And who's the little boomer?"

"This is Georgie; he's got your bedroom now."

"Hey, you take good care of my stuff, you hear?" DeeJay rang the popsicles and Joo-sees through the till and gave Jeannie the employee discount on them. "Just don't tell the boss, okay, he can be a real pill at times."

"So why haven't you come around to visit or something?"

"Oh, I don't know." DeeJay looked everywhere except at Jeannie's smiling face.

"What do you mean, you don't know. Come out for a visit. If you need a ride, phone, I'll come and get you."

"Ah, you don't want all your damn fosters showin' up for week-end barbecue, you'd be crowded out of a place at the potato salad bowl."

"Don't you tell me what I want and don't want. I'd'a come and got you a long time ago but nobody would tell me where you were livin', and when I tried to find you in the phone book..."

"Yeah, well, Patsy can't get a phone any more, she didn't pay her bill so many times they put her on the bad list."

"Welfare wouldn't tell me a thing!"

DeeJay was so pleased she thought she would jump up and down. "You mean it?"

"'Course I mean it. Why don't you make plans for your next days off. When *are* your days off?"

"Tuesdays and Wednesdays. But you don't want..."

"I'll meet you out front here at ten Tuesday morning. You be there, DeeJay! I mean it, now! You be there or I'll be here on Thursday and raise such a big stink your job will be past history."

Tuesday morning at ten DeeJay was waiting and had been for fifteen minutes. At five after, Jeannie's station wagon slid to a halt in the loading zone.

"Come on," she called, "hop in front. Don't let Georgie dribble that creamsicle down the back of your neck. Georgie, I told you, if you want to eat that thing you sit down and eat it properly, otherwise it's goin' out the window for the cats and dogs. And I mean it, mister, I'm not having the inside of this jalopy stuck up with ice cream and junk. Just sit your bum on the seat, do up your safety belt, and pay attention to that thing before it drips itself all over your arm. That kid," she sighed. "Honest to God, he's more trouble than the whole other tribe of 'em put together ever was. I'm gonna give him away to the first gypsy that comes by collecting."

"She means it, Georgie," DeeJay warned. "I wasn't good and she gave *me* away. And now you got that bed, fella, so take a telling."

"Now you've done it, you've scared the piss right outta him," Jeannie laughed.

Georgie didn't believe DeeJay any more than he had believed Jeannie, he just shrugged and slurped at his melting ice cream.

"So, do up your seatbelt, we're on our way."

"Where we going?"

"Home, a'course."

They had lunch on the sundeck and Georgie was allowed to use the long-handled fork to turn the wieners on the barbecue. "You can get him to eat anything at all as long as you give him a barbecued wiener," Jeannie said. "Then he gorps that down and you say Okay, you want another, you finish what's on your plate. And that's it, he scoffs that, too. He'd live on bloody wieners. When he first came that's all he knew to eat. First time I put a hot meal down in front of him he started to cry. We figured he thought it was gonna burn him or something. Anyway, he hardly ate at all that first week, then he saw some wieners in the fridge and he just about had a fit. So I cooked some up and from then on we had 'er made; cut the wieners into little bits, and put some mashed spuds on a piece, he'd eat the spuds to get the wiener. A slice of carrot and a bit of wiener, two green beans and some wiener, and now he'll eat just fine. As long as there's wiener. I mean this kid, really, he eats pork chops with wieners! I'm waitin' for him to eat strawberry shortcake with wieners. So, are you pregnant or is that a punkin growing under your shirt?"

"It's not a pumpkin," DeeJay admitted, blushing.

"Ah, baby," Jeannie shook her head. "You sure bit off a mouthful."

"Patsy wanted me to flush it but . . ." Her eyes filled. "I couldn't. I know it makes good sense and all, but . . . . So I thought about adoption a bit. Patsy did that, she gave one away."

"They try to match them up with people who are just about desperate and who can give the kid a real good home."

"Yeah," DeeJay nodded. "But . . . like, you know, you see these things on TV all the time, people who were adopted twenty, thirty years ago, and they've spent how long poking around in records and running ads and finally they drive six thousand miles or something just for the chance to stand bawlin' their eyes out over someone who's a total stranger."

"There's worse things."

"Yeah. And, like, I know if Patsy hadda done that with me I mighta done the looking part but if I wound up cryin' it wouldn't be tears of joy, you know. And I doubt I'd off-load my adoptive mom just for the chance to try to forge some kind of a bond with that bimbo."

"But you never came here after you left," Jeannie said softly. "Or phoned, or anything."

"Yeah. I just . . . what good would it have done? It woulda just made both of us miserable. Well, made me miserable, anyway," she amended.

"People's rights, people's rights, people's rights!" Jeannie dug into the potato salad bowl with a big spoon and plopped a generous dollop on her plate. "I get sick to death with all this goddamn 'rights' stuff, I tell you. Civil rights, legal rights, moral rights, religious rights, women's rights, gay rights, everybody's got such a heap of them except for the kids and the poor."

"Easy now, you'll have a cardiac arrest."

"Be lucky if I don't get another kind of arrest before much time has passed." Jeannie slid a look over at Georgie who had finished his wiener and was waiting for something else to eat. Jeannie gave him salad, green and potato, and another wiener with mild mustard on it. "Like someone I could name but won't because little pitchers have big ears," she continued. "Well, they say, he's not adoptable because he might be developmentally arrested. More of those damn arrests, right? No, he can't be adopted because maybe he's a gibble in some way. If he is, it don't show, believe me. Couldn't talk a word when he got here and two months later he's jabberin' away like a whole roomful of hyperactives. Natter natter natter, drive me nuts. He couldn't crayon a picture. So I got him crayons and a colouring book and I showed him what it was for and what did they say? Well, they said, he was still late doing it. No wonder, I said, nobody ever gave him crayons to do it with! So then they say well, anyway, they say, his mother might decide at some future time that *she* wants . . . so I said look, I'm not getting jacked around on this one. I don't care what *she* wants. I mean the woman wanted to sniff coke up her nose, and they didn't let her do that. The woman wanted to ram stuff in her veins and they wouldn't let her do that, either. The woman wanted to write bad cheques and hold up banks and they said no, so why just because she decides she'd like chance number two to drive this guy nuts do they think maybe they'll go along with it. Got a lawyer. And if I have to I'll be on fuckin' TV, I tell you, I've had about as much of it as I'm gonna bother even trying to enjoy." She moved quickly, got out of her chair, came around the table, hugged DeeJay and kissed her cheek. "I tell you, the day they hauled us down outta the tree and said you were going to have to pack your grip and hit the road like it or not, was the day *this* woman realized she had a gut full! When you drove off in that goddamn car with that stunned idiot whose wages come out of *my* taxes . . . . I went to my bedroom and I cried until I had to go to the bathroom and vomit."

"Ah, Jeannie," DeeJay sobbed.

"So I said, No more. Absolutely no more of this nonsense. You quit cryin', you'll give that baby colic if you cry."

It was such an incredible relief to realize Jeannie cared for her as much as she cared for Jeannie. And almost as big a relief to have some other mind-set, another head load of ideas to bounce things off as she attempted to figure out what she was going to do about almost anything you could name.

"Oh, now, don't do that, DeeJay! Don't get all stiff-necked and hard-nosed and rock-headed and *dumb!* You never made a mistake? You never acted like a total jerk? Listen, everybody in the world, up to and including the Queen of England, has been a jerk at one or two or ten times in their life. What's the absolutely worst thing that could have happened that night? Right, the worst thing that could have happened would be that he *did* make out with that woman. So there it is. The worst thing he coulda done. Number one, you aren't married to him, okay? Number two, he made no promises that you ever mentioned to me. And number three, every dog is entitled to one bite before they put a bullet in its heart. You know, if I'd'a done what you're trying to talk yourself into doing, Bud and I would never have got married, we'd never have had kids, or tried to build a life or done anything other than spit at each other. Sure, Bud was a fool, too. I think it's how they prove some damn weird thing or another to themselves. Or to other guys, I don't know. I gave up trying to figure all that out long ago. Yeah, Bud too! And whatever else you might say, you got to admit that boy is *trying.*"

"But he . . ."

"Well, who knows how their minds work or if they even have minds? Maybe he was trying to find out if he really wanted to choose something or if he'd just sort of wandered in and couldn't find his way out again. Okay, so he maybe did it. He didn't stay there! He made a choice. He tried it and it was nothing compared to what he went home to, okay? Give yourself a break. He's *trying.*"

And he was. He came out of camp and showed up at the Mini-

Mart looking as if he half expected her to throw the frozen juice section at him. He waited next door, in the coffee shop, until she got off work, then walked home with her, his hands stuffed in the pockets of his brand new jeans, his shoulders slightly bent. He looked somehow huddled and cold, in spite of the soft late spring warmth. "Listen," he blurted, "I'm sorry we had that big fight. I just got mad and kind of stayed that way. I got so mad at Patsy that I just let the mad spread over everything."

"Me, too," she agreed, glad she had talked to Jeannie, glad she had at least decided not to make up her mind how she would react before she heard what he had to say. "I can be kinda awful when I'm mad."

"Kinda awful?" he grinned. "Listen, sweetheart, drop the kinda and stick to the awful, okay?"

"Oh, and you're the Prince of Wales and totally reasonable, right?"

"Me? Nah, I'm on the Olympic asshole team. We even beat Russia last time out."

And he didn't even know about Rupert!

When he did find out two days later, he just stood and stared at her. Just stared.

"So if we hadn't talked it out and made up . . . what? You wouldn't have told me, I guess, huh?"

"And make you feel like you had your foot caught in a leghold trap?"

"Is that fair?"

"Is it fair to make you feel there's something you've got to do that you don't want to do but you ought to do it because . . . ?"

"Yeah, but *you* had *both* your feet in the trap!"

"And telling you wouldn't have changed that!" DeeJay was suddenly very angry, but even she knew it wasn't Sid she was angry with, it was something else, and not being able to explain what it was made up a large part of why she was mad.

"Well, my God, eh? Ain't that something?" And he moved to sit in the ugly, uncomfortable motel chair, still grinning. "So what do we do?"

"I think we already did it." She sat on the bed and stuffed the pillow behind her back.

"You want to quit work? Stay home? Rest up and kind of get things ready?"

"Quit work? Hey, it might not be much of a job but it'll buy diapers for Rupert."

"I can buy my kid's diapers!" he flared.

"Oh stop it," she laughed. "What in hell would I do stuck at home all day every day doing nothing but getting fatter by the minute? Maybe I could sign up for an apprenticeship with Patsy?"

"Get your ass to work," he laughed. "Nobody needs to apprentice to *her*."

They went out to Mr. Mike's for supper, and DeeJay concentrated mostly on the salad bar, except for whatever that awful stuff is that seems to be jello, old fruit and teeny marshmallows. When they'd eaten, they walked hand in hand along the seawall across the gas-rainbowed inlet from the hockey rink, behind the undertaking parlour, toward the yacht club.

"Sure is nice here when the weather is good," Sid said, lighting a cigarette with his free hand. "But it sure is the anus of the world when it's pissin' down rain."

"Which it does a lot of the time."

"So, what do you want to do? I have to tell you I'm not jumping over the moon with joy at the idea of you bunkin' in with Patsy when Rupert arrives. I'd just as soon he never set eyes on that wrinkled sack of spit."

"You're just mad because she told on you."

"I'm just mad because what she told was bullshit," he said firmly. "Jesus! Come lallygaggin' into my place with a story like that for my old lady and no more proof than a pinch of coonshit, stuffin' her ugly face and laughin' at me. I don't want my kid learnin' to be like that."

"Well, Patsy and I aren't exactly what you'd call close," DeeJay admitted. "And I don't suppose it'd break my heart not to see very much of her."

Nothing got decided that trip out, and she stayed in the apartment with Patsy while Sid was back in camp. Then he was out for a week and back in again, but came out for fire season.

"I'm gonna prob'ly be out for a while," he said firmly, "and even if we get some rain and go back in, it'll only be until the bush gets dry again, and then we'll be out for another coupla weeks, maybe more. So why don't we find a place and just kinda move in like we were before? Only *this* time," he hastened, "I'll have m'act cleaned up, okay?"

"Yeah?" She didn't dare begin to hope.

"DeeJay, I promise. Pee-ahr-oh-em-eye-ess-eee, promise. I spent a lot of nights lyin' on my back in the bunkhouse listenin' to tapes on m'stereo, trying to figure things out. And when I did get to sleep I had these stupid fuckin' dreams where I was walking, walking, walking down a railroad track, one of them twin tracks, right, with another one just alongside? And I'm walking and walking and there's trains coming like all hell on fire, and they're all goin' the other way. I mean there's *no train* in the direction I'm walkin', right! And Jesus you shoulda seen who was wavin' out the fuckin' windas of those trains. We had Bozo the clown, we had Ronny McDonald, we had relatives, we had friends, we had half the bloody world and they've got all these damn balloons, you know the kind where the guy blows 'em up and then twists 'em into little dogs or something? Night after night, and if it wasn't the train dream I was on this goddamn boat, but there's just me, no captain, no crew, no nobody but me. I could see all this food, and I knew if I wanted it I could just go get 'er, but . . . it was like the big boat in the movies, you know, where the whole packa oddballs decide to go on a cruise and some of 'em's nuts and some of 'em's stupid? Well, like that."

DeeJay couldn't believe this was Sid. Walking along chattering away as if he were Patsy, gab gab gab. She figured he was explaining something to her but she had no idea what it was. Taking a hike along the tracks, going on some boat that never existed, what was he talking about anyway, and why was he telling her? It all sounded more like something you should tell a shrink.

"And I'd sit and poke my food around on my plate and I guess I was doing a lot of muttering because this old guy grabbed my arm one night and drug me into his room and we sat on his bunk and he said So, he said, What in hell has *you* walkin' around like a whipped pup. And I don't know what got into me, DeeJay, I started running off at the mouth, and I told him about the train and about how we'd had this big fight and he give me a shove and sent me off his bunk onto the floor and he yelled at me. I mean he *yelled*. 'I thought you had more better sense than *that!*' he yells. And wouldn't tell me what he meant. So then I goddamn near cut off my own fuckin' leg because I was all in knots about us and about everything instead of paying attention to my work and that scared the old hee-haw right outta me."

"Why'd he yell?"

"Because he knew that I knew that even if I hadn't done what that bitch told Patsy I'd done—and I didn't do that, DeeJay!—even so, I shouldn't'a been out bein' a party type, I shoulda been home takin' care of business. I was actin' like a damn kid, and kids don't get an apartment and an old lady and all that, they get bubble gum and chocky bars."

"And Bozo the clown?"

"Only if they're good kids and someone takes 'em to the circus." He let go of her hand and put his arm around her waist, pulled her close in a hug. "So I won't do that again, okay? I promise."

DeeJay didn't know if she believed Sid or not. Sometimes she did. Sometimes she could almost see it happening, like a movie in her head, with Sid laughing and being Sid-at-a-party, boogying around and telling jokes. And this bitch deciding she'd mess it up with DeeJay so Sid would be on the loose and maybe angry and looking to show the world. Other times it was almost the same scenario except Sid was tomcatting around and doing more than just flirting, he was tapping on some of the women, and she didn't know which of the two movies fit the facts and which didn't. And she wasn't sure she wanted to know. In fact she was pretty sure she didn't want to know.

3

It was all sid's idea, anyway. DeeJay wished she had told him to fall on his top lip, but she hadn't told him that, she just nodded and tried not to let on she all of a sudden had a cramp in her belly that was about enough to curl your hair. After all, what would she know about what normal people did, what would she know about how ordinary people handled things?

"I think we should catch a bus or rent a car or something so you can meet my folks." He dropped it on her head halfway through the pancakes with maple syrup at Smitty's. "Can't have the folks not knowing what you look like," he added, grinning.

So he rented a car. Thank heaven for small mercies because it would have been just about total horror to have to sit in a diesel-reeking big old bus, with fat people eating garlic and drunks breathing stinkfumes and probably a kid puking in the aisle or something. As it was it was bad enough! By the time they got where they were going, DeeJay was just about ready to give it up as a bad job and a waste of time.

And there they were, waving and smiling and pointing, and she panicked. She might have crawled under the seat or climbed into the trunk if Sid hadn't taken her arm and smiled and said, real softly, "It'll be okay, sweetheart, you'll see."

It's a lot to get past all at once, though. His mom, two sisters, one of them with a couple of kids, and before DeeJay had any idea what was happening, they piled into the car with her and Sid, and everyone had to go by way of his grandmother's place so he could give her a big smooch and they could all sit like bumps on a log, smiling, smiling, smiling and sipping tea from those little cups that make your hands go clumsy so you spend your time terrified that you're going to drop ten dollars' worth of cup and smash it.

But for someone who knew nothing about grandmothers except what you see on TV, it was great. Tall, starting to put on weight, hair as white as snow and pulled back in a big bun on her neck, and these funny little silver-rimmed glasses, just like Mrs. Beasley. She put her hands on DeeJay's shoulders and stared into her face for the longest minute of DeeJay's life and then she nodded. "Don't let it overwhelm you, dear," she said softly, "they make a lot of noise, and they all talk at once, and it must feel as if you're drowning in family, but it will be fine. I'm glad to meet you, and I'm very very glad you came to see us. I think it's about the hardest thing a person can do and it ought to be forbidden by law."

"Yes, ma'am," DeeJay agreed.

Gran had probably ten dozen sandwiches. The kind where you butter a slice of bread, then spread peanut butter on it, then put some banana on it and roll the whole thing up until it looks like some new kind of sausage. She also had watercress and cucumber, that was a new idea as far as DeeJay was concerned, and thank heaven some egg salad and salmon salad and even some tuna fish with mayonnaise. Everyone nibbled politely and sipped tea and talked about things which meant nothing at all to DeeJay and then all of a sudden they were on their feet, the dishes were whisked away, Sid's sisters washed them, dried them, put them away and they were trooping out to the cars, with Gran, of course, who came with them to Sid's parents' place.

That was an eyeful. So this is the kind of place you could have if you had money. God. Wall-to-wall rug except in the little coat-room thing just inside the front door, where it was linoleum, for obvious reasons. And on top of the wall-to-wall, believe it or not, more rugs. Rugs on top of rugs for crying out loud! The wall-to-wall was sort of a beige-y colour, the kind you don't see, and the other ones sitting on top of it were the kind they put auction advertisements about in the TV Guide. Oriental, they called them. Nice colours, too, but you'd wonder about people walking on them, they looked like pictures that should be hung up on a wall or something.

Carpet going up the stairs to the second floor, carpet along the hallway and in the bedrooms. Carpets on top of the carpets in the bedrooms, too!

Sid and his mother went into a little huddle and the mother nodded but not with any show of a smile or anything, and then Sid took their suitcases into what he said used to be his bedroom. DeeJay followed. You could have put Patsy's entire apartment in this room. Well, if you discounted the bathroom and you might as well, the toilet ran all the time and the bathtub drain hardly ever did.

"You okay?" Sid asked.

"I guess your folks are rich, huh?" she almost whispered.

"My old man has his own logging company."

"So how come you don't work for him?"

"And have everyone say I only got the job because I was the boss's son?" He shook his head. "When I go to work for my old man I'm going in as a logger, not as the boss's wet-nose. You okay?"

"I'm tired," she admitted. "And kind of . . . you know." She waved her hands helplessly.

"Yeah, they're a bit much, especially when they're all together. You want to lie down for a while?"

"Probably wouldn't rest," she heard the quaver in her voice. "I don't know what I want to do!"

"Then let's go for a walk, I'll show you around."

That was nice, just the two of them, walking slowly together and not needing to talk or anything. He showed her the big old tree where his tire swing was still hanging. He pulled on the rope and shook his head. "Have to put a new one up before Rupert starts swinging. He'll break his neck on this old thing."

It was hard to picture Rupert here. She could picture Rupert at a playground, she could see him whapping a ball around on the soccer field, she could even almost see him learning to ride a trike along the sidewalk or going into the wading pool, but she had a real hard time seeing her kid here, with all those carpets and stuff. What if he spit up or something. Then what?

The first two days were pretty awful. She couldn't remember anyone's name and she was scared stiff. And then Sid announced that he and DeeJay were making supper. Everyone gaped. Sid laughed. "Go on, you think we don't know how to burn a pork chop? The whole lot of you find something else to do and leave her alone for a while, she's drowning in good will and kind sentiments." He even talked differently when he was with them, and when he did she wasn't sure she knew him very well.

It wasn't pork chops at all. They went to the supermarket and bought out the chicken thighs, then went back and DeeJay made her favourite, what Jeannie had called Paprika Chook. Supper did what all the rest of the time at the place hadn't been able to do, and by the time the double chocolate cake came out, DeeJay knew she had it aced.

Sid's dad shook his head and laughed out loud. "That's it, boy," he said loudly, "I'm serving notice. You give this woman any grief at all and she's hittin' the road, leavin' you high'n'dry and comin' to work for me!"

"Back off," Sid pretended to glower, "I found 'er first."

"G'wan, you never did take care of nothin', not your bike, nor your roller skates either. You'll mess it up and she'll get smart and see you for what you are, and then it'll be Phone the old man, line up the float plane and off she goes to make bigger money than she'll ever see comin' outta *your* pocket."

"I make good money."

"You make shit," and it was no joke now. "That gyppo bastard pays you about half what I pay my men."

"Yeah, but he don't yell at me," Sid said calmly. "And nobody in the bunkhouse thinks I got the job because my mother didn't want me hangin' around the house any longer."

"Come into camp with me." It was out in the open. "There's a place empty, you and DeeJay can move right in."

"Not yet." Sid opened the bag and let the striped tomcat out to run around the chocolate cake. "Gotta wait until after Rupert comes. Can't have her flyin' out in the middle of the night in the teeth of a storm."

DeeJay could have crawled under the table and died. Everybody looked at her.

"Are you getting married?" Sid's mother asked. Sid opened his mouth to say yes.

"No," DeeJay said firmly. The silence was so thick you could almost see it hanging over everyone's head. "I don't believe in marriage," she ploughed ahead. "They charge you sixty dollars to get married and then wait so they can charge you five thousand for the divorce."

"You planning a divorce?" Gran asked.

"No ma'am, but if you think I'm going cooking in Mr. McFadden's camp and then have Sid McFadden show up and expect to collect my wages for me then you aren't as smart a woman as I thought you were," and she grinned the cheekiest grin she could pull off under the circumstances. Sid howled with laughter, his dad nearly choked on his chocolate cake and both of Sid's sisters got the giggles. Sid's mother did not laugh. Gran almost did.

"And what about living in sin?" she pushed it.

"It's an old family tradition," DeeJay said agreeably. "I think it's something we were born to do," and everyone just left it at that and went back to the double chocolate cake.

But you knew it wasn't just going to be left alone. They didn't bother trying to pressure DeeJay about it, they put the screws to Sid. Well, why not, he was the one had the practice with all that.

Thank God for the trip home. She'd have gladly gone home on a skateboard if that was the only way to make the trip. They'd all been just as nice as you'd want anybody to be, and it had worn her out just getting through it.

"Don't think it's *you* they wanted to see," Patsy warned. "They just don't want anyone else having their son's kid, is all. Next thing you know it'll be Oh we just want him for a week, and then it'll be Let him visit for two weeks, and then it'll be boarding schools or something, you watch."

"They didn't even know about Rupert."

"Bullshit."

"They didn't, not until we'd been there for days. They're just nice, is all."

"Nice? Fall on your head. *Nobody* is nice. Some pretend to be, is all. You'll see, they'll be after that kid faster'n a cat goes after a mouse. People like that think they *own* kids."

"Put a sock in it."

They rented a house, and that felt more like home than the apartment had. Sid would have bought brand-new stuff from the furniture store but DeeJay nixed that idea.

"We don't even know where we'll be this time next year," she argued. "If you go into camp with your dad, and if Rupert and I go in with you, how do we get all this stuff up there? If it's new we'd lose a fortune selling it off. Why not just go to the Sally Ann and see what they have by way of reconditioned stuff?"

So they did. Sid didn't really like the idea but he wasn't going to start arguing about it. He was busy trying to make sure she forgot the last big argument they'd had.

It was too late in the year to get into the plant bulbs and flowers routine, and they told the landlord they weren't paying five hundred dollars for a mower to cut *his* grass, he'd have to do it himself. But it was nice to have a house, even a little one, and nice, too, that this time Sid didn't start to feel as if he was going to go out of his tree with boredom.

And then Rupert arrived. DeeJay wasn't sure there was much about that you'd want to call nice. She was fully prepared for the hurt part of it. In fact, as it turned out it didn't hurt anywhere near as bad as she was prepared for it to hurt. What she wasn't prepared for was the feeling scared. Even Sid didn't understand what it was she was scared *of*.

"Hey, cool down, calm down," he tried to soothe her, "women been doing this for thousands of years."

"Not this woman hasn't. And I notice you talk a good line but do I see you scoopin'er up and doing anything with her?"

"Well, if I did you'd never learn, now, would you?"

"As if you knew how," she scoffed.

Rupert wasn't a him the way they'd planned. Not that they'd have called him Rupert even if he had been what they'd planned. But they only had boys' names picked out and nothing for a girl.

"We could call her Michelle," Sid suggested.

"Forget that one." DeeJay stopped sucking up her milk shake

long enough to take aim and shoot it down like a clay duck. "I knew a Michelle in school and she was a damn suck."

"Well, there's, uh, let's see, uh, what about—say, we could call her Geraldine, after my mother."

"We could call her Rover after the neighbour's dog, too. Or Bozo after your friend on that other train you dreamed about that time."

"Evangeline," he laughed. "Evangeline Emmaline Ruth."

"Rosemary Ivy Pansy Rose."

"Minnie after the Mouse."

"Goofy after her dad."

"We could call her DeeJay Junior."

"I could split your skull, too. Besides, Jeannie's already got half my name."

"Well, what about April? I always liked the name April."

"Great, a kid named April who got born in November. I guess if we ever have a kid born in April we could call her January. Or Hallowe'en, maybe. I'd rather call her Rupert! Or Roberta, which is close enough."

"Yeah," he smiled, "and we could call her Bobbi."

"We could call her Spot if that's what you're in to. Roberta Marie because if we start naming her after relatives Patsy's gonna put in her two cents' worth and I don't want to go through *that* horror show! I don't know *anybody* named Roberta Marie."

"Great. Roberta Marie McFadden."

"Roberta Marie Banwin," DeeJay corrected firmly. Sid opened his mouth to protest, then closed it again and looked away.

And thank God for Jeannie! Patsy got it into her head DeeJay would need someone to help her when she first got out of the hospital, and of course Patsy was convinced that someone should be her. But Jeannie got there firstest with the mostest, was already installed with her suitcase unpacked and a roast started in the oven when Patsy showed up all set to take up residence.

"What'n hell d'ya mean? She's *my* daughter and *my* granddaughter!"

"I'm sure they'll appreciate your visit. And appreciate it when I give you a ride home, too."

"Did God die and put you in charge?"

"God isn't dead," Jeannie said sweetly, "she's on the Riviera with the beautiful people today. But I'm in charge all the same."

"Well, we'll just see about *that*."

"That's right, we will. We'll ask Sid what he thinks."

"Him! He don't think!"

Jeannie drove Patsy home after a two-and-a-half-hour visit that just about frayed DeeJay's nerves.

"You'd think she was Doctor Spock the child expert," Sid raged. "Did you ever hear such garbage? Don't cut her hair before she's two or she'll go near-sighted? What's her damn hair got to do with her eyes? Don't let her suck her thumb, she'll be buck-toothed. Jesus!"

"Calm down, stupid," Jeannie laughed, "you let her get your goat and she'll be back tomorrow to try for twice in a row. Let it blow off and she'll give it up."

"One day I'll bust her neck."

"Well, wait until DeeJay's back on her feet before you do, okay?" Jeannie winked. "I'm too old and too weary to deal with her, the kid *and* the cops."

All DeeJay had to do was sit in a comfortable chair, drink milk shakes and eggnogs, take her vitamin pills and nurse Bobbi. Jeannie did the rest and gave lessons in how to bath the baby, how to hold her, how to burp her, how to just close the door and walk away and let her cry.

"Now don't *you* cry," Jeannie lectured. "You have to remember, there's nothing wrong with her. She's fed, she's burped, she's warm, she's dry . . . what she's doing has nothing to do with being sick or sad or uncomfortable. That is all she can do right now. She's just getting exercise, is all. Which you could stand a bit of, by the way. Bundle up and go for a walk with your old man."

So they went for a walk around the block. Then went home because DeeJay felt as if she would die of cold.

"Tomorrow will be better," Jeannie said, so matter-of-fact Dee-Jay wanted to scream at her. "You go have yourself a rest, now, you'll need it."

Everybody thought they knew more about her and her life than she did. And what made it worse was knowing they probably *did* know more than she did, even about her own life.

Sid was back in camp until just before Christmas, and out until well past New Year, then he was home for a couple of weeks and back in camp again. In mid-February it snowed like hell and Sid came back for shutdown. He had all his stuff with him, clothes, stereo, tapes, the whole shiterooni.

"So," he said, sitting in the big chair and holding Bobbi while she sucked on her bottle of formula, "you think you'd like to move into camp?"

"And live on a raft?" DeeJay had been hearing some real horror stories about float camps.

"No," he scoffed, "we got us a real show, okay? What do you think, we're a buncha heathens? Hey, this place is on *skids*." he put down the bottle of formula, lifted Bobbi to his shoulder and rubbed her back until she belched, then went back to feeding her. And the whole time he was doing that, he was talking, and grinning. "We're not bobbing around like a bunch of ducks, at the mercy of the tide and waves, this is a first-class land-based show. We just drag 'em to the top of a hill and park 'em and then they slip'n'slide down the slope bit by bit so's by the time we need to move 'em again they've picked up some momentum and it's like jump-startin'em. And we drag 'em off over the mud to the next place, is all."

She thought he was joking. He wasn't.

It might have passed for a very small town or hamlet if it hadn't been for the skids. That gave it all away and you knew that these places had been dragged to different locations more than once or twice. The skids were made of what had once been enormous logs, their bark stripped off and the bottom side made smooth. "You just hitch 'em onto the big loader there," Sid explained, "and off you go. If you have to, you can put 'em on a barge or, if things get tough, you can drag the float-raft up to the beach and drag 'em onto *that* and tow 'em on to the next place."

"My God." It was all she could think of to say. Even with snow on the ground the place looked dreary. There probably wasn't a tree standing for a quarter of a mile or more. And beyond that just about all you could see were stumps. Some of the houses had what might have been intended as rose arbors, the roots rammed into half barrels or thick blue plastic pails, so when it was time to move the house, the garden could move with it.

But DeeJay had lived in worse. She had lived in lots worse. Before she took up with Sid, except for foster homes, every place DeeJay had lived had been one hell of a whole lot worse. And besides, Gerri, Sid's mother, had lived for years in places which didn't even begin to approach this. So DeeJay nodded and set about turning the place into something as close to "home" as she could manage.

They still weren't logging, but there was more than enough to do just keeping the camp together and getting ready for when everyone else came pouring back in again. Sid was busy from seven in the morning until suppertime and sometimes even afterward. He and Skip would sit sometimes with their grey wool socked feet almost but not quite touching the wood stove and drink cups of hot tea with generous dollops of rye, which Skip insisted was the only way to fight pneumonia. "Every night since I was sixteen," he offered as proof, "and I never had pneumonia yet."

Even before she opened the letter, DeeJay knew what it was going to say. It was the return address tipped her off: box 1000. Sure enough, Patsy was in the pokey again.

Predictably enough, it was a mistake, it wasn't anything to do with *her*, the police just wouldn't let her alone, it was a wonder she hadn't been arrested for something some man had done in China the way they tried to pin things on her. There was one law for the rich and they could get away with anything, but another law for the poor and this proved it, those legal aid lawyers couldn't find their arses to scratch them and why not send some pictures of Bobbi to brighten up the cell.

DeeJay felt weary. She handed the letter to Sid, who read it, then looked at her and shook his head. She was glad he didn't try to say something reassuring or, even worse, cheerful. Sometimes not talking was the best thing. And what in hell could you say about it? She didn't know if he told his dad or not. She didn't really care.

Spring rain washed away the snow and exposed the camp. It wasn't as bad as DeeJay had feared it would be. Between the houses there was grass and some of the places even had little garden patches scratched out of the rocky soil. One energetic soul had made a series of little boxes and filled them with what looked like good dirt, although you wondered where she'd found it around here. "Oh, seaweed and moss and stuff," Skip said vaguely, "she just kind of kept stacking it up and it'd rot down and she'd add more."

Turned out "she" was Gerri. "Got sick of it, I guess," Skip shrugged. DeeJay could understand why. Unless you wanted to start in on tea toddies at noon there wasn't a whole lot to do. But if Gerri could stick it out all that time, DeeJay could give it a try. It was just that Bobbi didn't take much looking after and the place was small and no sidewalks for a stroller, so if you wanted to go for a walk you had to put the kid in a carrypack and that was fine but she was first cousin to a moose and getting heavier every meal.

But Skip was smarter about it than Sid, probably because he'd lived through it a time or two. "Could you do me a favour, hen," and he put some crumpled papers on the table and looked hopeful. "Can you phone these numbers and tell 'em who we are and that I need this stuff? I'd do 'er myself but I'm up to my ears this week. Sure would appreciate it."

That took an hour or two, at least. Then he was bringing out the book with the hard red cover and explaining where she stapled the receipts and where she wrote in the amount. "See, money comin' in goes here, and money goin' out goes here. Payroll goes in the blue book."

"I don't know anything about accounting!" she protested, her stomach knotting. "You'll go broke and it'll be my fault!"

"Oh, I'm not askin' you to do the accounting," he said quickly, "we send out to a chartered accountant for that. Just keepin' track is all it is. I'm so damn busy here I hardly got time to drink my tea at lunchtime, and I'd sure appreciate it if you found the time. No sense askin' Siddley, he can't read his own damn writin'."

But even when the men were back in and camp was in full swing the days were long and time heavy. Sometimes she'd go over and help the cook but he was so scared Bobbi would burn herself, cut herself, pull something heavy over on her head or fall off the back steps that he worked himself into a nervous sweat and wound up so frantic his pastry was tough.

She wrote letters to Jeannie and got answers, but she didn't bother sending replies to Patsy's scrawled notes. What could she say? I'm sorry for your troubles? She wasn't sorry, she was bored with the whole thing, there had been too many years of it, too much bee-ess about it and too many lies. Most of the time she didn't even think about her, anyway. It was just every now and again she'd get this awful sinking coldness throughout her body, even her fingers would feel swollen and lifeless, her scalp would creep as if a chill had gone up her spine and she'd realize she was thinking of Patsy.

She took rolls of film and sent it out to get developed. Two weeks later, back came pictures of Bobbi. Bobbi standing grinning a wet one while staring up at some mammoth hunk of machinery. Bobbi wearing Skip's hard hat. Bobbi standing in Sid's caulk boots. Bobbi bent over with the pullcord of a chain saw, as if trying to start it up and shear the world.

"We should get her a puppy," Sid suggested. "Give her something to play with."

"A teddy bear'd do fine," DeeJay yawned. "I got no time for that. I don't even know how to do it. You don't just leave 'em to train themselves, I know that much."

"I had a dog." He seemed to be arguing with her somehow.

"Good for you." She rolled on her side and hauled the covers up over her shoulders. "I guess your mother looked after it for you." She was starting to feel as if she was drowning in Gerri's wonderfulness. Gerri did the books, Gerri did the payroll, Gerri put the kids in the outboard and ran them across the bay to the school in town, damn near an hour each way, Gerri this and Gerri that, Gerri jump in the air and bite your own ass. More than just Gerri, DeeJay was stuck in quicksand made up of Sid's family. His sisters wrote him long letters and then everyone seemed to expect DeeJay to write his answers for him. "They aren't *my* sisters," she told him, "and those letters all start off 'Dear Sid', so why don't *you* write back? What am I, your secretary?"

"Jesus, it's not as if you had too much to do!" he shouted.

"That's right, it's not anything like that at all," she agreed stubbornly, "I don't even *know* them."

"Never mind know, DeeJay, just answer the friggin' letter, will you? Christ, it's fulla questions; how's Sid, how's Dad, how's this, what's that doing, are they up to this or that . . . just answer the questions is all."

"Okay. I'll grab the old pen and paper and I'll answer. 'Snarly, okay, not much, no they aren't' and mail 'er off, will I? Sure, Sid, I'll write your letters for you. Maybe set up a little booth and scribe off letters for everyone else, too. Dollar a page. Better yet, a dime a word."

"Oh for fuck's sake," and he rolled over and pulled the quilt up over *his* shoulders and they lay back-to-back, stiff and ticked right off with each other.

Then Patsy wrote to say she only had two more months to serve. "I thought maybe I could come up for a visit, see where you're living and all." DeeJay didn't show that one to Sid. She just sat down and answered it. "Dear Patsy: Your idea about coming in to camp for a visit isn't the best idea you've had. For a start you'd have to fly in and that costs an arm and a leg. Besides which once you're here there is nothing to do. There is no hotel or anything and our place is so small already we're tripping over each other. And on top of that I don't think you and Sid get along very well and I would probably wind up killing both of you after one day of listening to the sniping. Better you just head for your apartment. I know you want to see Bobbi so I'll send some pictures and make sure you get a visit when we come out at shutdown time."

"And that," she vowed, "is all it will be. A damn visit!"

She expected Patsy to write back immediately, but Patsy waited until she was out, and home, then she sat down and tried to write a novel. The writing started out neat enough, but as page followed page it was obvious she was lubricating herself with something that had nothing to do with ink. The letter was more like a shopping list with additions. Patsy's feelings were hurt, after all she sacrificed for DeeJay she got told to butt out and eff off, and maybe she might have made one or two little mistakes in her life but who was DeeJay to decide that, it wasn't as if DeeJay had never made an error and anyway there was something unnatural about a daughter telling her mother to take a hike. First you don't bother to answer my letters and I wrote all the time, and then when you do answer it's to flush me off with some story about your house being small and at least you've got one which is more than I ever had but I still did the best I could by you.

DeeJay just threw it in the woodstove and let it turn to smoke and go to Jesus, maybe he'd want to write an answer.

"Ah, come on DeeJay, don't let her get to you. She's not workin' with a full deck and you know it. Come on, take a deep breath and blow 'er away, okay?"

"Sure," she agreed. She even smiled. It was Sunday and they were sitting on the riverbank with a picnic and cold beer. Bobbi was bare bum in the sand with a tablespoon, digging up pebbles and burying them, her skin tanned almost the colour of cinnamon, a frilly bonnet protecting her head, tied under her chin with a piece of ribbon. Skip was on a blanket, belly down, sleeping, and the air was thick with the smell of evergreen sap. The sky looked to be so far away nobody would ever be able to catch it, the same pale pale blue as old jeans when they've been worn so much the knees are always baggy and the backside is starting to fray. "The sun looks like a big penny. I never saw it like that before."

"Yeah?" Sid looked up, then jerked upright and jumped to his feet. "*Dad!*" He grabbed for his jeans.

Skip opened his eyes and lifted his head. Sid pointed up at the sun. Skip squinted at it, still more asleep than awake, and then he was awake immediately. "Come on!" Sid yelled to DeeJay.

"What?"

"Jesus, DeeJay come *on!*" He threw the picnic stuff in the middle of the blanket, grabbed the corners and lifted the whole thing like a tinker's bundle, spilling juice and ruining the salad. Skip grabbed Bobbi, rammed his feet in his boots and started running for the pickup.

The camp was already organizing, men driving equipment as close to the river as they could get it, other men soaking down the houses, someone riding the radiophone, trying to get an air survey of size and direction, and the cook starting huge vats of coffee. The fallers already had their chain saws fired up and were clearing the second, third and brush growth from around the camp, the dozer was scraping the earth bare as a tabletop and they had everything ready for a backfire, just waiting for Skip to tell them to set it alight.

"They got a plane comin'," the cook yelled. "Pack 'er up and get 'er out with the kid."

"But you're coming, too, aren't you?" DeeJay was so scared all she wanted to do was sit in the dust and cry.

"I'll be out as soon as this mess is over," Sid promised. "But we have to try to stop this or . . ." His face was pale, his eyes just about as big as saucers. "That's our wages going up in smoke, babe."

The float plane put down on the water and taxi'd to the dock. DeeJay handed Bobbi in to the pilot, and clambered in through the awkward little door. She tried to smile as Sid kissed her cheek, too shy to give her a real kiss with the others watching.

"You be careful," she whispered.

"I'm better'n just careful," he teased, "I'm scared shitless."

"Me too."

And then they were turning, slowly enough, and moving across the water, faster and faster, until the floats were in the air and they were climbing. "Looks bloody hairy down there, I'll tell you," the pilot shook his head. "Gonna be rough, so strap that kid in on your lap, we don't want her bouncing around in here."

"My God." DeeJay stared at the red lines peeking through sheets of thick smoke. "That's *awful*."

"She's crowned." The pilot swallowed, his face ashen. "They've got a real job on their hands controlling that mad bitch down there. If the friggin' wind gets into it, they've got trouble."

DeeJay could only watch, and wish there was something she could do.

"Sometimes the bugger burns so fast it takes the oxygen out of the air," the pilot went on, seemingly determined to write an encyclopedia on forest fires, "it starts pulling in the air from around it, until you get this goddamn wind happening, and the wind feeds the fire so it sucks more and you get more wind and she just goes fuckin' *nuts!*"

"How do they put it out?"

"They don't. It has to rain to put it out."

75

It didn't rain. Four days later Skip got off the plane looking as if his guts had been stolen from him. He had burns over his hands and arms, a bruise on his jaw and a lump on his head where the skidder driver had knocked him cold with a wrench handle. "We'd'a never got him out otherwise," the driver apologized, "he was all for headin' back in again, and there was no bloody use, we'd tried everything, but he was just about as crazy as a shithouse rat by then. I'm real sorry, Gerri. I'm sorry DeeJay. I'm as sorry as hell."

It wasn't just Sid. It was four other guys, too. After it rained, and after the fire was out, they went back in and they found what was left of the bulldozer, they even found a couple of belt buckles, what was left of the chain saws, the business end of a shovel or two and the metal parts of the portable water tank.

"We'll have a memorial service all the same," Gerri said, her voice shaking.

"You have it if you want," DeeJay sobbed, "I ain't goin'!"

"Oh, yes you are, darling. If you don't he'll never be dead and you'll ruin the rest of your life trying to believe he's just late for supper. Besides, those men worked for us. We owe them."

"I don't! They never worked for me. I don't owe them a thing."

But she went. She got out of bed, she had a bath, she put ice cubes on her eyes, she hauled on her new clothes, and she went to the memorial service. She never remembered as much as one word of what got said, and she was never clear, really, on what got done, but she was there and it was weird how much that seemed to mean to the families of the ones who weren't there.

"Oh my poor baby!" Patsy wailed.

"Don't touch me, Patsy. I don't need any hugs and slobbers. Don't touch me. I might break or something. I mean it." Patsy nodded and kept her hands to herself.

And then Jeannie was there, and DeeJay felt her legs give out, she started to sag and Jeannie had her. "Let 'er rip, baby," Jeannie sobbed, "and never you mind about that stiff upper damn lip."

"What am I going to *do*, Jeannie?"

"You're going to live, baby. That's what you're going to do."

DeeJay hardly saw Bobbi for almost a month. Jeannie took over and all DeeJay had to do was make it from getting-out-of-bed time to crawling-back-in time.

"Take 'em," Jeannie insisted, and DeeJay swallowed the pills the doctor prescribed.

"I'll wind up hooked like my mother," she warned. "Then you'll be sorry."

"Take 'em. If you wind up hooked I'll say Gee, DeeJay, you were right after all, and then you can play I Told You So. Come on, kid, if you've got that pill in you we're goin' for a drive."

"Soon as the pill starts to work I won't know if I'm seein' highway or sky."

"Good."

Jeannie drove them up and down the highway. They went to rivers and lakes and beaches and parks, they walked and sometimes they talked. But never about any of the things DeeJay felt she had to know or go nuts. Like had they passed out from smoke and never felt it? Everyone said that's probably what happened. But how would anybody know? And didn't everyone say stuff like that all the time just to avoid having to think about how fucking awful it must have been? She knew why Sid had been there, though. He was the boss's son and he just *had* to fuckin' prove over and over and over again that he got his job because he was a logger, not because he was daddy's little boy. And of course he had to take out the goddamn bulldozer and of course Skip had to let him take it out. God, how could Skip send someone else's kid out there to try to make firebreak? Sid *had* to go and Skip *had* to let him and wasn't that all just too stupid for words. "Bloody men," she sobbed suddenly, "rah rah rah and three fuckin' bags full! They shoulda just let the goddamn thing burn itself out! Who cares about a few old shacks? But no, we all had to be so bloody brave, didn't we?"

"Right on, DeeJay," Jeannie agreed. "I sometimes wonder, especially with stuff like this or those damned heroes they're always comin' up with when there's a war or something . . . do you think maybe they pump adrenalin faster than we do or something? I mean, I understand about adrenalin. But I got to tell you if I had fire on three sides and water behind me that adrenalin would *not* send me into any one of the three sides, it'd be what had me pulling oars on a rowboat so goddamn fast the spray behind that

77

boat would put out the fire on at least one side! Wouldn't you think they'd learn how to *run?*"

DeeJay suddenly felt as if she might make it through the rest of the day. "Oh, he knew how to run, all right. Trouble was, Sid always ran *into* things. Usually at top speed. And always laughin'!" And she knew, for whatever value it had or difference it did not make, that Sid probably had put the tap on what's-her-name. So what? He'd come back. And not because he had to, either. Like Jeannie had said, he came back because he wanted to. And that counted. Counted big.

4

GERRI AND SKIP WANTED DEEJAY to get a place close to them, Jeannie wanted her to move next door, and Patsy figured wherever it was DeeJay chose to live, Patsy would move in with her and help with Bobbi.

"No," DeeJay sighed, "we aren't living under the same roof."

"What kind of a daughter are you?" Patsy whined. "What did I ever do to you that you'd be so mean to me all the time?"

"You really want to know?" DeeJay could feel anger burning in her chest, and it was a physical effort not to swing a punch.

"That was a long time ago and a lot has changed."

"No it hasn't. You were a drunk and a hype then, and you're still one, you're just playing at rehab for a while because you're on parole."

"That's just what anyone needs! A big gesture of faith from their nearest and dearest."

"Your dearest has always been whatever it is you're getting goofed on, and your nearest has usually been whoever is paying for your dearest! I didn't have any say-so when I was a little kid but I've got some now. I'm not havin' my kid raised up with that crap and I'm not livin' with it, either."

"Boy, are you ever cheap. I didn't raise you to be cheap. You'll have a big place and lots of room and everything!"

"No."

DeeJay decided she'd find something halfway between Jeannie and Gerri; if it was just her she probably would have moved into a room in Jeannie's basement, but there wasn't just her. Bobbi adored Skip, Gerri adored Bobbi, and who knew how they were all going to feel about Rupert when he arrived.

Meanwhile she was staying with Jeannie for a few days, waiting for the papers on the house to go through. "Jesus but it's weird," she told Jeannie. "I found out about Bobbi after Sid'n me'd had this big fight and split up and all, and now this happens and guess who makes himself known. I mean it's almost weird."

"Nothing weird about it," Jeannie said flatly. "It's just how it all happened is all."

"You don't think it's kind of a co-incidoodly?"

"Oh, it's that all right, but nothing weird about it, they happen all the time. Look at yesterday, shopping, with the guavas."

They had split the shopping list. Bobbi was fussy and they wanted to get her home and into her crib, so DeeJay took the supermarket and Jeannie took the bank, where she could also pay the phone and hydro. Coming out of the bank and heading to the Italian grocery for black olives, good coffee and decent Parmesan cheese, she passed the fruit store. On impulse she went in and bought some fresh fruit for a salad. When she got back to the supermarket DeeJay was loading bags into the rear of the station wagon. "Look," DeeJay said, holding up a guava, "I got it and I don't know what'n hell it is! You ever eat one?"

"No," and Jeannie held up the one she had bought, "but they said it was great in fruit salad."

"How did you know I got stuff for fruit salad?"

"Oh, I'm psychic."

DeeJay thought about the guavas and finally nodded. It didn't seem quite the same as Rupert. She had thought it was stress, strain, fear and nerves had her period late, and with all the moving and settling in and trying to hold something together after the funeral she hadn't even really counted much until there she was, turning the page on the calendar and my God, is it really October?

Her first thought was the surprise at the date. Her second was a bolt of fear: oh crap Skip and Gerri'll think I've been screwing around already. She was so convinced they would think that, she almost didn't say anything, not even after she'd taken her little jar to the doctor's office. But she did tell them, and they just stared, then Skip started to grin and Gerri cried. But not the kind of crying she'd been doing ever since Sid went up in a puff of smoke. A soft kind, without the deep gut-wrenching sobs. Just a little warm trickle from her eyes.

"I don't dare live too close," she told Jeannie, "or they'll be there all the time and I like them but . . . I feel like if I don't get some space I'll just choke, or something."

"You better take some driving lessons and get yourself a car, so you can hit the old highway and bomb off when you have to. Otherwise you're gonna be flagging down the bus with a kid under each arm and a heapa suitcases in the dirt behind you," Jeannie teased.

"Me? Drive? I doubt it."

"Why not? You too stupid or something?"

"If I buy a car Patsy'll turn up in the dead of night and swipe it. She'll prob'ly take it through the plate glass window of the jewellery store, fill it up with stuff, back it onto the sidewalk and when she gets caught they'll hold the registered owner responsible."

"Patsy's too brain-dead to figure that one out."

She was pretty brain-dead, all right. Whatever she'd been into in the time DeeJay was trying to adapt to living in camp, it had burned some holes in her circuits. And whatever went on while she was in jail hadn't healed any of the holes or done any good to her personality.

"Why *won't* you loan me some money? Jesus, I'm dead broke and you got lots. You're up to your eyes in insurance money."

"I don't have lots, Patsy. And I'm not giving you money, you'll just sniff it up your snoot!"

"I shoulda give you away and kept the nice one!"

"No, you shoulda give both of us away! They oughta have a law that people like you can't even keep a cat. I don't owe you, Patsy. There's days and weeks of my life where I didn't even eat right because you were off spendin' grocery money on bein' a jerk. And you're not spendin' any more grocery money of mine. You ever think of gettin' a job and payin' your own way in the world?"

"Who'd hire me," Patsy said complacently. "Even the whoofare says I'm unemployable."

DeeJay couldn't think of a single person who would hire Patsy to do so much as stand in the field to scare the crows. She looked like someone who had spent her life fawning and earning herself kicks in the head. And Sid had died, damn it, for that insurance settlement. But he hadn't made the premium payments for Patsy.

At first DeeJay had considered buying a little house, maybe an acre or two of land, with some chickens so she could have her own eggs. Jeannie put her straight on that. "You know how to prune fruit trees? You know anything about chicken cholera or coccidiosis or flukes or worms? You know how to clean a chimney? How about replacing or repairing shingles on the roof? What are you going to do if your basement starts to leak? You know how to fix the Big-O drains? What can you tell me about septic tanks? What about upgrading the insulation or stopping draughts around the windows?"

"Can't you get someone? Phone someone to come in and do it?"

"Sure. They get paid about the same as a doctor, only no insurance to help you pay for it."

"I don't want an apartment on the tenth floor!"

"It doesn't have to be either/or, kiddo. It isn't a choice between back-to-the-land or concrete jungle. They got condo developments, they got townhouses, they got co-ops, they got . . . all kinds of stuff."

She wasn't convinced until she'd spent three weeks looking at houses. She didn't see a single one that turned her crank. You could buy a pile of problems or you could buy something that would hold together for ten years and then give you a pile of problems. And all that lawn to mow. Worse, all those neighbours mowing lawns, marching back and forth, back and forth, behind mowers of all sizes and colours while the enormous dogs of suburbia watched, mouths open, tongues lolling, waiting for the whirling mower blades to find the next festering heap, chop it into chunks and spray it back into the face of the one pushing the mower. Turn the belugas into dog food will you, well, here's the revenge. Now wear it!

And if she did get a place like that, how far was it to the closest playground? How far would she have to walk with Bobbi and Rupert so they could play with other kids and go nuts in the adventure playground, and why didn't they have someplace for the parents to sit while they guarded the kids because you sure didn't want to send them off by themselves, not with all the perverts, weirdos, oddballs and outright dangerous lunatics who were congregating near the sandboxes and swings.

She didn't think much of the place from the outside. There was almost no outside to be seen. An awful expanse of parking lot! Virtually bare walls, stucco with little patches of dark-stained cedar siding and a small probably three-feet-square window, then two or three steps up to a plain dark brown door with a little block of bubble-glass window set in it. And from the front it seemed as if it was going to be awful small!

Inside she couldn't believe the amount of room. It was as if everything in here existed in a different dimension, where an inch had nothing to do with an inch in the ordinary world. Kitchen, living room, bathroom, hallway, utility room, small back-up bedroom and a big bedroom downstairs, and upstairs three more bedrooms, another bathroom and a hallway you could have rented out as a parlour if you needed extra money or wanted to join the landlord society.

And still she hesitated. Finally, unable to believe she had any kind of judgement at all, she asked Jeannie to have a look at the place with her.

"This is great," Jeannie said firmly. "You take that little downstairs room and you put the toybox and stuff in there. That's got them within earshot but out from underfoot. A baby gate across here, where the counter goes almost but not quite to the wall and the little darlins can't get into the kitchen to grab the cord and haul the boiling kettle down on their sunshiny faces. Bud can fix up a kid-proof burglar-proof lock for that sliding door out to the back yard, and there you are, all set."

So, feeling as if she was taking a header off something very high, she signed the papers. After all, the price was about half what you'd pay for something twice as small on a city lot. You couldn't really argue with that. And included in the price was all this other stuff, like a guy to mow the lawns and clean the eavestroughs and make sure any other upkeep got done. Not having had any experience with upkeep, DeeJay wasn't sure what kind of it or how much of it was going to raise its ugly head.

They'd given their good secondhand furniture to the Salvation Army for re-sale when they went into camp, except for a few boxes of stuff she had stored in Jeannie's enormous basement. Bud delivered the boxes but DeeJay couldn't bring herself to open them. Pillowcases and the feather-stuffed quilt were only going to remind her and God knows there were enough other reminders, she didn't need to add to the crowd.

"Oh, god, darling, don't bother with the bloody catalogue," Jeannie warned. "You get stuff from the catalogue and all you're getting is more bee-ess than you need. First thing that'll come will be a little printed notice saying they are temporarily out of stock and will ship as soon as new product arrives. When it arrives it'll be the wrong size, the wrong colour, and so late you'll have forgotten you ever thought you needed it. Two weeks later it'll fall apart and you'll be sitting in a heap of splinters and little chunks of pressboard coated with glue. And they don't care. Send it back, it just drops in a hole, nobody even says gee, sorry about that. We'll do the rounds of the stores and you can start supporting the neighbourhood economy instead of mailing money back east where the bastards don't care if we live or die."

She didn't say a word to Patsy about going shopping for furniture. That was be all Patsy would need. She'd put on her glad rags and hike along as if her opinion were based on experience instead of warm and rising air currents. Patsy probably hadn't bought a stick of furniture in her life although she had likely managed to shoplift entire living room ensembles, hide them under her coat and waltz out the front door to pawn them and take the money to the bar with her.

"You sure got quiet taste," Jeannie remarked gently. "You might want to think about a dash of colour somewhere. Tan and beige and desert sand are nice colours but . . ."

"I just don't want them to, you know, clash?"

"Darling, so far they won't even purr let alone clash. Maybe we could find something that would, oh, I don't know, chortle once in a while? Maybe even a good giggle?"

"Yeah? Okay. What?"

"Let's start with some colour for the kitchen. I mean you don't want it to be so innocuous it vanishes; how would you find it to get your supper cooked?"

Jeannie put the ix-nay on the light grey ofa-say and put the nod on a dark blue with wild tropical flowers splashed across it, in white with leaves of two shades of green.

"Jesus, Jeannie, it leaps at you when you come in the door."

"It's supposed to. Besides which, in case you didn't notice, there are zippers hidden in it. See, the cotton-and-whatever blend comes off and can be washed . . . by *hand*, DeeJay, in *cold* water with a big handful of salt to keep the colours from running. Phone me when you take it into your head to do it and I'll come and help."

They had a near argument about the drapes. "No, Jesus, *no!* Not those rotten fibreglass things. DeeJay, it's a trap. They say you can wash them but it's a lie. Unless you've got six Portuguese washerwomen who are going to come in and dip the buggers clean in egg cups full of warm water! You do them or I do them and what you wind up with is this mass of yard-long spaghetti in the bottom of the bathtub. And you washed them in the bathtub because it's the only thing they'd fit into. If you send 'em to the cleaners they're going to cost as much to clean as to buy new ones." Finally, DeeJay gave in on the drapes. She thought she didn't much like the colour of the ones Jeannie said were perfect but once she got used to them she loved them.

And the great thing was, once it was delivered and in place it didn't feel as if it was Jeannie's place, it felt more like home than anything DeeJay had known.

"One sideways glare or one harsh word from Bud and I'm moving in myself," Jeannie decided. "You did a real good job, DeeJay."

"I didn't do it. You did."

"Me? Ah, pooh, a suggestion on the drapes is all. The sales clerk could have done more if he'd been anything other than colour blind."

"And the sofa."

"Me? No way, kiddo, you picked the style."

"You picked the material."

"I did not! I suggested. A splash of colour, I said. No, you picked it, DeeJay, and it fits the room just fine. It's harder to find the *form* to fit the room than it is to find the *colour*, you know. Great eye you've got."

The store delivered and with Bud joking and grinning, grabbing the other end and doing the talking, the delivery men even took the stuff to the very room in which it was going to live. In some rooms they even got it to the very place it was supposed to go.

"Oh, no, ma'am," the younger one blushed, "we're not supposed to take tips of any kind. Company policy."

"Good," Bud said loudly, "so we won't tip the friggin' company. And anyway, it ain't a tip. I'd crack a case of beer but they've got rules on top of rules about that, too, I bet, and we'd invite you to dinner, but they'd shit bricks in the office, so what this is, is by way of bein' a steak supper out for you and your wives because if we can't at least, by God, do that much to say thank you, then *we* are going to be upset and shit bricks. Come on, the lady was in a real bind until you came along, at least let her treat you to a McDonald's and a coke."

They grinned and nodded and Bud slapped them on the shoulders. DeeJay smiled and Jeannie smiled and they all walked back out to the truck to say goodbye.

"I thought I was going to be shoving that stuff around until this time tomorrow afternoon," DeeJay admitted.

"Ah, we'd'a had 'er done by midnight," Bud brushed it off. But he put his arm around her and gave her a squeeze. "You'll make out, darlin'."

She didn't sleep in the place that night, she went back with Bud and Jeannie because Bobbi was at their place, running herself ragged with all the fosters to play with and to spoil her by pretending she was a breathing play dolly.

Everything was at the new place except what they had on, their night stuff, and what they would wear the next day. And by noon even that was in the new place. Then it was off to do some grocery shopping, take it home, and put it in the cupboards. "Take the lid off the cinnamon," Jeannie suggested quietly, "then it won't smell so much like paint and brand-new in this place. If that doesn't work, boil some vinegar on the stove."

And then they were gone and DeeJay was alone in her new place with nothing to do but make supper for herself and Bobbi, bath Bobbi, and put her to bed. By eight-thirty she was sitting on her new sofa watching a program on her new TV, waiting to feel lonely. What she felt was a sense of real peace.

Sometimes at night she lay awake feeling Rupert squirming around and trying to get comfortable, wishing she wasn't alone. She missed Sid then, so much that she would have cried but Jeannie had told her that wasn't good for the baby. It wasn't the sex. DeeJay wasn't sure what all the fuss about sex was, anyway. It was comfortable and comforting, it was better than dancing but so was cuddling, snuggling and smooching. Whatever it was they meant in those stupid novels Patsy read, the ones that went on forever about pounding waves and surging emotions, or was it surging waves and pounding emotions, whatever all that was, DeeJay didn't know anything about it. Sometimes she'd felt with Sid as if she'd never be able to get close enough to him, never be able to hold him tight enough or long enough, never be able to stay pressed against him for enough time to be calm again, but she'd never wanted to scream and yell or slobber or drool or whatever all that stuff was about and she'd never felt as if she'd lost touch with life, love, the universe or the need to pay income tax once a year. But without him the bed seemed about five times as big as your average football field, and the sheets were cold and stiff.

Doug helped her put the swingset in the little back yard. Doug worked for the furniture company, sometimes driving, usually swamping. He was the younger one who had blushed when DeeJay tipped them as a thank you for their help. He had shoulders and chest that made him look like a triangle with the pointy end to the ground. He dropped by on his way home from work a week or so after DeeJay moved in; she found out later he'd driven by almost every night but hadn't seen her outside and was too shy to knock on the door.

She was pushing Bobbi down the parking lot on her tricycle, trying to introduce the kid to the idea the feet moved the pedals made the wheel turn and the trike move. "Got your work cut out for you," he laughed. "She's having too much fun with you pushing."

"I'll push her," DeeJay promised. "If she doesn't start doin' it herself I'll push her off the edge of the world."

"Oh, I bet you would." He turned off the motor and grinned at her from the cab of his pickup truck. "You get settled okay?"

"Yeah. It's great!" She left the trike and moved closer to the pickup so they wouldn't have to half holler at each other. Bobbi yelled a couple of times and jiggled on the seat, wanting to be pushed. "Do it yourself," DeeJay said comfortably, "I'm sure you know how, you're just being lazy."

They talked maybe five minutes, then she had to run off and grab Bobbi before she left the parking lot and took the trike out on the road.

Gerri and Skip wanted DeeJay to call the new baby Sidney James, after his poor dead father. DeeJay thought about that, on and off for months, then for three days and nights in the hospital. It wasn't the Sid Junior part of it bothered her or even the Little Sid, it was that what you get to name somehow Belongs to you, and he didn't Belong to them. And who wants to go through life trying to fill the shoes of someone who was playing a harp several months before you pushed your way into the world? There was enough reminiscing going on anyway, she was doing a lot of it herself, cradling her revisions to herself, erasing and expunging the less-than-golden-perfect parts, embellishing the rest and even pretending for some of it.

She didn't argue, though. She wasn't up to that. She just smiled and yet never quite agreed. And then there he was, with his little hospital nametag bracelet on his wrist, wrapped in a blue blanket, his hair standing up every which-a-way like the fluff on a newly dried chick, and she called him Steven Allan Banwin.

"But I thought you were going to call him *Little Sid!*" Gerri almost exploded.

"I never said yes," DeeJay answered, quietly stubborn. "I never said no, maybe, but I never said yes."

"But . . ."

"Stevie."

"But . . . Sid Junior . . ."

"No." And by her, that was that. Whose kid was it anyway?

Just calling the baby Stevie instead of Sid Junior or Little Sid seemed to hammer something home for Skip. DeeJay didn't want to look too closely at whatever it was Skip had been pretending to himself. Or maybe not pretending, maybe he believed in re-incarnation or something. All she knew was there was some kind of spunk that just seemed to dry up in him. And she knew for sure Gerri was as mad as a wet hen. Well, let her be. She'd get over it. Or not.

DeeJay took Stevie home to the new place and had sense enough to do it right. She carried Stevie in one arm and Bobbi's new rubber dolly in the other. Stevie had a blue blanket, and Bobbi's baby had a new blanket. When it was time to give Stevie his bottle, Bobbi's baby had to have her bottle, too. When Stevie had a bath, the rubber dolly had a bath. Stevie got powdered, the rubber doll got powdered, Stevie got cuddled, Bobbi and her rubber doll got cuddled, too. "Come on," DeeJay settled herself in the big chair and patted her knee, "smooch-ups, okay?" Bobbi hurried over, climbed up and sat leaning against her mother, holding her dolly in the crook of one arm the way DeeJay was holding Stevie. "Wanna switch?" DeeJay asked. And in seconds DeeJay had the rubber dolly, Bobbi was holding her baby brother and grinning widely. "So much for jealousy, eh babe?"

"Smooch-ups," Bobbi agreed placidly.

Stevie wasn't placid. Stevie was what they called a going con-cern. He slept until he was hungry; then, as his eyes opened, so did his mouth. The noise was incredible. "Must have vocal cords the size of a choker cable," Skip decided. "Only kid I ever knew who popped out and roared *whaa* in a bass voice."

Stevie ate, burped, belched, wriggled and went back to sleep for three hours. Then he opened his eyes, opened his mouth and roared. An hour later he was fed, burped, belched, bathed, changed, cuddled and nodding off to sleep another three hours. Day and night. He was four months old before he slept the whole night and the morning it finally happened DeeJay woke up, heard the silence, saw how light it was in the room and nearly died of fear. The baby had died, she knew it, otherwise why hadn't he wakened for his middle-of-the-night feeding?

He wasn't dead. He was still asleep. She hurried to get his break-fast ready in case he woke up roaring. He did. She changed his diaper and started feeding him, he stopped roaring and started packing it away, slurping and almost growling in his eagerness.

Doug showed up every couple of nights. Before Stevie was born it was "just dropped by to see if you needed any help with anything." But after Stevie was born things settled into something else. Doug visited DeeJay every day in hospital, brought flowers, even offered to drive her and the baby home when it was time.

"Jeannie's coming for me," DeeJay told him.

"Sure," he smiled and shrugged. Gerri didn't smile, Skip didn't shrug, they looked puzzled and almost hurt.

"It's not as if she's family," Gerri said finally.

"As close to it as I have," DeeJay answered stubbornly. "You sure can't count Patsy!"

"We're family." Gerri's voice was getting a bit hard around the edges.

"I haven't known you as long as I've known her. She's like a cross between my mom and a sister." DeeJay's voice was just a little bit harder around the edges than Gerri's.

And when Gerri and Skip showed up to see Stevie, not only was Jeannie there, staying a couple of weeks to help out, Doug was there, too, sitting on the floor, his legs spread, Bobbi sitting facing him, her legs spread, the two of them holding hands and rocking back and forth, chanting "rowboat, rowboat, rowboat." That went over like a lead balloon. They seemed to think he should jump up, grab his hat and run off down the road casting terrified glances over his shoulder. Instead, Doug smiled and nodded, and when Bobbi stopped playing rowboat and raced to Skip, Doug got up and went over to the kitchenette area to plug in the kettle and help Jeannie with lunch.

"Hey," DeeJay said clearly, when Gerri finally put it in words, "I'm not the one they buried, okay? He's a friend. That's spelled eff, ahr . . ."

"I know how it's spelled. I'm just not sure I know what that word means to you! Sid is hardly cold in his grave and . . ."

"Sid doesn't *have* a goddamn grave!" DeeJay yelled. "And by now the wind has blown him all over the coast! I'm not going to climb into a cave and sit there snoffling for the rest of my life, Gerri. And I'm not even going to tell you Sid would have wanted me to . . . whatever. It's got nothing to do with what Sid might have wanted or might not have wanted! He's dead. He don't want for a thing, okay? *I'm* not dead! If I wanna have a friend, I'll have one. Or two or three or ten if that's what I want. If I want to eat a gallon of beans and stand on my head in the corner farting Oh Canada, I'll do 'er!"

"I just meant . . ."

"Never mind what you just meant. I know what you just meant."

And he was a friend. A friend who didn't show up at suppertime unless they'd made plans for it, a friend who came over in time for the bedtime rush, who at first just sat on a chair grinning and watching as first Jeannie, then DeeJay dunked Stevie in his blue plastic tub set up on the table. "Look at those feet go," he marvelled. "The old fight-or-flight instinct, I guess. It's okay, beanpole, it's just water, they aren't gonna drown you. Look, Bobbi's baby isn't a suckyboy, Bobbi's baby isn't splashin' water all over the kitchen."

And then one night Jeannie looked over at DeeJay and winked. She was holding Stevie with one hand cupped over his chest, washing his back with the soft pale blue cloth. "Want to give it a try?" she asked softly.

Doug hesitated, looked almost wildly at DeeJay, then looked at Bobbi, who was doing her best to drown her rubber dolly.

"Sure," he gulped. "If Bobbi can wash *her* baby I guess I can try old Steve."

He moved beside Jeannie and slid his huge hand where hers was. She pulled her hand away and Doug swallowed nervously. But he knew what he was doing. "Oh, I got more brothers and sisters than the Protestant Children's Orphan's Home in New Westminster," he laughed. "My mom had kids, my dad had kids, then they got together and they had kids, then they split up and each of 'em had some more kids and since neither of them was much into looking after kids we all sort of had to look after each other. Hey, I got more experience at this than you have, lady."

"Yeah? Then how come you're so scared?" Jeannie teased.

"Because there was so many of us it didn't matter if we drowned a few, but this is half the sum total around here so far."

When Stevie was three months old Doug was spending a couple of nights a week with DeeJay. Jeannie was back at her own place by then, and Gerri and Skip only came by every few days to see the kids and check on DeeJay. The first time they showed up in the morning and found Doug sitting in his jeans, barefoot and bare-chested, having breakfast with Bobbi and spooning cereal glup into Stevie's mouth while DeeJay slept in, Gerri nearly blew her cork. It must have cost her just about everything she had not to go into a verbal eruption, but she bit down hard and pressed her top china clippers against her bottom ones, made her mouth smile and accepted a cup of coffee. She waited until Doug was in the shower and the kids were being entertained and amused by Skip before she brought up the Siberian tiger which had been lurking in every corner of the place since she had arrived.

"Is he going to be a permanent fixture around here?" she asked carefully.

"Probably not permanent, and maybe not a fixture, but he'll be around a lot, for sure," DeeJay agreed, making her voice as casual as she could manage.

Gerri nodded and swallowed the lumps in her coffee. "He seems nice," she said, going the extra ten miles.

"He is," DeeJay smiled, going ten miles or so herself. "And real good to the kids."

He knew how to handle bloody Patsy, too. She came out of the pokey with the idea she'd move in with DeeJay and the kids until she got herself "properly set up again." DeeJay said no. And Patsy started her version of the Chinese water torture. "Why not?" "What do you mean not enough room, you could lose a damn softball team in here." "Jesus Christ, your own mother, and you'd see her on the street I suppose." "Thanks a bunch, kid, I guess this is what they mean when they talk about family support being so important to rehabilitation of multiple offenders." "I don't see why not, I'd pay my own way." "Cheapskate bitch!"

DeeJay knew she was losing ground. She'd run out of answers and was reduced to merely repeating "No, Patsy." And when she got that low on ammunition it meant that she was as apt as not to give in, and wouldn't that be more fun than a frog-hopping competition.

"No," Doug said loudly.

Patsy turned and tried to flatten him with her The-Duchess-of-the-Realm look. "And who, pray tell, are *you?*" she snapped. "We know you have an opinion, but opinions are like assholes, every-body has one and a lot of 'em's shitty."

"I'm the one who isn't the least bit impressed with that disguise you're trying to wear." He stood up, filling at least half the room. "And I'm the one has heard DeeJay say at least three dozen times that the answer to all this goddamn go-round is no. Take a tellin', Patsy."

"Do I know you?" Patsy was, if possible, even more haughty.

"I don't know." Doug wasn't smiling at all. "You know a lot of people, I guess. Now me, I got no trouble at all remembering who I know and who I don't know, but I don't think my circle of acquaintances is as large as yours."

"Butt out, you fuckin' jerk!" Patsy lost her false cool. "Just butt the hell out!"

"Stop shouting, you're scaring my kids," DeeJay roared. Stevie started to cry, Bobbi moved away from the noise, went to her room and closed the door.

"I never scared the goddamn kids, *you* scared the kids."

"Shut up," Doug yelled. "Just shut the fuck up, okay? The answer is no. Enn- oh. Now if there's some part of that concept goes over your head, just tell me what part and I'll do what I can to explain it."

The nagging stopped. At least any time Doug was around Patsy buttoned her lip and accepted, with what grace she could muster, the fact she was going to have to make her own way in the world. When he wasn't around she bitched. Of course. "That damn motel unit is so small you couldn't swing a cat in it."

"Who'd want to swing a cat? There or anywhere else, for that matter."

"Well, if you wanted to swing it you couldn't."

"You don't even *have* a cat. If you did it would leave home."

"What a grouch you are."

"You're the only one thinks so."

"And *noisy?* You wouldn't believe the noise."

"I'd believe it. I lived in too many of them when I was a kid, remember?"

"Well, if you know how awful it is why don't you . . ."

"Shut up about it or leave."

"Some daughter you are!"

"Look at the mother I got stuck with."

"Well, why'n't you loan me your vacuum cleaner? That thing I got from the Goodwill don't hardly suck and that motel unit hasn't been properly done since Christ was a cadet."

"No."

"No? *No!* Why in hell not?"

"Because you'd pawn it. Then I'd have to drive down, find the pawn shop and pay to get my own vacuum back again."

"What a *lie.*"

Patsy dropped it though, because DeeJay did have to drive down that one time and hit the pawnshops looking for her rug shampooer. Patsy vowed up and down she wasn't the one pawned it, she swore on a stack of Bibles someone had swiped it from her. "I'd just finished doin' the rug and the manager came to say there was a phone call and I just ran over for a minute and I left the door open so's the rug would air out and start dryin' and then I came back and just like that . . . gone . . ."

"Right."

And who knew for sure. Maybe it had been someone else swiped it. Maybe Patsy was telling the truth. Maybe bureaucracy was the best way to run things. And maybe the cow really had jumped over the moon.

There were all these things Patsy seemed to want and need, things she seemed to expect, things she seemed to feel DeeJay ought to know, to do, and even to be.

"Guess you got that Jeannie a mother's day card, too, huh?"

"Of course I did. It was at Jeannie's place I found out what Mother's Day *was!*"

"And didja get her a boxa choc'lates, too?"

"No, I didn't," DeeJay said. She didn't bother to add she had bought Jeannie a nice little bush for her front yard, a magnolia the man said would have purple cup-like flowers on it when it bloomed. She might have got away with the lie-by-omission, too, if Bobbi didn't have a tongue, a mouth and vocal cords. She dropped the clanger about the nice flower tree they had bought for Grandma Jeannie.

94

"Magnolia tree?" Patsy glared.

"Not a *tree*," DeeJay backfilled hurriedly, "a bush. Maybe a foot tall is all."

"Lucky for her *she's* got a yard to put it in."

Patsy wanted a cake for her birthday. And more, she wanted no cake for Jeannie or Gerri, either. Patsy wanted them to have Xmas together as a family, just her and DeeJay and the grandchildren, with no sign of anyone else. When it didn't turn out that way, when she came into the house and found Gerri and Skip already there, up to their chins in wrapping paper, with Doug leaping around taking pictures, the flash illuminating the entire scene with light bright enough to make even those not the subject of the photo blink, the old green-eyed dragon surfaced again.

"Last one to arrive, I see," she muttered. "Must be nice to have a car."

It didn't help matters that Jeannie dropped over after the rush had died down at her place. All that meant to Patsy was that some people had *two* Christmases instead of only one.

"Don't you ever do anything like *normal* people?" she flared.

"What in hell would I know about normal," DeeJay said wearily for the umpteenth time. "Give it a rest, will you Patsy? Get off my case. If it makes you so friggin' unhappy to come, don't come."

"Oh and some people would just *love* that!" Patsy was getting herself all wound up for a real display.

Doug came over, stared down at her for a long and very quiet minute, then, so quietly only Patsy and DeeJay heard, he put in his two cents' worth. "Button it up, bitch," he said. "I can drive you back to your cage one helluva lot quicker'n the bus brought you here."

So she shut up. But DeeJay's stomach was in such a knot she could hardly force herself to eat her turkey dinner. She might not have got any of it down if she hadn't had a good supply of beer in the fridge to wash the ashes from her mouth.

"Listen," Patsy tried a new tack, "it's gettin' kinda late. Rather than drag anyone away from things I could just stretch out on the sofa with a sleepin' bag."

"Oh, no problem," Doug was on his feet immediately. "No problem at all, Patsy, be glad to be of help."

Sometimes, when she was fully in the bag, Patsy would phone and bleat into DeeJay's ear until DeeJay felt as if she'd like to join Stevie in his crib, just curl in a ball with her thumb in her mouth, and anytime something didn't sit right, open that thumby mouth and wail. "I might as well be a bloody mouse," Patsy griped drunkenly, "Then I could crawl into your walls and live in the corners of your life, come out after dark and stuff myself on the crumbs that fell from your table."

"You're not movin' in with us, Patsy," was all DeeJay could say, over and over again.

"Oh, there's room for that sausage with the big shoulders, but no room for your own mother. Nice. Real nice."

The problem was like one of those nails in an expensive pair of shoes; with cheap shoes you can find the nail right away, it's sticking up where it's impossible to not find it, but with expensive shoes, as soon as your foot comes out and your weight is off the sole, the leather assumes its own shape and the nail tip is hidden. Even if you run your fingers over the seams and joins inside you don't find the nail, but by Christ there's a scrape on your foot and the longer you try to wear the shoes the worse the scrape gets until you'd have a hole in your foot if you didn't have sense enough to throw the goddamn shoes away or, if you can't afford to do that, at least put moleskin over the rubbed place and slide in some cardboard or something.

You could also amputate your foot, of course, and not need to wear a shoe on it.

"If you give in on this one, kid, you're sunk," Jeannie agreed. "And other than just telling her over and over again that you're not going to give in, I don't know what to suggest. Unless you want to pay the bikers five hundred dollars to knee-cap her."

"Oh, they'd do it for two hundred, prob'ly," DeeJay sighed. "The woman is such a total pain in the ass I could probably get a grant from the federal government to pay the bikers to off her and dump her in the ocean."

"You could maybe talk to her social worker?"

"And then what? If *talk* is all I want to do about it I could get a bloody gerbil at the five'n'ten and talk to it while it ran around on its little go-nowhere wheel and shit oval pellets into its own food dish. I mean if *talk* is all I can do about it I've got Stevie. He's a great listener. Or I could just say Sure, Patsy, move in, and then Stevie could listen to her the way I had to listen to her all those years. He could also listen to all her bloody loser friends while they burned holes in the sofa with their cigarettes and other holes in the rugs and maybe even burned the place down around our ears. And we could all listen to them barfing all over the bathtub and fighting with each other and Christ, couldn't we just listen to the sound of all our furniture being dragged out and sold at the pawn shop for money for something to poke up their snouts. Mind you, they'd have to move fast to get anything before Patsy'd already took it."

"You must take after my damn parents," Patsy's shriek poured from the receiver. "They got a house as big as the bus station and more locks on the doors than you could shake a stick at! Locks on the windows. Amaze me if I found out they don't got a lock on the crapper to keep someone from stealing what they flush away. If it's money you're worried about I'll pay my way. I'm sick and tired of living in this cheap unit, I tell you."

"Then get a job, Patsy," DeeJay shouted. "Stop sucking tit and waitin' for your next whoofare cheque. Clean up your act, wash your face, and for a change, brush your hair. Go down to the market and get a job puttin' cans of peas on the shelf. Make some decent money and get a two-room upstairs with a view of the sea."

"A view of the alley and the roof of the garage, more likely. Even the whoofare says I'm unemployable."

"Leave me alone." DeeJay hung up and pulled the plug out of the walljack. If the place caught fire or Stevie choked on something she could always plug the sucker back in and phone out, but she wasn't waiting for the Prince to phone for an appointment to try the glass slipper on her foot so why did she need the damn thing anyway.

"In all the paperbacks she'd move in, be struck by lightning or maybe love for the kids, start going to AA or something, get herself sober and straight and make up for all the lost years, safe in the bosom of her loving family." DeeJay popped the tab on the can of Black Label and sucked morosely. "Even a damn leech will let go sooner or later. Maybe the world is lucky Patsy found booze

97

and junk, can you imagine what a fuckin' threat she'd be if she'd, say, joined the Army and been able to direct all this stubbornness at the enemy? People with that kind of need to win, win, win all the time must make real good generals. Of course, she'd be hard as hell on the enlisted ones, and the casualty lists would be as long as your leg, but I can just see her, slappin' her damn swagger stick against her leg and yellin' at John Wayne to put on his fuckin' red berry and Take that ridge, pilgrim. Only trouble is, I'm not interested in bein' John Wayne and this isn't any ridge, it's where I live. And it used to feel like home but not any more."

"Just keep the phone jack unplugged is all." Doug put his empty can in the case, got another and opened it. "Drink up," he grinned, "you're one behind me."

"Be four behind you soon, the way you're suckin'er back."

Doug sat down beside her on the sofa, put his arm around her shoulder and gave her a quick hug. DeeJay grinned at him and leaned her head back. He moved, shoved his beer can between his legs then reached up with that hand to shift her head from resting against the back of the sofa to touching his shoulder. "Supposed to put your head on my shoulder," he reminded her.

"G'wan, ya dumb tit," she teased, "I got my head on my own shoulders. You got *your* head on your shoulders."

"So, what say we invite some people over for Saturday night?"

"What's Saturday night?"

"That's what comes between Friday night and Sunday night, didn't they tell you about it?"

"Is it someone's birthday?"

"No."

"Anniversary or something?"

"No. Does there have to be a reason for a party?"

"Just have a bunch of people come in and mess up the house for no reason except it's Saturday night?"

"People do that, DeeJay. It's called socializing."

"Guess someone forgot to socialize me. I'll pass, thanks."

Doug sighed, and nodded. "It's your place," he agreed. He even bent his head and managed to kiss her on the forehead.

DeeJay smiled up at him and tried to concentrate on and enjoy the quiet that came once the kids were in bed and asleep.

"Don't you like having people over for supper or drinks or stuff like that?"

"I don't know many people." She looked up at him, her face showing her puzzlement. "I like going to Jeannie's place for a visit and a good yack, and I like it when she comes here. I don't particularly mind it when Gerri and Skip come over because the kids bounce around and laugh and have themselves a great old time and anyway Gerri and Skip don't stay long, usually, an hour or so and they're off again. I can take visiting them for a bit, but it wears on me when they want me to go for the whole weekend, because, well, we don't really have anything much to talk about except Sid and what's there to say that hasn't already been said ten times. And I've been thinking that maybe what they want is to have the *kids* overnight, so I thought maybe first chance I had to bring it up I'd tell 'em that if that's what they'd like it's fine by me. I never had a grandma or grandpa but Jeannie said kids really get off on doing stuff with them, so . . . far be it from me, eh?"

"And what will you do with yourself while the kids are spending a few days and nights with Grammie and Grampie?" He looked down at her and smiled gently. "Sit in this place and listen to music? Hon, you're like a bloody hermit or something."

"You're all the time talking, Dougie. And when you walk around you make little noises. You pick things up and put them down without even looking at them. You whistle while you're making coffee. You even make little whistles through your teeth when you're reading the paper, and you rattle the paper and you go hmmmm, and you do this little tsk thing if there's something in it you don't like and . . . like you're trying to fill up a hole or something, dribbling sand into it, or dropping in bits of grass and pieces of stick. It's like quiet is something you've decided to get rid of. And I like quiet. I like music soft and you crank 'er up so's you can hear it all over the house. It's funny how people can get along real good and still be totally different. You like to live in a crowd. I spent my life watchin' the crowd come and the crowd go and to me a crowd is just a whole buncha people and there's not many of them I'd walk across the street to see."

"Boy." He finished his beer and moved gently. She lifted her head and put it where she had wanted it to be all along, against the back of the sofa. "Want one?"

"Sure." She drained hers and grimaced at the taste of warm beer. "Sure, why not?"

The thing of it was, Doug had more family than you could keep track of without a printed program. Marlene and Fred, his mom and dad, had either been madly in love or lived in an awful cold house with only one way to get warm, because they'd had one kid after another. "All he has to do is drape his pants over the bottom of the bed and that's it, I'm pregnant again," Marlene laughed. "I got a couple of kids in spite of a diaphragm and Delfen cream, I got a few more playing Vatican Roulette, I got a couple strained through French safes. I tell you, if there'd been more ways of birth control I'd probably have had more kids."

"Fertile?" Fred laughed. "Listen, people'd come to the house and ask if they could borrow her, stand her in the field for a while, get the corn growing like hell. I had to learn not to mention her name or even think about her while I was at work, otherwise I'd come home and find a new set of triplets."

It was like being at Jeannie's place, except at Jeannie's she knew people and those she didn't know were so used to fosters of all shapes, sizes and colours passing through but not staying long that they hadn't fussed over her or acted as if they expected her to become important in their lives. Doug's family seemed to think she'd just signed a legally binding contract to become a very *un-*silent partner in whatever road show it was they were putting on for the world. His sister Nadine wanted her to join the bowling league, his brother Alex thought she'd be a good second base on the beer league team he and his wife Sally had organized. Lorraine, who was married to another brother but DeeJay couldn't remember which one and didn't ask because not remembering made her feel like a fool, phoned at least once a week and asked DeeJay if she wanted to take the kids to the pool for swimming lessons. DeeJay didn't really much feel like it, but the kids loved going so how can you say no. And every time she got to the pool there was Lorraine and her three kids and probably two sisters, a sister-in-law, four cousins and whichever of the neighbours had finished her laundry and come along, too.

And Doug thought it was great. He really figured his family was doing what any family was supposed to do, bringing DeeJay out of her shell, getting her back out into the world, opening itself to include her. Privately DeeJay thought it was a lot like being smothered. They might use a silk cushion instead of a stinking old feather pillow, but there you were, going blue in the face all the same.

"He's right, darlin'," Jeannie told her, leaning across the table and holding DeeJay's hand between hers. "That *is* what people do."

"Even when they don't really want to?"

"The only reason you don't want to is that you haven't done it much. You're used to not having someone around, so that's what you think you like. If you were born in the cat's litter box and grew up there you wouldn't really feel comfortable when someone emptied it and set you on the floor. You might even spend your whole life looking for another box of kitty litter to live in; or you might say goodbye to the catshit and start exploring the rest of the house."

"Oh."

"And people *do* things together. Dougie is used to having people laughing and talking and singing and, after all, it was his friendliness that made him stand out in the crowd, right? That's what you've always said you liked most about him. So why fall in love with someone because of something about them and then make both of you miserably unhappy by setting about to change the very thing about them you most liked?"

"I'm not in love with Doug," DeeJay said. Jeannie gaped. "I like him. I like him lots. But I'm not in love with him. I don't think."

"You don't think? You mean you don't know?"

"I'm not sure I know what 'in love with' means. I know love. I love my kids. I love you. I know if anything happened to any of you I'd go nuts. I can't even think about what life would be like without you and the kids in it. But I don't feel that way about Dougie. I mean I know if he took a hike next Tuesday I'd feel bad. For a while. But I can imagine life without him. It'd be just like it was before him. And I'd live."

"Then why is he living here with you?"

"Well, it seemed important to him. And I like him okay."

She thought about what Jeannie had said. Thought about it a lot. She had two hours every afternoon when it was quiet enough to think. Bobbi didn't exactly nap, but she did still have a lie-down time, and Stevie needed his nap or he turned into a miniature mass murderer. DeeJay loved that time. She made sure the phone was off, the door locked and the chores either done or caught up enough she could call them to a halt. Then she sat in her lovely living room and stared out the big sliding glass doors, flanked on either side by floor-to-ceiling windows.

The sliding doors opened onto her share of the back yard. The designer had put cedar fences between the sections of yard, separating unit 19 from unit 20 and 20 from 21, but there was no back section of the fencing, you could see your portion of the entire town, spreading wider and wider the further from the units you looked. And out there, half a mile or so away, was the harbour and beyond it little islands and rocks, and beyond that a misty blue strip that was the Strait and beyond that a long low bluish hump that was a big island and, speckled all over everything, boats of more kinds and descriptions than DeeJay knew, fish boats and tugs and barges and sailboats and who knows what they were all called.

She had columbine planted along her pieces of fence, and begonias in the half-shady places. In the corner by the house, where the sun seldom shone directly but the light slanted, she put sword fern she had dug from the bush with a shovel. There was a little patch of grass, too, and smack in the middle of it, a lilac tree that looked as if it wasn't sure if it was going to grow or not.

"I could put together a play area for the kids, " Doug offered. "You've got the swingset, I could rig up a slide and a teety-totter and maybe one of those riggins with ropes and nets to climb on."

"They can go to the play area," DeeJay said. "Christ, it's not but almost next door!"

"I thought maybe you'd want to keep an eye on them."

"I can do that easy enough. But thank you, Dougie, it's a nice thought. I just kind of like the back yard the way it is."

"Sure. Whatever," he agreed. "You're probably right, now that I think about it. Do them good to get on their own, meet kids their own age, learn all about the push and shove of social interaction."

"Yeah?" She was teasing him and he knew it. "Failing that they can have a helluva good time on the swings and slides, right?"

"You got 'er, kiddo."

She liked the way the hummingbirds sipped from the columbine flowers and the big fat-ass bumblybees came from the foxglove drunk on perfume and pollen. She watched the back yard and the cedar waxwings which sometimes perched on the fence, and she thought about what Jeannie had said.

"You still want to have a Saturday night get-together?" she asked quietly.

Doug stared at her, then nodded. "Yeah."

"So what are we expected to do?" she couldn't quite look at him and he didn't seem to expect her to.

"Oh, not much. Get in some beer, load up on chips and dip and peanuts and stuff. Everyone will bring their own stuff, drinks and that, and . . . and that's about it." He sat on the floor, his back against the sofa, her leg touching his shoulder. "You never party?"

"Partied hearty when I first met Sid," she said softly. "But it was different. It wasn't really at anyone's house. Well, sometimes it was but they didn't have kids. Everyone was sort of . . . well, like loose in their lives, right? Not like this is gonna be. People settled and all."

"It'll be fine, DeeJay, you'll see. It'll be fun!"

She fudged on Stevie's afternoon nap and didn't put Bobbi down at all, so by the time they were finished their supper, deliberately late because being hungry seemed to exhaust the two of them, and had their bath, deep and warm and thick with bubbles, they were more than ready for their pyjamas and cuddle-bears. DeeJay tucked them into bed and smooched them both, she rubbed their bums and backs, and sang a little silly-song to them, she promised she'd leave the night light on so if they woke up they'd see Minnie Mouse's ears and her big nose glowing at them, she said no, of course there were no boogers under the bed, but if it would make Bobbi feel better DeeJay would get down on her hands and knees and check. "Not even dust buggers," she said pleasantly.

"Sure?"

"Posi-hoochy, babe."

"Cherie's got boogers in her closet."

"Well I tell you, I'm gonna be as surprised as all get-out if we've got boogers because I distinctly told the real estate agent *no boogers* or I won't buy the house. We had the booger killers in to be sure; remember, we came to have another look and they were going over the carpets with a big machine and everything. 'Member? Even put that jigger-sucker on the drapes, 'member?"

"No boogers here," Bobbi agreed, sighing with relief.

"Darlin', any time you even *think* there's a booger, you call me. I'll be up here with the egg beater so fast your eyes will spin. And I'll egg beater that booger until it's all muddled up, tied in knots and squinched, okay? Because no booger is bothering *my* girl!"

If that goddamn Cherie didn't stop with her tales of boogers and spooks DeeJay was going to give her a taste of her own medicine, put on a scare mask and jump up at her bedroom window, gibbering and shining the flashlight on the Dracula face. Let her screech then! Find out what scared was all about, by God.

She showered and got into her good clothes, brushed her hair and fussed herself, then went to check on the kids. She leaned against the door frame and just watched them sleeping, both of them on their stomachs, Stevie with his bum in the air, Bobbi flat out with her head turned to one side. He had his thumb in his mouth, Bobbi had her half-curled fist up near her face but hadn't sucked her thumb since she was eighteen months old. DeeJay couldn't believe how much she loved them. It just started in her belly and swelled up and up and up until it was thick in her throat, she could taste it in her mouth, it was pushing against her eyes and filling her head. They were just so perfect! If you sat down, educated as any egghead, and tried to design something better, you couldn't. They were just exactly what they ought to be. They didn't need another finger on each hand or another leg to move faster or wheels to get them around corners without tipping, they didn't need more or fewer eyes or ears, they had just everything they needed or a person could imagine. And round and soft and yet their backs were straight and their legs as strong as little trees.

And they were hers. They had started in her body, grown there, and come out when they were damn good and ready, not a day sooner or later than they had decided for themselves. Her blood and her bones and her meat and she hadn't even had to think about it, and there they were, and they belonged to her the way her own hair and teeth were hers, the way her fingernails were a part of her, and if someone hauled them out with pliers they would still be *her* fingernails, they would never belong to that other person. She knew if they were on the other side of a burning wall she'd chew her way through the flames to get to them. She knew if they were sitting on the bottom of the ocean calling for her she'd grab the biggest rock she could find, hold it tight against herself, jump over the side and sink down, down, down to the sand and muck to be with them.

And why hadn't Patsy felt that way about her? What was it about her that was so fucking incomplete the stink of old beer in a bar had been preferable? Oh well, them's the breaks DeeJay.

"You ready, hon? Want a beer?"

"Sure. Love one. Hey, you look some nice, fella! You got anything planned for tonight? Maybe I could show you a good time."

"Sorry, lady, hate to bust your old heart and all but I got me a girl and we're going to party."

"Oh yeah? Betcha I could show you a better time than she could, whoever she is."

"Bet you couldn't. Nobody can show me a better time than *my* woman does."

There hadn't been any way to get out of inviting Patsy. DeeJay just knew Patsy'd get a snootful and do something ravishingly charming like upchuck on someone's chest or pitch herself headfirst into the potted plants or maybe with any luck at all she'd fall off her high heels and go ass over teakettle through the glass doors. Maybe she'd bring a date and he'd pitch a fit on the carpet and flop around until he knocked over the table and splattered chip dip over everyone's party togs. Maybe Patsy would have tried to get herself in decent shape by hopping on the old wagon and maybe she'd no sooner get in the unit than she'd go into the DTs and see spiders in the platter of raw veggies, the ones Doug called croo-di-tays. Well, if there was any crude around, Patsy'd be sure to find it, you could depend on that in times of stress and woe. Sure as there's poop-inna-goose.

Gerri and Skip brought a half dozen of Gerri's special meat loaf things, pat-tays, not to be confused with Patsy. They were already sliced, as thin as you could imagine, and fanned out like someone was doing card tricks with them.

"Oh *wow!*" DeeJay blurted. "Just about my all-time favourite stuff! Thanks, Gerri, thanks, Skip, that's great."

"Here, Doug, try this, see what you think." Skip scooped a slice with a cracker and held it out with a smile. A smile that must have cost him about three-quarters of everything he had ever hoped he would have because Doug, whatever else he might be, wasn't Sid, and it ought to be Sid living with DeeJay and playing horsey-back with Stevie.

"Good stuff," Doug agreed, "damn good stuff. How'd you do that, anyway?" and Gerri was telling him about how you needed veal and rabbit and this spice and that seasoning and boiled it and ground it and then baked it with some grated onion and what was left of its own juice that you'd boiled it in.

Jeannie brought potato salad and two quarts of home-canned home-smoked sockeye. "Got a bowl?" she asked. "I thought we'd just put this on the table with maybe a couple of forks and people could take their choice, be polite or be pigs, all the same to me."

Patsy arrived with a smile on her face and a case of beer under her arm, and of course nothing would do but put the beer in the fridge then go up to see her darlings.

"Don't wake them up," DeeJay hissed, "or we'll never get them settled again."

"What do you think I am, stupid or something? Of course I won't wake them up! But *my* kid didn't need to be wrapped in cotton batten just so's she'd sleep. *My* kid coulda slept on the head of a straight pin. Or the point of it for that matter!" There were all these things Patsy's kid could do that DeeJay's kids couldn't do. "Why I could just tuck her under my arm and head off with a spare diaper and a bottle of milk and she was at home anywhere we went. I coulda headed off on a safari to darkest Africa and my kid wouldn't'a played strange or fussed up."

Yeah, and you could leave her alone in a hotel room for three days with nothing to eat but a big paper plateload of cold French fries, too, and all she did was watch TV and sleep on the floor.

The brothers arrived with the sisters-in-law, the sisters arrived with the brothers-in-law and a boatload of cousins showed up, some of them bringing what they called housewarming gifts, some of them with what they said were "sort of" wedding presents. Dee-Jay just went into overload and accepted the fact there were dozens of people in her unit and most of them looked so much like each other they might have been coming out of the other end of a Xerox machine.

She just kept refilling the dip bowls and putting out more croo-di-tays. After a while she gave up trying to keep the chip bowl full and just ripped open the packages and left them where hands could reach in and move entire fields of spuds to chomping mouths. She took the two huge pots of chili and put them in the oven to warm up, she hauled out her pre-sliced French bread and smeared it with garlic butter and put that in to heat, she made sure there was coffee for those who wanted it, she took blocks of cheese and turned them into cubes that vanished before she got the crackers out of the package. She was just about ready to call the caterers on the emergency line when she realized everyone else had brought food, too, and they were bringing it out of the places where it was hidden. Someone opened the linen closet in the hall, brought out a cookie sheet piled high with sandwiches and set it down on the counter, someone else had half the celery crop of the state of California stuffed with cream cheese and speckled with pimento and olive. One of the cousins went out to the car and brought in a big blue cold-pack canner that looked to weigh six metric tons. "Can I put this on a stove burner to warm up?" she asked, and before DeeJay could even nod she'd done it. "Spaghetti sauce," she winked. "Now if you'll just steer me toward your biggest pot I'll start boiling up the spaghetti."

By midnight they'd eaten their way through enough food to keep a third world village alive for a month, and they'd packed away enough booze to float the HMCS *Magnificent*. By two in the morning DeeJay was ready to check herself into the hospital for a rest. They were dancing, they were singing along to the music, they were laughing, they were talking over the music, they'd got past the remember-whens and were into the jokes nobody but family would ever understand and Patsy was perambulating around as if she was a charter member of the whole mad bunch.

Fred was busy talking sawmills to Skip, who'd never worked in one in his entire life but seemed to know everything a person would need to know to run one singlehandedly. DeeJay understood bugger-all about what they were talking about, except they seemed to agree that by the time Stevie was grown up enough to need a job there wouldn't be a mill in the province that hired humans. "Robots," Fred said firmly. "The whole thing's gonna be robots, like the ones they got makin' cars in Japan."

"Used to be they'd say they'd never be able to totally mechanize the green chain," Skip agreed, "and they got more fuckin' buttons, switches and levers than you could shake a stick at and if it gets any more automated they won't even need people to buy the fuckin' product!"

"You got 'er. By the time they're through shavin', choppin', shreddin' and slimin' up the bush this entire bloody place is gonna look like one'a them polished rocks they got in the desert. Fuck of a shame if you ask me."

"Well, I don't know," Gerri was saying to someone DeeJay thought was probably one of Marlene's sisters, or maybe an in-law of some kind. "Every time I read about how there's someone else in the States shot every what is it, forty-eight seconds or something, I think, God and all my life we've only had a gap of maybe ten years at most keeping us from the same kinda thing. I mean for a while we thought it was incredible that they were all supposed to have *two* cars, and now we got two cars, know what I mean? They were the ones with the race riots and now we got Indians mad as wet hens all over the country. But it's spooky, you know, to think of people walking around like some kind of cowboy movie, with guns in their pockets, ready to just put a hole in your head if you bump into them on the street."

"I know, did you hear about that thing where there was a line-up for gas and this guy just jumped out of his car and started *shooting*. Jesus, if you can't wait a bit for your damned gas, you know? Of course," the cousin or whatever said firmly, "we've always known the whole damn lot of them might be nice if you take them one by one, but in groups and bunches they're crazy as hell."

Doug and one of his sisters were dancing together singing about how Leroy Brown was the meanest man in the whole damn town, meaner than a junkyard dog, and Patsy was blithely discussing the foolishness of a bloated bureaucracy. "If insteada welfare and whoofare and hawfare and feefare and foofare and unemployment enjoyment and compensation and old age wotzit and family whichit they just put everyone on a guaranteed annual income, poof, you get born, they mail in a form, and that's it, there's your guaranteed annual and it goes up as you grow up until you're an adult and there it is, comin' in on the fifteenth of every month, period. You got any idea how many bean counters, pencil pushers and their duplicate numbers who double-check the yellow slips, the blue slips, the pink slips, the green slips and we must *never* forget the buff slips . . . well, they'd all be retired and insteada payin' them sixty thou a year or whatever it is, they'd get the same guaranteed annual the rest of us got."

"Yeah, but what about the incentive to work?" the other asked.

"What incentive to work?" Patsy grinned. "Me, I never felt no huge incentive to hop outta bed and go cripple myself makin' money for some other sucker! The only incentive most people's got is they're hungry."

"Right, and gettin' a helluva lot hungrier, too."

Jesus Christ on a teetering cross, what did Patsy know about economics or bureaucracy or the national debt or the gross national product? How could she do it? Just stand there with her dyed hair gleaming from the overhead light and laughingly confess she'd never had any incentive at all to go to work and pay her own way in the world.

"Listen, you can bank on it. I'll take bets. When you got a bloody economy that's *built* on guns, bullets and bombs you don't *want* world peace! They no more'n get their gnawed-to-shreds butts out of Veetnam and what happens? The bottom falls outta the bag, the whole place goes for a poop, they've got unemployed ready to burn down entire neighbourhoods and they call it a recession. Well, what're they gonna do about it if not find some other place to get a dirty little war going. All they gotta do is find someplace where they can stir the pot a bit, get people riled up, put in their own puppet for a while, let him send the place to hell so bad the people start a revolution, then they say it's communism, and *bang* here comes another war and more money bein' made and the unemployed, they're back to work again and it's all in the name of freedom, God and right. Because they want their money right here and right now, by God!"

By three-thirty a few others were yawning, by four-thirty they were starting to leave and by six the place was empty except for her, and Doug, and the still sleeping kids. Her eyes felt like she had gravel behind the lids, her throat was raw from all the cigarette smoke but Doug assured her they'd all had a wonderful time.

"Leave the mess for now," he said. "I'll clean 'er up later on after we've had a bit of sleep."

They went to bed at six-thirty, for a bit of sleep. And it was a bit, all right, the kids were awake and up by eight. DeeJay got out of bed and went to do the cereal and milk routine, closing the door quietly so Doug wouldn't be disturbed. The kids ate their cereal and milk, then started in on the stale chips and wilted olives.

"Who had the party?" Bobbi demanded, "and why didn't I get to go to it? I *never* get to go to a party."

"Your whole life is a party," DeeJay yawned, "but if it means that much to you we'll have a party you can go to, too."

"When? Tonight?"

"Tonight we're having a slumber party," DeeJay agreed.

DeeJay got the idea of upgrading her education after Doug took a St. John's Ambulance First Aid course. He headed off two nights a week from seven until nine-thirty and in between classes peeked into his books for a half hour or so each night. When he needed to practise bandaging, DeeJay became the purported patient. And watching him, she learned quite a bit herself. Enough to become interested in what was in his textbooks. So she cracked them open and read them from front cover to back a couple of times, and then, when he was boning for his exams, she was the one would ask questions, most of which it turned out were not on the exam. Enough were, however, and Doug passed the course with good marks. He no sooner got his certificate than his pay went up by almost a dollar an hour. DeeJay did not miss the significance of the raise. It proved what she had heard other people say. She didn't expect her widow's compensation pension to go up no matter how much education she got, but she didn't expect to just sit on compy all her life, either. As soon as Stevie was old enough . . .

In which case why not use the time before he was old enough to get herself prepared a bit and maybe even equipped for something more than a job in the Mini Mart?

It wasn't hard to find a babysitter, the project was swarming with teen-agers who were willing to line up for the chance of a job which entailed little more than watching TV and getting paid to do it.

"You coulda asked me," Patsy glared. "I'd'a done it for nothing."

"I'd have had to drive over, get you, bring you to the unit, then drive you back when I got home."

"I coulda slept on the couch."

"I'd still have had to drive you back!"

"I don't like the idea of strangers looking after my grandchildren."

"Carlie is less a stranger to them than you are. She lives across the street, they see her every day!"

"I'd be less a stranger if you'd just make an effort."

"Make your own efforts, Patsy."

That first semester, the spring session, DeeJay took upgrading for her GED and was amazed when she managed, in just a few months, to get herself through what would have taken her two or three years of high school. "They must just teach you what you need for the tests or something," she decided. "They know ahead of time what'll be on the tests because they make them up and they just feed you the answers, I guess."

"Sure," Jeannie agreed, "and after all, if you shit on yourself first nobody else gets the chance, right? God forbid any of us think you were able to *do* something!"

"Well, I did it, sure, but . . ."

"But nothing! You did it. Period."

"Yeah, but how can they teach in a few months what they take years to . . ."

"DeeJay, there was a time when all you needed was to know how to sign your bloody X and you could get a job. Then you needed to be able to sign your name. Then they wanted reading and writing. Not long ago you could waltz out of grade eight and get a job that paid enough to support a family. Then you had to have grade ten to get the same job. Now they won't even look at the nose in the middle of your face unless you've got high school graduation. So all the people who would have been out working at age fifteen or sixteen or whatever have *got* to stay in school. And the school has to *keep* them in school or they'll be out on the streets protesting the lack of jobs! And what was an educational system has become a babysitting service. They could take all of high school and stuff it in your head in six months. They could probably leave the little tads out playing softball or something until they were fifteen, then put 'em in grade one and they'd still graduate high school at age seventeen. Most of what they're teaching you is to stay quiet, sit down, say nothing and find some way to either amuse yourself or put your own brain to sleep."

"Oh, come on."

"Come on nothing. I've got fosters who don't know as much about writing a simple letter home asking for money after they've finished grade eleven as the ones I used to have knew how to do after grade eight. And that, my dear, is the absolute cold truth. I've got fosters in grade twelve who can't do the math in the grade nine book from only ten years ago! And maybe some things change. I don't know, maybe English grammar is different than it was, but numbers are numbers and four is still four and as near as I know square root is still square root, only what they used to do in grade ten they can't do now unless they've got a bloody calculator in one hand and a computer keyboard in the other!"

"Really?"

"Darlin', last week one of my fosters came home with a report card, which, incidentally, it seems to me I see less often these days than I once did, and less on them to tell me what's going on, too. And on that goddamn report card were teachers' comments. I found two spelling mistakes and a clanger of a mistake in grammar . . . and this was the damn *teacher*, not the kid! Week before that a different kid comes home with a homework assignment about looking for examples of, and I quote, 'the indigenous plants that grow around here'." Jeannie shook her head and poured another cup of tea, almost slamming the pot back on the table in her frustration. "Where the fuck *else* would the indigenous plants grow? If they grew someplace else they wouldn't be indigenous! And when did the word 'that' start replacing the words 'which' and 'who'? And why is everything 'upcoming' and nothing is 'forthcoming' any more?"

"Huh?"

"Right. Huh, for sure. Half the time you don't know what the voice on the radio is trying to say!"

"Then you think maybe I could . . . ?"

"Darlin', I *know* you could! You've got your equivalency now. Come fall semester you can start taking courses for credit. Get enough credits and you can go for university level courses. DeeJay, whatever else you might be, stupid isn't on the list!"

"Yeah?"

"There's a daycare centre, for one thing. Won't hurt Stevie to play with the kids there instead of out in the project play area. You can arrange it so's you head for class when Bobbi goes to kindergarten. Stevie goes to school with Mommy. You take your class, pick up Stevie, walk back down the hill and pick up Bobbi just as she's getting out and . . . hey, the whole fam damily goes to school."

"I bet I could, too."

"You know it. *If* you want to."

DeeJay wanted to. DeeJay suddenly wanted to do just about exactly what Jeannie had outlined. Badly. And it didn't take any more effort than it would have taken to juggle six roaring chain saws and two razor-sharp sabres at the same time while standing on the top strand of a barbed-wire fence over a ditch full of snapping alligators.

"There are no difficulties," she insisted grimly, "just challenges, right?"

"Right," Jeannie agreed.

"Well, hell, if you'd wanted to go to school you shoulda done it at the time you were supposed to do it," Patsy yelled. "It ain't right them kids are pawned off on people they don't know! A little kid ought to just be out playin' in its own yard, not headin' off to bloody school with a briefcase, as if it was already a grown-up insurance salesman!"

"Patsy, would you do me a big favour? Would you go in the bathroom, look in the laundry hamper, find a dirty towel and shove it in your mouth? When did *your* kid get to play in its own yard? *Your* kid got left alone in some of the shittiest holes in town for days on end! Don't you give me the gears about leavin' my kids because the people I leave *my* kids with have been *trained* and they *know* and furthermore the kids love it."

"Well there's no damn need for it. I could . . ."

"You want to hear the patter of little feet? Is that it? Because if you do I'll buy you a white rat. At least it'd be able to look after itself and eat garbage if you just all of a sudden lurch off down the yellow brick road."

"I ain't drinkin' no more."

"No," DeeJay's voice could have cut steel, "and you ain't drinkin' no less, either, darlin', you don't fool me."

Patsy didn't answer, she just glared. She'd taken to putting a new rinse in her hair, one which was supposed to be rich auburn but which seemed to add a pinkish glow, especially at the front. When Patsy wasn't around DeeJay could sit down and figure out how old she had been when Patsy was the age DeeJay herself now was, and it made sense until Patsy herself showed up and then it all fell apart because she looked at least twice as old as she really was. Privately, DeeJay figured it wasn't so much the booze that had aged her, it was the chemicals she popped whenever she got the chance. They didn't call it speed for no reason at all, every cell in your body went into overdrive on the stuff so of course your old biological clock must start ticking two or three times as fast, each day using up a week or so of your life's energy, so after a while there you were, and chronological time no longer applied, you'd speeded away entire decades of energy and by damn it showed.

"How come you're all the time fighting with me?" Patsy asked piteously. "How come you can't talk nice?"

"You don't like the way you get talked to? Then hit the fuckin' road. You get what you dish out in this life, didn't they tell you?

I had to eat your shit and swallow your lies when I was little but I don't have to do it now. Don't tell *me* you aren't drinking because I can smell it from across the room, and don't give *me* the gears for going to school because basically it's none of your business, and don't try to make it sound like I'm doing something real bad to my kids because I won't get *you* to babysit them! I know how you take care of kids. I'm the kid you took care of. The *only* kid you took care of. And you might have thought that was good enough for a shitty little loser kid like I was but I'm telling you it isn't good enough for *my* kids."

"You never made a mistake, I suppose!"

"A mistake? A *mistake?* I bet if we both shut up for a while we'll hear the sound of violins sobbin' in the corner. Oh, pardon me ma'am, I seem to have made a slight error here. My intention was never to do that. I apologize. Do forgive me for ruining your childhood. How thoughtless of me. I was only exploring my own sense of adventure and searching the boundaries of my own horizons."

"Fuck, but you're hard."

"You can bet on it, Patsy."

The going to school part of it, the learning part of it was easy alongside what had to be gone through to get to it. DeeJay had to first get the kids up, dressed, fed and to daycare. She figured God had blessed her because neither Bobbi nor Stevie howled, yelled, screeched, screamed or turned blue in the face when they saw her waving and heading from the centre to her car. Some of the other kids practically decapitated themselves in their attempts to go with Mom or keep Mom from going. Bobbi looked on the daycare as a brief pit stop on her way to what really counted, kindergarten. The kindergarten teacher knew everything that was fit to know, and nobody else knew anything. "My teacher says" began to rule DeeJay's life. "My teacher says we have to drink lots of water."

"My teacher says we should always have kleenexes." "My teacher says don't sit too close to the teevee." "My teacher says sit up straight at the table." "My teacher says keep our rooms tidy."

"I said keep your room tidy and you didn't listen."

"My teacher says don't talk that way to people."

Stevie didn't know there was anything beyond daycare. When

he found out he would accept that as placidly as he had accepted everything else in his life so far. Stevie put his lunch and his snack'n'juice in the fridge, handed his cuddle-blanket to Daisy who put it on a shelf while reassuring him, "We'll put it where it will be safe and you can have it any time you want it." He stopped then, and looked at the blanket, probably to reassure himself, then he was off to the toybox. He didn't even fuss up when Bobbi left daycare to go with several others, under the supervision of Daisy, to the kindergarten. He just watched her leave, then went to the shelf and pointed. Phyllis got him his blanket immediately. "He usually goes to the quiet room with it," she told DeeJay, "and just finds a foamie, lies down, and goes to sleep."

DeeJay sometimes wished she could go to sleep. All this stuff and she hadn't known bugger-nothing about it. She'd expected to run into math she'd never experienced or needed, but she didn't know there was so much you could do wrong with the language you'd been talking all your life. The thought of people learning six or eight other languages was astounding. What really blew her mind was meeting people for whom her language was their second or third and then finding out they knew more about the rules of grammar and sentence construction than she did.

"Hey, there, it's the scholars comin' home," Doug laughed. He had supper started, that meant he'd got off early. "What did you learn today?"

"Nothin'," Bobbi decided. "Didn't learn anything. Melissa had a nosebleed, though. Nobody hit her or anything, she just started bleedin'. All over," she added grimly. "Her shirt and everything."

"Good heavens, what did the teacher do?"

"Stuffed toilet paper up her nose and said we should be good for the aide because she was takin' Melissa to see the doctor."

"Well, that was exciting." He scooped up Stevie and held him in a gentle hug. "And you, mister, what did you learn?"

"He din't learn nothin'. He scribbled on the blackboard. And he didn't use chalk, he used crayon."

"Oh oh, bad move, buds."

Stevie just grinned and started telling them the history of the Manchu dynasty in the original language. Whatever he was explaining involved a lot of arm waving and some loud laughter.

"By golly!" Doug sat Stevie on his hip and moved back to the stove. "You don't say. Well, I didn't know that. Good job you told me or we might have burned the spuds!"

"He's not talking, he's just making noises." Bobbi headed for the door.

"Where are you going?"

"I gotta go out to the swings."

"What about supper? It's almost ready."

"No, it's not, there's no meat or nothin'," and she was out the door, and off to see if the play area was still in place.

Some nights Doug had a late delivery and supper wasn't started. DeeJay turned on the TV to keep Stevie amused until she caught up with herself. After supper she stacked the dishes in the sink, soaked them in blistering hot water while supervising bath time and tucking kids into their beds. Once they were asleep she could throw a load of washing into the machine, do the dishes, tidy the kitchen and put the wet washing into the dryer. While it was spinning and fluffing she got to try to get her homework done.

"Oh Lord," Doug shook his head, "don't ask me, kid, I barely scraped myself through that crap and I think I forgot it ten minutes after they said I'd passed the test."

"I'm gonna die," DeeJay mourned. "I'm gonna read one confusing thing too many and my brain is gonna curl up and that'll be it, either I'll die or I'll spend ten years sitting in a corner, paralyzed."

But she stuck it out and got her piece of paper. She showed it to Jeannie; it wouldn't be real until someone else told her it was. Jeannie grinned, and then started leaking all down her face. "Oh, baby," she sobbed, "I'm so proud of you!"

"Ah, it's not that much. Any snot-nosed seventeen-year-old can do this."

"No they can't. Not dragging two kids behind them. Don't you downgrade what you've done! The world is full of people who'd pay a dime for the chance to take a slash at someone else's accomplishments, you don't have to do it to yourself, they'll do it for you."

"Feels strange. I've got this paper and yet I don't feel any different."

"Why should you be different? You were perfect before, and you're still perfect. You're wonderful!"

She'd have shown the paper to Patsy, too, but Patsy was back in the slammer, put away for a year for writing cheques on other people's bank accounts.

"Jesus, I don't know," DeeJay said to Jeannie, "seems to me if you're going to do something that's gonna send you off to the Crowbar Hotel, the least you can do is something big. You can almost have some respect for whoever it was pulled off the Great Train Robbery, but all Patsy ever does is little stupid stuff, the kind that gets you caught right away."

"Maybe she feels more at home in jail?"

"Why not, she's been there often enough. And each time she gets out she winds up in a different hole in the wall. Maybe they save her cell for her, give her the same one each time."

But she didn't really have time to worry about it, because she was busy figuring out what her own next move was going to be. She could take courses for credit now. If she wanted to she could bit by bit pick away until she had the first two years of university. She had no idea what she'd do after that, but she sure as hell wasn't going to just tread water while her kids learned to read and got good enough at it to recognize their grandmother's name in the hometown rag.

5

ONE THING YOU COULD BE SURE OF, everyone said, was that Doug wore his manners well. You could dress him up and he looked like a million dollars, but then you could also take him out and he'd charm his way through whatever was happening. Doug was the one at the wedding reception went over to where the aunties were sitting together in their mauve, lavender or pale lilac-coloured dresses and asked if he could have the honour of bringing them some punch; and would that be alcoholic or Sunday School kind. Doug was the one always volunteered to pick up whoever it was who didn't have a ride for whatever the occasion. He was the one would quite gladly grin refusal and say "nope, I'm drivin' to-night" so there would always be a sober ride home for those who needed it and he was the one went up on the roof in the pouring rain to lie on his belly, head down over the cement sidewalk, stringing Christmas lights. So of course a person put the hints and clues together and decided this was a man whose life was an open book. No skeletons in this closet.

DeeJay had been living with him four years before she even found out he had a kid.

"Nothin' to tell." His mouth grinned, but his eyes didn't. "I didn't say anything because there's nothing much to say."

"Don't you ever see him?"

"Nope."

"Why not?"

"Too much water under the bridge. It makes it easier for everyone if I just butt out and stay butted out."

"That's amazing!" She didn't believe it, even now. "You're so good with Stevie and Bobbi and . . ."

"The one's got nothing to do with the other," he answered easily. "It was all bad news right from the start. We just went out a few times is all. And then she dumped me and was going out with a couple of other guys, and then she learned how to count, I guess, and realized she was up a stump. So she never said nothing to me, she just packed her stuff in cardboard boxes and black plastic garbage bags and went off to stay with her sister. By the time I found out about it Phil was crawling around on someone else's rug and when I went to see them, to see if there was some way I could help out, I got told to take a hike, so . . ." The smile moved to include his eyes and he shrugged. "I took 'er. I can take a hint. Don't need the roof to fall in on me."

"Why didn't she want you to see him?"

"Oh, well, you'd have to ask her what her reasons are. All I know is she seemed real scared I'd go for custody or something. I don't know. I asked once if I could have him for a long weekend, maybe go to the PNE or something and she said no. Said if her kid wanted to go to the fair she could take him herself. I've sent her money from time to time and she always takes that, and his birthday or Christmas presents don't come back, but then she might give 'em to the Sally Ann or dump 'em in the garbage, I don't know."

"Why is she so . . . bitter?"

"Well, that's the thing, you see. She don't even *seem* bitter. Just . . . like it was and now it isn't, it happened and now it's over." He grinned again and shrugged again. "And she got this nice souvenir, I guess."

"Jesus aitch, eh?"

"Takes all kinds, I guess. So, you comin' to the ball game?"

"Of *course* I'm comin' to the ball game! Hey, kids, you ready?"

The beer league team practised every Thursday night and played their games on Sunday afternoons. There were some differences about beer league. The team had to have a woman pitcher. Of the nine players on the field at least four had to be women. Underhand pitches only. And no fast balls, spin balls, curve balls or spit balls. And anyone who hit a home run had to buy a two-four of beer.

DeeJay filled the hole in left field. That meant most of the time all she had to do was stand out there and pray nobody hit the ball in her direction. She was so afraid of the ball she wore a catcher's mask whether she was in the field or at the plate.

"No, I have never been hit in the face by a softball. And if I can help it, I never will be, either."

"How many people you heard of been hit in the face while playing left field?"

"So what am I supposed to do, volunteer to be number one, maybe? Why do *you* care if I wear the damn thing? *I'm* the one looks like a fool, not you."

"Well, if you don't mind lookin' like a chickenshit I guess it's fine by me."

"It better be fine by you because fine by you or not I'm wearin 'er! It's that or sit on the bench."

"But there's no reason to be afraid."

"Listen, what are you, my shrink or something? If I feel better wearing it what do you care?"

The kids watched bits and pieces of the game as they drifted from the swings and slides to the lemonade and potato chips, then back over to the swings again. "No, you aren't taking your drink over there with you. You want a drink you sit right here with it, otherwise the place'll be knee-deep in paper cups and you'll be wandering around with a shirt soaked through with spilled sticky. And if you don't want to sit down and drink it, don't drink it, fine by me, see if I care if you're thirsty."

"Well, this dumb game is *boring*."

"Then bring a book with you. Or don't drink anything."

"Other kids get to take their drinks to the swings."

"Other kids do *not* get to take their drinks to the swings. Other kids are sitting right over there."

"Not all of them. Other kids get to . . ."

"Other kids can jump off a cliff into the ocean. Does that mean you're gonna jump off with them?"

"That's stupid!"

"I know, but it's what my mother always said to me and I lived through it so you will, too. Now sit down if you want a drink."

"Boy, what a grouch."

"Oh for Christ's sake Bobbi, will you shut the fuck up and either drink this shit or don't drink it but stop nagging!"

"I'm not nagging, all I said was . . ."

"Bobbi, shut up," Doug said quietly. Bobbi flicked her eyes sideways, pressed her lips together and glared. "That's better. And shape up, babe, or we'll get a babysitter and you can stay in your room the whole damn time, okay?" DeeJay was shocked to realize she sounded enough like Patsy to be her twin. Almost numb with shock, DeeJay vowed then and there to be more like Jeannie.

Usually the games started somewhere between quarter to and seven o'clock, and ended just before nine-thirty. It made for tired kids Friday morning, but somehow they'd never been able to get the ball field for Friday night. And nobody was going to throw Saturday away, especially with Sunday being sacrificed for the game.

All too often Saturday morning got fed to the kids' soccer games, or lacrosse games, or baseball or T-ball or whatever else someone had thought to organize and the kids had decided to play.

"God, I hope they have fun," Doug muttered, shivering through the winter while Bobbi ran and slid in the mud, her knees blue, her legs red with cold. "Ever feel as if your whole damn life is dominated by kids?"

"I spend more time with kids now than I did when I *was* a kid," DeeJay agreed.

Book II

6

BETTY FIDDICK WAS FOUR YEARS OLD when her mother met Burt. Until Magda and Burt got married, Betty was just Betty, she got the Fiddick as part of the agreement. Magda had got Betty out behind the Speedway Dance Hall on a Saturday night similar to and yet not at all like every other in her life until then. The difference that Saturday night was she'd whirled around the floor dancing one polka too many and felt dizzy so went outside to cool off a bit, intending to be back in time for the schottische. A half dozen soldiers in khaki with Princess Patricia Canadian Light Infantry patches on their sleeves were drinking thirstily from large Mason jars in which the pale piss-yellow rocket fuel one of the locals made from a mix of corn, potatoes and pig chow was sold. By the time the soldiers were through and had lurched off into the night doing up their zillions of buttons, Magda didn't much feel like dancing a slow waltz, let alone the schottische. She just slipped into the bathroom, brushed her hair, got her coat and went out to wait in the big blue bus that drove those without cars back into town.

She didn't tell anybody about it. She didn't want anybody to know. She didn't want to see that look on their faces that said more clearly than words that any woman who went outside by herself might just as well strip naked and parade through town with a sign asking for what she so obviously was looking to get.

She had a cold knot in her stomach for the next week and a half and when her monthlies didn't come she knew right away what she had been expecting was going to happen. So she just waited until she was afraid the others at work would notice her growing pot, then she handed in her resignation, packed up her stuff and moved two towns further on down the highway. She rented an apartment and told everyone she was a Mrs., said her husband was in camp and people seemed to swallow it. Why not, just about every family had one or two guys off in camp.

Of course her own family knew the truth. They weren't about to let any cats out of the bag, it was too much like inviting the world to say things like Well, another case of history repeating itself. If asked how their second-oldest daughter was doing they just smiled widely and said She's doing real well, got a good job, married to a logger, seems to have the world by the tail.

Every couple of months Magda would just lie low for a while. If asked she said her old man had been home from camp. Then, just after Betty was born, Magda let it slip she'd split up with the bum. And people seemed willing to swallow that, too, everyone knew how hard it was to keep things running smoothly when most of the time you weren't even sure what he looked like and like as not on his way out of camp he'd stop for a few drinks and lose a day or two because he thought he was still single.

But Magda was terrified. Not so much that people would find out what a huge lie she'd spread. She was just terrified on general grounds. She knew how safe she was after dark because she tucked her proof into bed at seven o'clock every night. And the newspapers and TV sure let you know how safe you were at home, what with burglars and all. It got that she was afraid to set her nose out the door and afraid to be in the house alone.

So she found an apartment where at least if she had to start screaming there was a half a chance someone might hear. And that's how she met Burt Fiddick. She was doing her laundry in the bleach-smelling room in the basement, just alongside the room with the pool table, and Burt came in with a pillowcase stuffed with clothes.

"Hi," he grinned, and went to the other washer to dump in his stuff.

"Hello," she answered, getting ready to scoop up Betty and run for their lives if she had to do that.

"Cute little girl," Burt smiled. "She looks like you."

"Yeah? Well, she's a good little kid." She didn't really want to talk to him but if she didn't he might get mad and then God knows what he might do. She really wasn't sure how dangerous most men were, but men themselves seemed to think they were all powder kegs just waiting to go off in a big explosion of some kind. All the men writers put out stories about fighting in alleys or bars or just about anywhere else, and all the movies the men made had bullets flying and cars zooming around smashing into other cars and innocent bystanders being killed and male actors yelling at each other, so maybe they knew the truth about themselves and a person ought to take the hint.

"Can I buy a half cup of detergent powder from you? I'm out and I don't want to have to run down to the store in this pouring rain."

"You don't have to buy it. I've got lots," and she handed over the box. She handed over a lot more than just some washing detergent. She picked up every doubt and worry she had and stuffed them in a corner. How could a guy not be totally trustworthy if all he wanted from you was some Arctic Power?

They didn't run out of the laundry room and get married then and there, it took several months for them to progress to the will you and I do part of it. Betty was their flower girl. She went on their honeymoon with them, to the Empress Hotel in Victoria and when they came back from there she helped move Magda's stuff from her small apartment and Burt's stuff from his small apartment and they all fit nicely in one of the big apartments.

Magda kept working at the bank and Burt kept selling cars and everyone thought how nice they were as a family. Why, when Betty had to get her tonsils out, wasn't it Burt himself said she should just snuggle up in bed with him and Magda so that if she needed anything or felt sick, she'd have help right there and not need to try to call out, what with her throat being sore and all.

Her throat was healed and she was feeling fine before she felt the need to call out for help, but by then things were established in some kind of pattern, so she just squeezed her eyes shut and lay stiff as a board and tried to convince herself everything was fine, just fine.

She woke up in her own bed the following morning. Somewhere between the bathroom and the breakfast table, Betty decided there was nothing at all different, nothing had happened, she'd just been snuggled to sleep, like always. It was confusing to go to sleep in one bed and wake up in another but when you're not even six years old, a lot of things are confusing.

Magda just kept on with life as it was being lived at the time. She got up before anyone else, spent a half hour in the bathroom, then went to the kitchen all showered, made up, hair done, everything except the outer layer of clothes. She wore a terrycloth robe over her underwear and nylons, and cooked breakfast for Burt and Betty. Then, while they ate, Magda went into the bedroom and put on the rest of her clothes.

While Burt shaved and Betty got dressed, Magda had a cup of coffee and two cigarettes. While Burt got dressed, Magda had another coffee and another cigarette. When they were all of them ready, they went down and got into Burt's car and he drove Betty to the sitter, then dropped Magda off at the bank before he went to the lot to sell cars, new or used, if you want the best deal in town go see Burt Fiddick.

Betty was at the sitter's until Magda got off work at the bank. She took the bus to the corner, got off, walked to the sitter's, picked up Betty and walked back to the corner in time to catch the next bus which took them to within two blocks of the apartment building.

Magda took off her good clothes and pulled on her polyester slacks, the ones with the seam sewn down the front of the legs as if the pants had just come back from the cleaners and had been pressed carefully instead of chucked into the washer and dryer, then smoothed with the flat of her hand. She turned on the TV for Betty and started in making supper.

Burt came home somewhere after eight and before nine, unless he had a sale happening, and then he might be home more like ten o'clock, unless he'd taken the happy purchaser out for a drink or two, in which case he might be home at midnight or he might come home later. Magda was terrified the time would come Burt wouldn't come home. She was convinced that sooner or later he'd waltz off down the pike with someone younger, or older, or better looking, or shorter, or taller, or something. Maybe that's why she did nothing at all about the whimpering that sometimes came from her daughter at night. Maybe for Magda, Betty was as close to insurance as she could get. On the other hand, maybe she thought the kid had bad dreams, or pinworms. There was no telling.

And no telling what it was about the babysitter that Betty didn't seem to like. "What's wrong?" Magda asked when the car had stopped and still Betty didn't reach for the door handle. But Betty just looked at the tips of her sneakers and got that silent-as-a-stone look, the stubborn one Magda hated so much. "Well, go on, then." She opened the door herself and Betty got out of the car and walked slowly to the side door of the house.

It was all lots easier once Betty started school. Burt dropped her off at the playground at quarter to nine and when school let out at three Betty walked the few blocks home, went up in the elevator and pulled her key from under her shirt, where it hung from a thong around her neck. Once inside the apartment she turned on the TV, got an apple or something to eat, and sat quietly, waiting for Magda to come home.

By grade two she could be trusted to take the casserole out of the fridge, turn the electric oven on to three hundred, and put the casserole on the rack instead of dropping it on the floor. And she could also be trusted to stay in the apartment no matter how nicely the sun was shining or how much she thought she wanted to go play on the swings. More, you could trust her to answer the phone if it rang, and not sit ignoring it, scaring a body half out of her skin.

"How you doing?" Magda asked.

"Fine," Betty answered.

"You think you can get your own supper? I might be late."

"How late?"

"Not very. Can you turn off the oven and get your own supper without burning yourself?"

"Yes. When you comin' home?"

"Soon."

"Where you goin'?"

"Burt has a customer he wants to butter up a bit. So we'll be a bit late but we'll be there. You be good, now, you know what to not do, okay?"

Betty knew what to not do. Anything that had anything to do with electricity was what not to do. Anything that had to do with matches was what not to do. Sometimes there wasn't even a phone call, there would just be a knock on the door and when she asked who was there the voice would say it was the Pizza Platter. "Just leave it on the floor," she'd say.

"You sure?"

"Yes. I'm not s'posed to open the door to strangers."

"Okay, kid, good idea. You can watch through the peephole and once I'm gone you can just open the door and whip 'er inside before she gets cold, okay?"

"Yeah," and that's what she did. If it wasn't pizza it might be the Chinese place bringing some little cardboard buckets, or maybe Burt would come tearing in smelling of whiskey and plop some fried chicken'n'chips down before running back out again, or it might be something else, barbecued ribs and a couple of cans of Sprite, or maybe a couple of hamburgers. Whatever it was, she ate it and watched TV and waited for the phone which usually rang every hour or hour and a half until about ten. Around about ten Magda would say, "Hey, how come you aren't in bed, button?" and whether she was in bed or not Betty would say "I am in bed, I just hadda get up to answer the phone. When you comin' home?"

"Be there soon. We're just gonna hang the last dog and wrap up the deal and we'll be there. You go to bed, tuck yourself in good, turn out the bedside light and the next thing you know I'll be there." And sometimes she was.

No matter what kind of a mood Burt was in, Magda refused to fight or even argue. "Yes, Burt," she agreed. "Okay, if that's how you want it, that's how it's going to be from now on."

"Jesus Suffering Christ, woman, is that all you can say is yes Burt yes Burt yes Burt?"

"I'm not arguing with you, Burt."

"Oh shut up will you!"

"Yes, Burt."

Saturday afternoon Magda would give Betty money to go to the matinee at the Strand Theatre. Betty stood in line with her money in her sweaty fist, got her ticket, went through the door, handed the ticket to the man in the suit, then got in line for her treat.

Same thing every week. A medium popcorn, a can of Sprite and a red flat packet of McIntosh toffee. You put it in your shirt pocket while you munched the popcorn and by the time you were ready for the toffee it was soft and you could stretch it almost as long as your arm could reach.

She loved sitting in the darkness watching the picture on the big screen, she even loved watching the dust dancing in the beam of light from the projection booth up behind the seats in the balcony, the seats where kids weren't allowed to sit. Teen-agers sat up there, and adults, but the kids sat down here, maybe so they wouldn't get to jackassing around and fall or get pushed over the balcony rail where the tough boys put their booted feet. She loved the crunch of the popcorn, the slickery butter on her fingers, the sweet toffee taste on her lips and tongue. It was just about the best place to be in the world.

She shifted her weight, squirmed to a new position in her seat. The guy next to her was sitting with his ankles crossed, his knees jacked sideways, his arms on the arm rests. One knee pressed against her leg. She moved it, but only a few minutes later the knee pressed hers again. Betty shifted her weight again and for a brief time lost herself in the story. But then there was the knee again, and part of the hot thigh, too. She felt as if she were being squeezed into the corner. She had to sit way over on the left side of her seat because of the way he was leaning on the arm rest, and even so, there was that leg.

"'Scuse me," she mumbled, ready to move to the aisle. But he didn't draw back his legs, he didn't scrunch up in his chair. He just sat there, and she couldn't get past him without climbing right over his body.

She looked behind her. Some empty seats. Good. She stood up, climbed on her seat, stepped over the back of it to the row behind, then moved to the aisle and an empty seat in the center section. There was nobody on either side of her, now. She settled down, and before trying to get back into the film, she picked waxed paper from the sticky sucked'n'licked end of her toffee bar.

And then he slid into the seat next to her. She didn't really have to look to know it was the same guy, but she looked anyway, just to be sure. He smiled at her, and the smile made her feel sick to her stomach. He knew what he was doing. The look told her she could move every five minutes if she wanted to, but he'd move right along with her. Nobody would believe her. Nobody ever believed kids.

The beam of the flashlight cut the darkness, the man's face was suddenly illuminated. Other people in the movie turned toward the light, saw the face of the man sitting beside Betty. With the light still full on the face of the man the ticket taker spoke to Betty. "Would you like to sit up in the balcony, Miss? You might be able to see better up there."

She didn't answer, she just moved, and again she went over the back of her seat, afraid to pass in front of the guy sitting next to her.

"Thank you," she muttered.

"No problem," the old man answered calmly. "No problem at all."

The next time she went to the Saturday matinee the ticket taker recognized her, smiled and nodded, and she knew he kept an eye on her, made sure there was no guy sitting next to her trying to push his leg against hers or put his hand on her knee or something. There was a guy did that, the kids warned each other about him. He'd sit next to you and the next thing you knew he'd take off his jacket and put it over his lap, as if he was too hot or something. Then he'd put his hand on your knee. Put his other hand under his jacket. Bit by bit by bit, if you didn't move, his hand would creep from your knee up your leg. The thing to do, see, was just get up and move right away. Only if it was a real good show, and the place was full, you might not find another seat. What some kids did was make a group, fill up a bunch of seats, side by side by side, with big tough boys, ten or eleven years old, on the outside edges. Then if that guy with the jacket sat down, the big tough boys would just look at the guy and say "Back off, Jack." The guy was kind of simple and would sometimes say he hadn't done anything, why were they talking to him like that, all he was doing was watching the show, but that wasn't what he was there for, not really.

"The ticket man at the show said if I went down early on Saturday and helped him clean up the popcorn boxes from the night before, I could get into the show for free," Betty said.

You'd have thought Betty herself had done something wrong. Magda started off by saying no way, and worked herself into a frenzy of weeping and yelling. "They have people they *pay* to do that! Adult people!" and it went on and on and on until Betty felt as if she were being accused of something she didn't know anything about, nor want to, either.

"Why are you yelling at *me?*" she screamed. "I never done nothing! Why am I the one catching heck!"

"I'm not mad at *you*, darling," Magda yowled. But she kept on shooting off at the mouth until Betty just went to her room, climbed into her own bed, clothes and all, and lay curled on her side, her back to the bedroom door. She'd have sobbed herself to sleep if she'd been able to cry, but she couldn't, she was too mixed up to know what it was she'd even be crying about, and anyway, what good does crying do, all you get is a runny nose and a headache.

Burt took it into his head what they needed was a few aspirations, some of what he had begun to call Upward Mobility. "What you get is what you settle for getting," he told them repeatedly. "If you content yourself with setting up camp in the cat's litter box you'll spend your life choking on sand and cat shit. But decide you're going to live in one of the big houses on Beach Avenue and one way or the other you'll get there."

"Yes, Burt," Magda agreed. "Of course, your neighbours might snub you raw, but you'll be there."

"They'll only snub you if once you're there you act like you're still living in the cat's shitbox," he corrected.

So Betty had to take music lessons. They couldn't afford to buy a piano so she wound up with a half-sized violin tucked under her little pointy chin, sawing away determinedly, clumping her foot on the floor as she tried to keep time, stretching the third finger of her left hand as far as it would go so she could get that damn high one, the second note of Oh where tell me where has my Highland laddie gone. She started thinking of it as Oh *ouch* tell me where has my Highland laddie gone. When she had that one aced it was the bonnie banks of Clyde. The music teacher was a touch fixated on Scottish music. Annie Laurie. Flora MacDonald's

Lament. Mary of Argyle. But they were at least slow enough you could think about what you were doing until you got good enough to remember what came next.

By the end of her first year of lessons Betty could not only play her assigned lessons, she could play songs from the radio. The music teacher wasn't the one introduced her to them, she just sort of picked it up herself. She'd hear the melody line of a song a couple of times and the next thing she knew when she heard the music she'd see someone's fingers (whose?) moving on some strings. So there she was, Christmas of grade four, stuffed into a new dress she hated, with white socks to her knees and new patent leather shoes on her feet, trapped up on stage in a bright light playing Hark the Herald Angels Sing and, because she didn't know any other Christmas-y thing, Jesu Joy of Man's Desiring, which wasn't really that at all but something else some guy had written for the piano. But it did for the violin and the Christmas concert and everyone clapped so hard they said Betty had to go back out and play something else. She almost panicked. Everyone was looking at her. She knew they were looking at her even if she couldn't see their faces because of that bright light in her eyes. She hadn't wanted to go out there in the first place and now she had to go back out again just because she'd played well. It didn't seem fair! The kids who hadn't done well ought to be the ones made to go back out there and get stared at. But she went because she could just about hear what Burt would say about it all if she didn't. She hadn't been inside a church in her life, she didn't have any idea what might be right for a Christmas concert, and she was so scared of making a fool of herself she went out and played the thing she knew best, the one she most enjoyed playing when she was all alone and waiting for them to come home from the bar. Sometimes I live in the country, sometimes I live in the town, sometimes I take a great notion to jump into the river and drown. The next thing she knew someone out in that big white glare was singing along with her violin. Goodnight Irene, Goodnight Irene and then everyone was singing and some were clapping and a voice, it wasn't Burt's and it wasn't Magda's, echoed from about the middle of the bright light, *Merry Christmas, kid!* and Betty burst out laughing. So did most of the audience. Stop ramblin', stop your gamblin', stop stayin' out late at night, go home to your wife and family, and stay by the fireside bright.

It was the hit of the show even if Mrs. Delahanty, the music teacher, wasn't the least bit pleased and snapped something about inappropriate. Well, how could it be if everybody enjoyed it?

Mrs. Delahanty was a pain in the face at the best of times. She wore this grey dress most days, with big round red buttons that didn't do up down the middle of the dress like you'd expect, but off to one side a bit, just to the left of where the thing ought to button shut, and the kids all made jokes to each other about how that third button from the top looked like the tip of her tit. "Nice buttons," the boys would grin and nudge each other with their elbows. "Wouldn't mind having a couple of those for my own self," they'd snicker, as if they knew what they were talking about and not just repeating something they'd heard the big boys in grade seven say behind the bushes in the ravine, puffing on their badly rolled cigarettes.

"Think you're pretty much somethin', don't you," Teresa O'Reilly snapped at school on the first day back after Christmas holidays. "Standin' up on stage playin' a *pub* song for the concert! As if baby Jesus would be caught dead in a *pub!*"

"Ah, fall on your face why don't you," Betty answered. "Maybe you'd land on a rock and smash what you've got. And maybe that'd make you look better."

"No wonder you play pub songs, your mom and dad are both drunks."

"How come all you Irish got faces that look like *pigs?*" Betty screeched. It was true. There was no getting away from it. They did. Little blobby noses and round flat faces, just like Porky and Petunia.

"You're going to be sorry for that," Teresa O'Reilly promised.

"Oink oink oink," Betty laughed. "Oink oink oink, have another patata."

So after school Terry O'Reilly tried to beat her up. Betty ran, but nobody ran faster than Terry O'Reilly and she knew she was going to get caught, probably just about the time she got to the bottom of the hill. So before then, before Terry could give her a shove and send her into the gravel to ruin her knees and the palms of her hands, Betty whirled and swung her tin lunch kit. It connected, Terry started yowling and crying, one of the kids who had run along to watch yelled in alarm and Betty whirled, then ran as if the devils of hell were on her heels.

Terry O'Reilly wasn't in school the next day. When she showed up Wednesday morning she looked as if she'd been hit by a logging truck.

"What happened to you?" Mrs. Delahanty asked, her face and voice expressing her shock.

Terry just shook her head but Melvin Dugan spoke up, out of turn as usual. "Betty Fiddick beat her up," he said.

"Betty Fiddick!" Mrs. Delahanty glared, still mad from the concert.

"Not on the playground," Betty said self-righteously. "She was chasing me. She wanted a fight and she got it."

So they had to go down to the principal's office, and so did those kids who had seen the whole thing from the very beginning, when Terry came out from behind the bush near the monkey bars and made a grab at Betty. The principal listened as one faction tried to get Betty in trouble and the other put the blame on Terry. There were more kids glad to see Terry O'Reilly in hot water, finally, than wanted to put Betty on the hotseat because Terry had probably had at least one fight with every other kid her own age or younger and Betty had hardly ever had a fight.

The principal didn't give anybody a detention or the strap or anything, just sent them all back to class. "And *stop* this," he said sternly, "or there is going to be trouble."

"So *that's* what happened to your lunch kit and thermos," Magda glared. "You told me it was an accident." Betty didn't say anything. "You hit Terry O'Reilly with it! That's what dented it. That's what broke the glass liner of your thermos!"

"Yes."

"Well you just stop your damn lying! I can't *stand* your lying!" and it was a half hour or so of that, with a slap on the backside at the end of it all.

More and more often Magda and Burt came home when the bar closed, and Magda would head straight for bed. By the time Burt had showered and brushed his teeth, Magda would be out like a light, cold as a clam, sawing logs, zizzing with her mouth open, and Burt would take a detour on his way to bed. Betty didn't enjoy Burt's detours. But she learned how to squeeze her eyes shut, so tight she could see little coloured dots and yellowy squiggles where her eyelids ought to be. When she did that, when she squeezed so hard she saw dots and squiggles, she just went.

She didn't know where she went or how long she stayed away or anything else. She might have known if she had thought about it, but she made good and sure she didn't think about it. And after a while she got so good at it that as soon as she heard Magda bustling and lurching around in her bedroom, taking off her clothes and flopping into bed, Betty squinched shut her eyes. Eventually she got so good at it she didn't have to wait until the sound of Magda going to sleep started to tighten the knot in her stomach, she would check out as soon as her mother and stepfather came home from the bar. If anyone had asked, she would have said that as soon as she knew they were home, she went sound asleep.

By grade seven Betty had her life efficiently compartmentalized. There was the school part, the by-herself part, the outside world part, and then that other part, the one she wasn't even aware of any more, the one she had so well learned to set aside that she had almost divorced herself from it.

The school part had its ups and downs but was generally manageable, although never really enjoyable or even very interesting. The by-herself part was quiet and private, she could read books for hours at a time and never feel stiff or cramped or bored or anything except lost in the images and adventures. She could watch movies on TV and enjoy them in a very different way than how she had enjoyed the ones on the big screen at the Strand, where it wasn't only the storyline that counted but how they set up the story, how the backgrounds changed the mood, things you couldn't see on the little screen were suddenly there on the big one and it mattered whether they were driving a new car or an old one, and if what they were driving was a heavy Chevy then you just *knew* all this stuff about the people in the car, knew it without having to be told. Seen on TV most of that kind of thing diminished or vanished altogether and that's when you had to get yourself into the storyline and fill in the blanks for yourself, and that was fun, it was like what went on in real life, with people saying almost, but not all, never all, of what was really going on around you. Her outside world part wasn't as comfortable. That was the part where she felt, sometimes, as if she was back up there in that spotlight at Christmastime with some people approving but others disapproving and she had no idea at all what caused them to choose which side. She didn't know why the music teacher had given her the gears about inappropriate and she didn't know why the man in the audience had yelled and laughed. You didn't have any control at all over any of that. Sometimes she'd be going somewhere and she knew she was clean and tidy and her hair was brushed and her shoes shined, and then someone would say something to someone else and they would laugh softly. And Betty just knew they were laughing at her. She didn't know why, but she knew they were. And she knew, too, if she stopped and asked what was so funny, or what it was about her that made them laugh, they would look amazed, shocked, even hurt, and insist it had nothing to do with her. They might even believe what they said. But Betty wouldn't believe it.

She was drifting through grade ten, bringing in passing marks without having to try very hard at all, not interested in working for an A or even a B+, just passing the tests and moving on, only a little while left and then she could leave home and support herself, make her own choices, have her own place, with a great big deadbolt lock on the door, on every door if that was what she chose. Magda and Burt barely spoke to each other any more. They still went everywhere together, but more like a couple of people who had somehow wound up signing on for the same tour, seeing the same sights, but not together, not really. And Al Ridgely got taken to court.

Al Ridgely was the simple-wit the bigger boys had kept from the little kids by placing themselves at the edges of the groups. Al Ridgely was travelling with a half-empty suitcase, the lights were on but nobody was home, he'd gone to the picnic without his potato salad, there was no filling in his sandwiches, two and two didn't make four, there were planks missing in the wall and his roof leaked water. He still lived with his mom and dad, and for his birthday they had bought him a new bike, just the same as if he was still ten or eleven years old instead of what, maybe forty-five or something.

Old Ridgely and his wife were okay people and so were their other two sons and their daughter, who was married on Pete Dickson, who drove chipper truck for the pulp mill. Nothing wrong with them, nor any of their kids, either. Just Al Ridgely and if all you did was look at him you'd think he was the same as anyone else. He didn't look dozey. Didn't even have the kind of eyes they were always describing in books, just ordinary brown ones, not dull or muddy or flat or empty. Just eyes, for crying out loud. His smile wasn't loose, or sloppy, or vacant or even off-kilter, it was just a smile. His face was a face like a world full of other faces. He just didn't have all his marbles was all. Some said he'd always been that way, others said it was a fever when he was a little guy, some others insisted he'd fallen off the roof and bashed his head, and some said he'd been knocked off his bike. He didn't take fits, or limp, or lurch, or walk funny or look any different than anyone else.

But he couldn't even get a job, let alone hold one, and the only people he was the least bit interested in talking to were kids from about age ten down to maybe age five. Babies and little kids didn't even seem to exist for him, and he was afraid of the bigger kids, and probably with good reason. You could see him lots of times at the playground, happily pushing swings, giving the nine-year-olds good high rides, or maybe waiting at the bottom of the slide to catch the seven-year-olds who wanted to go down the big one but were afraid of what might happen when they got to the bottom. And he never bothered a kid at the playground. It was only in the movie he wanted to put his fingers where they didn't belong.

It wasn't as if nobody knew about it. Boys who had been bigger boys on the outside of a group when Betty was just first going to the movie were now grown-up and married, some with kids of their own. And they had mostly been warned by older brothers whose kids were now old enough to go to the movies and who headed off forewarned about Simple-Wit Al Ridgely.

And then some new people moved to town and nobody thought to warn them. The man was small and wiry and, as it turned out, as tough as hell, with a Scots accent you could only understand if you'd grown up with heather-hoppers as neighbours. He worked at the pulp mill and they said he could skip around on the booms like a bloody weasel, light-footed and never off balance. And of course everyone called him Scotty. Probably a third of the dads in town were called Scotty.

Scotty and Scotty's-wife, whatever her name was, had half a dozen kids, and people made quiet little jokes about how they must be Catholic and busy playin' Vatican roulette. One Saturday, one of the kids came home from the matinee complaining that it hurt when she went pee-pee. When her mother checked to see why the kid should hurt, she found her all red and swollen and with little flecks of blood on her underpants. Convinced the kid had some kind of bladder infection, Scotty's-wife hied herself off to the Emergency at the hospital, to maybe get some antibiotic pills from the doctor on duty.

The doctor looked at the kid and suggested Scotty's-wife go get a cup of tea in the cafeteria, or a coffee and doughnut or something.

"She might fret if I'm not here," the woman worried.

"Oh, I don't think she's going to fret," the doctor smiled. "After all, she knows I'm going to do what I can to fix this up so she can go pee-pee without it hurting her. Don't you sweetheart?" And he stroked the kid's dandelion fluff hair. Scotty's-kid smiled and nodded, so Scotty's-wife headed off for a coffee and when she came back the kid was about half asleep from a pill the doctor had given her, and was talking in a dreamy voice to the doctor and to a big cop who had a notebook open and was taking notes.

"What's this, then?" Scotty's-wife demanded, scared spitless to see a cop asking her kid questions. The doctor spoke to the kid before he answered Scotty's-wife. "You just rest here, darling, and the nurse will be right here if you need anything. Tell the man what he needs to know, and then, after I've talked to your mommy and told her how to use the ointment that makes the burning go away, you can go home to your own bed, okay?"

They went in the doctor's little cubicle of an office and the doctor talked quietly for a few minutes, then Scotty's-wife started to cry. The other cop showed up with Scotty, the first cop came from where he'd been talking to the kid, and he and the other cop and Scotty stood in the hallway talking, the one cop checking his notes a lot, the other keeping a close eye on Scotty. When Scotty got mad and started to yell they took him outside and gave him a cigarette and talked to him, real hard and real stern.

Scotty drove his weeping wife and sleeping kid home and the cops went over to Ridgelys' house. The neighbours saw the cop car pull up and park, and they all just looked at each other. At that point nobody knew it was one of Scotty's kids, but they all had a damn good idea what it was the cops wanted to talk to the family about, and they all sort of closed their eyes and thanked God, or their individual version of Her, that it hadn't been their kid.

Scotty lost it when all the kids were in bed. He ate his supper, he sat on his porch smoking one home-rollie after another, and he fumed. When the kids were in bed he went the rounds tucking them in and giving them kisses and then he came out of the bedroom and blew it.

"No fuckin' way!" he yelled. And he grabbed the car keys.

As the car took off in a spew of gravel and small stones Scotty's-wife phoned the cops. Scotty had no sooner got to the Ridgelys' place than the cop car came up and almost skidded to a stop. Scotty was on the porch arguing with Old Man Ridgely when the cop took him by the arm. The other cop drove Scotty's car home and put the keys and the spare set in his pocket. "Come down to the station tomorrow, Scotty, and you can have the keys back," he said gently.

"Ah hell, man," Scotty was shaking and almost crying. "Ah, hell."

"Yeah. Right. But I don't want to have to escort you into court, you know? I understand, believe me. I got kids of my own. If I was in your shoes I'd probably be right off the map about it. But he's shootin' blanks, that guy, and it'd be like beatin' on a little kid."

"Ah, hell." Scotty couldn't stop the tears and nobody ever held it against him. "He fingerfucked my baby, man. She's not even six years old! All she wanted was to see fuckin' Bambi, you know?"

Everybody felt guilty. Nobody had thought to go over and warn the new people about Al, or to tell them that if their kids went to Bambi the littlest ones should sit in the middle, with the older ones on the outside.

So they took Al Ridgely to court. Not the little court where the local judge passed out fines for speeding or impaired or disturbing the peace. They put him in the court where the out-of-town judge came to hear the charges. Nobody was ever sure what it was Al Ridgely got charged with because the court was cleared before the case started.

Al Ridgely went away for three months and then, when he came back, it was only for a visit. He was home one weekend and was never left alone. If it wasn't a brother or sister with him it was a sister-in-law or a brother-in-law. Then his oldest brother and Old Man and Mrs. Ridgely took him in the car, and drove him to the Shelter Farm, with all his clothes in boxes in the trunk and his bike strapped to the roof rack.

"Best place for him," everyone agreed.

"He'll be happier with others like himself," they decided.

"Shoulda been put there years ago."

"Not really his fault, but all the same . . ."

"Feel heart sorry for his poor mother."

"Sure glad it wasn't *my* kid," they kept insisting, as if their own kids hadn't ever gone to the movie, or had to change rows, or had to climb over the back of their chairs. As if their own kids may have been too intimidated to climb over the chair. As if their own kids may have just not dared to mention to anyone how much it burned when you went pee-pee. As if Al Ridgely was the only one in town who did things like that. As if worse things didn't happen just about every day or night of the week.

Betty didn't talk about Al Ridgely being taken to court, and she didn't say anything at all about him being taken to Shelter Farm. Magda talked about it and Burt talked about it, but Betty didn't say anything at all.

"Don't care *how* simple-wit he is," Magda insisted, "they shoulda done something about it years ago!"

"Shouldn't let people like that just walk around as if they were the same as everyone else," Burt agreed.

That's when Betty finally spoke.

"There's worse things get done," she said flatly.

They just looked at her.

"I guess the only thing that surprises me," she continued, "is that the cops did something. I didn't know the cops would do anything about stuff like that. I didn't know it was against the law," and she looked at Magda, eye to eye. "Nobody told me it was against the law."

Saturday morning, after Burt had gone off to sell cars, while Magda was still sleeping off the Friday night pub crawl, Betty cleaned the apartment. She got all the beer cases from where they were stacked in the hall closet and took them down to the parking lot. She loaded them in a shopping cart and pushed them to the bottle depot to collect the deposit. With that money and some other she had just lifted out of Magda's purse, she went to the hardware store. She went back home and got Burt's five-in-one from his toolbox, took the bit from its place inside the handle, and got the bolt screwed in place, one half of the riggins tight to the door, the other half to the frame. Then she twisted the bottom of the screwdriver handle to open it, put the bit back in place, put the screwdriver back in Burt's toolbox, went into her room, closed her door and slid the bolt into the latch part. She felt just exactly the way she had felt the day she had stopped running, whirled, and swung the lunch kit so it connected—*crack*—with Terry O'Reilly's pig-Irish face.

She didn't say a word to anyone about any of it. She made pork chops, mashed potatoes, gravy with onions and a salad for supper, then she did the dishes while Magda had a shower and put on her glad rags. "What you got planned for tonight?" Magda asked, sitting at the table and putting on her face by the light of the overhead.

"Thought I'd go to the show."

"You be careful," Magda warned.

"Oh, don't worry about me." Betty did not smile. "I'll be okay."

She didn't go straight home after the movie, she walked up one side of the main street and down the other, looking in store windows, sometimes stopping to talk to this or that group of kids standing around waiting for something to make Saturday night more interesting than any other night of the week. Hugh McKenzie asked if she wanted to go for a ride in his car and she said sure, so they did that and he dropped her off in front of the apartment at about half past midnight.

"You want to go up to the lake tomorrow?" he asked, as casual as if he didn't give a shit whether she said yes or no.

"What time?"

"When can you be ready?"

"Oh, just about any time you want. I could pack a lunch," she offered. "What's your favourite sandwich?"

"Cheese and onion with mayonnaise."

"*Yuck*, Hughie!" she laughed. "You'll prob'ly get egg salad or spam'n'mustard."

"Hey, whatever's going, darlin'," he laughed, as if they had promised each other something. "I could come around at, oh, ten-thirty in the morning?"

"I'll be waiting."

She didn't answer the phone and she didn't go to sleep. At half past two they came home and Magda tried to open the bedroom door. With the bolt in place it wouldn't open, so Magda hammered on it. Betty opened the door right away.

"Where in hell you been?" Magda yelled.

"I'm here, aren't I?"

"Well, why didn't you answer the goddamn *phone?*"

"I didn't hear it."

"You didn't *hear* it?"

"Maybe I was asleep or something."

Magda didn't know whether to believe Betty or not. Who can say what another person hears or doesn't hear. Hearing is a very private thing.

"Need your bloody ears washed out," she grumbled.

"Sorry," Betty shrugged.

Magda headed for her bedroom, and Burt moved toward the bathroom to take his shower. Betty closed the door, slid the bolt in place, went to bed and crawled under the covers. She heard the door rattle softly and she grinned. Then she fell into a deep, sound sleep.

When Hughie McKenzie drove his car up in front of the apartment building at quarter to eleven, Betty was sitting on the curb with a big bag of picnic packed and ready.

Hughie grinned at her. "That looks like a lot of tunafish," he teased.

"Yeah, well, you know what they say, the way to a man's heart is through his stomach."

"You're goin' after my heart, are you?"

"Sure, why not? You got any objections?"

Magda raised hell. Burt declared war. He never came right out and said he was doing battle because of Hughie, he never admitted anything much at all, he just stopped behaving as if Betty could ever do anything the right way.

"You be in this apartment by ten o'clock *or else,*" Magda warned.

When the phone rang at ten o'clock, Betty answered.

"What are you up to?" Magda asked.

"Watching TV," Betty answered.

"What program?" Magda dared. And Betty had the right answer to that one, too.

When Burt took it into his head that Betty was whoring at home with half the high school track team, and appeared without warning at half past nine, he found her alone, at the kitchen table, with her homework spread out in front of her. He even checked the other rooms. Went so far as to slide open the glass doors and check the little rectangle that tried to pretend it was a balcony. No track team. "You behave yourself," he warned, and left for the bar again.

But if people are on the prod you can't always cover yourself. Sooner or later they find a reason for being on the prod. That's when Magda would yell accusations until Burt took off his belt and started whaling away on Betty. The first couple of times he did it she wore long-sleeved blouses to school so nobody would see the inch-wide purple welts. Then one day she figured it all out for herself and from then on wore short-sleeved blouses so the whole world could see what a head case Burt Fiddick really was.

"What did you do to deserve *that?*" the gym teacher asked, looking at the crisscross of tattletale marks on Betty's upper legs.

"I didn't deserve it," Betty answered tartly. "I just got it. You know how it is, you don't always get what you deserve nor deserve what you get."

"Just say the word," Hughie offered, "and I'll pound sand up the bastard's ass until it scratches his tonsils."

"He'd call the cops," she told him, "and you'd wind up in hot water and then they'd have a reason for me not to be able to see you."

"Break his bloody neck for him."

"And go to jail the same as if you'd pounded on a human being?"

By the middle of grade eleven, Hughie was out of school and working on the green chain at the Eagle sawmill, making grown man's wages and starting to think of finding a place of his own instead of paying room and board at home. He was still the nicest guy you'd hope to find, but things between them had changed. They were good friends, they knew more about each other than they would ever know about anyone else in their lives, and they could as easily have been brother and sister. They didn't even neck any more, let alone spread the blanket under a tree and feast on each other's bodies.

"I feel funny about bringing this up." Hughie pulled a stem of grass and started crumpling the seed head between his fingers. "I don't know how to say what I want to say."

"Pretend you're talking to yourself," Betty suggested, and rolled onto her belly so he wouldn't have to look at her face.

"Well, I really like you. I never liked anyone the way I like you."

She beat him to it. "Why don't we agree that what we maybe ought to be doing is starting to see some other people?" There was a hollow feeling where her belly ought to be and a sense of loss like nothing else she had known, but she didn't feel like crying or like hanging on to something that wasn't what she'd first tried to grab hold of and get. "Maybe not exactly call it quits, maybe just once in a while, see how it feels." She knew how it would feel for her. But she didn't think it would feel like that for him.

"You're not mad?"

"I'm not mad, Hughie. I could probably never be mad at you," and she meant it.

"I don't know what love is, but it's probably a lot like what I feel for you. It's just . . . well, you know."

"Right." She could actually see him relax.

He turned and lay on his side, his head in his hand, his elbow pressed on the flannel blanket. He smiled, and winked at her. "I bet I never have a better friend than you."

"Yeah, but a guy needs a girlfriend, too, right?" and she reached for the sandwiches, brought out the cheese and onion, and handed them to him. "A bit of the old clutch-and-grab, a small touch of lust, maybe a bit of what spells awful close to the number between five and seven?"

"You got it, kiddo," and he winked again. Then they both started in on their sandwiches.

Two months later Burt hauled his belt out of its loops and got all set to lay a thrashing on Betty, and she scooped up one of the heavy chrome kitchen chairs.

"I'll bash your bloody head in if you so much as try!" she screamed. "You hit me and *I'll kill you.*"

"Don't you dare talk to me like that," he shouted, and took a step toward her. If he hadn't jumped to one side, out of the way, she would have hit his head so hard the force of it would have accordioned his spine and put his ears where his asshole was supposed to be. The colour drained from his face. Betty swung again, sideways this time, not up and down. Then sideways back to the left. Then sideways to the right, taking a step toward him. Sideways to the left again, and another step, and Burt backed away from her, his eyes wide. She shouted at him that she hadn't done anything wrong, she hadn't been misbehaving, she hadn't sassed Magda back. "Nothing but a couple of drunken bar flies!" she screeched, "and I've had all of it I'm going to take!"

She went into her room, taking the heavy chair with her. She slid the bolt shut, then grabbed the big two-toned blue backpack she had used for camping in the summertime. Twenty minutes later the pack was stuffed, and anything not in it she didn't want anyway.

She had twenty-three dollars in her wallet, a hundred and thirty in the bank, and in her heart a burning desire to never set eyes on either one of them again as long as she lived.

She headed for the door. Burt made one little move toward her, to stop her. She whirled, her face looking like nobody he or Magda had ever seen. "And from now on," she gritted, "you can fuck your hand."

7

SOMEONE, POSSIBLY EVEN SEVERAL SOMEONES, once wrote or talked about the banality of evil. Most people seem to prefer to ignore this idea. They want their villains to be huger than life-size, more monstrous than even the plastic ones given to children as toys, to play with, to enjoy, to become familiar with, perhaps in preparation for the larger, more monstrous, less playful versions reality will force on them all too soon. We cannot see Hitler as a homely little fart with the mentality of a pig farmer, we have to see him as a huge horror. What did he do? Gave power to some turds no more special than himself. And each little pencil pusher, each little bureaucrat, each little filing clerk added some small part of his own nastiness to the simmering stew until finally, there we were, with true evil at large, the whole being inevitably, sadly and horribly more than the sum of its parts, more than the mind can easily accommodate. But we don't want to look at that. We don't want to admit evil can be at home in someone who looks like Elmer Fudd. If we look at that, we might have to wonder if Elmer Fudd himself is capable of evil. If Elmer Fudd is capable of evil, might not Elmer Fudd *be* evil? And who are we if we lose Elmer Fudd?

The first few jobs Betty Fiddick had after she left home were about what anybody would expect someone who hadn't finished high school to have. Betty waited tables and lived in a rented roach palace in the city until she came to the conclusion the city was exactly the last place in the world anyone with limited education should live. A city is built for the upwardly mobile, only those with what some like to call disposable income can afford the cappuccino bars, the theatres, the dining establishments; Betty didn't even work in, let alone go to dining establishments, she just waited tables at the greasy spoon and what she made, combined with her tips, was enough to keep her in shoe leather so she could go to work to scrape by for a while longer. She couldn't afford to buy concert tickets, she couldn't even manage a ticket to a hockey game once in a while. And finally she figured she was expending a lot of energy getting nowhere at all.

She gave her notice to the bitter-eyed reject who was the landlord, and to the snarling marvel who was her boss. On payday she had her stuff packed and no sooner was her cheque in the bank than she was on a bus. Ten hours later she was looking around at the walls of a different but very similar seeming roach palace.

Of course Canada Employment was as much help as a wet toilet seat. Still, she went down every day and checked the jobs posted on the board. She applied for everything and eventually got a job standing on the side of the road with a sign in her hand, directing traffic past a strip of highway construction. It paid much better than waiting tables, and when that strip of highway was fixed there was another strip needed fixed a few miles farther on and Betty moved with the private contracting crew. She didn't have to get a new roach palace, she just had to be standing at the corner when the rest of the crew drove to work. A bike got her there, and it wasn't even a new one. She left the motel fifteen minutes early, pedaled like fury and got to the corner in plenty of time to sip a half cup of thermos coffee before her ride arrived. The pickup would slow down, and Betty would toss in her bike then vault into the bed and sit hunkered under the fibreglass canopy top, bumping and swaying, smoking a cigarette and sometimes exchanging early morning gossip with whoever else was riding back there with her.

She knew it was a go-nowhere job. She knew she would spend a fair amount of time on pogey, she knew she had better find a way to turn Unemployment Insurance into Unemployment Enjoyment, and she knew it would be only too easy to slide down the slope into the lake of suds where Magda and Burt were paddling their lives away.

Betty started paying attention to the kind of jobs other people did. She wasn't the least little bit interested in education for its own sake, she just wanted a job that wouldn't drive her crazy, and being a flagwoman was a job which might, after a year or two, turn your brains to butter and let it drizzle out your ears onto your shoulders. Unless some self-appointed slick in a Firebird managed to run you over for no reason other than to demonstrate his opinion of highway maintenance crews in general and flaggers in particular.

First Aid seemed like a good place to start. St. John's Ambulance Corps had a class every Thursday night at the high school. Nobody asked where you'd gone to school or how far you'd gone or how well you'd done, you just signed up, paid your money, bought your little black textbook with the silver Cross of St. John of Jerusalem on the front, and started trying to make sense of the bandaging diagrams. When you finally passed your test you had your lowest level ticket. You had to stay at the lowest level for a while, though, you couldn't just charge in and try for the middle level. Well, that made sense. If you could just forge on ahead you might wind up with a paper that said you could do brain surgery on the side of a hill with a can opener for a trepanning drill, when you still had never so much as put a band-aid on a blister.

Betty needed some experience, and she wasn't going to get much of that with a sign in her hand telling drivers Slow or Stop. And she wasn't going to throw away that job just to maybe get a chance at a job where someone might get hurt because she might be nineteenth in line for the chance to wipe dirt out of a cut. So she started showing up for the kids' soccer games on Sunday morning. That was good for a sprained ankle and some skinned knees and palms, and led her to other volunteer events, like the local dog show where she actually got the chance to treat someone who had hyperventilated. She put a brown paper bag over the man's face and told him to breathe as normally as he could. That seemed to fix him up in only fifteen minutes.

Her boss suggested it might be a good idea to get her driver's licence. The Young Drivers of Canada had a course going on

Wednesday nights so Betty signed on and started learning the rules of the road. Then for a while she got to drive around in a dual-control car. Somehow she expected the driving teacher to be a nervous wretch, like Bob Newhart in his skit, but the woman just sat there as calm as a clam, keeping close watch on everything and talking easily about nothing much at all. "You've got a good feel for it," the woman told Betty. "When you're nineteen you can take the air and vacuum brakes course and probably get a job as a driver."

Betty checked it out. They wouldn't take you for the local bus line until you were twenty-five and that seemed like six days past the far end of forever, but she could get a job driving local delivery truck. It paid less than standing on the side of the road with her slow-on-one-side stop-on-the-other-side sign, so she passed on it but didn't throw the idea in the ditch.

The highway repairs were done for a few months and she was on layoff, but before she had been off work long enough for her first unemployment cheque to arrive, she got a job holding a sign for a bunch who took a big chipper up and down the sides of the road cutting down brush and feeding it through the grinder. Two or three guys with brush cutters swarmed along the side of the road right-of-way cutting off elderberry, salal, Oregon grape and small alders and piling them up so the truck could move forward and a couple of other guys could chuck the piles inside what looked a bit like a garbage truck. Then there'd be this godawful grinding, grating, sawing sound and when that stopped they'd move on to the next heap.

The guy driving truck wasn't very much past nineteen. She filed that idea away near the top of what she intended to make a long and interesting list. The guy driving truck had a lot easier time of it than the bozos doing the cutting, especially the one who got sent up in the cherry picker to cut branches away from the overhead lines. One slip and that guy would be crispy critters for sure.

On payday she got one of the guys to pick her up a few bottles of wine and a case or two of beer. She kept it in her fridge and sipped at it while watching television before going to bed. It helped. It relaxed her so she could get to sleep without first spending a large part of the night staring at the blur that was the window.

Once in a while she'd go for supper with the crew, a couple of times a week she went to a movie, but mostly her social life wouldn't have made sparks dance in anyone's eyes. She didn't feel ready to get into any of that. It was such a relief to just go to bed and know that nobody else was going to wind up in there with you.

When the brush was cut there was a layoff, and then the phone rang and it was the repair crew foreman, so she went back to directing traffic around the roadwork. She knew there were probably thousands of people would think her life was too boring to even bother trying to live, but she liked it. She bought a little boat with a small motor and started going out to jig cod and troll for the last few salmon left alive in the Gulf. A few months later she bought a good camera and started taking that with her. There were some great things to take pictures of from a small boat, cliffs clustered thick with bird nests, small waterfalls leaping from between a couple of rocks and tumbling down, down, down to the chuck, seal and baby otter, herons perched on one leg, looking like feather dusters with beaks.

When she was nineteen she registered for trucker training. Two months of classes in the morning and lessons behind the wheel in the afternoons, and the most important thing of all was that walk around your truck before you got behind the wheel. She didn't want to be the one who just got into the truck, turned 'er on, threw her in gear and drove off with the undercarriage still down, because rip that off and there went two weeks pay deducted for the repair bill. And people laughing at you for years afterward!

Her first driving job was with the road crew. Not full time, but part time, and that was okay, all she had to do was wait until the bed of the truck was full of trash, dirt and old pavement, then drive it to the landfill and dump it. She could sit while the others filled the truck, and read a book or watch what was going on, or just turn her mind loose and let it wander in that place it liked to go, the one she wasn't aware of on any conscious level.

"You got your air brakes, don't you?" the foreman said idly.

"Sure do," she answered.

"Well, I was talkin' to my brother last night. He's got a contract to take salt up-country."

"Salt?"

"Road salt. You take 'er up by the dumptruck load, and there's all these little sheds along the Trans-Canada, and they have to be kept full so that if the highways crew needs to salt the roads . . . so he's got the contract but if he misses even one shed, he loses the contract, right? I mean, when they need that shit, they need it, right?"

"Yeah?"

"Yeah. He asked did I know anyone had an air brakes ticket and wanted a job." He grinned at her. "I hate to lose you, but he pays one helluva lot better'n this job does."

"Seasonal, though, I guess."

"Yeah, sure, seasonal, of course, on the other hand . . . it's experience, right?"

It was experience. It was also not the least bit boring. The truck was noisy as hell and the first thing she did was pay nearly a hundred dollars for a good back-support cushion that went under her bum and between her and the slat-hard back of the seat. A person could lose her kidneys, her gall bladder and part of her spleen just bouncing around in that old cab.

And while driving through the city was just about enough to curl your hair, once you were out of it you were all the way out and the highway just rolled under your wheels. After a half dozen trips she knew exactly what White Line Fever was. You just never got enough of it, the scenery changing every mile, and even if you were by yourself in the cab, you weren't alone, the road was full of others gypsying along. She liked the description one guy used, that they were like the blood in the veins of the country, she supposed it was a corny thought and probably not original with the guy who came out with it over coffee at the counter of some truck stop halfway between Hope and Spuzzum, but she liked it all the same.

Betty drove her pickup from her small apartment to and through the city, then a few miles past to pick up her salt truck. She parked, had a cup of coffee, talked briefly with the dispatcher in the office and maybe one or two of the other drivers, then checked out her truck and drove it to the load area. She backed carefully under the hopper and when she was properly situated, she set her truck and watched in the mirrors as the brownish road salt poured from the overhead hopper.

With her truck loaded and balanced, she drove off with a big thermos of coffee in the cab with her. The truck was noisy, but not unpleasantly, and the little yellow foam rubber ear plugs cut down the roar without blocking the sound of the radio or tape player. She wasn't sure how that worked. The engine noise was cut by more than half, but you could sit next to someone and carry on a conversation in a normal tone of voice. What will they think of next?

Most of the time she deadheaded back to the city. There wasn't much you could haul as payload in a gravel truck. She worked four days, and usually managed six loads in that time, then got in her pickup and drove back to her apartment, almost throbbing with the need for sleep by the time she got there. Two days with nothing to do but catch up on her rest, then it was time to get ready to head off again, time to pack her clean clothes, water the few plants, make sure there was nothing in the fridge that was going to turn into a science experiment in the time she would be gone, and check that the windows and doors were all securely locked. And then off, for more of the same.

Sometimes she worried about all that driving, especially since nobody needs to salt the roads when the weather is nice or the highways are in good condition. She wasn't so much afraid her truck would lose it on a curve and go over the guard rail to the canyon far below; her fear was that she'd turn the curve and find a couple of station wagons full of what had been happy suburban families spread all over everything. In one horror story she barrelled right into the mess and finished what summer tires had started, in another she got the truck stopped but then had to put her First Aid ticket to use on the mangled forms of kindergarten kids. Every trip she made she saw one or two nasty messes, it got so the first hint of a flashing light made her stomach tighten and the muscles from her neck to her shoulders go stiff.

You wouldn't think driving a truck back and forth on the Trans-Canada would be like some motorized version of one of those movies where the brave and hardy head off into unmapped territory with wagon trains. You wouldn't think there would be much to it other than get in, point in the direction you need to go and shove the pedal with your work-booted foot. We aren't talking some dirt track here, we're talking the link, the connector, the two million dollars per mile marvel.

She spent hours sitting waiting for highway crews to get snow slides off the pavement, she spent a couple of claustrophobic hours in a slide shed with one end blocked and the sick awareness that above her head, on the roof of the slide shed, was enough snow to entomb her for months. Without the shed she and the four other cars would have been swept off the road and over the side. Probably get left at the bottom of the chasm, maybe they'd put a little marker on the road, like the one at the scar left by the big slide just outside Hope.

But she didn't dwell on it. "It don't pay to get too focused on that shit," someone assured her in a coffee shop where the apple pie was about as good as any she'd ever tasted. "You take 'er as she comes and once it's behind you, well, you just make sure it stays behind you. Start thinkin' about it, or start askin' yourself What If and you'll go strange. Very strange indeed."

She was very aware all any one of them had to do was miss just one delivery and the contract was gone. Poof. No excuses. She promised herself she wasn't going to be the one to miss that delivery. She also promised herself if someone else missed, she wouldn't be one of the ones pointing her finger and laughing. It might sound easy, but if it was easy, everyone would be doing it.

Of course the job melted when the threat of snow vanished, but that was okay, she had plenty of UIC and she could probably go back on the brush cutting crew or something.

She had two weeks without work. She slept a lot the first week, then did housework until her apartment looked as if someone else lived there. She walked to the mall and sat watching people, picking up snatches of conversations which meant nothing to her, and she bought herself four brand-new pair of jeans, several nice pale blue levi shirts, and enough new underwear to almost fill the middle drawer of her dresser.

Then got a job driving a truck taking shake bolts to the city. She unhitched the double trailer, drove away, and went wherever it was she was told to go to pick up her load to take back to town.

Slings of lumber, maybe, or loads of reinforcing rods, it was never the same twice in a row, and she never deadheaded on her way back. Deliver whatever it was to the lumber company or the construction site, unhitch the cab, drive it to the trucking company, get out, stiff-legged and with that dull ache in the small of her back that meant she had been just a bit too long behind the wheel, then get in her pickup and go home for a good hot bath and at least ten hours, preferably twelve, in bye-bye land. And start getting ready to do 'er all again.

If she had wanted a social life, or a love life, or even a sex life, she'd have been ess–oh–ell. She worked, she slept, she did her laundry and once in a while actually got the chance to cook herself a meal, but mostly she worked, ate in truck stops and put her paycheque in the bank. And what's more, Betty Fiddick liked it that way.

Just about the time the job driving shake bolts was gearing down because the snowpack was creeping down the slopes, it was time to pack her clean clothes, get out her big stainless steel thermos, and head off to pick up a truckload of road salt and deliver it to the emergency sheds along the highway.

She stole her dog. When you drive the same road over and over again you get into routines and habits. The first few trips you try different truck stops, different coffee shops, checking out the bathrooms, testing the coffee, seeing if the special on the menu really is special, or just canned gravy on mystery meat with instant mashed potatoes and day-old warmed canned peas. After a few pleasant experiences and some sad surprises you know where it is you feel most comfortable, and after that, you'll drive ten miles with a full bladder rather than pull in at a different place.

Each time Betty began to slow down preparatory to pulling up at the New Moon, the dog was chained to the post beside the rickety-rackety uninsulated mess that was supposed to be a doghouse in the messy front yard of the big house beside the highway. Most of the time there was no sign of life. Day or night the place seemed empty. Either they slept a lot, or they sat in the bar, or something. And the mutt was there, alone. Whatever had been set up in the doghouse for it couldn't have been much, the dog seemed to prefer sitting shivering to lying inside.

It wasn't much of a dog. No purebred this or registered that. Just a dog. More white than black, looked as if Mr. Terrier had played a part in its genealogy, but not a little terrier, because the mutt was lab-sized. Well, a small lab, maybe, but at least twice as big as you'd expect a terrier to be.

She didn't ask who owned it, or who lived there, she didn't say a word about the dog. But sometimes, when there wasn't much to pay attention to and the miles were moving by easily, she'd get a mental image of that goddamn mutt sitting watching for something that didn't seem to come by very often. She didn't know if it was a male or a female. She knew bugger nothing about it except that they must feed it something from time to time because while it was as skinny as a rail and you could have used its ribs for a washboard, it didn't starve to death. Quite.

And then one night as she came back out of the New Moon with a nice big bowl of chili beneath her belt, there was the mutt. It hadn't broken its chain. It had slipped its collar. And was standing staring at her with those damn yellow eyes, not asking for anything, certainly not begging or pleading. Just looking.

She might have just shaken her head, got in her truck and headed back toward the city and her days off, but the damn thing whined. She stopped, looked at it, felt the raw bite of the wind coming off the mountains, and just could not do it. "Come on then." She moved to the passenger door. "Come if you're comin'."

And just like that the bugger was up in the truck. Betty closed the passenger door, walked around the truck, got in the driver's side and without a word stuffed her key in the ignition. Five miles down the road she stopped at a late-nighter and got a package of those little imitation hamburger things that try to pretend to be dog food.

"Don't pig out on them," she lectured, "I don't need to stop and hose barf off everything in the cab, okay?"

The dog ate two of the phoney-burgers, then curled comfortably on the plastic-pretending-to-be-leather of the truck seat, and Betty moved the draught lever so the warm air blew on the still shivering animal. The dog whined again, but not pleadingly, it was more as if she was trying to overcome the stinking trick nature had played on her by giving her vocal cords but the wrong kind of tongue to form words. "Yeah, well, you're welcome," Betty said.

She drove through the night and got back to the yard at four in the morning. By eight she was home, showered, and ready for bed. "You mess on the floor and you're toast," she said. The dog looked at her as if there was no need to get insulting just because you were short of sleep.

She wakened at two in the afternoon. She knew she could head for the jane, drain her bladder, go back to bed and roll on her other ear for another good long sleep, but instead she got up, went to the jane and then stayed up. She walked to the supermarket and bought enough chicken thighs for two meals, and a small sack of good dog mash, then went home and started making a decent meal. "I know you're not supposed to give chicken bones to a dog," she admitted to Mutt, "but you look like the only thing that has kept you alive is garbage and I wouldn't want you to go into withdrawal or something."

The landlord pitched a fit about the dog. "What do you mean ruin the carpet?" Betty laughed. "She won't hurt those old rags half as much as someone's kid will!" "What do you mean scratch up the goddamn paint? Why would she want to do that? At least she's not riding her trike into the wall and punching a hole in the gyproc!" But the landlord bitched. So Betty told him to go fuck his hat badge and walked away, closing the door in his face. After he'd yelled and shouted at the wallpaper in the hallway she grabbed the phone book and looked in the yellow pages. She looked under "trailer" first and didn't find anything so looked under "mobile" and found what she wanted. After that it was easy.

"Jesus, you're an expensive mutt," she scolded. "What other chow hound do you know who winds up costing thousands of dollars just for a bloody roof to keep off the rain?"

The landlord had this kiss-my-ass-bitch look on his face and she knew he had an eviction notice tucked in his pocket. He stood in the grungy hallway with his feet planted, obviously set to enjoy showing this long-legged bitch just who was and who was not going to tell who to do what with the badge on the hat.

"You still got that goddamn dog?" he asked endearingly.

"Got something else, too," she smiled winningly and handed over her thirty days' notice.

"What's that?" He took it suspiciously.

"A new hat badge," she smiled again, and closed the door. Mutt stood beside her, head tilted to one side, ears cocked, silently asking what was the big joke.

The Pleasant Valley mobile home park could have been set down anywhere and called anything. Sometimes Betty thought they should wrap it in yellow and write in black paint Generic Trailer Court or NoNameBrand Mobile or something. Hers was one of the newer, bigger, fancier and more expensive models, a three-bedroom double-wide complete with dishwasher and microwave oven. Personally, she thought she'd gone a bit overboard with it all but what the hell, they'd never be selling new ones any cheaper than right now, and all she needed was a place to sleep and cook her meals. Of course she could have slept in her pickup truck and cooked on a camp stove, but every now and again it does the heart good to splurge. Even if what you've splurged on sometimes seems a wee bit tacky.

It wasn't in a valley, it was on the side of a hill, and it might have been pleasant, but not after the heavy equipment moved in to carve roads and trailer pads. Over and above the payments on the double-wide, she had rent on her pad, and the combination meant she was paying almost double what she'd been paying for rent. "Christ, for the same money I could have had a *real* dog," she groused. Mutt made her strange noises that weren't whines and Betty laughed. "Sure," she said, "I know, you'd be worth it at twice the price, right? You might think so. The jury is out on the rest of the world."

The kids in the park loved Mutt. "If she was mine, I'd call her Princess," one of them scolded. "Mutt is an awful name for a nice dog like her."

"I'd call her Queenie," another vowed.

"Her name is Patch. Or ought to be."

"You call her whatever you want, she'll answer." Betty didn't really care if the whole world lined up to make a fuss over her dog. It was no skin off her nose. And the dog loved it. "Faithless bitch," she pretended to scold. "You'd go off with Ahab the Ayrab if he came around at the right time." And it was true. All you needed was for a kid to yell invitation and Mutt was off, tail wagging. But she always came home for supper, she was more than glad to jump in the truck and go off to work with Betty, and there wasn't a single night she was out running deer or killing chickens.

Sometimes Betty wondered if she'd set herself down in the middle of Peyton Place. This one was messing around with that one's wife, the other one was putting the tap on someone else's teen-aged daughter. The father of the teen-ager beat the snot out of the one trying to get cozy, it just unwound all around her, and most of it, she was sure, was the result of absolute boredom. The teen-ager screeched and yelled and wept and then vanished in the middle of the night at the same time the bruised-faced hubby and his Firebird hit the trail, the abandoned wife changed the locks on the doors and went to see the Family Court for a legal separation. She got full custody of all three kids and vowed on the blood of the lamb the sucker wouldn't set eyes on them again unless he paid child support, she'd had enough of his bullshit, by God, and she was ready to tell the details to the world, if anyone was willing to listen. Many were, but not Betty. She didn't care if the whole lot of them ran around fucking each other with mad abandon as long as nobody expected her to pick up the tab for it all.

"Don't you got a daddy?" one little jinny asked in wonder.

"Me? I'm a big girl, I don't need a daddy."

"My mommy's a big girl and she's got a daddy. He's not *my* daddy, though. *My* daddy lives in Port Hardy with the little bitch."

"Oh, *that* kind of daddy. No I don't have one."

"Don't you want one?"

"I've got Mutt," she laughed and the little jinny seemed satisfied.

Betty bought some cedar boxes and filled them with a rich mix of potting soil and sterilized steer manure, then planted fuchsia and busy lizzy, begonias and cascading lobelia. She hung the smaller ones from hooks she screwed into the overhang of the roof of the porch she'd had added to the double-wide, and set the bigger ones along the edge of the shaded two-by-four flooring. She paid one of the kids two dollars a week to water them when she was off working, did it herself when she was home, and fed them Alaska fish fertilizer. They repaid her by trying to take over the entire place, tumbling their blossoms and sending out new strong branches and shoots. She paid another kid to mow the lawn, it was cheaper than putting out the money for a lawn mower, gas to run it and tune-ups once or twice a year. She even went nuts and put in a small garden for lettuce, tomatoes and green onions, but resisted the urge to go any further than that. She didn't really think she wanted to wind up canning and freezing six tons of stuff, and since nobody she knew had ever made pickles she didn't think she'd be very good at it herself.

And she worked. She and Mutt drove truck, away from home more than they were in their own place. As luck would have it, and anybody's choice if it was good or bad, she heard about a job driving cross-country rig, taking whatever was loaded on for her back east and bringing new cars west to the coast. It paid better than anything she'd ever known, and satisfied her so much she wouldn't have called the queen her cousin. Her cab was roomy, new and clean, she had as fine a sound system as you could want, there was a comfortable bunk built in behind the seat, and all she had to do was move the load for as many hours as the law allowed, then find a safe place to park the thing and climb into her bunk and sleep the required number of hours before she fired 'er up and moved on again, carefully filling out her log book, so many miles so many hours heading from west to east, laying over a day, and heading back from east to west, ten days on the road and five days off, spring, summer, autumn, winter, always glad to get back to the trailer, always glad to leave and climb into the truck again.

If it hadn't been for keeping the log she might never have known the date. Time didn't mean much. Monday or Tuesday meant nothing more than Thursday or Friday, weekends were no different from any other day, and the seasons just fit into her schedule as if that's how life had been intended. There were times in the winter when she wound up sitting in the heated and comfortable cab waiting for a section of road to be ploughed, salted, gravelled and opened again, and more than once she wound up parked outside the truck stop, sleeping until she didn't need or want any more sleep because the road was still closed.

If anyone had told her she was hiding from something she would have laughed until her sides ached and her bladder was on the verge of flooding the world.

It was one of those two-day sit-without-wages road closures she wound up playing several games of pool with Dunc Green. And after the pool table lost any interest for either of them, they shrugged on their warm coats and went outside to take Mutt for a bladder break. Somehow they wound up sitting in his truck talking about nothing much at all, and somehow after that they wound up smooching for a while. Nothing more than smooching, but it was pleasant, and it reminded her of something she hadn't been the least bit interested in or aware of for a long time.

When the highway was finally open they headed through the mountains toward their days off, and even though they didn't work for the same company, it seemed easy and comfortable to meet him after the rigs were parked and the paperwork finished. They had Chinese food together, then she and Mutt went back to his apartment in the city and stayed the night. And she and Dunc made jokes about her stopping at the drug store for a tube of Delfen and a package of safes.

"Spontaneity my ass," he laughed.

"Yeah, and mine, too if I wind up caught!" She pinched his backside and teased him he was the embodiment of the furry-assed bum. "Why is it, you suppose, every other animal I know of might be covered with hair but not on or around its sex organs and here we are, with more fur there than anywhere else?"

"I always figured it was so the friction wouldn't cause blisters," he told her, straight-faced.

"Friction! Jesus. I'll friction you!" and they wound up rolling around on the bed until it looked as if the Russian Army had done field manoeuvres on it.

Their affair was easygoing and comfortable for most of the winter. They worked for different companies, and their shifts only partially meshed so they didn't see enough of each other for the sharp corners to get in the way of a good time. If Dunc was off, and at home when Betty came back, she would spend her first and last night off at his place; if he wasn't there, she went directly to her trailer, to sleep alone and catch up on her chores.

The first time Dunc showed up at the trailer on his days off he found Betty caught in the throes of springtime, dirt to her elbows, getting her flower boxes and hanging baskets ready, her begonia bulbs already showing circlets of green around the nipple where last year's growth had died back and been carefully picked away and discarded. "That all you got to do?" he grinned, coming around the corner of the trailer.

"It'll do for now," she answered, sitting back on her heels. "This is a nice surprise."

"Yeah? Well, they want to change my run and that'll change my shift and I didn't want you to think I'd run off with the circus and left you to cry your heart out every night wondering when I'd be back, or if I would."

"What're you going to be? Sword swallower? Fire eater?"

"Nah, I'm the fat lady." He nuzzled the back of her neck, and nibbled at her ear lobe. "You gonna fart around at this all day?"

"At what?" She brushed the dirt from her hands and stood, turning to him, moving into his hug. "Could I offer you a beer?" she teased. "Or maybe a cup of nice herb tea."

"If that bastard Herb's been around here while I've been off working, I'll tea him for sure."

The rescheduling changed more than Dunc's route and shift, it changed his address, too. With hardly any conversation about it, somehow his clothes wound up hanging in Betty's closet, his hunting rifle stored on the top shelf, his fishing gear in the small room supposed to be for laundry but used, instead, as a hell room.

It was nice to come off shift and either find him waiting, or, if he was already off himself, to find a card and flowers on the kitchen table. She made sure that the times she had to leave before he got back she did the same, a card, usually funny, with either a bouquet or maybe a black forest cake from the bakery in town. Dunc made jokes about his sweet tooth and was the only person Betty had ever met who could, over the course of two hours of B-movie and D-commercials, pack away four or five Oh Henry bars.

"Jesus Christ, and you wash them down with *beer?*"

"Don't knock it until you've tried it."

"Yeah? Well, everybody to his own taste, said the old man as he licked the cow's ass. A person'd think you were pregnant."

"I'm tryin'," he laughed, and so did she.

She didn't laugh when he suggested maybe *she* should get pregnant. "Be nice to have a kid around the place."

"Listen," she made it sound as if she was joking, but they both knew she wasn't joking at all, "if you want to hear the patter of little feet, you just say so and I'll buy you a cage and as many gerbils as it takes to satisfy your need, okay?"

"What you got against kids?"

"Nothing," she smiled easily, her eyes hard and flat. "It's parents I can't stand. Kids and I get along fine. They see my truck coming and they line up alongside the highway, waving like hell, and I always give 'em the air horn. They love that. I'll blow the air horn for any kid who waves. But I'd as soon run over their parents as look at them."

He opened the sack to let the family cats loose. "I'm a parent."

"I figured," she answered quietly.

"How'd you figure?"

"I don't know. Just figured. Were you married?"

"You betcha. Church, monkey suit, carnation in my lapel, the whole nine yards. Even had a guy there with a goddamn home movie camera to record the whole thing for posterity. Even at the time I figured it was a good job they were filming it because it was going to be one of those brief once-in-a-lifetime nine-day wonders."

"So why'd you get married?"

"Hell, why did the chicken cross the road, right?"

"And now you've got a kid."

"Kids." He got up, went to the fridge, took out a beer and twisted off the cap, then stared at it as if he'd never seen one before in his life. "I don't think the second one is mine."

"That's what they all say."

"Yeah. Don't much matter if it is or isn't, I guess. I mean even the first one was a total stranger until I actually *saw* him, right? And she's a nice little girl. Tough. I like 'em tough. Her mom wanted a little lady but I think she's already started to give up on that idea. This one was practically born wearing high-top sneakers with a lacrosse stick in one hand and a softball bat in the other." He grinned and Betty knew he wasn't kidding when he said it didn't matter if she was his or not. She was. In all the ways that counted, she was.

By the start of summer the baskets and flower boxes were bright with blooms, the reds, yellows, and blues softening the undeniably metallic outlines of the trailer.

"You're supposed to call 'em mobile homes," Dunc lectured, "not trailers. A trailer is something you go camping in, okay? I know because the guy who collects the pad rental gave me a half hour dissertation on the subject. Mobile home."

"Yeah? Take the wheels off and set them on a cement pad and they're about as mobile as the Rocky Mountains."

"Even so, you don't want to sound ignorant."

"Oh, of course not. Pre-constructed dwelling, you jerk."

They were sitting in the shade, Betty still tired from a long haul on a highway choked with tourist traffic, and they had just come out the other end of their first serious debate. Each was feeling at least half satisfied, each had come out ahead on at least half of the double-header; Betty had won about the truck, Dunc about the summer holidays.

The question about the truck had been hanging in the air since not long after Dunc moved in with her. He had come up with the idea they should finance their own rig, drive it together, doing long distance hauling. "We could take cedar shakes to California, where they sell like bloody hotcakes, and we could bring back fruit; probably go for organic, or what they're at least calling organic, get better prices for that, people pay double for the little label. I personally figure it's the same damn stuff grown the same damn way, but there you have it, there's always someone willing to get sucked in by some new marketing gimmick."

"I was talking to a guy who's an owner-operator. He isn't getting much more take-home than I am. And out of that little bit more he's got truck payments, insurance, tires, repairs and you-suck-and-name-it. By me, he's paying for the satisfaction of saying itsa-ma truck, and he's paying through the nose."

"Yeah, but he's building up an equity."

"Equity my ass!" she yawned, her voice lazy. "Put that money in the bank at ten percent interest and at the end of five or ten years you'll have something. Put it in a truck and you lose how much right off the bat in depreciation? Drive 'er off the lot and put a kilometre on the mileage and you've lost ten thou."

"Then why did you buy this house-trailer?"

"What has the one got to do with the other?" The laziness vanished from her voice. "I bought this because there are too many landlords just waiting for the chance to pick nits about my dog. Who is, by the way, hardly ever home, and seldom home alone, and never outside rambling out of control."

"But you sign the papers on a trailer and it depreciates. Bad as a truck."

"Sure, and it doesn't cost as much, not to buy, not for upkeep. I don't want to be an owner-operator. That guy I was talking to sounded like someone who didn't have a *job*, he had some kind of dysfunctional marriage or something. All these papers to keep track of, books to do, records to keep! I can look forward to my days off, he only sees 'em as days he's losing money."

"Yeah, but that's just it, Betty. With two of us workin', two of us drivin', two of us doin' it we'd haul twice as much, get paid twice as much and have twice as much to put toward the payments. We'd be able to afford to enjoy our days off."

"Nope." She shook her head firmly. "Life's too short. I watch TV. I've seen 'em lined up one behind the other, deliberately driving into downtown Vancouver and chokin' traffic on purpose in an attempt to get the arseltarts to pay attention. I've heard 'em interviewed and they were all saying the same thing. They can't afford it. They're being sold out on every side, and I feel for them, sure, but I don't want to join them."

He had facts, he even had figures, some of which she suspected he was skylining, which isn't exactly lying but is very close to creative conversation. And, finally, being very careful about the look on her face and the tone of her voice, she just put it to him. "Dunc, if you want to do this, you go ahead. But count me out. I do not want any part of it. It might be the best thing since sliced bread for you. It is *not* what I want."

"You're afraid of the responsibility," he said flatly. She stared at him and then smiled widely, shaking her head gently, as if in wonder. "What?" he snapped.

"Whatever you say," she agreed. "But if that's true why try to make me do something I'm afraid of? What would you prove? What business is it of yours, or anybody else's, whether I'm afraid of responsibility or not? Or afraid of flying, or afraid of crossing the street at busy intersections, or afraid of black cats or anything else? You want me to put my savings, my earnings and the next few years of my life into something I don't want to do but you do want to do. And I don't know you well enough to take that kind of risk. I don't know *anybody* well enough to hand years of my life over on a silver platter. And I really have enjoyed about as much of this conversation as my health can handle, okay? From here on, as far as I am personally concerned, any conversation along this line will be considered as the invitation to a fight. No. No, Dunc."

He stared at her, and for a minute she thought he was going to get up and start hollering. Then he looked away and stared at nothing, or something only he could see. He was angry. Angry on several levels. Bad enough she wasn't overjoyed at his idea, bad enough she was not only resistant but stubborn, but her last contribution to the debate had hit just about every bright red button he had. And he knew he could either like it or lump it. He wasn't used to having to do either. But he couldn't swing the financing by himself. Maybe she would be more willing some other time. Maybe if he just waited a while and broached it when she was in a better mood. Maybe.

He let it drop. Betty thought he had tossed it in the Grand Canyon of dead ideas. She thought they had just had a good discussion, a clearing of the air, an exchange of ideas and had come to a solid mutual understanding. She thought they had agreed to disagree. She even thought that if Dunc was still keen on the idea he would look for a way to make it happen for himself while respecting her own wish not to be included in any of it.

She felt so good about the way they could communicate with each other that she walked right into the one she didn't win.

He came back from his run looking as if he'd been pulled through a hedge backward. When she said as much he shook his head wearily and shrugged. "It's my kid," he admitted. "The whole thing is goin' to hell again. The cast of thousands is on stage, and they're all yappin' at the same time. My ex, my mother, her mother, my sister, her brother, everyone pointin' fingers and screamin' insults and I stop by to see my kid and bang, I get dragged into this go-round. Jesus Christ, anyway! I mean I'm sending money, God I'm sendin' money until . . . I pay through the nose, if it gets worse my beezer'll start to bleed, but I show up and it's natter natter the sneakers are worn out and nitter nitter what about a bathing suit for summer and yammer yammer who's supposed to pay for the summer camp and rah rah fuckin' rah."

"Tough," she agreed.

"And I say hey, hang on, how am I supposed to have the kid for half the summer holidays when I don't get my vacation until . . . and what do I get? What I get is Well, you *knew* the arrangement, you should have told them at work that you wouldn't be available, and I get Why is it *I'm* the one winds up always having to put *my* plans on hold and . . . Jesus."

She didn't understand ninety percent of it, she'd never met the cast of thousands, didn't know the faces let alone the names, and she didn't even have the name or address of a summer camp the kid in question could have attended. And the next thing she knew she had agreed that sure, the kid could come spend a couple of weeks.

"I mean what am I supposed to do with her in the city, right? At least here maybe you could ask around and find if there's like a babysitter or a daycare or something, you know, for when I'm out on a run, or whatever."

But she had forgotten one little detail. She was thinking in terms of kid, but what was excitedly packing clothes was kids-plural.

"Two?" She stared. "I told Mary-Lou Findlay *kid*. She agreed to take *a kid* while you were on the road. One."

"You knew I had two kids, Betty, Jesus, what do you think, we put one in a cold storage locker or something?"

"You go talk to Mary-Lou about it."

"Me? I hardly know the woman."

"Yeah, well you're still ahead of me. I don't know the kids."

"What do I say to her?"

"Duncan . . . I don't care what you say. I don't even care how you say it. For all I care you can set it to music and sing it. I'm tired. I just got in, I haven't even had a bath, I want just about anything else in the world other than the chance to walk four trailers over and talk to Mary-Lou Findlay about your kids. You go talk to her."

"All right! Okay! Fine, I will! I'd just like to know why in hell you made arrangements for one kid when there's two of them."

"Because I'm stupid, okay."

She didn't know why she'd overlooked a kid. You'd think they'd be impossible to overlook. And yet the world seemed to be crawling with kids someone had overlooked. The world seemed, in fact, to be ass deep in kids everybody had overlooked. They were starving on streets, in alleys, on TV, they were waiting for that one cup of milk a day, they were freezing to death, they were dying of thirst, they were scrounging on garbage heaps, and surely they all had parents at some point. Maybe getting mixed up about how many kids not her own were going to wind up crayoning on her walls wasn't such a big deal, all things considered.

Duncan was gone almost an hour. When he came back he seemed to be in a much better mood than when he had left. There was the faint smell of beer on his breath and a grin that said everything was tickety-boo.

"No prob," he announced before the door was even shut. "No prob at all. I drop 'em off when I leave and whichever of us is home first picks them up again."

"You pick them up when you get home," Betty corrected. "I come home and I have a shower and go to bed for probably ten hours."

"Jesus, Betty!"

"Then if you're not home I'll go get them." She moved to meet him, if not halfway at least a quarter of the way. "Believe me, Dunc, you wouldn't want me, short of sleep, wiping your kid's nose. I'd likely miss and wipe out an eyeball or something."

"You'll get used to it," he promised, his grin wider than ever. "You wait. You'll see. You'll love them."

Well, she'd wait, she'd see, and she hoped to Christ she did learn to love them, or at least like them. God knows they were going to be underfoot for long enough. "You want another?" she asked, getting up and turning toward the double sliding door that took up a large part of the wall alongside the kitchen-dining area.

"Ah, you know it." He handed over his empty can. "Might as well take advantage while we can, it'll all come to an end soon enough."

"That's my boy," she pushed her muscles into a tired smile. "Get me in a cheery mood, why don't you?"

8

B RADY ARRIVED WITH A SUITCASE half full of colouring books and crayons. Tanya came with a smaller, matching suitcase stuffed with what looked like most of the thick terrycloth training pants made in one year by the potty-training company.

"Well, *shit!*" Dunc exploded. "Why didn't someone pack things like jeans and socks and bathing suits?" Brady stood, wide-eyed and frightened. "Who packed for you?" Dunc demanded.

"I packed," Brady quavered. He pointed at his suitcase. "See? I got my bathin' suit. And socks. And I brought stuff for her to play with."

"Your mother didn't pack for you?"

"I packed. And I brought all her underwears because she pees 'em. I put in jammies, too," he hastened to add, rummaging in the little suitcase. "See? And her socks and . . ." His eyes flooded, and he looked totally helpless.

"Okay," Dunc sighed. "Okay, you did what you could." He looked over at Betty and for all the size and strength of him he looked about as helpless as five-year-old Brady. "Guess we have to do the shopping trip routine."

"Well, that could be fun, I guess," she managed.

It wasn't. Tanya didn't know Betty and didn't trust anybody she didn't know. She seemed to barely know her father. Brady was so anxious to be good he practically became invisible, except for his pale fingers, nervously picking at a button on his shirt.

"Kid's a nervous wreck!" Duncan hissed angrily. "They'll be putting him on tranks next."

"If they do they'd better wait until next payday because the way we're spending money on clothes we'll be lucky to buy groceries let alone tranks."

She supposed it would have been as fine a time as any to make some comment about Damn glad we don't have to make truck payments, but she figured she didn't need the mushroom cloud that would be sure to happen if she twisted the stiletto.

Betty headed off to pick up her truck almost a full day before Dunc had to hit the road. She left with Mutt sitting beside her in the pickup truck and a touch of headache sitting behind her eyes. Tanya. Tanya who was supposed to be three but seemed too babyish for three. Tanya who wouldn't eat her supper. Or her lunch. Or even her breakfast. Tanya who wanted to live on juice and Flintstone vitamins. Tanya who wouldn't take an afternoon nap so fell asleep at the supper table, was out like a light until eleven at night, then awake and full of piss and vinegar. Tanya whose big social achievement was the ability to scream and hold her breath at the same time. A person could exhaust herself trying to cope with Tanya and in the attempt to cope could well overlook poor Brady altogether. And Brady acted as if he was used to being overlooked.

"If I look like I'm going to fall asleep at the wheel, be sure to bite me," Betty muttered. Mutt sighed, lay down on the seat, put her head on her paws and fell asleep. "Poor Mutt. They've run you ragged, you poor thing."

She got home almost a full day before Dunc arrived, too. She parked her pickup truck, locked the doors because Tanya liked to climb inside vehicles and play with the switches, and headed up the few steps to the sliding glass doors. Once inside the house she headed immediately for the shower, and from there to the bed. Her eyes felt as if the sand of the Sahara were trapped under her lids. Her headache was back, not just a niggling behind the eyes but a full-blown thunder in the middle of her skull. She hit the bed belly down, managed to drag her coverlet over her, and she was asleep.

She wakened to the sound of Tanya wailing. "Oh God, life in

the buzzum of the fambly," she sighed. She got up, pulled on her terrycloth wrapper and headed for the source of the uproar.

Dunc looked about the way Betty felt. Brady was sitting at the table packing away bacon, fried eggs and warmed-up canned pork and beans, and Tanya was sitting on the phone book booster on a kitchen chair, mouth open, sound issuing forth. Dunc looked as if what he wanted to do was bury either his daughter or himself.

"Sorry about you getting woke up," he mumbled.

"Tanya, shut up," Betty suggested, moving to make coffee. "What time is it, anyway?"

"Four-thirty in the afternoon, on what might be the last day of my life."

"You're home early."

"Yeah." He didn't elaborate, just got up from where he'd been trying to get Tanya to eat something, and headed for the sink. He poured half a glass of water, reached up to the third shelf for the Excedrin and shook two into his hand.

"Why don't you go to bed?" she suggested.

"You sure you can handle it?"

"Oh, that's about what I intend to do," she agreed. "*Handl*e it." She went over to Tanya, lifted her off the chair and, with the mess that had once been a paper napkin, got the unchewed food out of the kid's mouth and off her face. Then she removed the Mickey Mouse bib and gave Tanya a little shove away from the table. The noise stopped. Tanya stared. Betty said nothing. Dunc frowned.

"She didn't eat much lunch," he warned.

"I don't care," Betty shrugged. "If she starves herself into a coma it's one way to stop the friggin' uproar."

"She has to eat."

"Is that what she was doing?"

He looked as if he had more to say but couldn't find the words to say it. His eyes were heavy-lidded and bloodshot, and nobody would think for half a minute he was in a very good mood. He just nodded and headed for the bedroom. Tanya watched him go, then opened her mouth to screech again.

"You do," Betty said conversationally, "and you're going to have a bright red ass and be in your bedroom with the no toys and the door locked."

"I finished my supper," Brady said nervously. "Should I eat more?"

"Do you want more?"

"No."

"Then by all means don't eat any more. Is there something you'd like for dessert? For that matter do we have anything for dessert?" She went to the fridge, opened the freezer and looked inside. "Aha! Fruit juice popsicles! What's your pleasure, mister? Red, green, or . . . orange, I guess. Ugly orange, but orange."

"Red, please."

She handed over a red popsicle and Brady removed the wrapper. "You can save these," he announced, "and when you get enough of them you win a prize."

"Yeah? When I was a kid it was peanuts packages you saved. I used to watch out for them on the street. I think people ate more peanuts then than they do now. Or maybe the streets are still littered with empty peanut packages and I just don't notice."

"Gimme!" Tanya reached for Brady's popsicle.

Brady would have handed it over but Betty shook her head, picked him off his chair and walked to the door with him half sitting on her hip. "You take it outside," she suggested gently, "and you find a nice place, all by yourself, and sit down and eat the whole thing."

Brady headed off eagerly. Tanya screeched. She yelled. She pointed at the freezer and wailed. When none of that worked she flung herself to the kitchen floor and kicked her feet. "Go ahead," Betty said agreeably, pouring coffee into her cup, "break all your toes. See if it hurts *me*."

She left the kid and her tantrum in the kitchen, walked down the hallway, closed the bedroom door so the decibels wouldn't bother Dunc, then went outside herself and sat on the porch wondering who it was had poured those rocks into her head, the ones which had displaced her brain long enough for her to agree to this guff.

"No wonder your mother was so eager to off-load you," she muttered. "You might be the bitch child from hell."

The tantrum stopped by five o'clock and at five-fifteen Tanya announced she was hungry and wanted cereal with banana sliced on it. Betty ignored her. By five-thirty Tanya was on the verge of another tantrum.

"You can eat your bacon, egg and beans," Betty told her.

"It *code!*"

"Yeah, so's cereal."

"Gimme!"

"Get stuffed, brat." Betty walked away. Tanya followed. And that was a good thing, too, because the tantrum took off all over again and even a closed door might not have protected Dunc from the noise.

"Well, I'm glad I'm not the only one," Mary-Lou Findlay laughed.

Betty turned and didn't even bother pretending to smile. "How do you *do* it?" she blurted. "And *why?*"

"Look after kids, you mean? Well, most of them aren't like that, for a start, and anyway, what else am I going to do? If I get a job-job I wind up looking for someone bone-headed enough to do kid care for *me*. This way I get to stay home, look after my own kids, save what it would cost me for daycare *plus* have some money coming in."

"Jesus Christ, you couldn't pay me to look after this one!"

"Pretty awful, all right." Mary-Lou sat in a lawn chair, sighing tiredly. "You want a beer?"

"Does a cat have fur? I'd love a beer."

Betty went into the trailer and came out with two, lids removed. "Pretend I brought you a nice glass, too, okay?"

"You mean this tapered crystal goblet here? Nice stuff. Family heirloom?"

"Yeah, my great-great-whatever brought it over from the old country." They drank from the amber bottles. The noise subsided, as Tanya turned her tear-streaked snotty face in their direction and stared.

"What does a person *do* with a hunk of misery like that?"

"Well, there's this woman brings her kids over a few times a week and she tells me that instead of dealing with the behaviour you should look for the cause of the behaviour and deal with that."

"Her kids are shitheads, too, huh?" Betty guessed.

"You got it. Front and centre all the time. Yap yap yap, as if they were the first on earth to have any idea at all, let alone a good one. Yap yap, gimme gimme, snatch, grab, and then fight like ferrets. So what I did was sit one of them on a chair and tell him to stay there. He wouldn't. So I tied him to the friggin' chair. That's when I got the lecture about looking for the source of the behaviour."

"Did you find it?"

"Yeah, I told her I figured the source of the behaviour was that the kids were assholes. Told her I had it worked out that the best way to handle them was to leave them with their mother. She still brings them over, she still gives me this argument about how I should look at it from the kids' point of view, and I still tie the little shit to a chair when he starts beating up on the other kids. Nothing changes. No modification of behavioural patterns or any of that."

"Tie the mother to a chair."

"And the dad, too. He can give the same argument. Easy for him, he handles the whole thing by putting in hours of overtime, might see the kid once or twice a week for five or ten minutes. Easy to be patient then, huh?"

"Patient? I'd like to turn this one into a patient! In a hospital about ninety miles from here."

"Try to pretend it's just someone's got the TV turned up too loud. Try to pretend it's got nothing at all to do with you. Oh shit," she sighed loudly, "it sounds as if some of *mine* have found out where I am. I was hoping I'd been put on the missing persons list."

The troops had found her. They swarmed around chasing each other, kicking balls, climbing up into the bed of Betty's pickup and jumping down again. Tanya watched them for a while then went over to join them. A few minutes later there was a holler of protest from another kid. Betty and Mary-Lou looked up in time to see Tanya catch a good one alongside the face. Tanya howled. Nobody paid any attention to her, especially not Brady who was racing after one of Mary-Lou's daycare kids. After a while Tanya stopped screeching and started chasing after the others.

"What makes them like that?" Betty asked, not too interested.

"I don't know. I've read all these books, eh. This theory, that theory, the next theory. Far as I'm concerned some of them are born that way. Some people say that the very things that make them impossible to live with when they're little are the things you'll like best about them when they're big."

"Some people say the damn-dumbest things."

"You got 'er.

They finished their beer and Betty suggested a second. Mary-Lou smiled agreement and yawned lazily. "This might be what I want to do when I grow up and can play with the big girls," she decided. "Sit in a lawn chair and have someone go get me a beer. Nice life if you can get it full-time."

"It amazes me Tanya is even awake. She usually falls asleep in the middle of supper and is out like a light until we go to bed. Then she's up and it's go go go."

"Yeah," Mary-Lou nodded, "but I didn't let her do that. Your old man warned me about it so when she tried to fall asleep at suppertime I put her in a cold bath and jarred her awake. She didn't eat, mind you, but she howled until half past eight and then went to bed for the entire night."

"You put her in a cold bath?" Betty couldn't believe her ears.

"Sure. Snapped her awake, I'll tell you."

"Jesus God."

"Well, it might sound mean, but the alternative is to put her head in the toilet and flush her away. I mean you can't have round-the-clock kid care, you know what I mean? Anyway, it doesn't matter what you do with them. One way or the other, whether you're Supermom or a total dud, they grow up and either they do okay or they don't. And from what I've seen you could have the best kid in the world until about age fourteen and then forget it, they all turn into horrible monsters and make your life miserable until they're big enough to leave home and give ulcers to the police."

One look at Mary-Lou and you knew she was up to her ears in kids most of the time. She even looked like a kid. A pudgy kid who was so eager for acceptance she spent her time doing the dishes, washing the countertops and scrubbing the ring off the bathtub after other people were finished. She probably grew up picking other people's wet towels off the floor and bringing the washing in off the line. So used to looking after people who didn't even bother to say thank you that she'd forgotten the words existed. She had a round pretty little face and a softly padded short-ass body you knew was never going to be like the ones in the magazines. If she moved into the weight loss clinic and lived there around the clock, obeying every rule, regulation and dietary law, she'd still be pudgy. She had probably given up on trying to look any other way or be anything else. She had probably been taken advantage of all her life, and probably didn't expect anything else. She was, in short, what people call a good-hearted soul.

At eight o'clock Betty filled the tub with warm water, plunked Tanya down in it and soaked off the grime. The kid came out of the tub pink and sleepy. She just stood while Betty towelled her dry and stuffed her into her pyjamas, and ten minutes after her head hit her pillow, she was asleep. Brady bathed himself, dried himself, brushed his teeth, got into his pyjamas and went to bed quietly. Betty stood in the doorway looking at them, wondering why it was a sleeping kid seemed like something so much nicer and more lovable than a wide-awake one. "It might be the only thing has saved your life so far," she said softly to the sleeping Tanya. "People come to the doorway with the axe in their hand, ready to do you in, then see you looking like that and go away, deed undone. Unfortunately, when you wake up in the morning you'll go back to being who you really are. Madame Misery."

She went to bed and fell asleep. She wakened to the sound of Tanya screeching angrily.

"Hey," she nudged Dunc, "it's your turn. It's your kid."

"Shit." He sat up yawning. "What time is it?"

"Time for you to go out there and cope."

The next time she opened her eyes it was because she could smell coffee and pancakes. She got out of bed and headed to the kitchen. Both kids were sitting at the table packing away hotcakes and syrup. Tanya grinned, her mouth smeared.

"Mo'ning," she said agreeably.

"Good morning to you, too," Betty yawned.

"Hey, thanks for letting me sleep," Dunc gushed. "I must have gone out like a light. How'd you manage?"

"I didn't." Betty poured coffee. "I just took a tip from Mary-Lou and tied her to a chair."

Dunc gaped, then started laughing. "Ah, g'wan, you did not!" He kissed her cheek.

"Mary-Lou ties her to a chair," Brady announced clearly. "And puts tape on her mouth, too."

"Jesus!" Dunc stared at Betty. "You don't think she *did*, do you?"

"If she did, it worked. I mean it's eating, isn't it? And it's not screeching. Jesus, Duncan, it even smiled!"

"Yeah, but . . ."

"Gotcha!" Brady said loudly. "Gotcha *good!*" and he laughed wildly.

Betty sat down with her coffee, privately wondering if Brady's joke was the part about tying and gagging the bitch child from hell, or about then pretending it hadn't happened. Part of her was convinced Mary-Lou actually had restrained Tanya physically; part of her didn't believe it for a minute.

Mutt had obviously gone crazy. She ignored Brady and glued herself to the bitch child from hell. See one, the other was within four feet. It wasn't as if Brady was mean to Mutt, and it certainly wasn't as if Tanya was nice to Mutt, although sometimes she might be, if it suited her. "Maybe the dog is trying to figure out how something so small can be so . . . so damn Tanya!" Betty suggested. Whatever it was, find one, find the other. It worked out great for Brady. For the first time in his life since Tanya had arrived to complicate things, he had time to himself. And something in the arrangement worked out for Tanya, too. By the end of the second week she wasn't quite as ready to destroy the entire world in the attempt to rule everyone around her. By the end of the third week she was at least bearable—not nice, not sweet, not loving, and not what you'd want to have inflicted on your life forever, but at least the noise level was down, and the disruptions of much shorter duration.

"Well, of course," Mary-Lou said placidly. "Put yourself in her place; who *is* this guy, anyway? And who *is* this woman who drives off for several days then drives back again? Where, by Christ, is

Mommy? And what is this tin box, and where is it, and why am I here and did anybody *ask* me about any of this?"

"So you *do* consider the reason for the uproar and try to deal with that rather than just dealing with the uproar?"

"No," Mary-Lou laughed easily. "No. But I try to direct my hatred at what's happening and not at who's making it happen. I figure however hard on them all this separation/visitation/custody/divorce crap might be they're still better off than four out of five kids on the face of the earth. I mean, they're eating, aren't they? Nobody's shooting at them or blowing up the house or bombing the playground or dropping toys from the sky that explode in their faces when they pick them up to examine them. We've got this stupid idea that childhood is great, best time of your life, all that stuff. And the only person I ever met who had a childhood that wasn't like something out of a Stephen King novel was so bloody *boring* nobody wanted to be around her!"

"Maybe we just got stuck with the wrong parents."

"Yeah? Maybe we just got stuck with the wrong idea about the glory of being a kid."

Mary-Lou had three of her own and no husband on the horizon. "Him," she wrinkled her nose, and shook her head, as if the breeze were coming to them over a swamp of skunk cabbage in bloom. "He decided none of this was what he'd had in mind, really. Said he had to 'find' himself. I told him be careful, don't look too hard, you ever find out who you really are you're going to get an awful surprise. You won't like you any better than anybody else likes you," and she laughed. "He found someone liked him well enough to run off with him. Off they went together. Lasted about six months, then he started phoning. Said he wanted to know how his kids were doing. I said to him, I said oh, them? They starved, I said. Ate up the last of the groceries Daddy had bothered to buy and then when there weren't any more they just starved in the corners. You better smarten up, he said. Me, I said, me smarten up? Hey, I'm a lot smarter than I used to be. And I was, too. By the time the sucker decided to do something more than whine into the phone he had nothing left to do but whine into the phone. Went to welfare first, and they send me around to Family Court and *they* gave me papers to sign and then when his honour showed up making strange noises *he* had to go see Family Court and sign papers. So he started his bullshit with them, right? Which was fine by me, eh? I mean he's playing games on their heads and they don't care, which, by me, is better than him playing games on my head because maybe it is going to upset me! So he can see them, there's nothing much I can do to stop that. But at least he has to do it on a schedule, has to let me know in advance so that I can at least have a life, eh. Had the idea he could just kind of sashay around whenever the mood struck him but I put a stop to that in a hurry. I know. He was hoping he'd see some other guy sitting here in his sock feet and use that against me in court. But he didn't. Nobody gets to put sock feet under *my* table. Well, someone could now," she laughed again, "but I made sure nobody did before the final decree went through."

"Does anybody stay together any more?" Betty wondered aloud.

"Nobody I know. It's like this game of musical beds or something. You just look around this trailer court. There's more kids on the weekend than hell would hold. And probably a third to a half of them live somewhere else with one parent and come here on weekends to get to know the other parent, and half the guys who live here are supporting other guys' kids while their own are off somewhere else being supported by some other guy and everybody bitching about how nobody is paying child support."

Betty was glad to get into her truck and drive off with Mutt on the seat next to her and the radio playing somebody done somebody wrong songs. All she had to do was avoid tourists, avoid impaired drivers, and make her way through some of the roughest country on the face of the earth. It was a hell of a lot easier than trying to figure out who was what to whom and why in the trailer court.

And then as quickly as they came, Brady and Tanya were gone again. Dunc was on the road so it was Betty packed the suitcases and cardboard boxes, loaded them in the back of the pickup and drove the kids down to the city with her when she went back to work. She left a couple of hours early so had plenty of time to take them right to their front door.

The woman who answered the bell flicked her eyes over Betty in a casual once-over that in other circumstances might have fetched her a poke in the eye, the kind of disdainful check a person might give to a dead cow lying on the side of the road. Okay, sister, Betty thought, two can play your dumb game. She smiled widely and put the cardboard boxes on the porch. "I'll go get the rest of it," she said brightly and hurried back to the pickup. The kids were still hugging and smooching and trying to tell the whole story of their month's holiday when Betty got back with the big black plastic garbage bag in which all the toys were stuffed. "This is kind of a jumble, I'm sorry," she said pleasantly. "I suggested they leave it all for next time but they wanted to bring it all home, so . . ."

"Okay," the woman nodded, and Betty knew she wasn't going to be asked in for coffee or tea.

She turned her attention to the kids. "So you be good for your mom, okay? And be sure to help her with the dishes, like you know how, and with the vacuuming, okay?" They nodded, and then Brady zipped his arms around her neck and gave her a squeeze that cut off her breath.

"See you soon?" he asked hopefully.

"And I'll send you postcards, like I promised, okay?"

She didn't bother trying for even one pleasantry with the ex. She just headed back to the pickup and drove off with Mutt whining and pawing at the door. "Oh, *stop it!*" Betty snapped, giving the dog a cuff on the side of the head.

The kids were back again two days after Turkey Day. The tree was decorated and took up most of the living room, the heap of presents waiting to be opened seemed to Betty to be an almost pagan display, and the kids were dead tired and crabby when they arrived with Dunc. "Why don't we open everything up tomorrow morning," Betty suggested. Tanya glared at her suspiciously. Maybe the Grinch would come in the middle of the night and swipe them. "We're having a big dinner and everything, just the same as if it was still Christmas," Betty coaxed, "so it would be nice to do it all, I think."

"Turkey?" Brady looked unimpressed.

"What am I, stupid?" She shook her head. "I don't care if I don't hear another gobblegobble for six months. No, I thought it would be nice to have something fun for supper."

"I'm not eating pig." Tanya said clearly. "No pig."

"How about wieners? On sticks. And pretend we're camping?"

It worked. Betty roasted a chicken, with mashed potatoes, gravy, cranberries, the whole nine yards, but she also let the kids sit with sticks in front of the propane fireplace in the living room and char their wieners to their hearts' content. Mary-Lou and her kids came for supper, and it was like Old Home Week for a while, the kids ran around inside the trailer yelling and breaking things, wrestling and quarrelling, and the adults sat in the living room ignoring it all and trying to talk.

"Nice to see them again," Mary-Lou said. "Must be nice to have them."

"Wish they could be here all the time," Dunc agreed. "I don't like some of the crap that's coming down for them, you know," and he started talking about his ex's boyfriend and what a bad example it was for the kids, people drinking and arguing and splitting up and getting back together again. Betty sat back in her recliner and wondered when and how Dunc had wound up with all this gossip and why this was the first she'd heard of any of it. "But Betty's not into it full-time and I can't fault her for that, I mean they aren't *her* kids, you know."

"Well, you can't expect someone to change her entire life just because your ex has a boyfriend you don't like," Mary-Lou teased. "Your ex and her boyfriend are probably sitting with someone right now, saying how they don't like the way the kids get treated when they're here or how awful it is that they come to visit you and wind up spending a third of their time with a sitter or something . . ."

"Yeah," he nodded. "The latest is they figure that the child maintenance payments should be increased because, get this, both Bet and I are working and making good money so we can afford it."

"We?" Betty yawned. "Like Tonto told the Lone Ranger when ten million angry Indians rode over the hill, 'what *we*, white man?' I got no kids. Why should I have to pay maintenance?"

"You better watch out," Mary-Lou warned. "The law says if you voluntarily act in a parenting role for two years or more you are as liable as a natural parent."

"Fuck that shit," Betty said flatly.

"Check it out," Mary-Lou suggested. "I know this guy, a friend of mine, he moved in with a woman who had a kid, and then they had one together and then about five years after they got together, they split up. She went to court and he wound up paying support for both kids. Court said he'd assumed the role of father and so was as liable as a father. So she's getting money from him for his kid and for her kid *and* she's getting money from her first old man."

"Nobody better get any ideas about dinging *me!*" Betty laughed, drained her beer and went to the fridge for more. "I figure I'm being the very soul of patient understanding just unlocking the door of the trailer and stepping out of the way to let them in. Anyone else?"

"Sure," Mary-Lou agreed.

Dunc shook his head, his eyes turned to the flickering flames in the propane fireplace.

That night, just as she was falling into a welcome sleep, he asked her what she had meant about unlocking the door of the trailer. "Are we in a partnership or aren't we?" he asked.

"Well, I guess so. You and I. A kind of unequal one, maybe, all things considered, but . . . I didn't sign on to pay child support or even to be a step-mommy."

"Well thank you ever so much," he growled. "I didn't know my kids were making your life miserable."

"They aren't," she yawned, "and believe me, they won't."

She had two more days with them and then it was time for her to head off again. Halfway through her run, somewhere between the middle of Alberta and the foothills, on her way home, she got caught in what anyone driving across Alberta in the wintertime can expect. For three days she sprawled on the plastic-covered bench seat of a booth in a diner which might as well have been totally nameless for all she ever remembered of it, watching out the large plate glass window at the white which blew and blew and blew and fell and fell and fell to be blown some more. When she could stand the sight and sound of the blizzard no longer, she went out to her truck, got in, locked the doors, climbed into her built-in bunk and slept. It was so friggin' cold she had the heater going all the time, her motor running, burning gas.

"Coulda driven to China the amount of gas we're burning," another trucker grumbled. "But what you going to do, eh. Turn 'er off and she's apt to freeze until the 24th of May."

"What makes you think anything'll be thawed by 24 May," the tired waitress quipped. "Last year we had a snowstorm for the first weekend in June."

"Fuckin' awful hole," a second driver decided. "Give it back to the fuckin' Indians if they want it."

"Fuck you, white guy," a Blackfoot trucker laughed. "You stole 'er, you're stuck with 'er. Take a lesson from it, be careful what you go after you might not like it once you've got it."

"Jesus, if you guys'd quit dancin' we might get outta here. But no, you gotta just keep doin' the rain dance and it freezes and falls on us and here we are, and *why*, I ask you."

"Because we're making plots," the Blackfoot replied. "While you're sittin' here burnin' up gas we're puttin' land claims against all the oil fields and *we* get the money you're spendin' on high octane."

"Look at that fuckin' shit come down."

"Talk about it all you want you can't *do* anything about it."

The same conversation, or ones with minor variations, got played over and over for three days. Then four very cold, very tired and obviously hungry highways workers stumbled in out of the still-tumbling mess. Over plateloads of hot food they announced they'd probably have the road clear in another three or four hours. "Get you at least fifty miles down the road to the next truck stop," one of them laughed. "That'll let the people fifty miles back get themselves down here. Just like some kind of kid's game, highway leapfrog or something."

"Hope the bunch comin' in next includes the supply truck," the waitress yawned. "We're gettin' to the point where if you don't like oatmeal porridge you're shit outta luck."

"Time to hit the road," Betty said loudly. "If there's one thing I can't stand it's oatmeal porridge."

The crew finished eating, then went out and got back on their huge machine. The trucks lined up behind the machine and crawled off down the highway. They made it to the next truck stop, made it beyond that one to the next one. Then the highway patrol made them all park and wait. Betty slept for three hours, and wakened to the sound of the patrolman's leather glove rap rap rapping on the side of the truck.

"You might want to put 'er in gear and get in line," he said, his eyes red-rimmed, his face showing his weariness. "They've got the pass open but God in heaven alone knows for how long."

"Thanks. You look like you need some sleep."

"Sleep?" He shook his head. "I don't know what you're talkin' about, lady."

She made it home only eight days late to find Duncan in a mood almost guaranteed to make a person dream of axe murder. "Sure screwed *me* up," he grumbled.

"Jesus, Duncan, beat me with a cat o' nine tails, will you? I mean how silly of me to make it snow like that. You'd think I'd know better than to schedule a blizzard when it wasn't convenient for you."

"Well how was I supposed to go to work without any idea of when you were comin' back? I mean what was I supposed to tell Mary-Lou?"

"I don't give a rat's ass what you told her. You coulda recited the Koran for all I care. Get real, will you?"

"Why don't *you* get real, Betty? What in hell kind of relationship is this, anyway? You come dancing in here a week late! I had to run around like a cat with its tail on fire just so's I could go to work my own self! Had to drop the kids off with Mary-Lou with no idea when I'd be back or if you were even *comin'* back! Then I had to tell 'em I could only do short run so's I could come back here, load the kids in the car and drive 'em back to the ex, and you seem to think it's got nothin' at all to do with you!"

"It's got nothing at all to do with me," she agreed. "Except it looks as if I'm going to have to pay for new wallpaper in the spare room because someone has scribbled crayon all over it. *That* has to do with me. That and the big mark on the carpet where someone's juice spilled; someone who knew damn well they aren't supposed to have juice in the living room."

"Who are you? Missus Clean all of a sudden? Jesus Christ! I mean, really! What's got up your nose anyway? We could be workin' for ourselves but no, Madam LaZonga here don't want that kind of commitment, so we wind up workin' to put money in other people's pockets. Madam LaZonga is more worried about the friggin' wallpaper than the kids, and the friggin' carpet ranks pretty high, too. A week outta my life doesn't count for frig all, I suppose."

"Yeah, well you know how it is," she said, reaching for her jacket, "it's the screwin' you get now for the screwin' you did back then," and she snapped her fingers. Mutt leaped to her feet, and they left the trailer. The door didn't come off its hinges, and that was only a testament to the workmanship of the people who had put it together in Winlaw.

Some things you can patch and the seams don't show. Some things you can patch and the seams show, but they don't interfere with anything. Some things you can patch and patch again, until the patches overlap and still the air leaks out and the balloon steadily deflates. They made it to Easter and made it through the kids' Easter holidays visit, but they didn't make it much further than that.

"Jesus *Christ*, Betty! All you gotta do is sign the dotted line for frig's sake. That is *all* you got to do. I ain't askin' you to drive, I ain't askin' you to make the payments, I ain't askin' you to do fuck all but sign on the fuckin' dotted line."

"And put everything I own on that dotted line! I am not going to co-jo this thing. I told you if you could put 'er together to go right ahead. *You*. Not me. Not us. Not me and my trailer."

"You and your goddamn tin box! You and your goddamn sardine can! You and your goddamn son of a bitchin' cedar boxes full of jerry-rain-ee-ums! You and what *you* want. What I want doesn't count, is that it?"

"If *you* want something *you* get it. When *you* can sign your own dotted line you're off to the races."

"And how'n hell'm I ever going to do that with my ex with her hand in my pocket up to her wrist? I don't even have a trailer as collateral for God's sake because I live here in *your* friggin' trailer."

"Well, tough shit, guy. I mean really, tough shit. How cruel things are for you, eh, you live here and you don't pay rent, isn't that a dreadful thing to have happen to you? No payments to worry about, no taxes to pay, no pad rental to have to come up with once a month, no insurance, no repairs . . . oh woe is you. Alas alack-a-day, Duncan."

"You're lucky you're a woman," he gritted, "because if you were a man . . ."

"*Fuck you,*" she shouted. "*You're* the one lucky I'm not a man because if I was I'd be just about as stupid as you are and that would mean I'd dump you on your ass on the other side of the friggin' door and send you down the road with a lump on your jaw."

"You want me on the other side of the door? Well Jesus, lady, you get what you want. You just bloody bet you get what you want. Keep your eye on the tick-tock, lady. Because when the big hand is here and the little hand is over here your wish will have come true."

"Don't forget your thermos," she snapped. And again she reached for her jacket. Mutt was on her feet immediately.

Betty got in her pickup and drove into town. She left Mutt curled on the seat, guarding the truck from all threats, and went into the mall. She bought new underpants, she bought new socks, she bought a soft yellow V-neck long-sleeved sweater. Then she went to the deli and got two smoked meat sandwiches and a half pint of milk. She drove to the lookout, parked and ate her lunch, watching the grey ocean heaving below, sliding crusts and scraps to the ever-hopeful Mutt, wondering what in the name of everything you ever got told was important had gone wrong. She didn't know whether to believe Dunc or not. She figured it was fifty-fifty whether he'd actually pack his crap and leave. He might be gone when she got home. He might be sitting in the big chair in the living room angrily waiting for her to come home so he could start in again about signing on the dotted line.

"Jesus, Mutt, even you understand what the word No means! What's with him that he thinks No means Later?"

When she got home he was gone. And so was his stuff. She checked the trailer; then, convinced he had actually gone, she got into her truck, drove back to the mall and got new locks for all the doors. He hadn't left his key on the table and she would be go-to-hell if he was coming back in when she wasn't home. If he

188

ever got back on this side of the damn door he'd come in wearing a different attitude, the world could make book on that.

She not only changed the locks on the doors, she got little sticks that fit along the frame of the windows so they couldn't be slid open. Of course he could always kick in the glass doors or break a window or use a can opener on the side of the trailer, but she figured the hint alone would do it.

9

PRACTICALLY THE ONLY FURNITURE Betty owned had come with the trailer when she bought it so there wasn't much to worry about or move into storage or pay someone to keep after she sold the trailer. Anyway, she found another place even before the final papers were signed on what she had begun to think of as the old tin box.

She quit her job, too. Just about the only part of her old life she didn't cast aside was Mutt. Privately, Betty figured there might be something to those psychological whatevers you read about from time to time; just about every move of any proportion she had ever made had been like a cancellation of an old life. She supposed she was somehow imprinted on getting rid of reminders and starting out fresh. She even left her cedar boxes and planters because, after all, you can always buy new begonia tubers, every nursery has a huge supply and selection and why wax sentimental over any one particular picotee?

The new job was such a stroke of absolute luck she could hardly believe it had come to her. All she had to do was drive the truck that took Her Majesty's Post from Powell River to Vancouver, drop it off to be lost in the labyrinth, pick up the sacks of sorted mail and take them back to Powell River.

Only a hundred miles from the city, the town was considered to be semi-isolated. Betty figured you could scratch the semi and just get down to brass tacks. She had to wait on the parking lot of the BC Ferries Corporation at Horseshoe Bay, then drive onto the Sunshine Coast ferry when it was finally time for it to leave. Three-quarters of an hour later she drove off that ferry and started the drive to the next. A sign alongside the highway claimed it was an hour and a half easy driving. But why rush? After all, when you got to the next ferry parking lot you had to sit and wait.

In Betty's opinion whoever had figured out the ferry timetable had, at best, dried bat shit in place of brains. "You'd think," she grumbled to Mutt, "if it's an hour and a half easy driving time from one terminal to the other they'd have the friggin' boats leaving every two hours. Two and a half at most, to give the sabbath creepers time to catch up to the rest. But no, we wait four fuckin' hours. If not bat shit, rat shit, and if not that cat shit, but shit for brains for sure." Mutt didn't bother to lift so much as one ear, she'd heard the grumbling too many times before to pay any attention to it.

The road was a horror. "They ought to erect signs on either end of this damn cow path," the grumbling continued. "That one they had in the Roman arena, abandon hope all ye who enter here. It's got to be some guys' answer to the overpopulation problem. Too many people? Hell, drive 'em off the cliffs."

But for all her nattering, nagging, mumbling, grumbling and bitching, she enjoyed the job, mostly because the scenery was nothing short of spectacular. Even at night, with the world swathed in darkness, her headlights picked up glimpses and mini-vistas of such beauty she sometimes had to catch her breath.

Mile after mile of highway, the settlements spaced along it like beads on a string. In what looked like just about the middle of nowhere there would be a sign, and four hundred metres or so farther down the road another, smaller road leading off to the left or the right. Somewhere down those little roads were hamlets or towns with names like Garden Bay, Irvines Landing, Madeira Park. Betty didn't drive down the side roads but took it on faith there really were places there, with piers and docks, with a corner store and maybe even a gas pump.

So much country, so few people. But the few who lived and worked there had left their mark. Miles and miles and even more miles of slash left behind after clearcut logging. Entire cliff faces blown away, for whatever whim or reason, the smooth channels cut by the drill bits showing where the dynamite had been stuffed. Once in a while a hitchhiker in faded jeans, denim jacket, sneakers and a baseball cap with someone's advertising on the front, Molson's Beer, Cat Diesel, D & D Logging, Peterbilt would start to lift a hopeful thumb, realize it was a federal truck and let the thumb fall, no hope of a ride here.

The ferry parking lots were where you found people. Other truckers like herself, tourists asking endless "why" questions about the ferry schedule, residents hashing and rehashing the ongoing years-long bitch that their Resident Permits had been cancelled and even though this was, for them, the last stretch of the federally financed Trans-Canada highway, they had to pay as much to take the ferry as outsiders did. After all, they pointed out time and time again, the ferries in the interior are free. Free, damn it, because they say they're a part of the highway system. Well, they said, what about us? Ours is part of the highway system, too. But *we* pay, by Christ, through the nose.

"Ah, well," some wit would sigh, "just wait until we get that bridge," and then everyone would laugh bitterly. They'd been promised a bridge half a century ago and even though everyone knew it was absolutely impossible to design and build a bridge covering that distance in those rough waters with so much marine traffic, every now and again some retard politician would dust off the old bullshit promise and give everyone a good chortle.

Her house was in what they called the Townsite, between the entrance road to the pulp mill and the turnoff to the municipal dump and incinerator. The house was old, and far too big, you could move Mom, Dad and four or five kids into it and still have more than enough room. In the city, or even near it, she wouldn't be able to afford to look at it as she drove by, let alone actually buy it. But here, six hours, two ferries and a dog's breakfast of a highway north of the city, set down between a couple of very offensive polluting stench-makers, she paid less for it than she got for her double-wide and cedar boxes in the valley.

The view was what actually sold her. The pulp mill with its belching stacks was to her right when she looked out her front window. All she had to do was angle her head just a little bit and she didn't have to see the filthy mess. Of course, if the wind was the wrong way or if the inversion layer was in place, she got the smell, but if you didn't exactly get used to it, you did learn to live with it. Or maybe enough exposure killed off some of the membranes that registered stink. Or maybe the dioxins, furans, and who knew what the hell else in the fallout killed off brain cells, the ones you needed to know that the scunge from the mill wasn't really the smell of bread, butter and new shoes for the baby.

Wretched as that all was, the house was worth it. Built in the time when if a board had a knot in it someone classified it as reject and threw it on the bonfire, it had hardwood floors and enormous windows. The living room was just about big enough to be used as a bowling alley and the stairs leading up to the second floor made you think of floor-length ballgowns and crystal wine glasses.

"Almost feel guilty living here in jeans and slippers," she told Mutt. The dog didn't feel guilty. She had her blanket in the hallway coming from the back door to the kitchen, near where the washer and dryer had been installed. In this house it was a hallway, in any other it would have been thought of as a long, thinnish room. At the end of it, beyond the doorway into the kitchen, was a room with a toilet and wash basin. Just in case you couldn't find your way to the bathroom on the first floor. Or the one on the second floor. There was even a shower, toilet and basin in the basement. "People who renovated this place musta been fulla shit," she decided. "And all those tubs and basins kinda suggest they were either awfully clean or awfully dirty."

Betty saw an ad in the local paper and phoned about it. The man who answered gave her an address, and she drove around to have a look, then drove home with an old Troy-built rototiller. There was a big patch in the back yard that had been used as a garden for years. The weeds had started to move in, but it didn't take long, or much, to get rid of them. There was so much garden space she didn't need cedar boxes or hanging baskets but she'd grown used to having them, and liked them, so bought nice ones at the nursery beside the lake and filled them with begonia tubers and fuchsia.

Of course then she needed hoses and sprinklers and a water-wand to get up to the baskets she'd hung from the underside of the roof over the huge front porch. She also needed fertilizer and a powder they said would set the blossoms on the tomato plants.

It all kept her busy in her off hours, and somehow one thing led to another. She had to fix her fence to make sure the neighbour's damn dog didn't come in and dig up the garden or pee on her new rose bushes and kill them. Then, with the missing pickets replaced, she had to paint, and the new pickets looked so much better with their fresh paint than the old ones did with their flaking and peeling stuff she wound up doing the entire fence. She stopped herself, though, before she started on the trim of the house or the back steps, which really did need Something, but not necessarily paint; maybe some outdoor carpeting.

The inside of the place was past empty, it was all the way to barren. She had a piece of foam on the floor of her bedroom with sheets and a blanket, but her clothes were still in boxes and the kitchen furniture consisted of an old table that had been in the basement when she moved in and a couple of metal folding chairs she'd found forgotten in the garage.

Just thinking about getting furniture made her feel weary. What in hell did she know about furniture other than that the stuff you get out of the catalogue isn't worth what it costs to ship it from the warehouse. She might not know what she did want, but she felt pretty clear on what she didn't. Imitation colonial or pretend scandihoovian, for instance.

Part of her would have been happy to just continue making do. The other part of her knew that a foamie on the floor and a couple of rickety-rackety folding chairs is a pretty clear sign of either ground-down poverty or emotional depression. Since she only had to look at her bankbook to know it wasn't ground-down poverty, she had to think about depression, which the articles in the magazines she read on the ferry told her was only anger turned inward. Only. *Only?* What else does it have to be besides only anger turned inward?

She wasn't interested in finding out what she was angry at; you don't need to know exactly what your temperature is as long as you know you're running a fever.

The articles said there were things you could do to combat depression. Keep yourself busy. Develop a positive attitude. Try to identify your feelings as you have them and not just stuff them down into the already over-full cauldron. Have routines and schedules.

Well, having routines and schedules was easy enough; there were those friggin' ferries to help with that one. The rest of it seemed like just about so much pony puckies. Who has time to identify each feeling as it comes along? Who has time to pull the truck over to the side of the road, light a smoke and say Well, what I'm feeling right now is more than a slight touch of annoyance because that dinkhead in the blue Ford creeps along on the bad parts of the road, then, when the snake-trail straightens enough for me to have a chance to pass him he shoves his pedal to the floor and takes off like a terrified titmouse. Who has the friggin' *time?*

Positive attitude. Develop one. One what? What was there to feel positive about lately? Well, you could be pretty positive that things were going to hell in a hurry; what had been done to the prawn fishery was about enough to make a person positive there weren't enough prawns left after the pollution to even sustain a healthy breeding program. And you could be pretty positive the number of fish was down, down, down thanks to that same poison and the effects of clearcut logging. The fleet had been cut, then cut again, the number of licences had been reduced, then the price of existing licences skyrocketed so only those who already had a pocketful of money could afford to buy them up, then the amount of time a person could spend out there trying to catch those few last fish had been cut back, then cut back again, and now they'd closed off enormous sections of what had been the prime fishing grounds. But nobody was doing much about the companies which blithely ignored the lenient regulations and if you were trying to be positive you could be damn good and positive nobody was going to do much about enforcing what was supposed to be the law. And she was pretty positive much of the crap around the damn ferry schedules was because the local representative owned every trucking company in the area and had the schedules fixed so as to give his own drivers an edge. Of course you couldn't exactly come out and say that or someone would put you in court for slander, you could be fuckin' well positive of that!

So she did little about the anger turned inward. She just got up

195

and made coffee, drank it, took herself off to work with Mutt tagging along contentedly. She did her work, she did it well, she bought most of her meals and bag-lunched it the rest of the time, and when her work was done she went home and slept on her foamie, telling herself each time she crawled into what she called her bed that this weekend for sure she was going furniture shopping.

And then the summer had pretty well slid past, and the soft colours of coastal autumn were showing on those hillsides not already logged bare. The road crews were checking the ditches and run-off channels to make sure there was nothing blocking them that would keep the rains from pouring off the shaved slopes and cascading down to stain the sea with the soil eroded off the sides of the hills and mountains. Most of the friggin' tourists had headed back to put their kids in school and the retirees in their motorized homes had caught and canned as many salmon as they could and were now on the road, headed for Mexico where they would do the same with shrimp; on their way to the shrimp grounds they'd sell their home-canned fish for more than enough to pay for their trip and on their way back up again in a few months they'd get rid of the shrimp, probably to the same customers, and turn up again with their pension cheques mercifully intact. Which was great for them but hell on the people who thought they could make a living commercial fishing.

And then Mary-Lou called. Betty was barely out of bed, the coffee in her cup still too hot to drink, and the sound of the bell was jarring. She jumped half out of her skin when she heard the phone, grabbed it with one of those fast reflex actions that ought to be saved for emergencies.

"Yes!" she blurted.

"Betty?"

"Yes." She could almost, but not quite, place the voice.

"It's Mary-Lou Findlay. Boy, are you ever a hard person to find!"

"This is a surprise."

"I finally had to call your old boss and ask if you'd left a forwarding address. You hadn't, but they said they thought they at least had an idea what town you'd moved to, so once I had that it was easier. How come you haven't phoned? Or written, or something?"

"Been real busy," Betty lied.

"Yeah?"

"You know how it is, moving, all that go-round. Bought a house, so you know what that's like. How are you?"

"Okay. You're sure that's all it is, eh? Busy with the new house and job?"

"Sure, what else would it be? Or did you think maybe my life had taken some new and exciting turn and I was off on a world cruise?"

"And that's all?"

"Yeah. Why?"

"Well, I was afraid maybe it was, like, well I was afraid maybe it was because, you know."

"No, I don't know. What are you going around the mulberry bush about?"

"You haven't heard?"

"Jesus, Mary-Lou, I've heard a lot of stuff. Music on the radio, voices outside my window, bats in the attic. Which of them is it?"

"Well, after you left, you know, and by the way the people who bought your trailer are real dick-heads and every time they have a party that goes on until three or four in the morning I miss you like crazy. Anyway, after you left and just before school let out, Duncan called and said he was in a bind. He said he needed someone to do kid care because his ex wanted him to take the kids for a full month and he didn't have any idea who he'd get to look after them when he was working, or how he'd arrange it. So could they stay with me while he worked. So I said yes, and we set a price on it and he rented one of those little rickety-tickety units by the lake for on his days off. So that worked fine for a while and then, well, it was time almost for them to go back to their mom and I guess we'd kind of got into a routine or something and so the long and short of it all is that we started seeing a lot of each other and I thought maybe you knew about that and were teed off or something."

"Why would I be teed off? Jesus, it's been over for months!"

"Yeah, but maybe, you know. I just wondered because of not hearing from you. And I didn't like to think it was because of that, is all."

"Listen, and I mean this. I don't care if you're hangin' out with him or if you're hangin' out with Prince Charles; neither of them is my type. And I'm gonna tell you right out, Dunc's a nice guy but he's a bit of a user."

"Oh, I know that!" Mary-Lou sounded happy, maybe she didn't believe anybody would pay any attention at all to her if she wasn't of some use to them. "And I know if he hadn't needed a place to get kid care he wouldn't have thought twice about me but so what, I say. I mean, we all got our reasons, right?"

"Yeah, I guess. So how are you?"

"Good. I'm fine. Kids are fine. Nothing much changes. Same old thing, you know. You're sure you aren't mad about it?"

"No, I'm not mad about it. Bon appétit, as the Quebeckers say."

"Oh, *you!*" Mary-Lou giggled. "We're gonna drop my kids off at my mom's place for a few days and see the bright lights of the city, have a break from everything. And come Xmas vacation we're takin' all the kids down to Disneyland while we can still afford it because once the new truck arrives we're going to be living pretty close to the bone for a while. But that's okay, nothing ventured nothing gained, you know."

"Right." Betty caught herself nodding, as if Mary-Lou could see her through the phone. "But do it while you're young or it might not get done at all, right?"

"Right. You got anyone new in your life?"

"Not me," she laughed softly. "No, not me. Not a chance. I've been too busy trying to decide what kind of furniture I want." She reached for her coffee, sipped it and sat on the floor, her back resting against the wall. "You ever feel like you can't make up your friggin' mind? I look at that shit and I think yeah, well, maybe. Then I head off without buyin' it. Tell myself I'm thinkin' it over. Next thing I know it's like a month later and I still haven't even picked out a lamp or a chair. I mean this place is so bare the mice left home because they got scared of the sound their feet made on the floor."

"It's probably the house," Mary-Lou laughed. "Probably you

don't even like the house very much. Probably that's why. You can't see your*self* in the house so how can you see furniture?"

"Anyone ever tell you that you might be a bloody genius?"

"Not lately. You're sure you're not mad at me? About Dunc, I mean."

She wasn't mad and she knew it. She wasn't even mad at Dunc for taking advantage of Mary-Lou. At least he was taking her to the city for a break, at least she'd get to Disneyland, even if she did have to pay for it by taking a troop of kids along and keeping their noses wiped.

"Get me one of those Mickey Mouse tee shirts, will you?"

"Sure! Glad to! What size?"

"Large."

"You aren't a large!"

"I didn't say I wanted to *be* large, I just said I wanted a large tee shirt! I might use it as a curtain over the window in the bedroom, or maybe pull it over a chair, for a slipcover. Hide this ugly friggin' furniture I'm prob'ly going to have to break down and buy soon. The floor is a cold, hard place to sit, you know? Listen, say hi to Tanya and Brady for me, and your kids, too, and give 'em a hug."

"Why don't you send them postcards or something? Keep in touch. It's hard on kids, you know, when people come into their lives and then just disappear like they'd fallen into a hole. I mean just because you and Dunc aren't a thing any more, is that any reason to just throw the kids away like old bread wrappers or something?"

"Okay, Mary-Lou, I'll make you a deal. You stop lecturing me and I'll send some postcards. But you have to stop lecturing me!"

She sent some postcards, then sent some more. She even got a highways map and inked in the route and fired off some of the tourist pamphlets that bragged about the lakes, the rivers, and everything else that was slowly being killed off by acid rain. She wasn't sure why she was doing it, other than that Mary-Lou had told her to do it. No way *she* wanted to throw kids away like bread wrappers. She hadn't exactly gone campaigning to have them in her life and couldn't say the times spent with them had been totally enjoyable, but still, no need to add to the burden. Mary-Lou knew more about it, she was up to her neck in kids all the time and in many ways had never left the queendom of childhood herself.

Betty wondered why it was important to her what Mary-Lou said or thought. She didn't know her very well. Not really. Living next door to someone didn't qualify you to say you Knew a person. You only Knew those parts of a person she'd felt easy to show you. If you actually Knew your next-door neighbour there'd be no murderers on the loose, someone would just pick up the phone, dial the police and say Listen, I happen to Know my next-door neighbour and he's the one did this ghastly deed.

What did Mary-Lou know about Betty? About as much as Betty knew about Mary-Lou. And yet it did matter, somehow, and enough that she got the postcards and even made herself write little messages, sitting on the ferry, with a ballpoint quick to hand, paying attention rather than staring glassy-eyed at nothing. Dear Tanya, Guess what, I just saw a bald eagle dive from the sky, hit the water with a splash and then come back up again with a FISH in her talons. You ever eat raw fish? I never did. Take care, Betty.

Why would Mary-Lou think Betty might be angry because Mary-Lou was mixed up with Duncan now? Did she think Betty had been just waiting for Dunc to phone so they could get back together again? Well, she hadn't. If he phoned tonight would she even talk to him?

She decided yes, of course she would talk to him. He wasn't Jack the Ripper. He wasn't Ted Bundy. He was just a guy who was used to getting things his own way, and who, if he couldn't get them right away, would wait and get them another way, but one way or the other, he'd get what he wanted. And was what he wanted so bad, after all? Was it too much to ask, really? His own truck so he could . . . what? Be his own boss? What a laugh. Nobody who depends on a company to hire him is his own boss! Nobody with big payments to make can really tell some arseltart to go fuck his hat badge. If you want to haul cedar shakes to California and bring back organic fruit and vegetables you still smile and nod and say Sure thing, be glad to. Anytime.

So why hadn't she just agreed, gone to the bank, put the trailer up as collateral, signed on the dotted line the way he had wanted? There was no way he could swing it alone, not with support payments taking first bite out of his income. Was that why? And was it the bite itself, or the knowledge that with more on the line than a damn truck, with Tanya and Brady to think about, he had still headed for the door? She had no idea what had gone on between him and his ex, but surely to God when you head for the door because you can't stand another minute of what's been going on, you could tuck one under each arm and get *them* out of it, too.

And what skin off her bum was it one way or the other? She wasn't mad at Mary-Lou. She wasn't even mad at Duncan. Why should she be angry? He wasn't the first person who thought the word *no* might mean almost anything else.

And maybe Mary-Lou was right. Maybe the reason she hadn't gone looking for furniture was because she didn't really like her house. Had she ever really wanted to live where she could see, hear and for sure smell a pulp mill? Had she ever really wanted a big lawn and a concrete walkway, three concrete steps down to the concrete sidewalk with the road on the other side of the phone and hydro poles? Well, what other options are there? You need a roof or you wind up sitting in the rain. And maybe she was just marking time but Jesus, you can mark it at least half-assed comfortable. All the economic experts who spouted advice from the radio and TV said that interest rates were going to have to go down soon, and, they said, when the rates dropped the market would pick up, house prices would rise, mortgages would seem to be more manageable and people would start to buy. Inevitably, things would drop again, house sales would either hold or drop slightly, then, after a while, people would stop worrying about the mortgage rates, they would think God if we don't buy now we'll never be able to buy, the market would come alive and off they'd go again, cycle after cycle and the trick, as near as Betty could figure out, was to hold tight right now and sell shortly after things started to move. So since things showed no sign of moving either far or fast, whether she was madly in love with her house or not, obviously she was going to hang onto it. So be comfortable. Just don't buy any distinctive crap which will only suit the house because if you're planning on selling . . . she sighed, and braked, slowing the truck so she wouldn't go right up the ass end of that dipshit idiot from out of province who was putzing along admiring the scenery, not seeming to realize if he didn't smarten up he was going to miss the curve and become a permanent stain on the rocks some two hundred feet almost straight down.

Damn, you just get one think halfways figured out and it leads to something else you have to figure out.

Like why, not an hour after Mary-Lou had phoned, why had the damn thing gone off again and her bloody *mother* spoken out of the plastic?

"Hello?"

"Is that Betty?"

"That's right."

"Betty, it's Mom."

"Mom who?"

"Oh you!" and Betty recognized the little laugh before she recognized the sound of the voice. "How many mothers do you have?"

"Hello."

"Is that all you've got to say? Hello? What happened to Nice to hear your voice, or something like that?"

"What do you want?"

"Because I phone you think I *want* something? Well, maybe I do. I want to talk to you, I want to hear your voice, I want to know how you're doing; it's been a long time."

"How did you find my number?"

"Well, I've read lots and lots and *lots* of police and detective stories. Mickey Spillane, Shell Scott . . . you read enough of them and you could get your licence and be a private eye yourself. How-*ever* did you wind up lost in the bush up there?"

"Oh, you know how it is. Wasn't hard."

"Why don't you write and let us know how you're doing?"

"You know me. I don't like writing letters."

"You could have phoned," still that teasing little undertone, that weird kind of sparring, that attempt to turn anything and everything into a little joke so there's never any reason to take offence, after all, ha ha ha I wasn't serious and if you object to what I said it's because, yuk yuk, you have a poorly developed sense of hee hee hee humour.

"Didn't have a quarter."

"Well, get one. If you take a dollar to the bank they'll give you four quarters and you can phone every week for a month."

"Yeah."

"You don't sound happy to hear from me."

"Why did you phone?"

"Why wouldn't a mother phone her daughter?"

"What do you want, Mom? Because if it's money, forget it, I'm no closer to being a zillionaire now than I ever was."

"Why would you think I *want* something?"

"Because it has been years. I mean *years*. People have died in less time than it's been since we talked. Babies were born, and now they're in school, okay? So can we just stop this evasive shit and get to the point before I watch while my hand reaches out and puts the receiver back in place?"

"Well, I can see time hasn't improved your disposition any!"

"No, it hasn't. I was an unreasonable bitch then and I'm still one. So what do you want? And before you say anything you have to know you probably won't get what you're after, especially if it involves sending you money."

"I don't want money! We've got money! We've got *lots* of money!"

"Great."

Jesus H. Christ on a blue suede cross but that idiot in front of her wasn't any smarter than the asshole behind her who had decided no more of this pokey-pokey for him and was pulling out to pass. She hit her horn, put her arm out the window and waved to get the joker to get back in his lane behind her and wait, the curve ahead was followed by another and there was no way to tell who or what might be coming, why did people think they had to be first in a long line of traffic, Christ what do you do, get to the scene of the accident six seconds ahead of the guy at the back of the line.

But the car behind didn't pull back in his own lane, he hit the gas to pull past Betty and her step van. The guy in front, oblivious to his mirrors or to anything except his vacation trip had no more idea of what was going on than he had of what was ahead of him.

And then the freight truck came around the curve. Betty hit the binders to give the idiot passing her room to get out of the way, room to slip just in front of her. But the dipshit tourist hit the binders, too, panicked by the sight of the big white Safeway truck. The Safeway driver hit *his* brakes, it was that or go right into Chummy coming at him in the wrong lane.

It was like something in slow motion and yet it happened too quickly to think. All she could do was depend on reflex and her years of experience. She knew that as long as the Safeway truck didn't broadside her and send her through the guard rail and down the bank, she'd be okay. Her step van was big enough and heavy enough to keep her from being crushed and killed. There wasn't much she could do about the assholes in the cars, all she wanted was to make sure she didn't wind up connecting with the freight truck.

When it was over there was a dent in the back of the step van where the car behind her had slid into her rear end. The freight truck was stopped in its own lane, the driver leaning out the window, puking. Betty got out of her own truck and leaned forward to help the Safeway driver call the Canada Geese. The fucking airhead who had been putzing around in front of her and the moron who had tried to pass were now as good as welded together on their way to heaven or hell, smeared into a crumpled and steaming mess maybe twenty-five or thirty feet down, on a ledge that looked as if given half a chance it, too, would bust loose. And if it did they might as well all just put on their good clothes and throw flowers over the side of the road, because no tow truck on earth would haul *that* back up to the pavement.

"Jesus, guy, are you all right?" she managed.

"Yeah. Where *did* that fucker come from?"

"I don't know but if he came from hell he's back home again," and suddenly she was yelling, "God *damn* all sabbath creepers!"

The Safeway driver climbed down from his cab, walked to the side of the road and peered past the twisted wreckage of what had been a steel guard rail. "Fuck," he sighed.

"Got a rope?" she asked. "You could tie one end of it to my bumper and I could . . ."

"Scratch that idea." He shook his head, his face still the colour of cottage cheese. "Nothing you can do for anyone in that mess, so the most that'll happen is either you'd get hurt or we'd dislodge that and send it the rest of the way to hell. You sure you're okay?"

"I'm not hurt. I just . . ." She turned away suddenly and gagged.

"I second the motion," the Safeway driver agreed. He went to his truck, climbed inside, and grabbed his mike. When he came back out of the cab he had a box of Kleenex in his hand. "Here," he said, handing it to her. "I think when this is finished and I can park the truck and call me a cab, I'm going to get it to take me to the closest hard-bar and I am going to get dee-ahr-yew-enn-kay."

10

DOUG HEADED OVER THE HORIZON and DeeJay decided she didn't really want to stay in the project much longer. It was beginning to seem rundown. What had started out as affordable housing had become something else; people bought up the units then rented them out to other people and the next thing you knew the upkeep wasn't quite kept up, there were places where paint had been touched up but not properly, so the new stuff was starting to peel too.

Too many kids tramped the grass flat in big brown patches of hard earth, and even though the regulations had some clear guidelines about pets, the dogs and cats seemed to own everything, and left their marks too. DeeJay had replaced the flowers in her brick planter so often she had lost count of how many geraniums, peonies and begonias had been put there only to be either uprooted by scatting cats or killed by what the cats left behind in the dirt. She tried putting chicken wire over the top. That worked only until the cats had managed to flatten it or claw it off and tip it over the edge.

"Jesus, Laura," she yelled, "if that friggin' Siamese of yours is smart enough to figure out how to get the wire off, you'd think it'd be smart enough to go into the bathroom, use the toilet, wipe its ass, then flush the stinky mess away so the rest of us wouldn't have to deal with it."

"Ah, get real, will you DeeJay? It's a cat for Chrissakes, what you gonna do with a cat? Train it to jump through flaming hoops or something? How much damage can one little cat cause anyway?"

"Easy for you to say. I notice you don't have any flower boxes or shrubs or anything else for that matter. How could you have with a goddamn pain in the ass of a cat like that spending every waking hour digging things up and killing them."

"Well listen, tell you what, when she comes in for supper I'll sit down in the living room and explain it all to her, okay? Maybe get her to join some kind of group therapy session or something. I'm sure once she knows how disappointed you are she'll bust her guts trying to atone."

"Bust your fuckin' guts you get too smart with me!" DeeJay muttered. Laura was okay except her kids were crazy and there was always the problem of the damn cat. Cats, half the time. The Siamese kept dropping litters, and the neighbours' kids trudged home with them, and nobody seemed to think of taking the damn things to the vet, so soon the kittens had kittens. DeeJay put mousetraps between her busy lizzies, and that worked, except it kicked off the next best thing to World War Three.

"Oughta report you to the SPCA is what I ought to do," the guy from across the way raged. "Goddamn kids are weepin' and wailin', and the cat's foot is swole up ten times its size, prob'ly got broken bones in there. How would you feel if *your* cat came home yowlin' and screechin' with a fuckin' mousetrap on its foot."

"Prob'ly about the way I feel when I step out the door and get greeted by a nose full of catstink! If you kept that damn thing at home where it belongs, or better yet fed it once in a while so it didn't come yowlin' around here . . ."

"Don't tell me what to do with the goddamn cat, y'hear? I'm phonin' the cops."

"Yeah, you do that. Dumb as you are you'll have to get someone to do the dialin' for you, though. I mean anyone as can't figure out how to keep a cat at home prob'ly can't figure out which enda the phone to talk into and which end to listen from. Although you sure don't listen much so it prob'ly doesn't matter."

"Keep it up, loose-lip. Just keep it up and you'll wish you hadn't."

"Oh God, mister," she laughed softly, "don't talk to me like that. You scare me so bad. I mean it, I am just so *scared* of you."

Someone swiped her mousetraps so she bought a spray can of ReePehl. That worked for as long as the bricks around the plants were dry. As soon as rain or even nighttime dew diluted the repellent, the cats were back.

She thought maybe cactus spines would discourage them. The cats peed on the cactus and that was the end of them. Even little firethorn bushes didn't help. In the end she decided to cover the entire top of the planter with boards. To hell with the flowers.

Three weeks after she put them there, the boards vanished. She supposed someone had taken them for bookshelves or something. She put more boards over the planter, and might have thought they'd been swiped for shelves, too, except her bladder hauled her out of bed in the middle of the night and halfway to the bathroom she heard sounds which sent her to her patio doors in time to see the flapjaw across the street taking the cat-cover apart and putting the planks in the trunk of his car.

She could have confronted him then and there, but DeeJay had grown up low-rent and learned early you don't get mad, you don't get even, you get vengeance and come out ahead.

She bought a special plastic spatula-type thing at the pet store. You were supposed to use it to sift the lumps out of the cat box. DeeJay sifted the dirt in her planter, collected more dried and fresh cat muck than the human mind would believe possible, and in the dead of night put it on the front doorstep of the mouthy neighbour across the street. He came out of the door on his way to his car to go to work, stepped in the mess and just about pulled the entire project apart. "No cat did that!" he roared. "Some god-damn *person* did that!"

DeeJay heard it all through the front window, but she didn't look out, didn't let him know she heard him, didn't do anything but sit in her big chair and smirk.

"Everybody says you're the one put the cat shit where that guy would step in it," Bobbi said flatly.

"Me?" DeeJay just looked at her daughter.

"Yeah. Did you?"

"Why me?"

"Well, he says it was you."

"Did he see me do it? If he did, why did he step in it?" She grinned. "I mean, if he *saw* me do it he knew it was there and if he knew it was there why did he put his size eighteens in it?"

"They say it's because the cat shit in your flowers."

"They," DeeJay announced, "say a whole helluva lot more than their prayers."

She had another go-round with the jerk but won it hands down. She had been in bed, but not asleep, and heard a sound that wasn't the same as the usual night sounds. Without turning on her light she looked out her bedroom window in time to see the guy from across the street leave her front porch and head back to his place.

She knew there was something on her porch even before she opened the door. She was ready for almost anything. She lifted the dead rat from her welcome mat, looked at it, shook her head and put the rat in a plastic bag.

Then she went down to the basement and out the back door. She didn't go directly across the street to return the rodent, she went up to the corner, crossed behind the triple-wide and went down the back way to the asshole's unit, and passed alongside it to his carport. Even if he'd been watching out his bedroom window, or his living room window for that matter, he wouldn't have seen her. She rammed the rat as far up the tailpipe of his car as she could get it to go. Smirking, she went back the way she had come, went in by way of her basement door, locked it, scrubbed her hands, stuffed the plastic bag in the fireplace with some newspaper, burned it all, then washed her hands again and went back to bed.

She didn't know how far he'd got before the rat up his tailpipe overheated everything and his motor burned out on him. She just decided to get the hell away from people like him. It was taking too much energy keeping one jump ahead of them. She started looking for a house in November and didn't find what she wanted until June. She didn't mind the wait, there wouldn't have been flowers in the planter during the winter anyway, and nobody was bothering her any more. Maybe the rat up the tailpipe had done more than blow the engine.

The house she bought was in the old section of town, so close to the beach she could smell the fumes from the speedboats and pleasure craft. The rattle and clatter of the sawmill was a constant background sound, the kind you knew would bother the hell out of you for three or four nights, then you'd be used to it and by the end of the second week you wouldn't notice it at all.

The house was enormous. When it had been first built the old section was *the* section of town, where the judges, lawyers, dentists and doctors lived, the second-and-third generation of new money, the ones with the new cars and huge well-tended lawns. Over the years money had moved but the big houses remained, becoming, in time, boarding houses or rental units. Bit by bit by bit the waterfront and foreshore had been taken over by motels, boatels and marinas, one by one the big old places had been bought up, let fall apart and all too often replaced by apartment buildings which pushed against every zoning restriction the town council had managed to put in place. The old section hovered close to becoming a slum. But DeeJay knew the town, and knew sooner or later what had been will be again. The place had grown but the roads hadn't kept up, people were sitting for half an hour or more to get from the new subdivisions to the downtown area. Sooner or later someone would wake up and smell the coffee, sooner or later the suburbs and exurbs would lose what tattered bit of appeal they still had and the old section would become desirable again. Already there was talk of moving the sawmill. The heaps and piles of sawdust, hog fuel and wood chips would be shoved around, flattened, called landfill, covered with a thin layer of soil and planted to grass, and on the former mess would be built very pricey townhouses and condos. Even if the inlet is rainbow-stained with spilled fuel, even if the off-sea breezes bring the stink of exhaust, it's waterfront, and it isn't going to stay low-rent for very long.

The move meant a change of schools but even the kids didn't gripe about that. The new house was five minutes from a beach, and besides, they were moving at the end of the school year. By the time classes started up again they'd have met kids at the beach, would know people, they would not walk into class with big targets painted on their foreheads, cursed and destined to be the butt of all jokes, taunts and barbs until the next new kids arrived.

DeeJay could have held onto the condo, found a tenant and

rented it out for enough to cover the mortgage on the house, but she decided against that. She didn't want the hassle. People phoning at any or all hours of the day or night to complain the toilet was plugged or a tap was dripping or they'd locked themselves out and needed yet another key to get inside. She didn't want to hear secondhand the kind of arguments she'd heard for too many months and years, she didn't want anything more to do, however distantly, with the yutz across the street. She sold. She could have held out for more money, but didn't.

"Hell, I'd'a been paying rent all that time anyway," she reasoned.

"Never mind what you *might* have been doing, you could have squeezed another five or six thousand out of them," Patsy lectured.

"Yeah? Well, I tell you what, Madam Trump; when you're clipping coupons and wheeling and dealing on the international exchange, maybe people will ask your advice on financial matters."

"One of these days you'll be sorry you talked to me like that. One of these days I won't be here and you'll wish I was."

"And the day after I wish you were here, they'll come with the coat that fastens my arms to my sides. Haul me away and put me in a rubber room."

"Sure, sure," Patsy waved her cigarette, brushing away everything DeeJay said and meant. "Until they do you can just get off my case. I think I'll take dibs on the big room at the top of the stairs, there. The one with the window looking out at the harbour."

"Take dibs on a dumpster out behind the Safeway, more like it," DeeJay warned. "The day hasn't come and never will when you move in with me."

"Hear that?" Patsy looked at Bobbi who was standing at the table, her body bent at the waist, elbows on the tabletop, chin resting on her hands. "You hear the way your mother talks to me? I bet if you talked to her like that she'd knock the spit out of you."

Bobbi half smiled and shook her head. Then looked at DeeJay, shook her head again and looked out the window. "Say it," DeeJay dared. Bobbi shook her head again. "Cat got your tongue?" DeeJay urged. "Seems to me your mouth works fine sometimes. Or do you already know what you've got to say is dumb?"

"It's not dumb," Bobbi answered, tone placid and easy.

"Then say it. You've got a perfectly good tongue in your head, speak up."

"What if you don't like what I say?"

"Hell, that never stopped you before."

"What if you think it sounds . . . cheeky to Gran?"

"If it's cheeky enough to make her stop yammering on about how she's gonna move in with us, maybe I'll give you a quarter."

"Fifty cents."

"You're on."

"Gran," Bobbi looked directly into Patsy's eyes, and even smiled. "We don't want you living with us."

Patsy gaped. "What?"

"We don't want you. I don't want you living here, Stevie don't want you living here and Mom sure doesn't. So why keep nagging?"

"Is that a nice thing to say to your grandma?"

"Is it nice of you to keep nagging? You know it upsets Mom and you do it anyway so I figure you only do it to upset Mom. So why do you want to upset her? You keep saying you love her but you keep upsetting her. And we don't want you living with us and upsetting her all the time. I don't think she likes you very much, anyway!"

"You going to let her just stand there and sass me like that?"

"Here's a dollar." DeeJay handed the money to Bobbi and winked at her. "The tip is for the extra good job."

"You're giving her *money* for talking to me like that?"

"Bobbi, tell your grandma to shut the hell up, will you?"

"Cost you another dollar."

Patsy was so angry she grabbed her fluffy sweater and left the new house. She stamped up the hill to the bus stop, waited, fuming, until the bus arrived, then she got on, dropped in her money and rode to the stop closest to the pub where she did most of her drinking. When she had packed away enough, she put a quarter in the pay phone and started maundering into DeeJay's ear, telling her what a rotten thing it was to raise a kid up thinking they could say just about anything at all to anybody.

"I taught you better'n that," she accused.

"Momma," DeeJay said clearly, "you didn't teach me a fuckin' thing that would ever, at any time, be of any use to me in polite company. You taught me hunger, you taught me neglect, you even taught me abuse and fear, but you didn't teach me much that I'd want to pass on to my own kids. So hang up the phone, you drunken old fart, and leave me alone for a while."

"Is that true?" Bobbi asked.

DeeJay whirled, surprised and suddenly very frightened. Bobbi was in her pyjamas, a small plate in her hand. On it a lettuce, tomato and ham sandwich dripped mayonnaise onto a dill pickle.

"You actually going to *eat* that?" DeeJay pretended to tease. "You'll be awake most of the night with indigestion."

"Is what you said true or did you just say it to make Gran butt out?"

"Bobbi . . ." DeeJay couldn't think of a thing to say.

"You're always telling Stevie'n me to tell the truth, you're always saying if someone asks you a question, answer the bugger, even if you know they won't like your answer. But you don't answer questions."

"There's stuff you don't understand, Bobbi, that's all."

"Never will if you don't answer questions." Bobbi turned away and headed for the living room and the TV. DeeJay could have laughed it all off if Bobbi had been angry, or even insulted. What she couldn't laugh off was the disappointment.

DeeJay followed her kid into the living room and sat beside her on the sofa. "Talk to me?" she begged.

"Sure," Bobbi munched determinedly, looking at the TV screen.

"So . . . what do you want to know?"

"What you said to Gran. About what she taught you. Abuse, you said, and fear. Is that true?"

"Yeah babe, it is," and DeeJay was horrified to hear the sobs in her own voice. Hot tears stung her eyes and trickled down her face.

"She was mean?"

"And drunk."

"That's why you don't touch the stuff?"

"You got it."

"We got a kid in my class phoned the Child Help Line because of getting beat up. They moved her."

"They moved me, too."

"Then why don't you just tell Gran to take a hike?"

"I've told her," and DeeJay started laughing. "But I guess I just can't be as mean and ugly to her as she was to me. Which doesn't mean I'm a better person, it might just mean I've got more rocks in my dome."

"Bummer, huh?"

"Yeah. Bummer, for sure."

"You want a bite of this sandwich?"

DeeJay knew she was being offered something much more than bread and filling. She wiped her traitor eyes and shook her head, grinning. "Jesus, kid, if you want to get rid of me, just say so. You don't have to *poison* me!"

Bobbi grinned and squirmed on the sofa, rested against DeeJay and munched quietly. "I like the old *Star Trek* better, don't you?" she asked, her mouth full, her words muffled. "I mean, I like *this* captain better'n old Kirk. He always looks like he's standin' there with all his muscles stiff so's he'll look like a hunk or something, and this one, well, he can't *talk* any better but at least he isn't so stupid-looking. But even Doctor Crusher is a fuckin' pain with her stupid gadgets . . . if those gadgets are so great how come they need *her*, they could just feed the crew into the gadgets, you know. And Troi, well, she's just dumb is all . . . and Geordi, he can't act for shit, everything he says sounds like what he *means* is holy moley Batman! But the stories were better in the old *Star Trek*."

"Boldly go where no man has gone before? You like that better than Boldly go where no *one* has gone before?"

"Ho, and then where do they go? To some place where they've already got all kinds of stuff! So someone or something or some *something* is already there!"

"I just wish they'd quit tugging on their uniforms. Can't fit very well if they're always tug-tug-tugging at the damn things."

"Yeah. And Wesley Crusher is a wimp. All he does is smile and look cute cute cute. Did you see the old one about the guy that got all burned and was in this machine to keep him alive and they took him to this place where everything is a fantasy and he *thought* he was young and healthy and handsome all over again and they left him there? I liked that one just about the best of all. He was happy, you know? I mean he knew it wasn't true, he knew he was still practically dead and living in this machine-thing but even though he knew that . . . he *believed* he was okay. How does that happen? That you can *know* one thing and *believe* something else?"

"I don't know, darling. But every day people do it."

"How come we don't go to Sunday School and church and stuff?"

"You want to go? Go."

"I don't want to go! I just asked how come."

"Because I don't want to go, either! And I could never see sending you, it seemed it was a thing where if the kid was to go the mother ought to take her. And I didn't want to go. So," she laughed softly, "ruined your life, huh?"

"Oh, prob'ly. Well, hell," Bobbi snorted and reached for the zapper to change channels. "Another of those stupid stories where some unknown *thing* comes blippin' through the electricity! See what I mean about the stories were better before? Every second one in this new bunch it's some *thing*—a spark, or what they keep calling 'an entity' comes blitzin' through the wires and everyone says *Captain, what was that?* And old baldy says *Gentlemen, I do not know.*"

"Beam me up, Scotty always did sound more fun than that Make it so," DeeJay agreed. Then she squirmed. "Jesus, Bobbi, you aren't gonna watch *this* shit, are you? Bang bang bang."

"I could turn to the music channel."

"And watch that crap? Gimme a break."

"Well, jeez, Mom, you oughta know if you want to see something good you don't look for it on TV, okay?"

DeeJay had known when she bought the old house in the old part of town that she was facing a huge job bringing everything up to snuff. She had thought her time in the project would have taught her what she needed to know to do what needed done.

She very quickly learned she could paint, but detested the job. She could wallpaper, but would rather have gone to the dentist. And when she found out what all you had to do to get old lino off the floor she felt boredom come crashing down on her head with such a thump she had the yellow pages open before she was aware she had made a decision.

And Jeannie had been absolutely correct when she had said they charged as much as doctors. "It's going to totally wipe out what I'd put aside for holiday money," she told Jeannie over coffee. "But I figure I've lived this long without seeing Disneyland, the kids can wait another year, it won't kill them. I am *not* spending my evenings down on my prayer bones with a little bitty hot air blower-thing scrape, scrape, scraping away at something someone else paid big money to glue to the floor. These guys have a *big* heater thing, they can do a square yard in the time it would take me to do a square inch. I got better things to do with my life."

"Of course you have," Jeannie agreed.

DeeJay nodded, reached for the teapot to refill their cups. Jeannie seemed preoccupied, almost hesitant.

"You act like someone who has something on her mind."

"Yeah."

"Good something or bad?"

"Good. I guess."

"You don't sound like someone with something good on their mind."

"Bud . . ." Jeannie hesitated, then jumped in with both feet. "Bud wants to sell the farm, buy a motor home, drive to Arizona, look around the place for a while, then get set up in one of those places where you can spend the winter in the sunshine."

"The winter? The entire winter?"

"He says he's been his whole life in the same place and he wants to see what else is out there."

"What about the summer?"

"Well, what he's talkin' about is travelling in that motor home."

"You mean . . . not come back?"

"Oh, we'd visit. For sure we'd visit!"

"Visit."

It felt like having something pulled out from under you. It felt like having something you thought was there and then found out really wasn't there pulled out from under you. DeeJay wanted to snivel and ask what about me?

But she didn't. It wasn't up to Jeannie and Bud to worry what about DeeJay. It was up to DeeJay to worry what about her. And what about her when Jeannie was down in Arid-zona?

"You gonna send postcards? Maybe you can smuggle me back some baby cactus?" She knew the smile on her face was as convincing as a plastic Jesus.

"You can just bet on it. And a big bag of the sand they grew in so they don't have to get used to something different. Things sometimes have a setback when they get transplanted."

"Yeah. But I guess if they don't die, they adapt, right?" and they both knew they weren't talking about cactus at all.

She had the downstairs walls painted before the workies started on the floors, and while they heated the lino to melt the glue so they could scrape off the old covering, the other team of workies painted the walls upstairs.

"I got no time for all that bee-ess," DeeJay blurted, "I want to spend my time here, with you, so's when you're gone I don't sit giving myself shit for having missed any chances."

"I know. I feel awful. I know Bud wants this, and I want him to have what he wants, he's earned it. And I want to go, too, it's just . . . God *damn* but I'm gonna miss you."

"Yeah. I love you, Jeannie."

"I love you, DeeJay. You're not a foster, you're my kid."

With the worn-out lino lifted, the floors turned out to be hardwood. "You've got about one sanding left in them," the workie told her, "and they aren't going to look brand new. I mean, you won't wind up with these absolutely perfect looking things you see in the new houses."

"Still look better than anything I've seen in the floor covering store. Can you put that stuff on? I don't know what it's called, plastic stuff, varathane or whatever."

"No problem."

"So, if it was your place, would you go for the hardwood or try to find something not too obnoxious to cover it?"

"If it was my own place I'd go for the hardwood. I don't know why so many people covered up so much good flooring, but they did. All the fashion, I guess. Yeah, I'd go for the hardwood. And you wouldn't really want it to look brand new in a nice old place like this, would you?"

And about the time the place was finished, Jeannie and Bud drove their brand-new motor home off to Arid-zona to see what had been on the screen in all those cowboy movies. DeeJay kept a brave face until she was in bed that night, then she bawled like a kid, bawled the way she never had when she was a kid.

She was sure it was the absolutely worst time of her life. But as bad as it is, it can still get worse. And it did.

11

BETTY CAME IN FROM WORK AND HAD SUPPER, then soaked in a nice hot tub until all the tension of all the miles was gone and she could actually move her shoulders without wincing. Then she dried herself, pulled on her terrycloth bathrobe and, barefoot, went to the living room to check the TV listings. The little red light on her answering machine was blinking so she pushed the message button.

She didn't want to phone her mother but five messages, one after the other, were too much to ignore.

"Oh, thank *God!*" and then it was tears-into-the-telephone time until Betty lost her patience.

"Listen, it's costing me money to hear you bawl. You want to bawl, do it on your own nickel and do it to someone else. What's so important?"

Less than an hour later she was in the ferry lineup. She'd lied to her supervisor, but the last thing she was going to tell about this trip was the truth. Now and forever more, the last thing she would tell was this particular truth. So she lied. So what, she'd been doing it for years, one way or the other. She'd said her mother had a stroke. Well, a stroke of bad luck, maybe, or a stroke of horror, more like it. Magda had often trilled on in a half-cut haze about what a stroke of luck she'd had when she met Burt. Well, they say it balances out, equal measures of shit and sugar throughout your life, and it looked as if sugar was going to be in short supply for quite some time.

Himself wasn't there. Himself probably wouldn't be there for at least a few weeks, unless Magda had socked away a tidy sum, and the thought of Magda saving anything was about on a par with the thought of a duck learning to dance.

Betty had known before she even got on the ferry that it was going to be hard on her to return to the place she'd walked away from those years ago. She thought she was prepared. She wasn't. She wasn't anywhere near prepared.

She parked on the street, unable to bring herself to pull up next to what she knew had to be Himself's car. Who else would feel compelled to flaunt whatever it was got flaunted by an El Dorado? She locked her vehicle, walked to the front door of the apartment building, pressed the buzzer and waited. Magda must have been sitting on it trying to hatch something, because she answered quickly. And when Betty had crossed the lobby and went up the stairs, Magda was standing in the hallway, in front of her open apartment door.

"Oh, thank *God!*" she shrilled. "I thought you'd never get here!"

"I'm here."

"It took long enough. I thought you'd at least hurry."

"Hey, settle down, okay? I had to arrange time off, for one thing. And for another, the ferry leaves when it wants to, not when I want it to."

"Well, anyway, you're here. That's what matters."

The apartment was painted different colours, the fridge was new, the dishwasher was new, the electric stove was new, the tables and chairs were new, but it was the same place. Magda had supper ready, all it needed was to be put in the microwave and nuked until it was hot. Betty wasn't sure she'd be able to eat, her belly felt hungry but her throat kept trying to lock shut; even getting words out was a chore, she wasn't sure food would go in, and if it did, she wasn't sure it would stay.

"I've got your old room all ready," Magda smiled.

"I'll be spending the night at a motel," Betty tried to smile. "I think it would be easier that way."

"At a motel? No way, you stay here!"

"Hey, they pay people at the motel. Pay 'em to do the beds, change the sheets, do the laundry, clean the tub . . . why make work for yourself."

"But I've got your room ready!"

"It won't rot."

Magda got all set to cry. "I don't want to be alone."

"Don't cry." Betty's voice was so calm, so level, and so quiet she surprised herself. "If you start crying I'll just get up and leave. You aren't using emotional blackmail on me, Magda. I'm staying at a motel. I need to think."

"Well, you can think here."

"No. I can't think here," and she knew no matter what Magda said or did, Betty was staying at the motel. Furthermore, she knew she could eat her supper and even if she couldn't enjoy it, she could keep it down.

"It's all lies, of course," Magda said repeatedly. "Just lies from a streetwalking little bitch. But the police are so paranoid, now, with all that stuff in the paper about those Catholic priests, and all."

Betty just ate, and listened.

"And the lawyer says our best defence is character witnesses. And he said we need you to testify, said it would look funny if Burt's own daughter didn't stand up for him."

"I'm not his daughter."

"Well, as good as! After all, he's the only father you ever knew."

"Right. And that pretty well makes me the fatherless child."

"*Why* do you have to be that way? My God, nobody knows what I went through, and what thanks do I get? Wait until you have kids of your own, you'll know then how hard it was for me. Then you'll be sorry!"

In the motel Betty sat on her bed and stared at the TV screen across the room. She just could not figure out what the story was supposed to be. Nothing about it made any sense at all.

Their appointment with the lawyer was for two in the afternoon. Betty's phone rang at nine-thirty in the morning and she knew it was Magda, so Betty didn't answer. She got dressed in a hurry and left the motel, drove to Smitty's for breakfast, then made a point of making herself scarce until it was time to go sit in the waiting room at the law office. Magda came rushing in all fluster and yap and only five minutes late.

"*Where* have you been?" she demanded angrily.

"Sitting here waiting for you to show up."

"No wonder I'm late! Running around trying to find you!"

"I told you I'd be here. I'm here. No need for you to run around looking for me."

"I phoned and you weren't there."

"Why is it people say that and make it sound as if you owe them an explanation?"

"Where were you?"

"Since I don't know what time you phoned," Betty fudged the truth again, it was easier, "how can I tell you where I was?"

"I had breakfast ready for you."

"I went to Smitty's. I always have breakfast at Smitty's."

"And lunch? A person would think you'd spend at least a little bit of time with me. I am, after all, your own mother."

"Hey, we're spending time right now, aren't we?" and she even made herself smile. "Don't make such a big deal out of everything, Magda. I told you, I don't want you going to any trouble, you've got enough to deal with already."

The lawyer finally called them into his office. He sat behind the big desk in a comfortable-looking black leather chair, while they sat in plainer, less comfortable chairs facing him across a polished expanse you could cover with green felt and use for billiards. The look he gave Betty told her more than everything Magda had been talking about so compulsively.

It felt like riding an inflated inner tube down the Nanaimo River rapids. You knew you weren't going to die, you knew this wasn't really "white water rafting," you knew you were about as safe as you could be, all things considered, and it was still scary. Betty wanted more control over her life than this. She wanted enough control over her life to be able to get up out of the chair, leave the office, drive up-island, get on the ferry, and not be seen or heard from again.

And she sat in the chair, watching the lawyer's face, watching his eyes, knowing he figured Burt had about the same chance as a small snowball carefully set on the inner hobs of hell.

Then Magda started talking about how everyone at work would testify, and the neighbours in the apartment building would testify and she could get letters of reference, too.

"Momma," Betty said clearly, "all any of that is going to do is spend every dime you've got. Didn't you hear the man? He's seen the RCMP video, the kid came through with flying colours."

"So what? Nobody cross-examined her! Anyone can tell any old lie at all and if nobody questions them they sound good. But put some heat on and watch the lie fall apart! And when do *we* get to see that video? I bet I could poke holes in the story myself, and I'm no lawyer! You just wait until we get *you* on the stand. *You* know! *You* lived with us for all those years, who better to know?"

Magda was looking at her, the lawyer was looking at her, and all Betty could do was look at the floor. Finally, she sighed. "Well, it's your old-age security, not mine. You want to spend a fortune on lawyers' fees, that's your business. I just want you both to know right now, up front, I don't have any money to help pay the bill."

There was nothing she could do, and less than nothing she wanted to do, so Betty went home. Magda screeched and wept and sobbed and even pleaded, but Betty went home. Magda didn't want to be alone, said she was afraid she'd have a nervous breakdown if she had to stay alone, but Betty went home.

It all drags on. They say it takes time because the lawyers need to carefully prepare their cases. Everyone deserves the best defence possible. There are formalities, rituals, procedures, and they all take time. Papers to file, other papers to pick up after the other side files them, i's to dot and t's to cross and depositions to take and through it all Betty just sat on her inflated inner tube and let the current do it all. She concentrated solely on keeping her head above water.

And then they were in the hallway, sitting on the old oak bench outside the courtroom, not allowed in until after they had testified. Magda looked fine but sounded as if she was just about ready to go into one of her soon-to-be-patented tirades. The lawyer was talking to her, calming her, reassuring her, but Betty had no idea what he was saying, she felt as if there was a wall between her and the rest of the world, a wall which buzzed faintly and muted all sound.

And then she saw a woman probably the same age as herself, walking down the corridor with a kid of perhaps eleven, or twelve; thirteen at the oldest. Betty knew she and Magda had never moved together so trustingly, so companionably as those two. All a person had to do was look at them and you knew these two could quarrel, then laugh about it later. The woman had her arm around the kid's shoulders, and was smiling down at her, encouragingly. The kid was looking up, nodding, and something about the way she walked, something about the set of her shoulders, something about . . . something . . . told Betty absolutely everything she needed to know. She stood up and the woman looked over at her. For just a second the woman stopped walking, and the eye contact was so strong it was like an electric charge. The kid looked over, too, and Betty knew the girl was half a step from terrified, and only her own courage and determination had got her this far.

Then the woman was moving on down the hallway, and Betty was walking toward Magda's lawyer. He looked up, smiling. Betty watched the smile fade from his face. "We have to talk," she said.

DeeJay and Bobbi sat in the little room, waiting for the whole thing to kick off. The Prosecutor had brought a glass of juice for Bobbi and a cup of coffee for DeeJay, then sat down and smiled encouragingly.

"You just answer the question, Bobbi. Don't tell him anything he doesn't ask, okay? Like if he asks if you went to the movie, you say yes. You don't tell him the name of the film, or the names of the actors, or how much popcorn you ate. Just say yes, you went to the movie. If he asks you about soccer practice, same thing. Yes, I had been at soccer practice. You don't bother with details like who did what or how much you enjoyed it or didn't, just yes, soccer practice."

"Okay." The kid seemed easy enough about it, but she had dark circles under her eyes and hadn't eaten enough to keep a cat alive in more than a week and a half.

Doug came into the little room then, and DeeJay was so glad to see him she could have jumped up and kissed him. It was Bobbi who did that, though.

"Listen," Doug said gently. "I'm going to be in that courtroom, okay? I think there won't even be any reporters or anything but he," Doug tilted his head in the direction of the Prosecutor, "found this thing that says if a guy acts like and fills the position of dad to a kid for more than two years, then legally he has the same rights as if he was a real dad. And what all that means is, I'm in there, kiddo. From start to finish, okay? And if you get scared, you just look over at me and you *know*, Bobbi, you know I believe you, I trust you, I love you like crazy, and I'm on your side, okay?"

"I'm scared, Doug."

"Yeah. Well, it's a scary thing."

"What if they don't believe me?"

"Then fuck 'em," he winked, "and the horse they rode in on, eh? No matter if, no matter what if, no matter anything at all; we believe you."

And then the noise started in the hallway, some woman screeching and yelling and caterwauling like hell. DeeJay was off her chair and out the door, her nerves shot, her adrenalin pumping. What if it was something like happened in the States, guys with guns racing around shooting witnesses in drug trials or something. Bobbi was right behind her, every bit as terrified as her mother.

The young woman who had been sitting on the bench and had stood up as DeeJay approached was standing, almost casually fending off the swings and swats of the older woman, who was dressed like Rita Respectable but had the skin tone and tired eyes of a dedicated barfly. And, as quickly became obvious, the voice of a muleskinner and the vocabulary of a dock whalloper. The dude in the month's-wages worth of suit was trying to hold back the barfly, while a couple of sheriff's deputies in their brown uniforms rushed to help him.

The deputies grabbed the woman and took her off down the hallway, and the guy in the fine threads said something to the younger woman, then came hurrying down the hall toward the little room. The Prosecutor whispered, "Excuse me," and brushed past DeeJay. Then the other one, in the suit, took the Prosecutor by the arm and started to talk five miles a minute.

The young woman looked over at DeeJay. That look was almost enough to make her jump out of her skin, the intensity of it left her shaken, and wondering. The Prosecutor was gesturing for her to join him and the guy in the suit. Just before she did, the young woman did just about the last thing DeeJay expected. She winked, then smiled at Bobbi.

12

DEEJAY HAD THOUGHT THE WORST PART OF IT ALL was going to be sitting in the courtroom listening to Bobbi tell what had happened. DeeJay had a too-clear idea because Bobbi had been open from the minute she had come in the door, her eyes still wide and glassy with fear. "Phone the cops, Mom, please," she said clearly, and if her voice shook, she could be forgiven that sign of weakness. DeeJay hadn't asked why or what or how or even who, she just grabbed the phone and dialled the emergency number. By the time the cops arrived her own voice was shakier than Bobbi's and her hands trembled with the need to reach out and grab the bastard by his saggy throat.

He may not have zeroed in on Bobbi, but he had it planned, he had to have been watching the soccer field, had to have the whole thing clear in his sick mind. Because it all went slick as it could go.

The practice had been a good one, busy and full, and by the time it was finished, Bobbi was tired. She hauled her sweat pants and jacket over top of her team uniform, changed from cleats to hightop runners, then went to her bike. Most of the other kids were piling into cars and taking off, and Bobbi took the time to wave at them.

And wouldn't you know it, her damn back tire was flat. Worse, some light-fingered hooligan had nicked her little bicycle pump. She was going to wind up pushing the thing home, damn damn damn.

"Got a problem there?" The guy was dressed in sweat pants and a long-sleeved sweatshirt. She wasn't sure, but maybe he was one of the guys who looked after the field. She was pretty sure she'd seen him talking to her coach.

"Flat," she mourned. "And some yahoo swiped my pump."

"Some people would steal a bag of dog doo-doo just for the chance to steal Something," he agreed. He hunkered, had a good look at the rear tire, then stood again.

"C'mon, toss it in the trunk and I'll take you home, you can get this fixed tomorrow." He looked around, did this little frown-thing, and shook his head slightly. "Dark's coming in pretty fast," he reminded her.

So the bike went in the trunk, Bobbi got in the car, everything was going just the way he had said it would, right up until the time he didn't turn right, but headed on toward the lake instead. "Hey," Bobbi protested. Then she saw the look in his eyes and knew the only person who was going to keep him from cracking her neck was herself. From then on, she didn't say a word and neither did he.

He left her at the lake. She didn't waste any time crying or telling herself she'd been a fool or mourning the fact her bike was still in his trunk. She just headed for home, thanking all the gods and goddesses she was still alive so she could go home. Of course, first she had to gather up her sweat pants and team shorts from where he'd tossed them. She didn't have to look for her under-pants, they were still on her, the crotch ripped open and flapping like some kind of primitive kilt. She almost hauled them off and tossed them in the bush, but she remembered the hour-long show she'd watched with her mom and Stevie, and what they'd said about evidence and all. So she left them on and didn't make the mistake of washing away the blood in the cool water of the lake.

She didn't have a full licence number, but enough to start nar-rowing things down for the police. Besides which, there weren't all that many mint-condition big old Caddies in town. The guy denied everything, of course, and they never did find the bike, but they got paint chips off the rim of the bottom of the trunk, where he'd just dragged out the bike any old which-a-way and dumped it in the toolies. And Bobbi certainly remembered his face!

DeeJay believed her kid. Even before they took Bobbi up to the hospital for a check-up, even before she saw the blood smeared on her daughter's inner thighs, even before she saw the ripped panties, she believed her kid. The panties had nearly unnerved her, though; white cotton and on them a design of little yellow ducklings, each with a big umbrella. DeeJay had bought them at Woolco, and she and Bobbi had laughed.

"Still think I'm a little baby, do you?"

"Darling, for as long as you live you'll be my little baby. And for as long as I live, too, for that matter, although I expect I'll go to glory before you do."

"Well, I should think so! What with you being such an old thing and all," and they laughed. "Just think, I've got four more whole and entire years to go before I'm as old as you were when I was born."

"Yeah? Well, don't bother to outdo me and have a kid younger'n that, you won't get as good a set as I got."

"Triplets, I'm gonna have triplets. One for God, one for Queen, one for country . . . and I don't want one of my own. I've got enough to handle puttin' up with you."

And when DeeJay saw the panties, stained and ripped, she had all she could do not to start screaming. The nurse knew it, too. One minute she wasn't there and the next she was, putting a chair behind DeeJay so when her legs gave out she didn't hit the floor.

No sooner had her rump touched the chair than something was sliding into her arm, something cold. "Thank you," she said clearly.

"I'm going to get the kitchen to make you a cup of tea." The nurse was making strong eye contact, it gave DeeJay something to hang onto, something to distract her from this need to howl like a gutshot dog.

"I appreciate what you're doing for me," she said, brushing at the tears. "I thought I was okay, but . . ."

They'd had counselling from the women at the Rape/Assault centre, and that helped. They'd joined a support group, and that helped, too. What helped the most was the long distance phone call from Jeannie and Bud, and Jeannie's offer to fly home if DeeJay wanted her to be there, to help. And for a moment, DeeJay did, desperately, want Jeannie to just walk in and put things right again, wrap her and Bobbi both in cotton batten and stand over them, keeping the world at bay. As she opened her mouth to say so, she knew the phone call was going to be more than enough to hold her together. Just knowing she wasn't all alone in the world helped.

Predictably enough, she hadn't seen or heard much from Patsy that was of any help. In fact, Patsy was using the whole sad episode as an excuse to swim in an ocean of suds.

"I'm going to be all right," DeeJay said, and meant it. But there was still the court thing to get through and DeeJay wasn't sure she was going to be able to hold it together with her kid up there being questioned. And she knew if the defence lawyer started cross-examining and ripping the kid's story to shreds, DeeJay was just going to lose it completely.

DeeJay hadn't asked the kid the kind of questions Chummy in the fancy threads was apt to ask. She hadn't asked if Bobbi had been sexually involved prior to the incident, she hadn't asked about the pain, she hadn't asked all the tacky intimate and embarrassing details, she knew everything she needed to know; she believed her kid, it had happened, and the kid hadn't done a thing to entice, encourage, or willingly participate. What DeeJay really wanted to do was chop that turkey-throated waggle-wattled old creep into little hunks and feed those hunks to the gulls.

But it wasn't anywhere near as awful as she had anticipated. For one thing, the courtroom was full. She hadn't expected that. The only men in the place other than Doug, who sat beside Bobbi and held her hand, were the police, the judge, the lawyers and the accused. The spectators, except for dear loyal Doug, were all women. Almost a dozen women in Salvation Army uniform, another eight in the white dress and veil of the nuns from the convent. The Rape/Assault women were there, and if the judge had let it be known ahead of time he would not tolerate any political messages on tee shirts, the Rape/Assault crew had ways around that; each of them was wearing a totally plain white tee shirt; for one mad, confused moment DeeJay thought they were more nuns. Women wearing tee shirts bearing the logo of the Transition House sat near a group of young women from the women's studies program at the college. The judge got to look out at a silent message, but there was no way to tell from his professionally expressionless face whether or not he appreciated what he was seeing.

Maybe if there had been a real trial it would have turned into the horror DeeJay feared. But it was obvious, from the get-go, that whatever the woman in the hallway had said or done, the starch was well and truly taken out of the defence. Basically, the turkey-necked old coot threw himself on the mercy of the court. Just looking at him you knew he'd spent his first couple of days in jail enduring the grip of DTs; he was even more of a barfly than the quiff in the hallway.

DeeJay sat by the aisle, her right hand gripping Bobbi's left, and on the other side of her kid sat Doug, holding her other hand. DeeJay could feel Bobbi trembling, and she wanted to say all the right things like Relax, it'll be okay, but she kept her mouth shut because she was strung so tight even the kid would have known she was lying; especially the kid would have known.

DeeJay had steeled herself for a couple of days of move and countermove, examine and cross-examine, and instead, it was all over and done with in an amazingly short period of time. She wasn't exactly sure, ever after, what had been said, because mostly what she heard was a loud humming in her ears, as if she was about to fall flat on her face. And then the judge was speaking, and it was the reaction of the Rape/Assault women drove the reality home for DeeJay. They didn't jump up and applaud, the judge would have had a screeching fit if they had, but they smiled. The nuns smiled. The Salvation Army women smiled, and DeeJay felt Bobbi relax suddenly, and slump against her.

Doug let go of Bobbi's hand and put his arm across her shoulders, his fingers gripping DeeJay's upper arm and squeezing gently. "Time to go home, darlin'," he said softly.

"What?" and DeeJay knew she was possibly in the worst shape she'd been in since she'd wakened in hospital with the hot pain in her pelvis.

"Five years is what." Doug stood, and he and Bobbi helped DeeJay to her feet. "Five years. I'd'a sent the fucker off for life but I'm not a judge. I'd'a give him life hangin' from his own balls, but we know I'm a vindictive prick, right?"

"Oh, right." Bobbi sounded as if nothing at all had ever come down on her. "I don't know why we bother with you."

The hard part came later. Not because of the newspapers, they were under orders from the judge to protect the identity of the one the judge called the victim and the women from Rape/Assault called the survivor. The hard part came because of, who else, Patsy and her pinned-in-the-middle-flapping-at-both-ends tongue. She, whose inside information was no more than what was in the newspapers plus the identity of the kid, was having a picnic in the pubs swilling down free beer while she told the story, again and again, of how the bastard had grabbed her poor little granddaughter. "And to think," she maundered, "of the number of times they've sat at a table with me, sipping suds and talking as if they were normal people, same as any of us."

When the flow of free beer seemed to be slowing down, Patsy would add some embellishments, things she didn't know, things which probably hadn't happened, things of her own boozy invention. Details known only to Bobbi or the fart himself were strung out as if Patsy had been sitting on the hood of the El Dorado throughout the entire attack. Each bullshit invention got passed on by the ones buying the beer, and each of the people they tried to impress passed it on to several others until the whole damn town thought it knew what had happened to Donna Jean Banwin and Sid McFadden's girl Roberta Marie. They paid more attention to Bobbi than they did to that babyfucker Burt Fiddick.

"*He's* the one they should be yapping about," DeeJay wept.

"Ah, darlin', darlin', don't do it to yourself." Doug put his arm around her shoulders and squeezed gently. His girlfriend got up, went to the bathroom, came back with a handful of toilet paper and gave it to DeeJay.

"I don't know how I'd have got through this without you," Dee-Jay sniffed. "I'm so goddamn mad I feel like I'm gonna burst. And when they're not yapping about Bobbi, they're yapping about Betty Fiddick, the asshole's daughter, as if she was in the wrong, too."

"You have to learn to live with it because it's all over town and it isn't going to go away," Doug said firmly. "And that stinks, but there you have it. Reality."

"That goddamn Patsy! Running off at the mouth as if she knew something. The goddamn woman wasn't even in court! She doesn't know diddly-squat, but does that slow her down or give her pause?

No, it sure as hell doesn't. Some of the stuff they're saying is just total BS, but what can we do about it? Rent space in the newspaper to run rebuttals?"

"Well, we know as much about Patsy as we'd want to, don't we? How are Skip and Gerri taking it?"

"They've been great. God, they've been great! When the kids were just about goin' nuts, afraid to go to school because of all the teasing and stuff, Skip just stepped in and got a tutor to come to the house. And he says if the kids don't want to go to school after summer holidays, he'll just keep on paying for the tutor or, if they'd rather go to boarding school, he'll pay for that too. He even said if we wanted to pack up and leave town he'd buy us a house and take care of all the details about selling this place."

"Take him up on it," Doug told her. "Get the hell out of here. And don't tell Patsy where you're going, either, or she'll be trailing along behind you, letting everyone in the new place in on the sordid shit, too."

DeeJay couldn't go anywhere without the sideways glances, the pitying looks, the people nudging each other and whispering. Several people had come up to her and very quietly offered her words of what they undoubtedly intended as encouragement and support. It wasn't their fault DeeJay cringed inside until her stomach cramped. She managed to say "thank you" each time, she even managed to force a smile, but then she went home and lay on her bed and trembled, wanting to yell and shout and holler and curse, wanting to wrap her kids in cotton batting, tuck them under her arm and run to someplace safe.

Betty wasn't having any easier a time of it. Nobody in town knew much about it, no more than they'd gleaned from the sparse reports on television, and as far as she knew none of them had put two and two together and decided Burt Fiddick was in any way connected to Betty Fiddick. The world might not be swarming with Fiddicks, but every town has probably got a couple of them.

Anyway, Fiddick wasn't her name, not really. She didn't feel any attachment to Magda's maiden name, nor to Magda's stand-offish family, either. In fact Betty felt very little connection to anybody.

She wasn't even connected to whatever it was that was going on inside her head. She lay awake at night wondering how many kids there had been between herself and Bobbi Banwin, kids who hadn't dared say anything, kids too young to be able to memorize bits of licence number or recognize the kind of car, kids who might never have been hurt if Betty had blown the whistle years earlier.

The thing was, she'd had it all so effectively blocked. Right up until she listened to Magda babbling into the phone, Betty had been able to split herself off from all those terrifying incidents. And now, one by one, two by two, like watching a sick movie and not being able to shut it off, it all replayed itself, over and over and over again.

She lost probably twenty pounds, and sometimes when she lit a smoke she saw her hands were trembling. Several times she had no sooner finished a meal than she had to head to the jane because it was making a round trip.

It didn't help the least little bit to read in practically every self-help book she bought that the trauma doesn't surface until the person is ready to deal with it, has all the skills she will need to cope, to endure, to survive. It didn't help any more than a frosty toilet seat on a damp cold morning.

The only good thing to come out of any of it was the violin. How in hell's name can a person overlook those lessons, those hours of practice, even the very existence of the instrument? But she had. She hadn't taken it with her when she left, hadn't so much as looked at another one in a music store window, and had erased it from her memories; then all the stuff she'd tried to put behind her came pelting down on her head. She wouldn't have been able to explain anything about it, but there she was, at the music store, putting three hundred and fifty dollars down for a made-in-Japan violin.

Amazing how much you can remember when the bung is knocked out of the barrel and the contents begin to flow.

She sat on her front porch in the evenings and deliberately ignored the pulp mill, fixed her attention on the long low blue hump that was the island, with spring sunset colouring the sky above, and she played, softly, all those old Scottish ballads she'd had to learn when she was a kid. Sometimes the neighbours would come out on their porches, too. The first couple of times she noticed them she started to put the violin away, but the elderly woman next door had called "Oh, please, dear, continue," so Betty did. She was next best thing to flabbergasted when she realized they were on their porches to listen to the music, not to watch the contaminated crud pour out of the mill stacks.

She wondered what they'd have to say if they knew she had been such a cowardy custard she'd given herself the first cousin to a case of amnesia and in doing that, endangered how many other little kids. Probably they'd pay for the chance to dump shit on her head. Instead, there she was, false-faced bitch, at the OpenAir market every weekend, up there with decent people, nice people, kind and normal people, playing music for the townsfolk who showed up to buy home-grown produce, home baking, honey and crafts. People smiled at her, waved at her, applauded after each song; boy, if they knew they'd buy those free range organic local eggs and chuck 'em at her for her sliminess and cowardice. She told herself those who don't speak up condone, and those who condone, do. She told herself she was as responsible as he was for what happened to those little kids.

Some nights, when sleep refused to come to her, she lay on her belly with her face buried in her pillow and she sobbed, deep racking sobs that usually gave her the hiccups. Damn, she mourned, damn damn damn damn *damn!* But the release in no way diminished the scenes and the guilt which haunted her. She supposed she was cracking up and they'd wind up hauling her off to the bin.

DeeJay followed Doug's advice. She didn't say a word to Patsy. She and the kids very quietly packed their clothes, loaded the boxes into the back of the pickup, closed and locked the canopy door and headed out of town.

"Anyone got any suggestions?" she asked. "We've got the whole damn world to choose from, you know."

"I'd like to go and see that woman. You know, the one from court. I'd like to tell her thank you."

"I didn't know you felt that way."

"Well, I do."

Trying hard to make a joke and lighten their mood, DeeJay

quoted the one which usually made Bobbi crack up laughing. "Your merest wish my dear is my command; I am more than your servant, I am your slave."

"Well, then, head north, slave," and Bobbi tried hard to smile.

"To Alaska?" Stevie tried, too, and DeeJay could have wept with pride, they were so young, and both of them were somehow so gallant.

They stopped halfway up-island and got oyster burgers at a roadside shack, then took them to the closest picnic site and sat at wooden tables watching the waves lapping against the driftwood logs.

"You're sure you're okay about this?"

"Yes," Stevie said firmly. "I'd like to live somewhere else, someplace where everybody doesn't know the one in the newspaper is my grandmother," and his lip trembled.

"Oh, shit, darlin', if I could, I'd reinvent the world for you, you know that. I'd give you a whole new family, one that didn't make you feel embarrassed."

"You don't make me feel like that, Bobbi doesn't make me feel like that, Grandpa Skip and Grandma Gerri don't make me feel like that, but *she* does. No sooner out of jail than she's back in again, and each time they write this thing in the paper about it and make sure everyone knows it's the tenth time, the eleventh time, the fourteenth time she's gone to the crowbar hotel. And all the kids know she's our Gran."

"Not mine," Bobbi laughed. "She's nothin' to me. Anyway, I don't want a whole new family, either. I've got all I can do to keep this one straight, all those names and faces and all."

The idea of reinventing seemed like a good one, though. If they moved, and if they didn't let Patsy know where they'd gone, and if Skip and Gerri could just go along with it, and if, and if, and if, they might be able to expunge a couple of skeletons and dust out the closet, give it a good airing.

The ferry trip over was one of those things in your life you knew, even at the time, you would never forget. DeeJay didn't want to talk, in case even the sound of their voices detracted from the dreamlike quality of the crossing. She sprawled on the life raft storage boxes at the back of the ship, and with every turn of the prop, she felt herself loosening, just a tad, then another tad, and another.

Others were out here in the sunshine, and not all of them because it was the only place on the boat where a person could light up a smoke. The sun was warm, the sky and sea different shades of blue, the clouds were like little streamers of something puffy stretched across the horizon, and the sound of the engines was soothing, like a deep-throated murmur she recognized from some time so long ago she couldn't remember.

Stevie stretched out too, and was asleep in no time. Bobbi leaned on the rail, and anyone who didn't know any better would think she was a kid who had never had a moment's worry in her life. She turned, and saw her mother looking at her. She smiled, then made a little mid-air kiss and turned her attention back to the scenery. When the ferry finally docked, DeeJay was sorry the trip couldn't have just lasted forever, sorry she couldn't spend her life floating somewhere between here and there, drifting gently, cut off from everything they insisted was the real world.

Just up the hill from the ferry dock was a motel, with a Vacancy sign.

"Good enough for me!" DeeJay turned the car into the driveway.

"It'll do for me, too," Bobbi agreed.

"Yeah," Stevie chimed in, "and there's a pizza place right across the street. And that is a hint, okay?"

Betty had more changes in her life than just the violin. She came home from work one evening, and as she walked in the back door she had what she would have described as a case of double vision. She saw her kitchen, and the hallway leading to the living room, but at the same time she saw another image, like a double exposure photograph, and she liked the new one better than the old. Instead of just whipping something together for supper and sitting on the cushion on the floor to watch TV, she had a fast shower, changed into clean clothes, and drove into town.

The furniture store was open until nine at night on Fridays and Saturdays. And they were more than willing to deliver.

She didn't fill the house up on that one trip, she took her time, and enjoyed every step of the process. She could have done the painting and re-papering herself, but she didn't much feel like it. She picked out the colours, she pored over the books of wallpaper samples, she decided every little detail, but she paid a crew of four guys to actually do it. And she knew they had done a much better job than she ever could have.

As much as possible she chose things which looked as if they had been designed the same year the house was built. She also made sure what she bought was actually made of wood, not some kind of sawdust and chips held together with epoxy glue. When she couldn't find a kitchen table and chairs that she liked in the furniture store, she went to the woodworking store and ordered a set made special.

The cabinets in the kitchen were nothing to write home about, even if you had a home to write to, and were the first things to go. The crew was careful about taking them down, and more careful about patching the wall once the cabinets were gone; they even recommended someone who they said made the best custom jobbies a person was apt to find anywhere.

She got a sofa and two chairs for the living room, but passed on a coffee table. They all looked as if they'd come out of a cereal box. Instead, she asked the cabinet maker if he could make her something which could serve as a coffee table without actually being one. What he made looked like an old blanket box, and the first time she saw it she knew she'd been waiting all her adult life for it.

The valances came down in the living room, the walls were patched and repainted. One by one she took on the bedrooms, snugging herself in until she felt totally at home in any room in the house. She had flower boxes made for the front porch, and positioned them in exactly the right place, and when the sweet peas grew up the strings Betty had fastened to the top of the porch fronting, she could sit out there of an evening and not see the mill or the mess it vomited because of the bright-coloured blossoms. Of course she could still smell it, perfume or not, but probably even the apples in Eden had the occasional worm.

The nightmares didn't stop, the sleepless hours didn't diminish, but at least if you have to have insomnia you might as well have it in a comfortable bed in a lovely room.

DeeJay and the kids looked at houses until they were damn near sick and tired of looking at them, and at the smiling faces of the commercially pleasant real estate agents. And in the end, it wasn't a house they bought. Not really.

They were bored, and with nothing better to do, they went for a stroll along the pier near the ferry dock. And there it was, with a small hand-lettered For Sale sign in the window.

"I want that," Stevie said.

"Yeah," Bobbi breathed, "wouldn't that be *great!*"

"You're kidding."

"Momma, I am not kidding," her son said. He didn't look up at her, he didn't try to flarch her into anything, he just stared at the boat.

Probably at some point in its long life it had been a big tugboat, or maybe a fish boat. DeeJay didn't know enough about boats to be able to tell. Whatever it used to be, it had been expertly re-done, and whoever had worked on it had loved it.

"We don't know the first thing about running a boat!" she argued.

"What 'run'?" Bobbi countered. "Nobody said anything about riding off into the sunset in it. You could keep it tied up here year-round and *still* love it. And no lawn to worry about, either."

On her own, DeeJay would have walked away and talked herself out of anything so different. She'd spent so much of her life trying not to stand out in a crowd, and this would stand out anywhere. But the kids were determined, and she went along with it, hoping some huge flaw would hit her between the eyes and give her some ammunition to talk them out of their bright idea.

But she couldn't find a flaw. And by the time the owner had shown them around, DeeJay was as much in love as her kids were.

The bedrooms, four of them, were below, and so was the bathtub and shower. The plumbing was attached to a flexible black plastic pipe which ran from a connection below the waterline to the big metal sewage pipe built along the dock. "You have to pump the holding tank," the owner explained, "because there's no way you can get water or anything else to run uphill, but it's no big problem, I just kind of do it as a matter of course once I've finished having my bath at night. By the time I'm dry and in my jammers, the tank is pumped out and flushed clean."

The main deck was like one big open room, except for the small walled cubicle where the second toilet was installed. The windows had been covered there, but the rest of it was encircled, with the glass actually curved at what would have been the corners, if boats had corners.

"Got them out of an old ferryboat," the owner explained. "Stroke of luck that I even heard about it. Most of the wood, too, I salvaged from that ferry; some of it had been too frapped in the beaching, but for the most part it was all still good and you just can't imitate it, somehow. I mean old is old, right?"

"And the table? Did you get that from the ferry?"

"Indirectly. Used to be a door. Nice, eh? Those are real brass fittings, too. They probably don't even make them any more. Not that heavy, anyway."

He had juice for the kids and poured beer for himself and Dee-Jay. She sat at the table, sipping and looking out the windows. Well, you'd have to train yourself not to pay too much attention to the big gas tanks there, but you probably wouldn't be too interested in that direction anyway, nothing over there but town. The rest of the view was incredible. She supposed it would look one helluva lot different in the wintertime, with grey sky, grey sea, and the pier black with water, but there was no denying that anytime things were nice, and right now they were gorgeous, the view was beyond description.

Of course there were some changes to be made. For one thing, she would want a window seat all the way around, so she could just plunk herself down any old where at all and enjoy to her heart's content. And she'd get rid of the damn doilies, too. She wondered if this guy's wife or girlfriend or someone had made them for him, they were just about everywhere you set your eye. What's more, there'd be more than just one or two little flower boxes out there on the open deck space beyond the windowed walls. And the upper half-deck area wasn't going to be bare, either.

"So why are you selling?" she asked outright. "If it was mine, I sure wouldn't."

"I've got cancer," he said conversationally, as if he was telling her he had just bought a canary in a cage. "And they've told me there's nothing they can do for me. So I'm selling and using the money to go down to Mexico to try some of that off-the-wall stuff." He smiled gently. "I don't expect to get a miracle, but what the hell, at least I'll get to see some of Mexico before they put pennies on my eyes."

"Gee, mister, I'm sorry," Bobbi blurted. "That's a real bummer."

"It's been a good life, darlin'," he smiled, as if there wasn't a thing wrong anywhere in his world or his life. "And hell, you know what they say, sooner or later you have to die of some damn thing or other."

Skip didn't even say she was nuts, let alone tell her she was making the world's second biggest mistake. He and Gerri came over to have a look, and he walked around inside, grinning from ear to ear.

"I'll tell you what, darlin'," he finally said. "If ever you decide you're fed up with this place, you just phone me, because I'd move in here in a minute."

"I thought at first you were, well, a bit foolish," Gerri admitted. "I guess I thought in terms of a float camp, and God knows I spent too many years of my life in a float camp! But this is just fine."

"Take one of those courses they have every few months, the power squadron course, teaches you all about navigation and what-not; then you can go cruising in the summertime."

It was a great idea, but DeeJay knew it wasn't one she was going to follow up on. Bad enough staying on top of car engines when you at least had the chance of phoning a tow truck, no way she was going to be to hell and gone out there in the middle of the chuck trying to figure out why the motor wouldn't do what it was supposed to do. But she just nodded and smiled, as if Skip's dream was her own.

"I'm going to miss you all like crazy," Gerri's voice quavered but she refused to allow herself the luxury of tears. "I guess I'm spoiled, because most grandparents don't hardly ever get to see their grandchildren any more and I've had lots of visits and cuddles. And maybe I *am* spoiled, I don't care! I'm still going to feel as if the sunshine's been swiped outta my life."

"You just get in the car and drive to the other side." DeeJay didn't know she was going to hug Gerri until she was doing it. "You leave the car over there, catch the ferry, and walk the few feet from there to here. I'll give you a key to the door, and that fourth bedroom down there is yours."

"Just don't bring grandma Patsy with you," Bobbi warned, "or it's over the side with a brick tied to your foot."

"If that old bat shows up here, whether I've taken that course or not, I'm firing up the motor and we're heading off, over the bounding main, even if it's into the teeth of a gale."

And less than an hour later, it was done, the signatures were on the dotted lines, the notary public had done her thing, and they could head back to the motel to start packing their clothes again. They took Skip and Gerri out for pizza supper and invited them to stay over with them, but Gerri said no, she wanted to get back and put her house up for sale. "If they did it with one boat," she teased, "someone'll do it with another one if I pay him enough."

They moved in four days after the paperwork was all ticketyboo. The previous owner had done little more about moving out than to pack some of his clothes and send the rest to the Salvation Army, and then he was gone, leaving his damn little doilies behind him. "Get rid of those things," DeeJay warned, "I hate 'em."

She didn't really want to go below at night but didn't want to sleep in the living room and maybe wake up to someone peering through her window at her. She had thought she would lie awake listening to the comings and goings of other boats and people, but she was asleep within minutes. In the morning she took her coffee outside and sat on the half-deck sipping it and feeling luckier than she deserved to be. It seemed a million miles from the string of two-bit roach palace motels in which she'd been raised.

Betty recognized the kid before she was all the way out of the car and moving toward the steps up from the sidewalk. She felt as if she'd been sitting out here, playing the violin, and waiting, waiting,

waiting for weeks, even months. She didn't wave, or smile, or anything except get up out of her chair, go in the house, put the violin away, and move to open the back door. The kid was just coming across the porch, and when she saw Betty, she stopped.

"I wanted to tell you thanks," she said clearly.

"That's funny. I wanted to tell you the same thing. Come on in, we'll have tea or something."

The boy was shy, and so was his mom, but not Bobbi. She and Betty talked together as if they'd been doing it every evening since the kid first drew breath.

"I feel bad," Betty confessed, "Maybe if I'd spoken up sooner they'd have done something about him, and maybe if they had, you wouldn't have had to go through it all."

"They've been putting my mother in jail on a regular basis for years," DeeJay blurted, "and it never stopped *her* from going back to her same tacky tricks. So stop doing a number on your own head. What is, is, and it can't be changed. By me, what counts, is that you were there when you were needed, and what you did made all the difference in the world."

"He was on his way to the pokey, anyway, even his own lawyer knew that. I guess Magda, my mother, was the only one who didn't know the old bugger'd had the bird."

"How's she taking it?"

"Who gives a shit?" Betty laughed. "Who knows, maybe at this very minute she's sitting in some stinkin' pub somewhere swillin' suds with *your* mother," and they all laughed, even Stevie.

"It was nice of you to drive all the way up here just to say what you said." Betty felt shy, and awkward.

"Wasn't much of a drive." DeeJay looked down at the table top, and ran her fingers along the grain of the gorgeous wood. "We moved here a month and a half ago."

"Why here?"

"Well, Bobbi wanted to see you and say thank you, so when we headed off, we came here first. And just never quite bothered to move on."

"We bought a boat," Stevie spoke up for the first time. "It's really neat, you should see it, and Mom's got all these ideas to make it even greater," and he started describing the bedrooms, the

242

bathroom with its old old tub, the brass fixtures. "I get to shine the brass, too," he bragged. "Lucky, huh?"

It was easy then to put the nastiness aside, to look at it, admit it, recognize it, even name it, and then turn away from it. They moved out onto the front porch with their second cup of tea, and were so comfortable together they didn't even need to talk, they could share silence and not feel awkward.

Summer slipped past them day by gorgeous day, like a seamless carpet of sunshine and cooling breeze and the scent of salt, iodine and that special comforting smell that is a well-cared-for boat. DeeJay's flower boxes and hanging baskets burgeoned, spilling blossoms and petals, adding the perfume of nicotiana to the evenings. Scorning all the ozone warnings, DeeJay, Betty and the kids lay on their half-deck and soaked up the sun, tanning darker than they'd ever been before, and if they got too hot, they just had to lower themselves over the side and the deep green water cooled them off in a hurry.

When not lolling around on their half-deck, they were lolling on one of the many quiet beaches. Most of the tourists only found those close to town, and Betty introduced them to other, better ones, where only the locals went. Just about any hour of the day or night you could go to a clean beach and, if it was jammed, you'd have to put up with the laughter of no more than a dozen other people. You could actually go to the beach and smell the salt-impregnated logs, the drying kelp left tangled on the sand when the tide went out, instead of the coconut oil smell of suntan lotion or that other chemically smell of sunblock cream. Not ten minutes by car and they were at a beach where they could sprawl in the shade of mammoth maple trees while tossing bits of crust to the tamest, cheekiest raven DeeJay had ever met. The bird seemed to recognize them. No sooner would they have their blanket spread and their picnic stuff safely in the shade than the raven would be in the branches above them, making an almost crooning noise. When Steve tossed the first piece of crust, the bird was down like a shot, hopping across the sand, coming closer and closer until it was actually on the blanket with them.

Kids brought dogs to the beach and threw sticks for them to

chase, and just beyond the sandy area a concrete strip ran down and into the water, and people came with boat trailers hitched to pickup trucks, backed the boats into the water, disconnected them, then drove the trucks up to park them before going out catch salmon.

DeeJay kept waiting for something to happen and smash the dream, but then it was time to get the kids new clothes for school. Time, too, to get a municipal bus schedule and work out which one they should take to get to and from classes.

"Too good to last, I guess," Bobbi mourned.

"On the other hand, old Gloom'n'Doom, there'll be another one next year, okay? And they'll call that one summer, too."

She knew she didn't want to just sit staring out her windows at the scenery, however gorgeous it was. And there didn't seem to be one helluva lot of choice when it came to jobs, but there would be something, and she knew she'd find it. She could have joined lawn bowling or horseshoes, she could have joined the Ladies' Aid or the Hospital Auxiliary, she could have volunteered her time at the Transition House or the Women's Centre. Instead, she joined the local writer's club, and then embarked on an affair.

Joining the writer's club was a big step, a person would have thought big enough to satisfy anyone's need for something new in her life. DeeJay had done what she called "a bit" of writing, you can't get through upgrading and university courses without having to do the occasional and often odd composition, but she hadn't really thought much about it until, as if it had walked across the water and jumped up to bite her on the nose, she had the idea to join the writer's club. She didn't expect that one night a month to jar her into several hours a day, nor had she expected the several hours a day would lead her, rapidly, from ballpoint pen and lined loose-leaf paper to an IBM clone and a XyWrite III program. But there she was, with the desk set up in the roomy area they still called the "living room," spending as much time staring out the glass at the ever-changing sea as she spent staring at the words taking shape on the screen.

From the one grew the other, and it happened so easily she sort of slid into rather than walked into something which ought to have scared the very bejeezus out of her, and didn't.

The kids were in bed, undoubtedly asleep, and DeeJay and Betty were having tea and peanut butter cookies. Betty had just finished reading the latest version of DeeJay's most recent short story, and they both reached for the same cookie at the same time. Neither of them got it. They wound up, instead, fingers touching, both of them holding the prize.

It was like being an awkward teen-ager all over again. Except DeeJay didn't remember ever being that awkward-feeling with Sid. She wondered if it had been easier because he was expected to take the initiative, all she had to do was follow along, unprotesting.

Betty froze, then stared at the cookie as if salvation was hidden inside it. "I, uh, guess it's, uh, about time I, uh, packed it up and, uh, headed home," she managed, at the same time praying heaven would intercede and keep DeeJay from knowing a bolt of lightning had just come from the sky and impaled Betty totally.

"Uh, sure, if that's what you want," and they both let go of the cookie at the same time.

DeeJay knew, better than she knew her own name, that Betty knew what DeeJay was feeling. And DeeJay could only wish harder than any other wish she'd ever made, that Betty not get so upset she would take off at full speed and never come back again. Betty was convinced DeeJay knew what was going on with her, and was itching for Betty to get her depraved self to hell and gone out and away, far away forever.

She looked up and saw DeeJay blinking rapidly. For one brief moment Betty almost thought DeeJay was weeping because their friendship was finished. But that brief moment passed and they each let realization sink in, then, slowly, each relaxed.

"Well, holy old badly, eh?" DeeJay managed. "Now what the hell do I do? Or you, for that matter?"

"I know what I'd like to do, I just don't want you to drop the anchor on my head if I try."

"Really?"

"Really."

"Do you feel kind of . . . clumsy?"

"That's a mild way of putting it. I feel . . . lost."

"Me, too. Lost and confused."

They moved from the table to the living room and sat side by side on the blue carpet, shoulders touching, hips and thighs touching, holding hands and looking at the lights of Courtenay, across the water. "So I guess the question is, are we going to do anything about this?"

"I'm going to do as much about this as I possibly can."

She wasn't sure how it was going to feel, or be, or even how to kick it off and get started, but turning her face and leaning forward to kiss seemed like a good start. That first kiss was so hesitant, so gentle, so much like a phantom touch she couldn't be sure she'd actually been kissing another woman, she might have been kissing mid-air. So she kissed again, and there was no doubt that time, she wasn't kissing mid-air. And it wasn't mid-air kissing her back.

Nothing went much further than that. Not that night. They kissed, lots, and touched, often, but nobody hauled off anybody else's clothes and nobody was driven by desire to do much more than more of what they had already been doing. Betty stayed the night, but not in DeeJay's bed. They didn't even go to bed, they just drifted into sleep right there on the carpet, fully clothed.

DeeJay's inner alarm wakened her before the kids were up and moving around. She had coffee made and the cereal and bowls on the table before the sounds from below wakened Betty. They were drinking their first cups of kickstart when the kids came up from below, dressed and ready for school.

"Stayed over, huh?" Bobbi said casually. "Did you have a good sleep?"

"It's like being rocked in a cradle or something," Betty agreed.

DeeJay packed the lunches and gave the kids her usual hug and kiss, then watched them head off down the pier toward the bus stop at the foot of the hill. She turned then, and looked at Betty.

"Could I interest you in seeing what's down below?" she said quietly, "or would you rather have cereal or pancakes or something."

"I would far rather have 'something,' but pass on the food," and as if they had been practising for years, they moved together toward the polished wooden steps leading below.

It was well past noon before they were in any shape to make sense when they spoke, and then they didn't waste much time talking.

"I wish I'd known about this years ago," Betty yawned.

"I didn't know you years ago." DeeJay nuzzled close, her mouth against the warm curve of Betty's breast. "And I'm not sure it would have been as much fun learning from someone else."

"You know, of course, I fully expect the lived-happily-ever-after part of it all?"

"Oh, for sure. No disagreements, no arguments, no quarrels and no screeching matches, just day after day of calm, peace, tranquility and love. Right?"

"Excuse me, I might barf," and they were laughing softly, turning to each other, touching, stroking, exploring.

"I feel as if I've known you forever," she said.

"Oh God, you're so beautiful," she said.

"Nothing in my whole life has been anywhere near this good," she said.

"I feel as if I've finally come home."

13

DEEJAY WAS AT THE REGULAR MONTHLY MEETING of the writer's club when she heard about the job. Actually, she only half-heard and was too shy to ask more about it, so when she went home, all she knew was the alternate school was looking for someone to be a combination counsellor, advisor and role model for those kids who didn't fit into the regular school system.

Having never felt she fit into the regular school system herself, DeeJay was sure she was eminently qualified. She also knew her feelings weren't necessarily going to convince the hiring committee so she spent three afternoons at the computer, calling on all the skills and tricks she'd picked up at the writer's club, working on a resume and covering letter. By the time she was even halfway satisfied with it, she figured she'd be more than willing to hire this person herself.

Even so, she was surprised when she was called in for an interview and flabbergasted when informed the job was hers. She expected her kids to be at least as astounded as she was, probably even more, but they seemed to feel there wasn't another soul on the face of the earth more deserving.

Betty insisted they have a celebration dinner at her place and it took no convincing at all to get DeeJay and the kids to agree. She roasted a chicken, whipped the potatoes to a fine froth, made a very garlicky butter to pour over the French-cut beans, and put together a salad that was practically a meal in itself. She had a dessert, too, but nobody had any room for it. Sitting at the gorgeous table in the quietly pleasant kitchen DeeJay felt as much at home as she did when she was at her own table on the boat.

The kids cleaned up the dishes, then moved to the living room to turn on the TV, do their homework, and natter at each other until they were both yawning and bleary-eyed. It took only the barest hint to send them upstairs to "lie down for a while," and once they were asleep the TV was off and Betty and DeeJay were in Betty's bed.

If the kids were surprised to wake up somewhere other than their own beds, they kept it to themselves. There was time after breakfast to nip down to the boat for a quick change of clothes before DeeJay drove them to school.

Then she spent the rest of the day looking through the stores, picking and choosing carefully, putting together a wardrobe for work.

Her stomach was tied in knots that first morning, and it stayed that way for the rest of the week. At first, the knot was because it had been so long since she'd tried to hold down a job, especially one she had to practically define for herself, since she was the first person to do this kind of thing and even the principal wasn't clear on how to do it, even though everyone agreed it was well past the time someone do *something*.

That new-job anxiety faded rapidly, and the knot tightened as DeeJay realized just how big a chunk she'd bitten off, and how hard it was going to be to chew on it. She might have thrown up her hands in despair if she hadn't been able to call on memories of Jeannie and how she'd treated her fosters, because that's what the job required. Someone willing to become a part-time foster mom to fifty-seven very fucked up young people, most of whom let her know by one belligerent means or another that they didn't figure there was any reason in the world for them to talk to her.

She might have wound up staring out a window while the kids bit hunks out of each other's throats, but for an instinct, and the way she acted on it. When she was just about at the peak of frustration, almost convinced her barbarians were never going to open up and discuss their problems, she suddenly realized there was no reason they'd want to. After all, what was she sharing with them?

She didn't know if the superintendent would approve, she had no idea how the board of trustees might react, and she didn't really care. Her responsibility was to the kids and to do her job she had to make connections with them. So she asked for, and got, what in other times would have been called an assembly. And found herself facing more suspicious and distrustful eyes than she'd imagined. She didn't lecture them on the need for trust, she didn't give them chapter and verse of the theories, she just stood without notes and talked to them. Afterward, she remembered only a few of the things she'd said. She remembered telling them she'd been raised in a situation that didn't even deserve the term "dysfunctional" because it was totally *non*functional. She told them a bit about Patsy. She told them about the welfare, the foster homes, and Jeannie. She even told them about the foul old fart who hauled her out from under the bed, and how she'd wound up in hospital.

"And that's who I am," she finished. "And probably each one of you thinks your pain is unique, and that only you have had to put up with, cope with and deal with what's coming down around you. But you aren't alone. And I want you to know that between fifteen and twenty percent of our population is as good as lost to society because of abuse of one kind or another. Whether physical, mental, emotional, psychological or sexual, abuse scars us and we have to learn how to function in spite of it. We're all crippled to some degree, and we'll limp our way through life with less trouble if we have the guts to dare to reach out and grab the hand some other cripple is offering. And thank you very much for listening to me, I appreciate it."

She came within an eyelash of losing her job, but she didn't care.

"I wouldn't have been able to do the job, anyway," she told Betty. "So if you don't dare try to do it, you might as well quit, right?"

"You are something, woman, you are really something!"

They didn't line up at her door the next morning, but at least when she waved, they waved back, at least when she said "Hi, how's it going?" they would answer her, and not snarl while doing it. And one by one, they began to find their way to her office. She made tea or coffee and didn't rush them into anything, she just chatted. How's socials, what are you taking in shop.

She found it took two or three such innocuous visits before anything serious got shared. But once the door was open, the shit poured forth as the kids unburdened themselves. More than once, DeeJay let the tears flow, and shared her box of tissues with a weeping youngster. Some of what she heard upset her so much she would lie at night in the circle of Betty's arms, and shake.

And yet, by the time the school year was finished, she knew there was no other job on earth she would rather be doing. She didn't even care that the job was so demanding she had given up the writer's group.

"It's not as if I was going to be the world's next Pulitzer Prize winner, you know," she teased.

"Then I might as well pack away my violin because I'm never going to be the next Rubinoff, either."

"Right," Bobbi added, "and I'll just quit school right here and now because I'm sure not going to be the poster kid for the Year of the Scholar."

"And I can quit because there's no sense just one member of the family going," Steve put in his two bits' worth. "After all, I'm going to make a fortune in the NHL, right?"

"You? Hell, you can't hardly skate."

"What difference does that make? I'll be the goalie, you don't have to do much skating to be the goalie."

"How did I wind up tangled up with such a pack of total goofs?" Betty threw a small cushion at Steve. He made a grab for it, and missed. "Some goalie," she laughed.

"I didn't say I was going to be a good one."

The last ferry of the night loaded and left the dock, and as soon as the throbbing sound of its engines faded, the docks became quiet. The big striped matriarch who lived on the *Bonny Lady* pressed against the windows, rubbing her entire body, purring hopefully. She had never been allowed inside, but hope glowed in her greenish-yellow eyes. When nobody herniated a set of muscles leaping up to let her in, she swished her tail a few times, then jumped to the pier and sat with her tail curled around her feet.

The kids went below to get ready for bed. Betty and DeeJay

turned off the TV, then the lights, and sat in the half light looking out at the sea, at the lights of the receding ferry, and listened to the lap of the water. "I'm going to go check on them and do the tuck-into-bed routine," DeeJay yawned. Betty nodded and grinned, and DeeJay headed down the steps. Steve was already in bed, his little foam earphones on, his fingers tapping to the beat of the tune coming from his radio. DeeJay kissed him goodnight, gave him a cuddle, and left to check on Bobbi.

She was sitting up in bed, obviously waiting. DeeJay sat on the side of the bed for a smooch.

"So." Bobbi couldn't quite look at her. "Is it true you and Betty are lezzies?"

"Pardon me?" DeeJay stalled.

"Is it true?"

"Yes. Does that bother you?"

"I don't know. Some of the kids at school said something about it and I didn't know what to say back, so I thought I'd better ask. I guess some people really get their knickers in a knot about stuff like that, eh?"

"Yes, darling, a lot of people get bent out of shape about it."

"Is that why sometimes we spend the night at her place and sometimes she spends the night here?"

"Yes." DeeJay hoped she wouldn't burst into tears then run screeching from her daughter's bedroom.

"So is it like, you know, being with a man?"

"No. And yes. Some things feel the same. The wanting to be with her, and enjoying listening to her talk and wanting to laugh when she laughs just because the sound makes me feel happy. Other things are, well, totally different."

"Better or worse?"

"Different. Not better, not worse, but really different. I guess there's stuff I don't have to explain to her, and other stuff, well I don't have to explain it but if I did, I'd be able to and she'd understand me."

"So if I say I don't like it and it makes me feel weird . . . will you stop?"

"No."

"So I can like it or lump it?"

"That's not what I mean, Bobbi. I don't want you to feel you have to lump it. I don't want any uproar at all. If you decide you can't stand the idea, and you'd rather live with Skip and Gerri, I'd cry my eyes out but I'd agree."

"I don't think I want to live with them. I just felt like I needed to know something. Was it okay to ask?"

"It's always okay to ask." For the first time since her daughter was born, DeeJay hesitated to hug, to kiss, to smooch, and she hated herself for the hesitancy. But Bobbi didn't seem to notice, and her hug was so intense the hesitation vanished. "I love you kiddo. And I want you to know I have never felt like I got 'stuck' with you."

"Was my dad a nice guy?" Bobbi whispered, still holding tightly, her face turned toward the curve of DeeJay's neck.

"Your dad?" DeeJay laughed softly. "Oh, babe, he was about the most fun a person could have. Most of the time we got along really good, and when we didn't the fight was legendary."

"Did you love him?"

"Yes. I don't know I ever relaxed around that; Patsy didn't do much toward teaching me about love, or being loved, so it took a while for me to know what it was I was feeling. And when I did clue in, well, it was . . . it was just so different from anything else I'd known I felt . . . maybe self-conscious? Something. But yeah, I loved him."

"As much as Betty?"

"Darling, your dad was the first person I'd ever been involved with, and, as you'll find out soon for yourself, there's something about that first relationship that is special. Overwhelming. It damn near *eats* you, swallows you. So yeah, I think I'd have to say I loved him as much, probably more in some ways."

"And Doug? Did you love him?"

"No. I liked him, enjoyed his company, trusted him, and had good times with him, but no, I didn't love him. Why?"

"Well, like, I still really love him lots, and when someone says something about 'dad' I think of Doug, but . . . he's not with us, and I probably won't see much of him and so if you weren't, like, well, as hung up on Betty as you'd been with him, then maybe she'd be gone soon, too. Does that make sense?"

"It makes sense. I don't know what's going to happen. In lots of ways this is as much a first for me as your daddy was, and I can't predict anything. But nobody can predict anything and promise it will happen a certain way; and if they try, they're lying. There's no promises in life."

When DeeJay went back upstairs, Betty barely looked at her. They sat on the carpet in the living room area, looking out the windows, watching the night darkness deepen, the lights on the boats seeming to get brighter.

"Bobbi had some questions," DeeJay finally admitted.

"I figured. You were down there a long time."

"She might want to talk to you at some point. About . . . us."

"She figured it out?"

"She had help from some of the kids at school."

"If the kids at school have clued in, sooner or later the trustees will get wind of it, too. Then what? What if they fire you?"

"Oh, they can try," DeeJay said quietly, "but they'll need dynamite to shift me."

"You'll fight them?"

"All the way to the Supreme Court if that's what it takes. I'm not doing anything wrong. Nothing I'm doing is any reason to fire me."

"I'm glad. I was afraid you were going to call it off. . . . I didn't know what I was going to do if you did."

"Call it off? Call what off?" She moved so her head was on Betty's lap and all she had to do was turn her face sideways and she could press her mouth against Betty's belly.

School dismissed for the summer and it quickly became obvious DeeJay was going to see almost as much of some of her students as she had during class time. Singly, in pairs or in bunches, they found their way down the dock to the boat. None of them actually knocked on the door, they sort of just hung around, sitting on the bleached planks with their legs dangling over the side, waiting to be noticed. "I hope those lemon growers in California are busy working overtime because we're going to need a bumper crop the rate we're going through lemonade here this year," DeeJay pretended to grumble, but she loved every minute of it. Everyone knew she was doing more than serving lemonade, offering and receiving more than casual summer visits.

Half a dozen kids had dropped by with cans of cold pop, and were sprawled on deck sipping, sunning and gabbing. The one-thirty ferry had just docked, and a long line of freight trucks, pickup trucks, campers, you-name-it up to and including four big motorcycles were disgorging. Walk-on passengers slogged their luggage up the walkway and along the decking to where private cars and a few public cabs waited.

DeeJay had let the kids know she wasn't spending the entire afternoon visiting with them, she had potato salad, cold cuts and all the other necessities for a picnic ready to pack into the cooler and had her late afternoon planned. But into every ointment a fly, and she looked up to see the fly tippy-tittling down the pier toward her. All she could do was sigh. She had boxes of flowers around the rim of the deck, and more boxes up on the half-deck, she had hanging baskets and even a half barrel in which grew a flowering vine; next to it she had a box of kitty litter in case the matriarch hauled her scraps-fat self over in search of a new scat site. The sun glinted off the water, she squinted in the glare, the sky was the colour of faded jeans, and if they had been anywhere except right on the water, they'd have been too hot to be comfortable but here, with the coolness rising from the water and the breeze playing coolly against their skin, they were probably the most comfortable people in town. Until the damn fly came on the scene.

Patsy had a suitcase dangling from one hand and it was just about big enough she could have packed her car in it, if she'd had a car. She was togged out like the very embodiment of the worst possible taste, the tacky tourist personified. Dangling from the shoulder not weighed down by the mammoth suitcase was a large straw purse on a bright red cord. You couldn't see how bloodshot her eyes were because she had on a pair of sunglasses almost guaranteed to make people gawk, and on her head she wore what was probably the ugliest straw sunhat ever seen on the West Coast.

"Oh shit Mother, I can't dance," DeeJay mourned.

"And we're too fat to fly, right? What's wrong? Want us to snuff someone for you?" one of the boys offered.

"You see that? That little short pitty-patty witch coming down the dock? Well that, boys'n'girls, young men and young women, is my mother." She sat up, wishing there was some way she could warn Steve and Bobbi, but they'd be home soon and would walk into it as unprepared as she had been when it walked in on her.

"I think maybe I'll just bop off and leave you to the big reunion scene," the same boy decided.

"Sure, that's it, abandon me," but she was glad to see them go. Kids shouldn't see their counsellor/role model grab her mommy by the throat and strangle her.

"Well, don't go away just because I'm arriving," Patsy chirruped as the kids left. "Maybe one of you could help me get this heavy suitcase down to the boat?"

"Leave the suitcase up on the dock," DeeJay ordered, her voice cool and calm.

"Now, don't you *start!*" Patsy laughed her false little laugh and did this flippy-floppy thing with her fingers that was probably supposed to be some endearing feminine gesture.

"Why're you here?"

"I came on the ferry." Patsy gave up waiting for someone to give the poor dear little old lady a hand and awkwardly got herself from the dock to the deck. She didn't lose her big straw purse, she didn't even lose her ridiculous hat.

"I know you came on the ferry, it's the only way to get here. What I asked was *why*."

"Isn't a mother allowed to visit her own daughter? Isn't a grandmother allowed to see her own flesh and blood?"

"How did you know where we were?"

"I'm not stupid, you know!" Patsy pronounced it "stooooopid." "You can't keep a secret long in any town, and you can't keep one at all in some. I was to the Bingo game and was talking to someone I know and she said she'd been told by someone who knew the next door neighbour to a good friend of Gerri's that they'd been up here to visit and found you living on a houseboat. Of course," she was probably glaring daggers from behind those silly sunglasses, but her tone of voice didn't change, it was all saccharine and false ladylike restraint, "of course, I had to pretend I knew what it was she was talkin' about, but I never blew my cool, I just said yes, well, and it's only to be expected after the hard time you'd all been through lately. A change is as good as a rest, I told her."

"Not too original, but it fits."

"Then not a half hour later, I won the big pot, and I thought to myself, there you go, Patsy, it's a sign from heaven, you find out where they are and then God sees to it you win more than enough money to be able to go and visit. And here I am."

"Here you are, indeed."

"And I brought enough clothes I can stay a coupla weeks, easy."

"No, actually, you won't be staying here at all." DeeJay didn't raise her voice, she didn't shout, she didn't curse, she didn't even have to say mean, nasty and hurtful things. She just told the truth. "I have no control over who visits this town, but I have a lot of control over who does and who does not move in with us, and you aren't moving in, you aren't spending so much as one night with us. I'll get you a glass of cold lemonade because I'd do the same for anybody. I'll even let you eat potato salad at the beach with us, but after that, well, either you get yourself a hotel room or you catch the ferry back to the other side. There's one at four-thirty and another one at nine. You can grab a cab over there and connect up with a bus heading back down; you can probably spend tonight in your own bed."

"My God but you're hard," Patsy said flatly.

"Momma, let's not get into it, okay? I can look back on my life and I can honestly say the sun didn't start to shine for me until the first time I was put in a foster home. And after that, it was sunshine when I was away from you and rain when I got moved back in with you, and I'm not losing any more of the days of my life to any of that old stuff."

"I'm your mother!"

"Yes."

"I'm entitled to . . ."

"Nothing. You're entitled to absolutely nothing at all from me or from my kids. And I don't intend to argue with you about it. You can either have a glass of lemonade or you can hike off without one, it's no skin off my ass either way."

"What if I just flat-out refuse to go?"

"I'll phone the cops. I guess you can sleep in the pokey as well here as anywhere else."

Patsy glowered. DeeJay got her mother a glass of lemonade and even put in three ice cubes. They sat outside, barely exchanging words, and when Bobbi and Steve arrived home from the beach to get ready for the picnic at a different beach, they stared at Patsy, then looked at DeeJay, then, after a very brief "hi," went inside and headed below to get themselves ready.

"Not very friendly," Patsy grumbled.

"Patsy, what did you expect?"

"Expect? What did I expect? Some common courtesy is what I expected!"

"Yeah? Well, finish up your lemonade and we'll head off to the beach."

"I have to go to the bathroom. Or do I just pee on the wharf in front of the entire fishing fleet?"

Patsy dawdled her way to the top jane, her eyes taking in as many details as possible. By the time she had done what she went there to do and made her way back out to the deck, she had stored away enough to keep her stocked with verbal ammunition for weeks. DeeJay could visualize it, Patsy sipping suds while trying to find words to describe the wraparound windows, the view, the brass fittings, the undeniably unique and gorgeous home. Somehow, she would manage to make it sound as if the entire place had been offered to her and only her loyalty to her friends had brought her back to the dear old home town.

They drove to Gibsons Beach and set up their blanket in the thin shade from the maple trees. Had she wanted to, DeeJay could have left a message for Betty to meet them at Dinner Rock, but she didn't want to share that pink-granite place with Patsy, she didn't want to explain about the black volcanic "chimneys" which cut through the sun-faded rosy cliffs. She didn't want to share, and obviously the kids didn't, either, because neither of them suggested they show dear old granny the nicest of places.

Betty arrived with a small cooler full of 7-Up, ginger ale and orange Crush, the cans packed in ice cubes. She sprawled on the blanket, her top lip lightly beaded with sweat, her bare skin tanned golden, and watched Patsy exploring and examining the bleached logs, the abandoned kelp, the salt-encrusted rocks.

"She walks like one of those ladies of the Chinese imperial court who had their feet bound. She teeters, y'know?" Betty sounded as if she was on the verge of a big yawn.

"Teeters for sure. Probably walks better drunk than she does sober because she's had more practice."

Patsy waved at the kids, swimming off the big sentinel rocks. Steve waved back, but not enthusiastically.

"Jesus, by the time she's finished with the story she'll have convinced herself Stevie was just begging for her to go in the water, too," DeeJay grumbled.

"Yeah. It's like she's heard other people say things like Well, I spent a week visiting with them and they couldn't do enough for me; and she wants to be able to say the same thing. She probably sits brooding into her beer envisioning the uproar when Skip and Gerri show up, and feeling sorry for herself because she's not a part of that. And rather than admit it, she takes what she imagines things to be like for them, and spins tales about it being that way for her!"

"Well, she's about far enough off the wall to believe it," and an enormous surge of emotion welled up from someplace deep inside her. DeeJay nearly burst into hysterical weeping. "God, I don't know what's happening!" she blurted.

Betty reached out, took DeeJay's hand in hers, and squeezed softly. "Babe, just dig yourself a little bit of a hole in the sand and put the whole mountain of shit in it, then cover 'er over and write The End . . . and go on with your life."

"She is such a sad, dreary, *evil* old bag of shit!"

"Yeah. And I bet she knows it even better than you do."

"It's not that I hate her so much I wish she'd die, I wouldn't want to be responsible for anything awful happening to anyone. I just wish she'd *go away!*" She fought for some semblance of control, and knew Betty was all there was holding her together. "I don't hate her . . . I don't feel enough for her or about her to be able to hate. I could live the rest of my life without spending five minutes thinking about her. And I really do want her to just *go*."

The kids came out of the water and sat on the warm sand, their skin goose-bumped, their lips dark with chill.

"I'm about ready to sit down and eat everything in the world," Steve announced.

"Me, too," Bobbi agreed. "Up to and including the Rocky Mountains."

Patsy joined them and the way she put away her supper could have been heartwarming if anyone had been inclined to have their hearts warmed. When the potato salad had been packed away and the cold cuts had disappeared, when the last stuffed celery had been munched and the jar of olives was empty, Betty stood up, gave the kids each a strong take-the-hint look, then walked off to throw a stick for one of the dogs who seemed to live year-round at the beach.

DeeJay was stuck on the blanket with Patsy. Patsy seemed to know Betty had taken the kids and effed off on purpose. And finally, because while she might have been all kinds of fool, she wasn't stupid, or totally blind, Patsy asked the question that was really none of her business at all.

"So what's the deal with *her*?" and she tilted her head in the general direction of Betty and the kids.

"Who her? You mean Bobbi? Or Betty."

"Not Bobbi."

"Then you mean Betty."

"So, what gives with her and you? She seems . . . awful chummy."

"She is wonderfully chummy," and DeeJay laughed, feeling tons of crap just dropping off her.

"You hinting at what I'm thinking?"

"Patsy, stop talking in circles. How in hell would I know what you are thinking unless you tell me what that is."

"So she acts like someone who thinks she's got dibs on stuff where you're concerned. You and her queer for each other?"

"Yes. In fact you couldn't get queerer if you tried. Queer as a three-dollar bill. Queer as a four-peckered owl."

"My God." Patsy's voice dripped disgust. "I never raised you to be a gearbox! That's disgusting!"

"Patsy, let's face it, you didn't raise me at all. And if you think two women together is disgusting, please give me your opinion of a grown person and a little kid."

"I want you to take me back to the ferry place. Right now. I don't want to spend any more time than I have to with that queer hangin' around as if she was family or something."

"Ah, madame, you know, your very merest hint of a wish is

like a commandment from God," and DeeJay started laughing.

They stood outside the little waiting shack until the gangplank was lifted and the ferry began to move slowly away from the dock. Then they moved along the catwalk, along the dock, and turned back down the planking toward the flower-bedecked converted boat. The kids went inside and turned on the TV as if the big family reunion meant no more to them than the presence of ants at a picnic. DeeJay and Betty sat on deck chairs watching the ferry move through the water, away from them.

"So much for that," Betty yawned.

"Yeah. So much for that. I feel as if I've just done two weeks work in one afternoon. I almost ache, I'm so tired!"

"Why don't you head below? I'll sit here a while longer, then I'll chase the kids to their dungeons when it's time . . . then I'll head below, too. Unless you'd rather I went back to my place."

"I'd like you to be here tonight. I really feel like I want and need someone . . . chummy," and she laughed softly. "Awful chummy, that's what that woman said. Awful chummy."

"What woman?" Betty stood up, reached down, took DeeJay's hand and tugged her to her feet. "Go to bed, you're seeing things."

261

Books by Anne Cameron

Novels

A Whole Brass Band
Kick the Can
Escape to Beulah
South of an Unnamed Creek
Stubby Amberchuk and the Holy Grail

Short Stories

Bright's Crossing
Women, Kids & Huckleberry Wine

Traditional Tales

Tales of the Cairds
Dzelarhons

Poems

The Annie Poems

Story for Children

The Gumboot Geese

Northwest Coast Legends for Children

Raven Goes Berrypicking
Raven & Snipe
Spider Woman
Lazy Boy
Orcas's Song
Raven Returns the Water
How the Loon Lost Her Voice
How Raven Freed the Moon